In the Belly
of the
Bloodhound

OTHER BOOKS IN THE BLOODY JACK ADVENTURES

Bloody Jack
Being an Account of the Curious Adventures
of Mary "Jacky" Faber, Ship's Boy

Curse of the Blue Tattoo
Being an Account of the Misadventures
of Jacky Faber, Midshipman and Fine Lady

Under the Jolly Roger
Being an Account of the Further
Nautical Adventures of Jacky Faber

L. A. MEYER

In the Belly
of the
Bloodhound

Being an Account of a
Particularly Peculiar Adventure
in the Life of Jacky Faber

Harcourt, Inc.

Orlando   Austin   New York   San Diego   Toronto   London

www.HarcourtBooks.com

Library of Congress Cataloging-in-Publication Data
Meyer, L. A. (Louis A.), 1942–
In the belly of the bloodhound: being an account of a particularly peculiar
adventure in the life of Jacky Faber/L. A. Meyer.—1st ed.
p.   cm.—(A Bloody Jack adventure)
Summary: Jacky Faber and her classmates at the Lawson Peabody School for
Young Girls in Boston are kidnapped while on a school outing and transported
in the hold of a slave ship bound for the slave markets of North Africa.
[1. Orphans—Fiction.   2. Seafaring life—Fiction.   3. Kidnapping—Fiction.
4. Sea stories.]   I. Title.   II. Series.
PZ7.M57172In   2006
[Fic]—dc22   2005033562
ISBN-13: 978-0-15-205557-8   ISBN-10: 0-15-205557-6

Text set in Minion
Display set in Pabst
Designed by Cathy Riggs

First edition
C E G H F D B
Printed in the United States of America

Once again, for Annetje…
and for my editor, Karen Grove,
without whom Jacky would still
be out beggin' in the streets

In the Belly
of the
Bloodhound

PART I

Chapter 1

Any old port in a storm. That's what I'm thinking as I carefully weave my little boat through the ships in the crowded harbor. I've seen many ports and I've weathered many storms and good old Boston Harbor is looking right good to me at this moment. *Hmmm...* be wary, though, girl. There's three British warships lying over there at Long Wharf. Got to steer clear of them, for sure, as the men on board could have heard of the price that's on my poor head and might be of a mind to try to collect it. My head, that is... Imagine that... a reward of two hundred and fifty pounds, and all for the body of one insignificant girl— a full Royal Navy captain's pay for a year, and wouldn't some lucky sailor like to nab that?

As I clear the end of Long Wharf, I pull my cap further down over my face and sail on. *Don't mind me, Sirs. Just a simple fisher lass heading home, nothing more.*

Now I start working my way over to the land. I'm remembering that there's an open bit of gravelly beach between Howard's and Codman's wharves, and that is where I'm of a mind to land. The wind is fair and my sail is drawing well and I'm cutting neatly through boats and ships that are anchored out. I pull in a bit closer and look over at the warships. They could see me from where they lay, if they cared to look. *But who cares about some fishmonger's dutiful daughter out plying her family's trade?* That's what I'm thinking. Or hoping. *But, oh Sirs—you, my fellow countrymen and fellow sailors—if only you knew what has happened at Trafalgar, you would not be sitting so peacefully here.* It's plain they haven't gotten the word yet.

Codman's Wharf passes on my port side and I throw the tiller over and bring the sail in close-hauled. When I hear and feel the scrape of the bottom on my keel, I loose the sail and the *Morning Star* slips her nose up elegantly onto the beach. *Pretty neat sailing, old girl,* I'm thinking, patting her gunwale affectionately. *I know it's been a long trip for the both of us, from Trafalgar to here, that's for sure, and now you just rest.*

For a moment I sit there in wonder at being back in Boston again, then I go forward and loosen the halyard, letting the sail and its booms collapse to the deck. I'm about to gather it in and wrap it up, when there's a noise behind me and I spin around in alarm, my shiv out of my vest and in my hand. *By God, they're not going to take me without—*

But it is nothing but a boy. A very ragged and dirty boy, to be sure, but just a boy. He is the very picture of a wharf rat, a breed with which I am very familiar, having once been one myself, back when I lived under London's Blackfriars Bridge as a member in good standing of the Rooster Charlie Gang of Naked Orphans. Blackfriars Bridge was real close to the docks on the Thames, so, yes, I know this kind of boy quite well.

"Need some help, Missy?" he says with hope in his voice. It's plain from the ribs sticking out under his too-short shirt that he hasn't eaten in a while and he looks real willin' to earn a penny. Well, I can't argue with that, as I'm all for youthful spunk and enterprise. I slide my knife back in my vest.

"Well, maybe. Help me stow the sail."

He leaps on board to help me wrap the sail around the boom, and we lash it down tight with the mainsheet and secure it to its stay post.

"There, Missy, tight as a drum. Anything else? Polish your brass, shine up your brightwork, varnish your oars?"

This one is younger than me—maybe thirteen, fourteen. His hair is held back with a piece of old twine and I can see both his knees through the rips in the trousers that end raggedly at his calves. He is, of course, barefoot.

"You can see, young Master Wharf Rat, that the *Morning Star* has neither brass work nor brightwork, nor do her oars need varnishing," I say severely, in my best Naval Officer voice, "but you may, if you wish to earn a penny, watch over her till I return, which might be today, or might be tomorrow. If you know a place where she can be moored..."

"Oh, yes, Missy. See that pier over by the market? I'll tie it up there. So many fishing boats go in and out of there that they'll never notice us."

"All right," I say. I dig in the purse that hangs by my side and pull out a penny and flip it to him. "Go spend this on something to eat first and then tend to moving her. And mark me— This is the *Morning Star* and she is a *her*, not an *it*. Do you get that?"

He nods.

"You can do it by yourself?"

"Oh, yes, Missy, I'm a thoroughgoing seaman! I'll get her anywhere you need her."

I give a quick snort. "Very well, Seaman...What is your name, boy?"

"Tanner, Missy. Jim Tanner."

"Why are you not in school?" I ask, suspiciously. I can't let anything happen to the *Star* after getting her all the way here.

"Done with that. Learned all I needed to. I can read and cipher some. That's all a seaman needs, I figure."

"Who are your parents? Where do you live?"

"My mother died havin' me. Dad was lost at sea a year ago. Ain't got no other people. I sleep under the docks, mostly, sometimes in woodsheds when I can find one that ain't locked." He looks a bit defiant when he says this. *Hmmm*...dirt poor but possessed of some pride, at least.

"Surely you could find a better place to sleep, up in the town."

"Maybe, but then Wiggins'd catch me and indenture me to some farmer and I don't want that. I'm a seaman, as I told you."

I know the fact that I am dressed in my serving-girl gear is why he's being as familiar as he is being. Time to put him straight. "Very well, Seaman Tanner, you may carry on with your duties. When I return, you shall see another penny. But I warn you, if you try anything cute, like stealing my boat, then things will go very hard for you. *Very* hard."

He nods, unconvinced, I know, of just how hard I could make things for him should I want to. I decide to convince him of this.

"Do you know of a John Thomas? Smasher McGee?" I ask, drilling my eyes into his. I name a few more of my more colorful Boston pierside acquaintances. "They are my

6

very good friends, and they would do anything for me—
anything—including running down, gutting, and making
fish bait out of a treacherous wharf rat. Do you take my
meaning, young Master Tanner?"

It is plain that he knows at least some of these sterling in-
dividuals, for he gulps and nods. "I wasn't gonna mess with
your boat, Missy," he says, looking hurt.

"I know you weren't, Seaman Tanner," I say, more kindly
now and feeling a little bit sorry for doubting him, "but I
was just making sure."

With that I turn to go down into the cuddy to change. I
dive into my seabag and choose my black school dress,
black bonnet, and lace mantilla. I have to leave the hatch
open for light.

"Turn around, Master Tanner, and face away," I call out
to him. He ducks his head and does an about-face.

After I have put on my clothes, I come back up and I
look him over. He stands there expectantly, shuffling his
feet. I decide to trust him.

"I now leave the *Morning Star* in your hands, Jim Tanner.
Take good care of her, for she has taken good care of me.
And maybe she will take good care of you, as well." I put on
my bonnet and throw the mantilla over my shoulders.
"And, by the way, my name is Nancy Alsop. That is *Miss*
Alsop to you."

With that I once again place my foot on Boston soil and
head up toward Union Street.

Chapter 2

No, I didn't sail the *Morning Star* all the way from Cape Trafalgar on the coast of Spain to here in America. I'm good with a small boat, but that would have been sheer folly to attempt, even for one as foolhardy as I. What I did was steer blindly for the transatlantic shipping lanes as soon as I was clear of the scene of that horrific battle, where scores of ships were still burning and sinking, and the men trapped in them were screaming and dying, and the very sea itself ran red with blood. As grateful as I was for my deliverance from death and capture, my heart was still low, very low, from having seen so many of my dear friends killed or wounded, and from knowing that I, myself, by the act of joining the battle, had caused the death and wounding and maiming of many of the enemy's men and boys. I know I will have a lot to answer for when my time of accounting comes. And then I thought of seeing Jaimy, maybe for the last time, looking out at me as I made my escape, but still... still I managed to steer the lifeboat in the right direction.

Wiping the tears from my eyes, I made myself take stock of the boat and my situation. The boat, which was about twenty-, maybe twenty-two-foot long, was rigged as a cat-boat. It had the mast placed well forward and only one sail, and that sail was gaff rigged. All of which was to the good, for it made the boat easy to sail single-handed. Just haul on the sail halyard and the top boom goes up, and the bottom boom anchors the sail. Then pull in the mainsheet till the sail goes full, tight, and stiff, and you're sailing. Easy to reef, too, when the wind starts blowing hard.

Which it certainly did that first awful night after the Battle of Trafalgar.

The wind had started picking up around dusk and increased in volume hourly after that. I shortened sail and went to inspect the cuddy cabin up forward, but if I had any thought of crawling into the cuddy and sleeping, that was cruelly dashed by the onset of the storm. At least I managed to get on my oilskins, stow my seabag, and batten down the cuddy hatch before the sheets of stinging rain came slashing at me. I don't ever want my friends to worry about me when I'm away from them and in possible danger, but on this night I could not help but wonder what was going through Jaimy's mind as he saw the storm approach, and me being out there all alone in a small boat. *Well, I gotta tell you, it's gonna be rough, Jaimy, but better out here than back there, bound and trussed and ready to be delivered back to London for a certain date with a noose.* Or so I thought.

That night was one of the worst I have ever spent, be it on land or sea. It was all I could do to keep the boat's bow on to the waves, with huge swell after huge swell rolling at me over and over, one after another, and all it would take is one slipup with the sail and tiller so that the waves could take me broadside and I would be rolled over and lost, lost in that cold, dark water. It was hour after hour of desperation and terror, until at last I lost all hope and heart and gave in to deep despair and counted myself finally, after all my struggles, doomed to die. *Good-bye, Jaimy. I hope you have a happy life without me, for I know you shall see me no more. But please know that I died happy in the knowledge that you did love me... You will think of me sometimes, won't you? Oh, but don't think of me as dead and gone, think of me instead as having drifted down to the bottom of the sea, to once again lie on the deck of my beautiful, lost* Emerald...

I guess when I start waxing stupidly poetic, it is a sign that things are about to turn for the better, and sure enough, it was then, as I snuffled and whined and said my last tearful good-byes, that the sky started to clear and the seas grew calmer and I could see the stars once again. Through a break in the clouds I could see Polaris, the North Star, and I steered for it as the dawn began to break. As the sky lightened and the stars began to wink out, I saw Venus, the morning star, shining up there, as always, the last to disappear. It was then that I named my sturdy little boat after her. I gave heartfelt thanks for my deliverance, trimmed sail, and continued heading for the sea-lanes.

On the first day, I spotted a British warship tearing down to Trafalgar—*a bit late, lads, to share in the glory, but on the other hand, very lucky for your own dear bodies, which did not have to share in the carnage that paid for that glory in blood and pain and death*—and I stayed well clear. They soon disappeared over the horizon, having absolutely no interest in a foolish fisherman who was far, much too far, at sea. I kept steering both north *and* westerly 'cause I wanted the ship that picked me up to be too far out on the ocean to kindly consider taking me safely back to England. That would be very gentlemanly of them to do, of course, but would be disastrous for me, the Admiralty having made it very plain that, while they wanted all of me back in the warm embrace of their custody for interrogation, and, I suspect, torture, they would settle quite nicely for my head in a sack.

It was on the third day that I spotted what was to be my ride across the Atlantic. I was quite hungry and *very* thirsty by then and was willing to settle for any kind of floating garbage scow, but what I found instead was a big, trim merchantman under all sail on a fine day and heading for America.

I tied down the mainsheet, secured the tiller, and let the *Star* sail herself while I rushed forward, put on my serving-girl skirt and hooded cloak to cover up my lieutenant's jacket— had to be presentable, of course, or else I would be treated badly, and, after all I had been through, I certainly didn't want that—then I sailed toward them, waving a white petticoat back and forth over my head and *halloo*ing loudly. I was soon gratified to see the glint of a long glass lens that could only have been trained on me, followed by the sight of their sails going slack and the great ship slowing and then stopping.

The crew of the *Enterprise,* a Yankee trader bound for Newport, Rhode Island, with a cargo of fine British linen and woolen goods, was obviously astounded to find a lone female in a small boat far, far out to sea.

"Ahoy, mates!" I sang out as I pulled the *Morning Star* alongside the towering ship. "Got room to take a poor lost girl to America?" I asked as I put on my brightest smile, grinning up at the amazed faces looking down at me.

It turns out they did have room, and not only for me but also for my *Star.* The skipper of the merchant, a Captain Billings, was none too pleased to see me, sailors' superstitions about women on board being bad luck and all, but he cheered up considerably when, upon gaining the deck by way of the ladder that was lowered down to me, I curtsied low to him and announced that I could pay for my passage, and "maybe a little extra if you big strong men could stow my dear little boat aboard." Orders were barked out and the *Morning Star* was quickly dismasted and hoisted aboard by crane. She was overturned on the forward hatch and lashed down securely, but not before I retrieved my seabag and was shown down to my stateroom by a *very* presentable young officer, who blushed mightily as I allowed him to lead me to my quarters. *Hmmmm…There certainly are a lot of pretty boys in this world.*

That young officer, one Andrew Billings, who was both Second Mate *and* the Captain's son, turned out to be a courteous, fine, and very shy companion. Course I had to tell him I was promised to another, as I once again am, but still we passed many pleasant days on the deck with the wind blowing through our hair. Maybe holding hands a bit and such like—but I was good, mostly.

They were right pleasant to me on the way over, in spite of the stupid superstition about women on board—hey, I figure I've brought some ships some actual good luck by being aboard…But then again, some not. Discipline not being as tight on a merchant as on a warship, I soon was able to pull out my whistle and play a few songs and dance a few dances, and in no time I was the darling of the ship, and all was well. There was a fiddle on board, too, so I was able to practice that. The fiddle's owner was no Gully MacFarland, but he was a decent cove and I learned a few new tunes off of him. And he off of me. I had left Gully's fine, fine fiddle, the Lady Lenore, as he had named her, back in London for some minor repairs when I left for what turned out to be my last voyage, and it's well I did, else the Lady Lenore would now be at the bottom of the sea, being badly played by mermaids. Or, worse, mermen.

Letting one of the crew—that one being the aforementioned beautiful, bashful Andrew—have some sort of claim on me, I did not have to fend off any other advances or attentions. And, as the Captain's son, Andrew does enjoy a certain privilege. I mean, who's gonna mess with the Captain's son's girl?

Although I am usually quite free with my kisses, I held myself back and did not let it get to that. A little hand-holding is all, though I did take his arm as we promenaded the decks. As I've said, I was good, mostly, for, after all, am I not newly re-promised to Lieutenant James Emerson Fletcher? This I had to tell the crestfallen Mr. Billings after he asked me to marry him, one week into the voyage. "But, Andrew, if it were not for that, I would surely take you into my affections and give myself in marriage to you. Really, I would, for you are the kindest and sweetest of young men..." *Right, Andy—get in line behind Randall Trevelyne, Robin Raeburne, Ishmael Turner, Joseph Jared, and a few others, and not necessarily in that order. And maybe Arthur McBride, that Irish devil, too...*

It was, by and large, a most pleasant journey, and three weeks, five days later, we pulled alongside a pier in Newport. In no time at all, my *Morning Star* was put over the side, rerigged, and I bounced down the gangway, with my seabag on my shoulder, to get into her. Before leaving the ship, though, I lifted my face to Andrew Billings and gave him a good one on the lips to remember me by. I do believe I gave the shy Mr. Billings something to remember and think about, and possibly in his next encounter with a female, he will have more confidence in himself and I will have done some good in this world. I'd like to think that.

I steered out away from the *Enterprise*, for I wanted these good-byes to be quick and final—no hanging around sad-eyed young men for me, no sir, not when there's work to be done. I trimmed the sail, threw over the tiller, and pulled away for New York, waving to my friends of the past month till I was well out of sight. Then I reversed course and slipped into the docks on the south side of the town, where I figured I would not run into any members of the *Enterprise* crew, they being well occupied in off-loading their cargo.

I had told them that I was headed for New York, in case anyone came around asking them questions, but I wasn't headed there at all—no, my plan was to outfit the *Star* and cruise up the southern side of Cape Cod and then across Massachusetts Bay to Boston.

When last I saw Jaimy Fletcher, he was standing on the smouldering deck of the warship that had taken on board the survivors and the wounded of the smashed and sunken *Wolverine*, looking out at me as I pulled away in the lifeboat that was to become the *Morning Star*. In the midst of the destruction, I stood up and semaphored to him the word *Boston* so that he would know where I was intending to go, so's he could come collect me, should we both survive.

Better do it this time, Jaimy . . .

Ah, but I know he will, and there is to be no more doubting, not on my part. If he is able to come for me, he will.

Chapter 3

It turned out to be a very good thing that I left the *Enterprise* in the quick way I did, considering what I found tacked to a wall not an hour later. I had tied up the *Star* and gone off joyously shopping. I was outfitting my dear little *Star,* now the flagship of Faber Shipping, Worldwide, after all, and was quite excited about it—some line and a small anchor, an oil lamp, bedding, spirit stove and fuel, teapot, tea, sugar, water jug, cups, and all to be carefully stowed in my cabin. There's something in me that loves doing this sort of thing... saying, *This will go here and that will go here... no... there.*

I carried all these things back and happily stowed them in the *Star* and again went into the town to look about. I strolled up Thames Street, looking in all the shops, blissfully thinking nothing amiss, and—*Hooray!*—I found a post office, where I was able to mail my letter to the Home for Little Wanderers, in London, telling everyone that I had made it over all right and to please get word to Jaimy. Leaving there, I rolled on, feeling the strangely solid land beneath my feet once again. I spotted a likely looking fiddle sitting in a pawn shop window, and although my money belt was getting mighty light, I bought the fiddle, figuring it would help me pay my way up the coast. I tried her out in the shop, and while she was no Lady Lenore, she did have a certain spirit and I knew I would learn to love her.

I was carrying the fiddle case back to the *Star,* thinking I was done shopping and would spend the night in the cuddy cabin, merrily rearranging things by lamplight, when I spied a piece of paper tacked to a post.

Uh-oh...

Publick Notice

Hear ye, All ye Citizens of the Americas—Desired by the Gov't of His Majesty, King George III of England, the Quick Apprehension of the Notorious Pyrate

Jacky Faber

a Female, Aged about 16 years, on Charges of Piracy on the High Seas, Theft of Royal Property, and Other High Crimes and Misdemeanors. The Miscreant is Distinguished by having an Anchor Tattoo on her Belly and a Peculiarly White Left Eyebrow due to a Scar Beneath. She is extremely Small and Slender, weighing Approx. 90 Pounds, and has been known to Disguise her Person as a Boy by Donning Male Clothing. The Girl is a British Citizen, so Citizens of the United States should not think it Amiss to Apprehend her on Behalf of His Gracious Majesty. A reward of

— 250 Pounds, Sterling —

is offered for the Capture and Delivery of said Criminal
Alive to any of His Majesty's Consulates or Embassies.
She may also be Bound Over and Delivered to any of
His Majesty's Royal Ships that Commonly Lie at
Anchor in Major Harbors. A Reward of 100 Pounds
is offered if the Female is taken Dead, her Head and
the Patch of Skin Containing the Tattoo, Preserved
in Alcohol, being Considered Sufficient Proof
for the Claiming of the Reward.

WARNING!

This Female is Known to be Extremely Clever and
Duplicitous in Bending Unsuspecting Males to her Will.
Although Godless and Without the Morals and
Sensibilities usually Ascribed to her Sex, She is said to be
Charming and Fair of Face and has been Educated and
can Ape the Manners of her Betters, but

Beware

She carries both Sword and Pistol, as well as a Knife
concealed on her Person, and is to be considered
Extremely Dangerous, having Killed, by her own Hand, a
Considerable Number of Unfortunate Men.

Looking furtively about, I kept myself from running off
in a blind panic. Seeing no one watching, I reached up and
ripped off the poster and stuck it under my arm. And then

I hurried, but not so fast as to raise suspicion, back toward the safety of my boat.

They sure didn't miss much, the scurvy sods, I thought as I climbed down the ladder and dropped into the *Star.* But how did they know about the tattoo, I wonder? *Hmmm...* Although I consider myself a girl of some virtue, it is true that I have in the past become separated from my clothes in the presence of more than one young man...but neither Randall nor Robin nor Jaimy would peach on me. And neither would Petey or Higgins...*Ah,* but of course—that damned book that Amy Trevelyne wrote about me! Wherein she told the entire English-speaking world about the Brotherhood of Ship's Boys of His Majesty's ship the *Dolphin* tattoo that rests on my right hip. *Ah, Amy, if your aim in writing that book was to get me, well, you got me good.*

I quickly stowed my new fiddle, threw off the lines, hoisted the sail, and headed out of Newport Harbor, fuming over this latest bit of trouble. I particularly don't like the thought of my head floating in a crock of alcohol— don't they know that I have sworn that spirits will never again pass my lips? And here they want to put my whole head, lips and all, into a crock of pure alcohol. *Damn!* This poor Cockney's noggin might yet end up in an anatomist's jar, for all her struggles to avoid that fate. And while we're at it, my tattoo's on my *hip,* not my *belly,* which you Admiralty sods oughta get right. After all, I am a lady...well, most of the time, anyway...and ladies don't have tattoos on their bellies.

When well under way, I wasted no time at all in getting back into my sailor togs—not only for comfort and ease of movement, but also so that if anyone put a long glass on me and wondered what I was about, they'd figure me for a boy out fishing and think no more of it. Boys get to do what they want in this world, and girls do not.

About an hour later, I pulled into a little cove, which my newly acquired chart told me was Sakonnet Cove in the lee of Price's Neck and which gave me and the *Morning Star* an excellent, calm anchorage next to a pleasant beach. In the light of my little lamp, I saw that some sort of town was over there to the west, but the lights winked out at dusk and there didn't seem to be much going on, which was all right, 'cause since my scare over the WANTED poster, I didn't want to go ashore. Not just yet, anyway. Besides, outside, the weather was working up.

I went on deck to make a final check that my anchor wasn't dragging and all was well, then went below for the night. I lit my little spirit stove and made tea and fried up some bacon, which I ate with bread and was content. I thought about doing some reading, but with the sea kicking up and the *Star* bucking about, I decided against it— couldn't have my lamp turning over and setting my boat afire. So I crawled into my bunk and pulled the covers over me and tried to settle down to sleep.

I was worried that the nightmares would come again, and it is not an idle worry, for they do come often. I have always had nightmares. I had them back in the kip under Blackfriars Bridge when I was with the Rooster Charlie Gang, and I had them on the *Dolphin*. I had them especially after the pirate LeFievre put a rope around my neck and swung me out to hang. I had them in the dormitory of the Lawson Peabody School for Young Girls, awakening the whole place with my howls, and I had them on the *Enterprise,* where several times I had returned to consciousness shaking in the arms of Andrew Billings, who had entered the sanctity of my room, thinking my innocence was being attacked. I had them on the *Wolverine,* too, rousing my poor fellow midshipmen out of their slumbers, and on my *Emerald* as well, coming back to my confused senses, terrified and soaked with sweat, to find Higgins at my bedside, trying to soothe and comfort me out of my night horrors. Not only do I relive in my dreams the terror of being hanged by LeFievre or nearly being burned alive by Reverend Mather, but now the slaughter of Trafalgar presses upon my mind as well, and it presses on my mind not only when I have the night dreads, but even in the daytime, when I let myself dwell upon it—*The arms thrusting through the ports of the* Redoubtable, *arms made bloody from my sword held in my hand, which was piercing them, through flesh and touching bone. Bloody arms, so much blood, and so many friends lost—* and a black cloud comes over my mind and sometimes doesn't go away for too long a while.

In my bed I shake my head to banish such thoughts. *You will think on cheerier things, girl.* I turn onto my side, wrap my arms around my legs and pull my knees to my chin, and smile to myself, thinking back to the *Enterprise.* I imagine the crew of that good ship has by now seen the WANTED poster concerning the "Notorious Pyrate Jacky Faber." While Andrew didn't get anywhere near seeing my blue tattoo, my unmistakable white eyebrow would be a clincher on any suspicions anyone might have that I was the WANTED one. I chuckle into my pillow as I picture Captain Billings fuming in front of the damning flyer, his Yankee trader heart breaking over the loss of the 250 pounds sterling reward that had been seated at his table for the past three weeks or so. I can also see in my mind's eye the same Captain Billings storming into his cabin and calling Andrew to him and slapping a copy of the poster in front of his young son, together with dire warnings about the "Pernicious Nature of Some Females"—*Oh, soft and pliant and yielding in their appearances, with soft sighs and melting eyes, but oh so cunning and devious as well. Take warning from this, young man, beware, oh beware, lest you again clasp a serpent to your bosom.*

But I don't think young Andrew will take warning at all, nor will he beware. Truth to tell, I think he will relate the tale all through his life, when sharing a cup of cheer with his friends, of how he once courted and nearly won the heart of a famous pirate queen. It's all right, Andrew, you can tell tales on me, I won't mind. I just hope you don't believe all that stuff about me, 'cause it ain't all true— but let that go, as maybe it's best you think of me as a bad girl so that you'll give up all thoughts of me and find a nice, good girl to live your life with. Of course, in the retelling of our time together, you will embellish the romance, throwing in fevered kisses on the quarterdeck, with ragged breath and torn bodices and heaving bosoms and all, but so be it. Enjoy the tale, Andrew, and enjoy your life, for I found you to be an excellent young man. However, as a friend, I must tell you this: Should you marry and share a bottle of wine with your lovely bride, do not get so deeply into your cups that you are foolish enough as to tell your wife the story—she just might believe it.

One thing they didn't describe on that poster was my new blue tattoo. No, it's not a real tattoo, but, like the one on my hip, certainly one I didn't want to get stitched on my skin. It is a small spray of little blue dots that radiate from the outer corner of my right eye. The dots are powder burns that I got when sighting over a cannon on the *Wolverine* and not getting out of the way fast enough after I pulled the firing matchlock. The burnt powder spit out of the touch hole and got me. They are hardly noticeable now and I can cover them with a pat of powder or a lock of my hair pulled down, but they are there. *Come get me and marry me, Jaimy, and on our wedding night we shall strip me down and play count-the-scars. Won't that be ever so much fun?*

Good night, Jaimy. I hope you are safe and well. I wish you were snugged up here beside me, I do wish that. But, maybe someday...

Chapter 4

Log of the *Morning Star*, November 22, 1805. Anchored in Sakonnet Cove, Rhode Island, U.S.A. Storm continues. Hope to get under way tomorrow. Bottom sand and mud. Seas very rough. Anchor holding, thanks be to God.

I decided to keep a log of my journeys on the *Morning Star*, as I did on the *Emerald*. It became a habit during my time on Royal Navy ships, and once I get into habits, I find them hard to break. It is the fussy part of my nature, I suppose, but so be it. It gives me comfort to do it and it may well be that, in the future, I might find these entries amusing...or maybe nostalgic, even. *You sit still, young Master James, while your grandmother reads to you from the sea logs she kept when Faber Shipping, Worldwide, was just beginning. Here! Leave your sister alone! You want a smack, young man? I thought not. That's better. Ahem...Now, where were we? Ah. All right, yes, well, I was just getting over the setback of the loss of my dear* Emerald. *I was back in Massachusetts, alone on the* Morning Star... *What? Your grandfather? Well, at the time I didn't know. After the Great Battle, I guessed that he would be assigned to another ship. I did hope that he would* come to get me, though, but I couldn't blame him if he didn't, it was such a turbulent time, those years of war with that Napoléon...

Actually, I hoped that this log would meet a somewhat better fate than the log of the *Emerald*, which now rests at the bottom of the sea. If any mermaids can read, I hope they are enjoying both my ship and the contents of the log.

Morning Star log, November 23, 1805. Ain't going nowhere. Storm still raging. Am bobbing like cork. Cannot even make tea. Eating dry biscuits. Got belly cramps. Nightmares. Am sick and miserable and feeling very sorry for self.

Morning Star log, Nov. 24. Ain't got nothing good to say. Seas still high. Black clouds out there and black clouds in my mind. To hell with this. To hell with everything.

Chapter 5

Morning Star log, November 25. Skies clearing. Seas subsiding. Mood much improved. Hauled anchor, stopped whining, and set sail on Course 079, making for Horseneck Beach on Cape Cod in Massachusetts.

The *Star* is fairly ripping along, and with the wind in my hair, my hand on the tiller, and my foot up on the gunwale, I am feeling much better. The Black Cloud that sometimes comes over my mind is gone, but I worry that it might be back soon, and I just cannot let it. I know it's because I've seen so much blood, so much death, but death is so common, why should I care? One can as easily die from a fever as from a French cannonball, I know that, but it doesn't make it any easier for me somehow. I shall try to keep the Black Cloud off. But I don't know...

This morning I was able to make tea and biscuits with butter and warmed maple syrup and it was good and I am content. Really.

Star log, Nov. 25, cont. Have made landfall at Horseneck Beach. Have tied up at dock. Am now in the state of

Massachusetts. Looked about for opportunity to work at my musical trade. Found none. No taverns. No inns.

I was hoping to find an out-of-the-way tavern where I could play a couple of sets, but no luck. At least there were no WANTED posters starring my own poor self, and I got to pass a pleasant evening tied up to a dock. There was a tannery there and I was able to buy a small jar of brown leather dye. When I was back on the *Star,* I used it to color my white eyebrow. It's not an exact match with my other one, but it will do.

Star log, cont. Bought fish from boy on dock. Cooked it. Ate it. Practiced my new fiddle. Disturbed no one but the gulls. Threw off lines and anchored a little ways off for the night, for safety's sake. Note to self: Buy a stout lock for cabin at first opportunity. So to bed.

I have named my new fiddle the Lady Gay, in the tradition of the Lady Lenore. No, my Gay is not in the same league with Gully MacFarland's Lenore, but still she has some depth, and she has a friskiness about her that I find appealing. I named her after that old ballad in which this mighty Lord Arlen is off at the King's court, consecrating King Henry the Eighth or somesuch, when this boy, this page as they were called, from back at his castle, rushes all breathless up to him, fairly bursting with news. Lord Arlen asks him what's up with his castle and his farm and how's his wife that he left behind, and the little snitch opens his mouth and:

> *No harm has come your house and lands,*
> *The little page did say,*

But Matty Groves is bedded up
With your fair Lady Gay.

Course all hell breaks loose then and Lord Arlen roars off to settle things with his wife and this Matty Groves, and most everybody ends up dead as usual in these kinds of songs, but still it's a great tune and I thought it a good name for my fiddle, as she is a frolicsome young dame, too.

Star log, Nov. 26. Wind from the south. Fair skies. Decide to avoid New Bedford due to risk of capture and so set sail directly across Buzzards Bay, on Course 075 for small harbor called Woods Hole. Hope to make passage through Devil's Eye to save time. Chart so far proving good and true.

I found out why it's called Devil's Eye. After a fast and very pleasant ride across the bay, I entered the passage between the Elizabeth Islands and the mainland of Cape Cod and was not even fairly into it when I encountered a tide rip so fierce as to make the very ocean itself writhe and foam like a mighty, raging river. I was able to hold my head in the torrent for a few moments, but I made a slight wrong move with the tiller and was turned violently around in the current and nearly sent tail over teacups, with the *Star* spinning around drunkenly, her sail flapping like a wild thing, and her boom swinging back and forth, threatening to brain me and send me overboard. *Finally,* I despaired, *for all my efforts and all my troubles I am going to end up as mere fish food, after all.* And on such a beautiful day, too, with blue skies and gentle breezes and all to lull me into complacency. Just goes to show, never trust the sea. Sometimes Neptune is your friend, and sometimes he ain't, and I vowed never to forget that again.

After being spit back into Buzzards Bay, I regained control and put in to shore to wait for the tide to turn, hoping no other sailor saw me sent all *a-hoo* like that. Would hurt my nautical pride, it would.

The tide did turn and I went through the Eye again and, this time, slipped right into the charming little port of Woods Hole. It has a perfectly protected inner harbor called, I found out later, Eel Pond, which didn't sound too cozy, but what the hell, I didn't see any slimy eels trying to climb aboard, so I pulled next to a likely looking dock and...*Aha!* If that ain't a right jolly tavern right there, then my name ain't Jacky Faber, Singing and Dancing Toast of Two Continents. Three, if you count the time in Algiers last summer, on the tabletop in that hashish den, with my emerald—the jewel, not the ship—stuck in my belly button and...well, never mind.

After I scouted the little town and satisfied myself that there were none of those WANTED posters around, I marched into the tavern and pronounced to the landlord that I was the renowned musician and singer Nancy Alsop and that if he was lucky enough to have me perform in his establishment for one, maybe two nights, I would do these sets in return for lodging, a bath, and whatever tips I might earn from the crowd. He, of course, would gain from the selling of his beers, wines, and whiskies to the increased crowds. When he looked doubtful, I pulled the newly christened Lady Gay from under my arm, put her under my chin, and whipped off a bit of "The Queen of the County Down," sang a verse, and ended with a rattle of my hooves on the floor.

Entertainment of any kind, good or bad, is rare in these small towns, and I am hired, in spite of my youth and gender.

As my bath was being prepared, I wandered through the town, playing on my concertina and announcing that I would be playing at Landlord Prosser's that evening and that all should attend for a night of good fun and entertainment. It did not take long to make a circuit of the village, but I thought that would be enough to get the word out.

It was. We had a good crowd the first night, and a full house the second. Got men, young and old, and women, and yes, kids, too. Entertainment is hard to find and cruel winter's coming on.

Being that Cape Cod was a seafaring place, I kept my act generally turned in that direction, with merry songs of the sea like "The Kangaroo"—"*a China Rat and a Bengal Cat and a Bombay Cockatoo, all on board the Kangaroo.*" And sad songs like "The Lowland Sea"—"*and he crossed his hands upon his breast and he sank to the bottom of the low-land, lowland, lowland sea...*"

Of course, "Cape Cod Girls" goes over real big here— "*Cape Cod girls ain't got no combs, they combs their hair with codfish bones, boys...*"

I sprinkled the act with Irish and Scottish tunes, too, 'cause that's where a lot of these people come from original-like, and I go back and forth from fiddle to concertina to pennywhistle, peppering all with dancing. And I end off, as I always do, with "The Parting Glass"—"*Good night and Joy to you all*"—and I always think of Gully MacFarland, him who taught it to me.

Course there were a couple, well, maybe more than a couple, of the local youngbloods who would like to get to know me better, but I put them off, saying they should pay attention to their local girls as I am sure they are much worthier than I, and not to think that I have any great worth for merely being a stranger. And besides, while you boys are so very pretty, and so very charming, I *am* promised to another.

Back in my room, with some more jingle in my purse, I prepared for bed. First, I tapped the little wood wedges I carry with me under the door so it could not be swung inward. Then I took off my clothes and crawled into bed and I must admit that the bed did feel awfully good. Although my bunk on my dear *Star* is much loved, it does sometimes tend to be a bit damp, and this bed is not. I burrow in, knees to chest.

Good night, Jaimy. Your girl is off again in the morning.

Star log, Nov. 28. 07:30. Under way on Course 053. Winds from southeast, 10 knots. Seas 2 to 4 feet. Weather clear. Fine day. 09:35 altered Course to 045. 12:12 altered Course, 033. Heading for Poponesset Bay. 13:50 sighted town of Mashpee. 16:45 moored alongside pier in Mashpee.

Star log, Nov. 29. 07:30. Under way on Course 047. Winds fair, but chill. Hope to make Yarmouth.

Mashpee was good. Another ten dollars. But I've got to get going. Winter is setting in.

16:30. Made Yarmouth. Moored. Bigger town than the others. No WANTED posters. Play at Bull and Moose tonight.

Looks to be a rowdy place. Must be careful here. Self notes that while Landlady Willendorfer seems upright and kind, Landlord Willendorfer has a roving eye, it roving mostly over me. When Mrs. Willendorfer is not watching, Mr. Willendorfer makes his interest plain to me.

The night's show went well, and I made a neat twelve dollars and left the stage to great applause. Dressed, as always in these shows, in my serving-girl gear to set the crowd's mind at ease as to who and what I was, I did my usual set and added to it two new songs that I learned from the fiddler on the *Enterprise*. One was "Billy Broke Locks," about a jailbreak, which I could certainly warm to, having been behind bars more than a few times myself, and "Three Jolly Coachmen," a slightly bawdy little piece that I used to get the crowd roused up and singing along. If you can get the audience to do half the work by singing the chorus, why, all the better, I say, and this song has a lot of repeated lines that make it just right for such a thing. I started out the song on my own...

> *Three Jolly Coachmen sat in an English Tavern,*
> *Three Jolly Coachmen sat in an English Tavern,*
> *And they decided,*
> *And they decided,*
> *And they decided...*
> *To have another flagon!*

By the second line, the crowd, seated at tables grouped around me on three sides, got the idea and they would come in and repeat the first line once and the third line twice.

Next there would be a slight pause, and I would come in at the last line, the hook, as we performers call it. Then on to the next verse, which also serves as the chorus...

Landlord, fill the Flowing Bowl until it doth run over,
Landlord, fill the Flowing Bowl until it doth run over,
For tonight 'tis merry I'll be,
For tonight 'tis merry I'll be,
For tonight 'tis merry I'll be...
Tomorrow I'll be sober!

That gets a laugh, as does the next verse...

Here's to the man who drinks water pure and goes to bed
* quite sober,*
Here's to the man who drinks water pure and goes to bed
* quite sober.*
He falls as the leaves do fall,
He falls as the leaves do fall,
He falls as the leaves do fall...
He'll die before October!

Back to the chorus again, and with each verse, I draw out the pause longer and longer before the last line for the best comic effect. Now to the maid who steals a kiss...

Here's to the maid who steals a kiss and runs to tell her
* mother,*
Here's to the maid who steals a kiss and runs to tell her
* mother,*
She's a foolish, foolish lass,

She's a foolish, foolish lass,
She's a foolish, foolish lass...
For she'll not get another!

There are cries of *"Hear! Hear!"* from the younger men, who look across to meet the eyes of the young women seated with their parents, and then it's on to the last verse...

Here's to the maid who steals a kiss and stays to have
*   another,*
Here's to the maid who steals a kiss and stays to have
*   another,*
She's a boon to all mankind,
She's a boon to all mankind,
She's a boon to all mankind...

And here I let the pause go on seemingly forever, till at last I put aside my concertina, puff out my belly and grab it with both hands, and sing out the last line...

...For soon she'll be a mother!

There are roars of laughter and admonishing fingers waved in the faces of young women by the fathers and mothers of same. From the hot glances I see cast around the room twixt the young men and young women, however, I don't think their warnings are gonna do much good in the end.

One more chorus, which fairly shakes the rafters, a restatement of the melody on the fiddle, a bit of a dance, a bow, and off.

As always, when I'm between sets in these taverns, I don

the apron and help serve the crowd. They are getting more customers because of me being there, and the landladies are glad of the help and it puts them on my side. Plus, I get some more tips that way. All I have to do is dodge the more rascally hands and all is well.

Because the crowd was jolly and the money good, I had planned to do another night, in spite of my desire to get to Boston as quickly as possible, but events of that evening changed my mind on that.

For when I got back to my room, I noticed that the door opened out into the hall, so I couldn't put my wedges under to secure it. There was a crude lock and I was given a key, so I chided myself for being overly concerned about the door—*Hey, this is a respectable house, you big baby*—and prepared for bed. Soon I'm in my nightshirt and under the covers, and after knocking off a quick prayer for the safety of those friends of mine who might still be alive and the salvation of those who ain't, I curl up and drift off to sleep, thinking amorous and, by the standards of almost any religion that I know of, highly impure thoughts of Jaimy.

In the past I have noticed that when I am suddenly startled, I feel the muscles above my ears tighten, and I have always felt that that was the animal in me trying to prick up its ears...and it was happening now and it brought me quickly up out of sleep. *Was that the lock rattling?* I turned over on my back and my eyes popped open just as a hand came across my mouth and I saw the landlord leaning over me, clad only in nightshirt and cap.

"Shush, shush, now dearie. We're just going to have a little fun," he said. "Shush, now..."

I figured he was aiming to get a little more entertainment out of his entertainer, but I also reckoned he wasn't gonna get it. I jerked my head to the side just enough to get my mouth clear of his hand and then bit down *hard* on the finger I felt on my cheek. He cried out in pain and jerked his hand from my jaws, and I screeched out, "Help, help, help!" And anyone who has ever heard me bellow out an order on a ship knows that for my size, I can really shout.

I succeeded in rousing the house, or at least I got up old Mother Willendorfer, who came charging into the room in her own nightdress and cap, with fire in her eye and a frying pan in her hand, and the landlord wailed, "Now, Mother, I was just seein' if she was settled in right." But she wasn't having any of that and she swung her frying pan up alongside his head with a mighty *boooonnng* and he went careening out the door and she got him again and he tumbled down the stairs to the great hilarity of those who still sat about the fire in the great room.

I ran to the top of the stairs with my shiv in my hand, my nightdress billowing about me, my hair all undone and looking a sight, I know.

"Well struck, Madam!" sang out the residents of the inn, who were pouring out of their own rooms in various states of undress, and who plainly did not have a very high opinion of either the landlord's generosity or his character, and adding, "Let's have another for the cheap bastard, him who won't fill a pint up to the proper top! And another for the poor girl! Oh, the poor thing!"

The poor thing herself continued to watch the mayhem in astonishment. The unfortunate Landlord Willendorfer was now on his hands and knees, bum in the air, and his missus gave him a swat there, too, then succeeded in kicking him moaning and groaning back to their quarters, where I am sure he did not pass a very pleasant night. I wondered what had gone on in his mind when he planned his little visit with me. Did he really think I'd just go *tee-hee* and comply with his wishes? Men, I swear...

Later, when all is quiet, I'm thinking that maybe in light of what happened with the now lumpy-headed and very sorry landlord, I should not have sung that "Jolly Coachmen" song, for perhaps it might have given him the wrong notion as to my own character, him figuring me to be free and easy in my ways. Which I surely am, in some ways, but not in all. Still, the song was not *that* bad, considering the words to some I know. Tucked deep in my seabag I still have the book *Laugh and Be Fat* that I bought back in Ireland, which is filled with the awfullest, most gross and foul jokes and songs in the world, all of which used to send both me and Mairead Delaney into fits and howls of uncontrollable laughter back in my cabin on the *Emerald* during that time she sailed with me. *Dear Mairead, you of the flaming red hair and fiery spirit, I do hope you and Ian are well and happy...*

Note to self: Never, never again sleep in a room that cannot be locked from the inside. And maybe lay off the naughty songs when you don't know the lay of the land. So resolved, and so back to bed.

Star log, Nov. 30. 05:00. Under way on Course 090. Weather clear, winds fair and from the southwest. Making good time. Bound for Chatham.

And so it went, from Chatham to Eastham, from Wellfleet to Provincetown, and, on a terrific, tearing beam reach, from Provincetown across Cape Cod Bay to Green Harbor. Thence to Scituate and then, on the next day, into Boston Harbor.

I played in each of those towns, and in each made money, and all in all, my voyage around the Cape was most pleasant. I could happily do this for a long time, plying the musical trade I have learned, seeing places I have never seen before, meeting good people and bringing them a good time, but winter's about to set in, and I must find out what's happening at the Home for Little Wanderers and what's up with Jaimy, and what is to be my own fate as well, so I press on.

I anchored this last night in the lee of one of the many islands that dot Boston Harbor. I made myself a nice dinner and ate it, then sat sipping my wine and watching the sunset. No black clouds, neither in the sky nor in my mind. This journey has been good for me, I reflect, putting my hand on the tiller of my lovely *Star*. In a way, a very small way, to be sure, I am again Tonda-lay-o, Queen of the Ocean Sea.

Tomorrow, Boston.

Chapter 6

The coast seems to be clear. Having left the *Morning Star* in the care of my newfound coxswain, Jim Tanner, I'm peeking around the corner of a warehouse and peering up and down Boston's Union Street, but no, I don't see anything that looks like a British soldier, sailor, officer, or spy, so I continue watchfully on my way down to my intended destination, that destination being the office of Ezra Pickering, Esquire. Before I left the *Star,* I had gone down into the cabin and changed into my old black school dress, the one I had once so proudly worn as a student at the Lawson Peabody School for Young Girls. Well, *sometimes* so proudly worn, that is—there was that time when Mistress Pimm stripped it from my back for bringing shame and disgrace to her school, and I was put in serving-girl gear in punishment for my crimes against ladyhood. Ah, yes, those good old golden school days…

I also donned my mantilla, the black lace one that Randall Trevelyne gave me that Christmas at Dovecote, and wrapped it around my head, shoulders, and face for both warmth and disguise. It is a cold day and there is, after all, a hefty reward out for my capture. I wonder if they've gotten to Boston yet with their damned posters. I haven't seen any, but that doesn't mean there ain't some around.

I go through the Haymarket Square, past Faneuil Hall, then go right onto Union Street.

Was it only the Christmas before last that Randall gave me this shawl? It seems like a century ago, that—*Ah, here we are...*

Damn! Ezra's door is locked! Where the hell could he be?

*Hmmm...*I'm thinking he's probably in court, today being Monday and him being a lawyer and all. Well, I can't stay around here—too suspicious looking, a lone female hanging about the streets—so I'll walk up to Court Street and see if I can catch him there. Shouldn't be any danger lurking in an American courthouse, 'cept maybe from that swine Constable Wiggins, who for certain would still enjoy getting his piggy paws around my blameless neck.

I start back up in that direction and get over to State Street, looking about me with fondness on this town where I washed up two years ago and which I've grown to love. I had some of the best of times here, as well as some of the worst, and it is here on this soil that I have made some of my finest and truest friendships. Ah, well, enough of that...

I trudge up State—*oh, and there's The Pig. Ah, how I would love to stop in to see Maudie and...no, not yet. Careful now, girl, you've no wish to dance your last dance at the end of a rope*—and step onto Court Street and there's that hateful jail of which I have no fond memories whatsoever, having once spent a *very* uncomfortable night there, and there's the courthouse where I was tried and convicted, and there...

And there, from that same courthouse, comes a chattering gaggle of women. I know from the brightness of their dress and the amount of rouge and powder on their faces, they are Mrs. Bodeen's girls, once again having got into trouble with Wiggins and once again being released from custody—after a suitable bribe was paid, of course. They are followed shortly down the stairs by the plump form of Ezra Pickering, Attorney at Law and Clerk of the Corporation of Faber Shipping, Worldwide. And my dear friend and protector, as well. Having done his duty for Mrs. Bodeen and her girls, he is plainly headed back to his office, his sweet little half smile still in place, as always. *Oh, Ezra, how good it is to see you again!*

I keep on walking toward him, my head down and my veil carefully tucked about my lower face. As we draw near, he doffs his hat and murmurs, "Good day, Miss," but instead of nodding in return, I whip around to link my arm in his and commence walking in step with him.

"So, Ezra," I say, "and what is the state of Faber Shipping, Worldwide, then?"

He is ever the cool one. Though I could feel his arm tighten as I slipped mine in his, he does not even break stride.

"Ah, Jacky. So good to see you. Or part of you," he says, gazing at my eyes above the veil. "Are you cold?"

"No, Ezra," I say, "but there *is* a bit of a problem."

He sighs and pats my hand. "Of course."

We get back to his office, I doff my mantilla, we joyously embrace, and then I lay it all out before him—my time on the *Wolverine,* the taking of the prizes, including the *Emerald,* the buccaneering, the eventual loss of my ship, my own capture, the great battle, and my escape over the ocean back to here.

"Astounding. Absolutely astounding," he says when I am done. He shakes his head in wonder. "So the charge is piracy?"

I nod. "Aye. And a few others. I think they are especially miffed at my taking the *Emerald* without asking permission."

"You are probably right in thinking that. And *miffed* is hardly the word. The British Lion does not like having his nose tweaked," says Ezra, "particularly by a young girl barely halfway through her teens."

I look down at my hands in contrition. "I know, Ezra, that I tend to be a bit impulsive at times, but it all seems so *reasonable* at the time I do these things, and so *un*reasonable when everyone looks back at what happened and what I did."

"Well, I must say I expected nothing less of you, given your nature. But since you are quite obviously guilty of the crimes with which you are charged, we cannot fight this in any court, we can only contrive to hide you till this all blows over, if it ever does. You are sure Lord Nelson is dead?"

"Yes. It was the last signal I saw as I sailed out of range. I'm sure that both the Royal Navy and the country itself are devastated. For a little man, lacking an arm, one eye, and, sometimes, common sense, he was much loved by all who knew him."

"I'm sure. England's joy at Napoléon's fleet being destroyed and the homeland being saved from invasion would be severely mitigated by news of his death," says Ezra. He rises from his chair and clasps his hands behind him as he paces the floor, thinking. *Good Ezra, keep on thinking and get me out of this mess.* "However, we can turn this to our advantage," he continues. "There are three British warships in the harbor right now..."

"I know. I spotted them on my way in. His Majesty's ships *Sirius*, *Aldebron*, and *Revenge*. I stayed well away from them, you may be sure."

"Good. Now I shall put out word about the great victory and the death of Nelson and they will all be gone in the morning, rushing back to Britain to pick up whatever pieces need picking up. Carlson, come here!"

A young man appears from a side room. *Hmm... Ezra must be doing better—he has hired himself a clerk.* Carlson looks over Ezra's shoulder, mystified at the sight of me sitting here looking all Spanish. Ezra gives him quick, concise instructions, and then the young man leaves to spread the word to the British ships. I can well imagine the uproar.

"Well," says Ezra, sitting down opposite me at his desk, "that takes care of that. I believe we shall be Brit free very shortly. Except for you, of course."

I sit quiet for a while and then I say, "For all of it, Ezra, the thing I regret most is the fact that the home for orphans that I had set up with my prizes will now go begging... My poor, dear grandfather."

"I did receive your letter that you had sent from Waterford, hinting at what you had been up to," he says, "and I think I can set your mind at ease as to the London Home for Little Wanderers. Miss Amy Trevelyne, upon hearing the news of your letter, immediately directed me to forward all the proceeds of the book she had written concerning your early life—and those proceeds are considerable, believe me—to the orphanage, in your name."

Well, I'll be damned... I guess that book did some good, after all.

"...and that brings me to another point. I have recently met with Mistress Pimm at the Lawson Peabody School for Young Girls, trying to pry out of her very tight fist the tuition money you had left there so that you, or your orphanage, could have the benefit of it and I could finally get my commission out of all this, but she would have none of it." He pauses. "However, she did say that she had learned of the circumstances of your actions when you were last in Boston and that she was prepared to receive you back at the school, under certain conditions."

I am astounded. "But I thought the school was burned to the ground, and that I had caused—"

"You caused nothing. It was not your fault. The Lawson Peabody is being rebuilt and it is almost complete—and this time with bricks, not wood. The girls will be returning after Christmas."

"Oh, and Constable Wiggins?"

"Well, he has said he would like to question you about the fire."

"I bet he would," says I, putting my hand to my neck, which not so long ago had been encircled by that same Wiggins's hand as he hauled me off to jail and deep disgrace. "Probably with the aid of a five-foot rod laid across my backside. I think I'd best be on my way."

"Now, wait, Jacky," says Ezra, coming around his desk. "Think on this: While the British have no jurisdiction here, there is nothing to prevent them from secretly nabbing you on the street should they spot you. The school would be an excellent place for you to hide until this thing blows over. You know that Mistress Pimm would never allow an unwelcome male through her doors, no matter what the reason, if there was a threat to one of her girls. She was a patriot during the Revolution and has no love for the British government. Your tuition is paid and winter is coming on. It is warm there and you have friends. Your only alternative is going to the frontier, and I don't think you would like that. It is very harsh there."

I think on this for a while, and I begin to see the wisdom of what he says. Winters here are cold, and if I do the singing-and-dancing thing in the taverns, I'm sure to be spotted by someone anxious to collect the reward. Even if I go back down to the Cape or over to New York or Philadelphia, it would be the same. British Intelligence has operatives everywhere. Maybe he's right...

"I still can't believe Mistress would take me back."

Ezra sits again and smiles at me. "I believe she considers you an especially challenging...project."

"*Hmmm.* She is up at the school?"

"Yes, overseeing every nail, every board, every bit of trim. The school is being put back *exactly* as before—except that it's bricks this time, not wood. For obvious reasons. That and the fact that it's now a law. Right after you left, as a matter of fact. The embers hadn't even cooled on Beacon Hill before the town fathers passed an ordinance forbidding any more wooden buildings within the city limits." Ezra leans back and smiles expansively. "So...*sic transit Jacky!*"

"Very funny, Ezra," I say, and go silent for a while. Then I put on the Look and stick my nose in the air and say, "And Amy Trevelyne. What of her?"

"You must go see her. She has not been herself since you left."

"Why? I should think she would have felt well rid of me."

"I know what you are thinking: That she betrayed you to the Preacher's hired thugs. But that was a misunderstanding. When I received the letter from you and told her of it, she asked to see it and I reluctantly gave it to her. Her immense joy at knowing you were still alive and well was immediately dashed by the realization that you thought she had betrayed you."

I know I look doubtful, and still I say nothing.

"You must do this for her, Jacky."

I take a deep breath and then say, "Very well. I shall now go and pay a call on Mistress Pimm. And then tomorrow we shall go see Amy."

"That is both wise and good of you, Jacky. However, the coach does not run down to Quincy tomorrow."

"Just meet me at Codman's Wharf, Ezra, at eight o'clock in the morning," I say, "and we shall go to Dovecote. Bring a coat, and maybe a bit of brandy, as it might be chilly." I get up, take his hands in mine, kiss him on the cheek, and leave his office, my mantilla wrapped tight about my face.

The school is on the same spot, built on the same foundation, but it is now made of brick, red brick, and it has a slightly different kind of roof—but it is essentially the same, right down to the widow's walk perched up top. I imagine Mistress insisted. The stables have been rebuilt, too, but not the church. The churchyard remains, and I guess always will remain. I pause for a second by Janey Porter's grave on the other side of the stone wall, same as it was that first day I came upon it, except that now there is a gravestone put at her head.

Here Lyeth ye Body of
Jane Porter
A goode girl cut down in the prime
of her Sixteenth year.
1802
Requiescat in Pacem

I do hope you are resting in peace now, Janey, I do.

I stand for a while, and then I turn and enter the kitchen door, which is where it always was, opening through the stone foundation in the back.

It's like nothing had ever happened. Peg is standing at the steaming stove as usual and the girls are dashing about getting ready to serve dinner. Annie's mouth drops open upon seeing me and she gasps, "Jesus, Mary, and Joseph! It's Jacky!" I'd planned on saying something arch and clever, but when Peg turns and sees me and I see her sweet face, she who was like a mum to me, I start bawling and hold out my arms to her and am folded into her warm embrace.

Eventually I recover somewhat and we have a joyous re-union. Everyone's here 'cept Abby, who married the other Barkley boy and is now great with child, and I'm told Betsey and Ephraim will marry in the spring when they are fully set up in the furniture-making business. Annie still carries a torch for that Davy, and Sylvie Rossio and Henry Hoffman are still hand-fervently-in-hand and will marry as soon as their parents say they are old enough.

There are two new girls, the jolly Ruby McCourt, who's a cousin of the Byrnes sisters, and Katy Deere, a tall, thin, and very reserved girl from the frontier, who I am told just showed up one day at Peg's kitchen door, half starved and looking for work. She is very solemn and not much given to smiling.

We chatter on deliriously, and although I want to stay there with them forever, these, my sisters of the Dread Sisterhood of the Lawson Peabody Serving Girl Division, I must get something done. After gratefully accepting an invitation to spend the night with Annie and her family, I ask about and am told that Mistress's office is in the same place it used to be, so I climb the stairs to the second floor and approach the door. I smooth down the front of my dress, take a deep breath, and knock.

"Come in," says the voice from within.

I open the door and enter. All the furniture is new, as are the rugs and curtains, but the white line is still drawn upon the floor. Although I have seen and done a lot of things since last I left this place, I go up and put my toes on the line and I am once again a schoolgirl. Mistress Pimm, Headmistress of the Lawson Peabody School for Young Girls, is seated at her desk, her iron-gray hair drawn back in that same severe bun.

"Good day, Mistress." I fix my eyes on a spot on the far wall and wait.

She looks up and says, "Ah, Miss Faber. So, you have returned to us." She regards me without expression. "I do not, however, recall having dismissed you when you left last year."

"No, Mistress, but at the time it seemed the best thing for all concerned." Being that the school and church and stables were all burning down, largely because of me...well, totally because of me.

She smiles slightly at this and says, "Perhaps so. Well, I have spoken with your attorney and informed him that you are welcome to come back to resume your studies, as you still have tuition on the books, and, if I guess right, you still have not attained your majority. That is, if you are still innocent."

That again.

"Yes, Mistress," I say, and think to myself, *It was a close thing a few times, but...*

"When last I asked that question, you blushed. This time you did not. Why is that?"

"Much water under the bridge, Mistress."

She nods. "Will you come back?"

"I would be honored, Mistress," I say.

"Where are you staying?"

"I'll stay the night with the Byrnes sisters. Tomorrow, I must go see Miss Trevelyne. I hear she is poorly."

She considers this. "Very well. But when you come back into this school, you will be completely under my guidance and tutelage. Is that understood?"

"Yes, Mistress."

"Good. Now you will join me for dinner." She reaches up to pull on her tasselled cord. Far off, I hear a bell, and I know that Annie or one of the others will be on her way up. "And you will tell me of your travels."

I will and I do.

Chapter 7

"You know," says Ezra, "this is not entirely un-pleasant."

He certainly had looked dubious about the whole notion of getting to Quincy by boat this morning when first he shakily boarded the *Morning Star*, but now, as we cut cleanly through the calm waters of Boston Bay under a sky of brilliant blue, he appears to have changed his mind. He relaxes against the railing, then says, "Ah yes, me, for the life on the open sea. And I did not even need my coat. Yo, ho, ho."

I have to smile at the notion of the newly nautical Mr. Pickering. "Indeed, it is a fine day, Ezra," says I from my place at the tiller. "But you can never trust the sea completely, as Father Neptune can turn nasty in a minute. It is his nature to suddenly test those who would presume to ride in comfort upon his ocean."

"I shall take that advice to heart, Miss Alsop," says Ezra, using my alias for the benefit of Jim Tanner, who is trimming the sail and who, while proving to be a good lad, cannot be completely trusted yet. Two hundred and fifty pounds is a lot of money and would be a mighty temptation to a penniless boy.

"Here, Master Tanner, be so good as to take the tiller. Steer between those two islands up ahead. I must check the chart." Saying that, I get up, hand the tiller over to him, and duck down into the cuddy to get the map. He squints up at the sail and alters his course a bit. It seems he does know a good bit of small-boat handling.

Jim is now decked out in new shirt and trousers, of which he is most proud. If he proves worthy, he shall get shoes and, when winter really sets in, a monkey jacket that will hold him in good stead if he continues to follow a sea-faring life...*Have your monkey jacket always at your command, for beware the cold nor'westers on the Banks of New Found Land,* as the song goes. I intend to put both the *Star* and Jim to work. When we return from Dovecote, I will buy some fish-and-lobster traps and Jim shall tend them with the *Star* so we'll make some money so I'll be able to pay for his keep. I really don't think I can chance playing in any of the local taverns, and Mistress ain't gonna allow me out, anyway. Buying the traps and keeping Jim fed will be a drain on my meager finances, but I should see a good return on my money. I don't have much, but I do have a sturdy little boat and a promising young coxswain.

Yesterday, after I had dinner with Mistress and before I headed to the Byrnes's place, I went back down to the docks and found that Jim had indeed found a more permanent and secure mooring for our *Star* and was standing by, as ordered. I noticed, too, that he had bailed the bilges completely, without being told to, and that pleased me greatly.

So pleased was I that I took him up into the town, bought him a meat pie from a vendor in the marketplace, and then went into a dry-goods store. There I purchased the pair of trousers, the drawers, and the blue striped shirt he now wears, all of which I refused to let him put on just then. We then proceeded up the street till we came to a wash-house that I knew of. As soon as Jim saw just what I was up to, he tried to run, but I grabbed his arm and held it tight and said through my teeth, "You do this and I'll allow you to sleep inside the cuddy from now on. But you will not climb dirty into my *Morning Star* bed, count on it, boy." *Besides, if you want to work for Faber Shipping, Worldwide, you must be clean and presentable, by God.*

"Here, Madam," I said to the washerwoman, who stood between her steaming tubs of water. "Wash this down thoroughly and then dress it up in these clean clothes. Spare not any part of him with your brush." He squalled, but the old woman took him by the scruff of his neck and tossed him inside. I paid the woman the amount she demanded for the task at hand.

"You are sure you know how to get there by boat?" asks Ezra, when I come out of the cabin with my chart.

I fix him with a gimlet eye. "You're asking Jacky Faber, Queen of the Ocean Sea, if she can find her way about well-charted Boston Bay?" I snort.

Ezra cuts his eyes to Jim, back at the tiller.

Ooops...

But I don't think the boy heard me stupidly use my real name, he being too concentrated on making a good showing of his sailing ability on this, our maiden voyage together. And actually, he's doing quite well.

"I meant no offense, Miss," says Ezra.

"I could never take offense from you, Ezra, you know

that," I say, plopping down next to him and spreading the chart out on my lap. I'm wearing my maroon, gray, and dark green riding habit, the one that Amy gave me for Christmas two years ago, in hopes that the sight of me in it might warm her now chilly heart. I'm starting to feel a little nervous about this coming reunion. "See that big island there? That's Thompson Island. Right here on the chart." I point to it and Ezra looks at it. "We'll leave that to our port and steer directly for Quincy. When we go past the mouth of the Neponset River, we'll know we are near Dovecote, as that river forms the northern boundary of the Trevelyne estate. Jim, come a few degrees to starboard. There, that's good."

We are heading in toward Dovecote's boathouse, with me again at the tiller and Jim up on the bow, looking down for rocks. I suspect there will be none, otherwise the boathouse wouldn't have been put where it is, but one can't be too careful—I'd hate to show up at Amy's place, drenched and bedraggled from having hit a rock, swamped and capsized a mere twenty feet from the shore. As we slowly work our way in, I look at the beach and think of the many hours Amy and I spent there, she sitting on the bank reading from a book of poems or some dreary political stuff, me with my skirt off and my drawers rolled up, wading in the water. Me turning over stones to see what was under them, she begging me not to eat what I found. The scavenging orphan in me does die hard, I must admit, and I know that sometimes I am a scandal to other, more well-bred people—in this and other ways.

"All clear, Miss. I can see the bottom now and it seems to be smooth mud or sand."

"Good. We'll moor starboard side to. Ready about. Hard a'lee."

I put the tiller toward the boom, spinning the boat about, drop the sail halyard, and slip in next to the dock, pretty as you please. *You may be pleased with your own performance today, Jim Tanner, but* this *is what's called good boat handling.*

Jim jumps over and secures the lines, and Ezra and I begin our walk up to the main house.

"Make her secure, Jim," I say over my shoulder, "then go up to that house there. Go in through the kitchen in the back. I'll make sure they give you something to eat. On your best behavior, now. Remember you are a representative of Faber Shipping, Worldwide."

The other two members of that same corporation link arms and trudge up the hill toward Dovecote Hall.

After renewing acquaintances with the downstairs staff, I am informed by a serving girl named Charity that she is about to take a dinner tray up to Miss Amy, as that is her usual wont these days and... *Oh, Miss, she won't eat hardly nothin', and almost never comes out of her room, she don't, and she's gettin' awful pale...* "Well, we'll see about that, won't we, Charity," I say and take the tray from the girl and go up the stairs and down the hall to Amy's room and knock on the door.

A faint "Come in" is heard from within.

I open the door and say, "Your dinner, Miss."

I see her there, seated at her desk, facing the window. She has on her black school dress and has gone back to putting her dark hair up in the severe bun that she had worn before she was graced with the dubious joy of my friendship. Her head is down and she is scratching away at a paper with her quill. She lifts that selfsame quill and dips it in her inkwell, and then resumes writing. She does not turn around.

"Put it there," she says, gesturing toward a side table.

"Yes, Miss," I say, all meek, and put down the tray. Her room is as it was before, all yellow and white and cheerful. Course last time I was in this room, I was on my hands and knees, throwing up into that chamber pot and covered in shame and disgrace.

I go back to the door and open it, then shut it as if I had just gone out. Then I go back, as silently as I can, and stand behind her and look over her shoulder at what she is writing...

When sad Melancholy in all his gray and dreary dress,
Comes to worm his way once again
Into my wan and wasting mind,
To writhe and bide in my distressed soul,
It is then that I rise and...

Christ, Amy, don't you ever cheer up, and such a pretty day out, too. It seems she is struggling to come up with the next line. I think a bit and then say, "How 'bout... *and tell him to bugger off.*"

She drops the quill, ruining a perfectly good piece of paper as well as a very bad poem. I see her shoulders begin to shake and tremble. Then she slowly turns around and looks at me, mouth open in astonishment. I flash her my best openmouthed, foxy grin, but she says nothing and only looks at me as if I were a ghost.

Abashed, I back away and drop down into a curtsy.

"I am sorry, Miss, if I intruded upon your privacy and startled you. If you want to put me out, I shall certainly understand." I start to retreat to the door. I *knew* this was a bad idea.

She gets shakily to her feet, her eyes filling with tears. Her chin is quivering and I fear she's going to faint dead away, but she doesn't. Instead she gasps, "Oh, Jacky, I've been so desperately worried. I've been..." Then she puts her face in her hands and starts crying, and I put my arms around her and gather her to my chest and make soothing noises and tears come to my own eyes, too.

"There, there, Amy. Come now. Take this handkerchief. Come, let us sit on the edge of your bed."

"How could you go off and leave me like that?" She sniffs. "You knew how I loved you, how you were my dearest friend in all the world..." She has lost a good deal of weight and there are dark circles under her eyes.

I poke at her ribs and say, "We're going to have to get some sausages down you, Miss, that's for sure. You're fair wasting away."

She continues to sniffle.

"Well," I say, in answer to her question, "when I left Dovecote in total disgrace, I was sure you hated me—after my drunken behavior at the ball, and Randall, his handsome face smashed because of me, and all. Then when I overheard those men, the ones who had kidnapped me and handed me over to the Preacher, when I heard them say that *you* had told them where to find me, I just figured you would be happy never to see the front of Jacky Faber again."

Her back bucks and she starts bawling into her hands again. "Th-that you could think that I could ever b-b-betray you..."

"I didn't blame you. I figured I had it coming. I usually do...have it coming, I mean."

"My f-father had hired those men to bring you back to us at Dovecote, that is why I told them where I thought you would be. I did not know they would take you to the Preacher."

"Back to *us*?" I ask, all innocent.

"To me...and Randall."

Ah.

"And how is young Lord Randall, and the lovely Clarissa, his bonny bride-to-be?" ask I, carelessly arranging the folds of my skirt about my knees, as if I don't really care what the answer is.

"That is off. Randall sent her back to Virginia the day you left."

Hmmm. I'd better watch my back very carefully if I ever again meet up with my old classmate and chief tormentor Miss Clarissa Worthington Howe. It'd be all right with me if that never happens, that's for sure. We loathed each other from the start, Her Ladyship and I—she figuring *me* for the upstart lowborn guttersnipe I really am, and me figuring her for the spoiled highborn snotty arrogant aristocratic brat that *she* really is. Well, maybe she'll stay down in Virginia and bother them that's unlucky enough to be around her, and not bother me.

"All right, Sister," I say, banishing Clarissa Howe from my thoughts. "Collect yourself and I will tell you what has happened since last we saw each other. But, please, *please*, do not take out your quill for a while—you've already made me famous enough, thank you. But first..."

But first there is a pounding of boots and rattling of

spurs on the stairs outside and the door flies open and there stands Randall Trevelyne, his own beautiful self, wearing a huge grin and looking perfectly splendid.

"Mr. Trevelyne, how good to see you again." I stand up and start to curtsy but he sweeps me up and I bleat out, "Now you put me down, Randall!" with my feet a good foot off the floor.

"I'll put you down when I'm ready, my girl! Well met, oh yes, very well met, Jacky!" Randall is wearing a ruffled white shirt, open at the collar, and from the smell of hot horse on him, he has been riding. Or was riding till he got word that I was here.

"I may be well met, but I ain't your girl, Randall." I put my hands upon his shoulders and look into his face. "But I was very sorry to hear that you were hurt in trying to protect my honor when last I was here, and when I was in a helpless state."

"Protect your honor? Hah! What nonsense! I was merely trying to haul you off myself for a bit of ravishment of my own when that miserable Flashby interfered. Now, give us a kiss."

"I don't believe you on that, Randall." I put my fingers to his cheek. "Is that scar from that time?"

"I count it a badge of honor, my dear."

"And well you should. Thank you. And I mean that."

He cocks his head to the side and peers at my temple. "What are these blue specks by your eye? Surely they can't be the latest fashion idiocy from Europe."

"I did not think they were noticeable, Sir."

"They aren't. Only when one gets this close." I can feel his breath on my face. He is angling his mouth toward mine. I duck my head and put my fingers to his chin and gently push him back.

"I must tell you, Randall, that I am still promised to another, and you really must put me down." I say that, but I cannot help but smile at the rogue as I say it. Randall Trevelyne may be a spoiled rake, but he's damned handsome and dashing as all hell.

"And I must tell you, Jacky, that I've heard that foolishness from you before, and I'll tell you this, too: I do not care if you are promised to a hundred men, as long as I am one of them. Now, enough idle talk. Off to my chambers with the two of us, to drink deeply from the Cup of Love!" And the dog actually turns to carry me out the door.

"Very poetic, Mr. Trevelyne, but I fear you mean the Cup of Lust, not Love, and though your offers are charming"— *and though I have never recoiled from the thought of a bit of a tumble with the beautiful Mr. Trevelyne, I must be good*— "nay, we shall not drink from that cup," I say firmly, trying to wriggle free and not succeeding.

"All right, plenty of time for that later. One kiss and tell me about the blue speckles and I'll let you down, I promise."

I put my head forward and kiss him on the forehead and say, "They are powder burns I got from leaning over a cannon."

"Why were you leaning over a gun?" he asks, astounded now.

"I was aiming it. At the French. At Trafalgar."

He is even more astonished now. He puts me down and my feet once again touch the floor. He steps back and gives a quick, formal bow, his face now set and unsmiling. "Forgive me. I did not realize I was mishandling a damned war hero." It is plain that he has heard of the Great Battle, and this information is not going down well with him.

It has always rankled Randall that though he is a lieutenant in the local militia, he has never been tested in combat, while I, a mere girl, have been. *Count yourself lucky, Mr. Trevelyne, you who have both your fine arms still hanging by your side and both your fine legs still under you.*

"Those specks are a true badge of honor, not a counterfeit such as I wear. I salute you. You should wear those marks with pride."

"I wear them because I must, and you must not mistake them for signs of valor, as I have none. I hold male concepts of honor in no great stead. I count myself a coward and have trembled and shaken through any danger I ever was in."

Randall gives out a snort. "Still, it must have been very exciting to be at that battle. Reports of it have been sweeping the town. They are calling it the greatest naval battle in history."

Ezra's man Carlson has done his job well, I reflect, and then say, "I don't care about history, and no, it wasn't exciting. It was horrible. I lost many dear friends that day. I hope that I never see anything like it ever again."

He stands and appears to think on that for a moment. Then he crosses the room and throws himself into a chair. "So now you have two blue tattoos. One upper and one... lower." He throws one booted leg over the other, his spurs jingling. He seems to be recovering some of his old cheek. That is good—I prefer him this way.

"Even so, Mr. Trevelyne," I say, giving a slight bob. Randall is one of many, I'm afraid, who have seen my Brotherhood tattoo in the flesh, as it were. I do consider myself to be a good girl, but I do seem to lose my clothing quite often in certain highly charged circumstances.

"So what brings you back to dull old Dovecote?"

"Ah, well, I'm in a spot of trouble with the British government and must hide out for a bit." I go over to Amy and put my arm around her shoulders and shine my countenance down upon her. "Actually, Sister, I'll be going back to Lawson Peabody to hide till things get less hot for me."

"Oh, Jacky, I am so glad!" exclaims Amy, clasping her hands together and squeezing her eyes shut in great joy. *Amy, my dear friend Amy, you should already know that a little of Jacky Faber goes a long, long way.*

"I, too, am glad," says Randall, getting to his feet once again. "It will give me time to work on what might be left of your virtue."

"Randall has been expelled from college for the rest of this term," says Amy, primly. "For duelling. That is why we are honored with his presence. It was the headmaster's son in whom Randall put a hole."

"The little prig should have borne his honorable wound with pride," says Randall, looking put upon. "But to hell with it. I am sick to death of schoolwork, anyway."

"I believe the British Army is hiring cannon fodder for a campaign against Napoléon," say I, wickedly, the old evil rising up in me, "if you are so bored with student life, or life in general. Oh, and the Austrians, too, will be needing soldiers, as Boney's after them now. And with your experience, why, you would surely be made a private, at least. Maybe even a corporal."

Randall looks at me with fire in his eye, but he nods and decides to smile at my banter. He gets to his feet, bows low, and says, "I believe I saw my sister's fat friend Pickering down below. Shall we all go to dinner and hear more tales of your adventures?"

Hey, Ezra ain't fat, he's...well...sleek is what he is. Sleek, like a well-fed seal. Or, hey, maybe even a Silkie...

Dinner is a jolly affair, with Ezra seated beside Amy, and me next to Randall. Randall drinks too much wine, but that's to be expected. At least he is not the kind to get mean when he's in his cups but is more likely to sing and tell rude jokes and put his hand on my knee. He actually gets on well with Ezra and refrains from insulting him, which surprises me. Maybe he figures that it wouldn't hurt for one as reckless as he to have a good lawyer as a possible brother-in-law. He's probably right.

"You said the British were looking for you?" asks Randall. He gestures for his glass to be refilled, and it is. "What do they mean to do with you if they find you?"

"I think they mean to hang me. I believe it's been decided that this would be the best resolution for all concerned," I say, as I let my eyes go all hooded. "'Cept maybe for me."

"What? But why?" This from both Amy and Randall. Ezra already knows, of course, and he sighs and gives out with a wry "Why, indeed..."

I put my hand inside my jacket and pull out the WANTED poster that I had torn down that day in Newport. I hand it to Amy. "That is why. Soon these will be all over Boston. When that happens, I will have to stay a virtual prisoner at the school. As for now, if I keep my face hidden, I believe I shall be all right."

Amy's eyes go wide, yet again, as she reads. "Oh, Jacky,

no!" she says, as she has said so many times before in regard to me and my ways.

Randall reaches over and snatches the paper from his sister's hand and reads. "Well, I'll be damned. You *have* been up to some serious mischief. Not only do you single-handedly save Mother England from destruction, you also dip your dainty little toe into the waters of vile piracy. Amazing!" He brings the palm of his hand loudly down upon the table. "I demand that you become my mistress immediately! It has been ordained by the gods of war and of love. One such as you and one such as I? I will hear nothing against it."

"This cannot be true," exclaims Amy. "Is it?"

"Wellllll…" The corners of my mouth pull down in a rueful grimace. "It all depends on how you look at it."

"Perhaps you had best start at the beginning," suggests Ezra.

"Yes," says Randall, beaming at me with all the lust that's in him. "At the very beginning, and spare us nothing in the telling of it."

Amy says nothing, but only looks very, *very* anxious.

And so after I take a sip of wine, I take a deep breath, then begin to tell it, and, as I did with Mistress, I mostly tell the truth. However, so as to spare Amy's Puritan sense of propriety and so as not to give Randall even more reason to try to jump me, I leave out the naughty bits. Most of them, anyway.

Later, lying in bed, with Amy sleeping contentedly beside me, I look off into the darkness and smile. *Ah, it's good to be back at Dovecote and forgiven my wanton ways, once again.*

Chapter 8

"Till later, Ezra. Have a good day, and I thank you for everything."

We have returned from our short stay at Dovecote and are back in Boston, Jim having brought in the *Star* neatly and tied her securely to the dock cleats.

Ezra steps carefully off the boat and climbs the ladder to the pier. Jim had found this excellent mooring for her tucked in between the Crane and Woodward's and the Hollowell's wharves. There's a little floating dock attached to the pier that goes up and down with the tides, so she's easy to get in and out of. This is good for Ezra, 'cause he ain't much of a sailor. But he's game, for a landlubber, I've got to give him that.

When he has gained the top, Ezra turns and tips his hat and smiles his little half smile down to me.

"And a very good day to you, too, Miss Alsop. Please do be careful. And watchful."

I assure him that I will be both and my dear Mr. Pickering heads back to his law practice.

This is a really good mooring for another reason, too, I reflect as I look across the harbor. I can see any British ships that might pull in next to Long Wharf, without them seeing me first. And they *always* moor at that wharf, it being the biggest and best in the harbor. There are none there now.

"Very well, Jim, I'm off for a while to see about the traps. Clean her up a bit, if you would. Then grab something to eat, and maybe see what Gardner's has got in the way of some small portholes for the cabin. I do hate not being able to see out from the cuddy when it's all battened down."

"Aye, aye, Captain," says Jim, and though I know he's being cheeky, I do like hearing it.

It takes me longer than I'd thought it would to bargain for the traps off the crook who was selling them, him taking me for a dumb girl and therefore to be stripped clean of any money she might have—and *she* getting steamed and contemplating physical violence—but eventually we come together and agree on the sale of five lobster/crab traps, and five fish traps, which is about all I figure Jim can handle. I also buy two clam forks for when the tide is right and the opportunity for taking some clams presents itself. Bad luck for the clams, lobsters, crabs, and fish, but good luck for Faber Shipping, Worldwide, I figure. I cannot see how we will not prosper, even if only in a small way.

I arrange to have my fishing gear picked up later, and feeling right bold because of the lack of British warships in the harbor, I work my way up State Street and duck into my beloved Pig and Whistle, scene of my first musical triumphs, for a reunion with Maudie and her man, Bob. After the joyful cries of surprise and delight on all sides, she quickly brings me up to date on how things are going... "Good, but not as good as when you and Gully MacFarland was bringin' in the crowds, and speakin' of that, Gully's been around lookin' for ye."

Gully MacFarland. *Uh-oh* ... I draw in a sharp breath, and twist around to watch my back, then ...

"But don't worry, dear, he seems to have straightened himself out a bit. Besides, he's back at sea again. Says the ocean air was good for him and he's given up the drink. I don't know if that's true, but he was a lot cleaner than when last I saw him ..."

The last time I saw Gully MacFarland, I had tied his drunken self to a wheelbarrow and delivered him to a Royal Navy ship that would take him out to sea and out of my life forever, I hoped. He'd have killed me right then and there if he'd had the chance, I know that.

"No, Jacky, he said he was thankin' you for it ... He was only looking to get his fiddle back."

"Well, Maudie, the next time you see Gully, you tell him the *Lady Lenore*'s back in London but in good hands and I'll give her back to him *if* ever I see him again and *if* I happen to have the Lady in my hands and *if* I happen to be in a for-givin' mood, in which mood I might not be, considerin' I ain't forgot how he laid his mark on me that last night we was together, so it'll have to be at arm's length, and in the presence of some of my larger friends, like ... like John Thomas there just come in the door ... John, so good to see you! Come here and give your Jacky a hug! And Smasher, too! And as pretty as ever! Tell me, who else in the old crowd is still about? Maudie, a pint for each of my friends!"

I've been gone for longer than I had planned to be and I'm hurrying back down to the docks, as I want to get started on setting the traps, so's they can get to catchin' stuff, but it was good, oh so good seeing everybody again. I wanted to do a set tonight, but I can't, I just can't do that, and when I left them, I had to say, "Now remember, if anybody asks, you ain't seen me."

I'm thinking we'll put a string of the traps on the other side of Spectacle Island. I like the looks of the bottom there. I bought ten wooden buoys to mark the traps, and I imagine I'll paint them white with a blue stripe, those being the colors of Faber Shipping. Gotta get these things settled, 'cause I ain't gonna have much freedom once school starts up again, that's for sure.

I step off the pier, go down the ladder to the floating dock, and hop onto the *Star*, where I see Jim splayed out there in the bilges, facedown. The two new portholes are lying beside him. What? Asleep on duty? Or *drunk*, even? No, I won't have that, I— Ah, no...it's not that, it's—

Horror.

I turn him over. He has been severely beaten. Blood pours from his mouth. There are thick little pools of it on the decking next to his face. His eyes are swollen and closed. *Oh, God, no.*

He stirs and tries to lift his head. Then he chokes and sobs, "I didn't tell 'em. I didn't tell the lousy bastards nothin'. Didn't give 'em the key, neither."

I look over and see that the door to the cuddy has been tried, but it looks like it didn't budge.

"Jim. Can you stand? Can you..."

"Run away, Missy. They want you. Run away now. They might be back." He's got his two skinny arms stuck down between his legs, and there is some vomit mixed with the blood on his shirt, so they must have punched him in the belly... and maybe kneed him down below, too.

"How many?"

"Two... One of 'em held me and the other one hit me." Another spasm of crying, gasping, sobbing, breath caught in his throat.

"Come, Jim, we've got to get you out of here. Up with you. I know it hurts, but we've got to get you some help."

He groans as he struggles to his knees. "But they might come back, Miss, they might get you—"

"Don't care. This is my fault that you're hurt. Don't worry about me. Up now. Put your arm around my neck. That's it. Up now. Let's get over to the side."

My mind seethes with fury. I wish now with all my heart that I still had my pistols. *The dirty sonsabitches! Damn them! Damn them to Hell!*

I get him over onto the dock and we stumble up the street. I see a man working at stacking spools of rope outside Gardner's Chandlery.

"Sir! Please help!" I cry. "Go out and hail a coach! This boy is hurt bad!"

"Why, it's our Jimmy! What—," says the man, his mouth hanging open.

"Just get the coach, Sir! *Please!*"

The man drops his coil of rope and runs down to the head of the pier and disappears around the corner of a warehouse. Soon, but not soon enough by me, a single-horse hack comes barrelling around the corner and pulls to a stop next to me and my sagging burden.

"Hold on, Jacky!" says the driver and he jumps down and helps me get Jim up onto the seat of the open coach. I don't know how he knows me, but right now I don't care.

"Thanks, Mr...."

"Strout, Jacky. Ed Strout. You and me was together in Mr. Fennel's and Mr. Bean's production of *Midsummer Night's Dream*. I was always in makeup as a donkey, which is prolly why you don't recognize me. Here...lift him up... There! Get in and we're off!" He leaps up into the driver's seat and I jump into the open coach with Jim. "Where to, Jacky?"

"The Lawson Peabody School, back door, Ed, and thanks!"

We lurch off.

I put Jim's head in my lap as we head off.

"Don't you worry, Jim. We're gonna take care of this, you'll see, you'll see, by God, you'll see."

Jim moans and says, "They had a poster...said you was the Jacky girl they was lookin' for. I said you was named Nancy Alsop and they should sod off, but they grabbed me and...I'm sorry, Missy...they messed me up and they messed up the *Star*."

"You did just fine, my brave, brave young Jim," I say, tears pouring out of my eyes and onto his face. I kiss his brow. "Just fine, you did...And I *am* the Jacky girl they're lookin' for, I am, and I should have trusted you with that so you could be more careful, but I didn't and now it's come to this...I am so sorry."

"I knowed you was that girl. I heard you talk with your mates, so don't...," he burbles through his blood-filled mouth. He grows quieter as his gasping stops and his breathing becomes more regular.

"Jim," I say softly into his ear, "what did they look like? The two men."

His cracked and bloody lips open. "Black jackets. White shirts. Black round hats. Heavy boots. Both had mustaches...dark hair...I..."

"That's enough, Jim. That will do. You rest now...Rest..."

We clatter up Center Street and onto Beacon and soon pull up to the school. Ed Strout is off the driver's seat and the door is pulled open.

"Here, Jacky, let me help you..." But the clatter of our arrival has roused the kitchen staff and the door bursts open and Peg hurries out, followed by Annie and Betsey and Katy, and they gather up Jim and take him inside. They have seen me, myself, dragged through that very door in a very similar condition to poor Jim, so they know what to do. They lay him out on a tabletop and take hot, wet cloths and wipe off the blood and check the wounds. He looks so small lying there like that. I bite my knuckle and try not to cry.

"If he needs a doctor, get him one," I manage to choke out. "I'll pay for it."

Peg pokes around at his ribs and feels his arms and legs. "Now, now, we'll see. Nothing broken...These boys are pretty tough...Made of leather and bone, they are. The cuts will heal...Wait, Jacky! Where are you going?"

But I am already at the door. "I got some business to settle," I say, and am out and gone before anyone can stop me.

_____

Somewhat later, I'm peeking around the corner of State and Union. Those thugs are undoubtedly still about... *There! Coming out of the Bull and Crown!* I sidle a little bit closer so as to get a look at them. I'm somewhat mystified by their presence, since I haven't seen any of the WANTED posters around Boston. They are putting on their broad-brimmed round black hats and hitching up their trousers after what was surely their dinner at the tavern and they step out into a beam of sunlight and... *Well, I'll be damned! It's Beadle and Strunk! Those two coves what kidnapped me and sold me to that crazy Reverend Mather when last I was here!*

It's plain to me now: Ezra had told me that those two had been banished from Boston, their license to practice their dubious trade as private investigators having been revoked after their dealings with the Reverend were brought to light. According to the town fathers reviewing the case, snatching me, a landless, underage girl, was perfectly all right and completely legal—*as long as I was delivered to the person who had hired them,* which was Colonel Trevelyne, not the Reverend. So it was merely a question of bad business practice, a breach of contract, not out of any concern for me or my wishes in the matter of my disposition. Go figure...

So Beadle and Strunk must have set up their nasty business again in either Philadelphia or New York and seen the posters when they were tacked up in those places. Recalling me from our last encounter, they figured that I'd probably be hiding out in Boston, where I knew my way around, and since they knew what I looked like, they came up here in hopes of a quick reward. *Hey, sell her once, sell her twice,* they must have joked, winking at each other as they climbed into the coach that would bring them here, *this girl's a walking industry for us, she is, and bless her for that.*

I step out and start walking down State toward the *Star.* Beadle and Strunk walk toward me. I wrap my mantilla more tightly about my lower face and cross the street so as to avoid the men. They notice this, and I see Beadle nudge Strunk and nod in my direction. Then they both quicken their pace and come at me.

I gasp and spin and start running back up State. *"Stop, there! You stop!"* I hear behind me, and I reach down and pull my skirts to my waist and turn on the speed. I dash past the Plow and Stars and then there's Mr. Yale's print shop, and then the good old Pig and Whistle, and I'm leavin' 'em behind 'cause nobody ever catches Jacky Faber in the riggin', or on foot, neither, and then I step on a cobble wrong and trip and go head over heels and I cry out in pain and get up lame. I hear shouts of triumph behind me. *We've got 'er now, by God!* but I hobble on and duck down into the alley between Mrs. Bodeen's and McGraths', and I can hear 'em pantin' behind me. I go to the end of the alley and then I stop and turn to face them. I fold my hands in front of me and I stand there quiet as they come puffing into the darkness of the narrow space.

"Ah, dearie, now that's a good girl," says the one named Strunk. He pulls a small length of rope from his pocket. "You just stand right there and be good. Put your hands out in front of you now and..."

...And then John Thomas and Smasher McGee step out of the shadows behind Beadle and Strunk. In their hands they hold heavy belaying pins, and their dark, grim faces are set. There is scant mercy to be seen in either of them.

I turn away from the sounds of struggle and head back to the school. And as I walk, I do not limp, for I didn't trip over no cobblestone back there on State Street, no, I did not.

Did two bodies wash up on the next morning's tide? I don't know, as I didn't ask. I do know that I never again laid eyes on Beadle and Strunk.

I know also that things will soon grow even hotter for me here and that I must get Jim and the *Morning Star* to Dovecote to lay over till spring. And I will have to stay in the safety of my school.

That's what I gotta do.

Chapter 9

And so it was that Jim and I and the *Star* went back to Dovecote—me to stay till school started again in January, Jim to stay there with the boat, at least until spring.

Jim had recovered enough to travel the next day, so we left early in the morning, right after a big breakfast, with Peg and the girls all fussing over him, which I know he enjoyed, although he blushed and said he didn't. Jim had to eat slowly, carefully placing the food between his bruised and split lips, but at least those two rotters didn't get any of his teeth. He might limp for a day or two, but he's young; he'll get over it.

On the way down to the *Star*, we stopped to buy Jim his heavy jacket, blue cap, and boots. And I bought him a bit of blue ribbon to tie back his curly brown hair.

We found the traps and buoys I bought the day before piled on the dock next to the boat as promised. We loaded them on board and I returned to the chandler's once more to buy some rope and blue and white paint. The money belt that I wear about my waist is getting very light.

Star log, December 4. 09:30. Under way on starboard tack from Boston to Quincy. Winds light and from the south. Will have to tack all the way to Dovecote.

Back at Dovecote, the farm kids find Jim to be an exotic—a handsome boy who wears a striped jersey, bears evidence on his face of a recent fight, walks with a swaggering roll in his step, and knows how to sail a boat. The boys, of course, want to pound him, it being in the nature of boys to do that, but I asked Edward, the stableboy I had known from before, to keep the others from beating him until he has fully recovered from his wounds, and then they could. They agree, and by the time he has healed, they are all friends and so they forgo that particular male ritual, as I thought they might. The girls, on the other hand, have something else on their minds, oh, yes, they do, and I know for sure there is more than one calico bonnet cocked in his direction—my female sense has noticed that Claire, the thirteen-year-old daughter of George Findley, the head hostler in the big stables, has for certain set her own sights on our unsuspecting Jim. We are not there many days before the clever Claire has taken his blue cap and embroidered *Morning Star* on the headband in white thread for him. *Smart girl. For that you shall get all of Faber Shipping's needlework contracts. Right now we need a new flag for our masthead. White background, two foot by three, with blue stitching. A fouled anchor, see, like the one I've drawn here...*

All in all, Jim Tanner does not lack for companionship. Nor do I.

———

And so December passed.

Jim's first task was to paint the buoys, which he did in the Great Barn with Claire in attendance, of course, *ooh*ing and *aah*ing over his skill with the brush. Then, after the paint had dried, we rigged and baited our traps and placed them out in the bay. It was with great joy and anticipation that we dropped them over the side, one by one. We vowed that we would not check them for three whole days, but when we stood on the shore and watched the buoys bouncing all jaunty out on the waves, well, we couldn't wait and were out on the second day, pulling them up. We didn't catch anything that day worth keeping, just some small crabs and trash fish, but it was wildly exciting, seeing the traps surge out of the cold water and wondering just what they might hold. Over the next few weeks, we moved the traps around till, at last, we did begin to draw some riches from the sea.

Amy is my constant companion, but Randall always seems to be around, too, which I really don't mind. Oh, he's always looking for ways to get me into his bed, or at least to that place we were that time down on the banks of red roses when...Well, never mind. It was just a close thing, is all, but now it's mostly banter, wordplay twixt the two of us, like, *So, Jacky, all I have to do is go over to England, put my sword through this Jaimy Fletcher, and then you'll consent to be my mistress?* And me back at him with *Which you might not find such an easy thing to do, milord. Lieutenant Fletcher also has a sword, and a very fine one, too...Perhaps his blade would slide between your ribs, instead. Hmmm?* All of which is all right, being just words. I mean, I know Randall would cheerfully seduce me and bring me to ruin, but he wouldn't force me. He is a gentleman, after all, and I think, beneath all his rascally exterior, good at heart. I do notice, though, that in his fanciful future plans for me, it is always as mistress, never as wife. The scoundrel.

Colonel and Mrs. Trevelyne have returned from the city and pronounce themselves delighted to see me again, which is big of them, considering the fact that I almost caused an international incident when last I was in their house. I think they put up with having me around mostly because I seem to bring some cheer to their children.

Christmas approaches and we have a fine, deep snowfall, and horse-drawn sleighs are rigged and we bundle up and go out caroling and wassailing. It is great fun, careening about the countryside and pulling up in front of houses, their lighted windows buried up to their sills in the snow, us piling out, getting into a group somewhat resembling a chorus, and belting out "Good King Wenceslaus," to the great hilarity of all. We are then invited in, to great house or small, and if the people within have a treat to give us, they give it. If not, then we give treats to them.

Toasts are drunk—in the rich houses, great bowls of wine that have spices like cinnamon and clove and nutmeg in them, and little pieces of toast floating, a piece of which is gathered up with each cup, and hence, a toast is said and drunk—and eaten, if the chunk of toast ends up in your mouth. In the poorer houses, some simple cakes are offered and we accept them in the spirit in which they are given. When we go, we leave more than we take.

Amy says that in the country, this custom is not just for fun—though I do find it great, glorious fun to be crammed in the back of a crowded sleigh, wrapped up in mufflers and scarves, thigh to thigh with Randall, his arm around my shoulders, all of us singing at the tops of our lungs, our breath, puffs of white fog in the cold winter's night. No, another reason for this practice is that it is an excuse to check on your neighbors without them taking shame or offense, to see if they are going to get through the winter all right— for we stop at the poor cottages, too, as well as the rich ones. To see if old Widow Crenshaw has enough wood stored in her shed, or if the Winslow family has enough food put up in their root cellar to feed the four children till spring, and if not, then steps are quietly taken to make things right— stacks of wood cut the proper size for the fireplace for some, sacks of potatoes, beets, and a few hams brought in for others. I find I like my country friends more and more, day by winter day.

Christmas Eve comes and we decorate the tree in the Great Hall and sing more carols, and all the people of Dovecote come with their children and we have a huge roaring party. The hall has a small stage on one end, and it doesn't take long for Jacky Faber to be up on it and doing a set. When I finish with a flourish of fiddle and dancing feet, I get generous applause, which, as always, warms the very depths of my show-off soul.

Christmas Day is quieter, with just family and me. We have a great feast, then later, when we are seated about the fireplace, we exchange gifts. I get some lovely dress fabric from the Colonel and his missus, a fine new fiddle bow from Amy, and a silver comb-and-mirror set from Randall. I protest that it is all much too much, and I can only give them something small and worthless: To each, I give a piece of the whalebone scrimshaw I had made on my whaling voyage. A naval battle scene goes to Colonel Trevelyne, an angel playing a harp to his wife, and a spouting whale to Amy. All say they like them and shall display them proudly.

When I give Randall his, I ask him to unwrap it in private, and he looks intrigued and slips it in his pocket, but the Colonel will hear nothing of it—"Come, come, let him open it now! We'll have no coyness here! Say you will allow it, my dear!"

I blush and nod.

The piece that I gave to Randall pictures a very saucy mermaid sitting on a rock. She is playing a pennywhistle, and, well...maybe she looks a bit like me.

PART II

Chapter 10

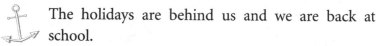 The holidays are behind us and we are back at school.

Being January, it was too cold to take the *Star*, so we had to come by coach, and we clattered up Beacon Street and piled out at the front door of the Lawson Peabody School for Young Girls. The vile Dobbs came out, surly and ill-tempered as ever, and carried our bags inside and put them in the foyer, whereupon they were carried up to the dormitory by the serving girls, all of whom I warmly embraced, having once been one of their number and treated very kindly by them as well. The vile Dobbs was not allowed up there without Mistress being with him, thank God. He gave me an especially black look, me having caused him some trouble in the past.

More coaches were pulling up, and other girls were getting out of them, and many fathers and mothers were saying farewell to their daughters, the mothers primping them up and the fathers shaking fingers in their faces, no doubt telling them to be good. As if we could be anything else but good here.

Now there is another, louder clatter of hooves from outside and I peek out the little side window and see that it is none other than Clarissa Worthington Howe, being delivered in a full coach and four. It seems that I am not to be spared the joy of her company, after all. The door is opened and out steps a large man, finely dressed and one plainly aware of his own importance. He reaches up a hand and it is taken by Miss Clarissa, a vision of pink-and-white silk-and-chiffon loveliness as she floats to the ground, light as a feather. That big fellow must be her father, poor man.

Father and daughter see each other off with bow, curtsy, and quick peck of a kiss, while five large trunks are put on the pavement. Dobbs begins hauling them inside.

I step away from the window and wait for her to come in.

"You be civil, now, Jacky," warns Amy, who stands by my side.

"Oh, I will be, Sister, and I will be careful, too. I well remember our past encounters." I have a neat, semicircular scar on my forearm, a mark left upon me by Clarissa's perfect and oh-so-well-bred teeth when she sank those self-same teeth into me. I don't really blame her for that, though, since at the time, I was trying to beat her senseless myself. But I do blame her for plying me with strong but oh-so-sweet-and-smooth bourbon liquor at the great ball at Dovecote, she pretending that we would be friends from then on, and me, stupid me, believing her and drinking down what she offered to my trusting self. Oh, yes, I do blame her for that, and I know that things ain't over between us, count on it.

"...and don't scratch my things, my man, or I'll see your pay docked. Damn, could you be any more clumsy and slow? The help here, I swear." I hear Clarissa say this to the bent-over and mumbling Dobbs as she sweeps into the room before him. He puts down the trunk and heads out for another. "You, there," she says to Annie and Sylvie, who have just come back into the room. "Take this trunk upstairs. You know where it goes. Do it."

"Yes, Miss," murmurs Annie, and she and Sylvie each take an end and struggle up the stairs with it. I give them a sympathetic wink, and I know they appreciate it, especially when I hold my nose and glance toward Clarissa.

Clarissa senses something going on behind her. She spins around and spies me standing there, hand brought quickly off my nose and back to my side. Not quickly enough, I suspect. She starts but quickly recovers, a little spot of pink appearing on each of her flawless cheeks.

"So. You, again. I would have thought they would have hanged you by now," she says. She looks me up and down. "A pity they have not."

"So good to see you, too, Clarissa dear." I give the very slightest of dips without taking my eyes off hers. "I am sure that since last we met, you have been passing the time in doing good works that bring relief to your fellow man and reflect honorably on your name."

"I am as sure of that, Jacky *dear*, as I am sure that you've been off whoring," she says shortly.

My hands hook into claws, but Amy's hand is on my arm and I hold back. I ready a retort, but then I say nothing, for there comes into the foyer something that makes my jaw drop in disbelief: It is a young black girl, simply dressed in a maid's uniform of white linen dress, apron, and cap. She stands there, hands folded, and awaits instructions from her mistress. Clarissa has brought a *slave* back with her. How could she do that? How could...

Clarissa sees my reaction and turns to the girl. "Go up-stairs and put my things away. You know how I like things done."

The girl nods, bobs, and turns to leave.

"Till later, then," says Clarissa, with a nod to Amy. "I must go greet Mistress and tell her that I have arrived. And register my protest that scum such as *she* has again been al-lowed into our midst." And then she, too, leaves.

I am astounded and speechless. For a while, anyway.

"How can she get away with that?" I ask Amy, whose stand against slavery is well known to all who know her. "This is Massachusetts!"

"Yes, it is, but Massachusetts outlawed slavery only two years ago—and then only by a judge striking the practice down, not by a popular vote, you may count on that."

I'm standing there steaming, and Amy takes my arm and gives me a bit of a shake. "Come, now, we'll talk about that later. Right now, here comes Dolley...yes, and Martha, too."

And as they come in, joyous greetings are exchanged. *Dear, dear Dolley, you who are the absolute best of us! And Martha, so good to see you! Oh, please, come and embrace me, for you could not be more well met!*

All thirty of us arrive. I greet the ones I know and am introduced to the new ones. Exclamations of gleeful sur-prise—"It can't be you." "Oh, yes, Jacky it is!"—at seeing me back in black dress and back in school. And from my own amazed mouth: "Rebecca, little Rebecca, how you have grown!" Everything is a whirl of ribbons and bows. Every-thing is joyful, giddy, and gay.

But I just can't get that black girl out of my mind. *Damn that Clarissa! Damn her straight to Hell!*

Chapter 11

"In the classic Greek play, we have the stage divided into the following parts: the proscenium, which is where the main action took place, the...Ahem! Miss Faber, could that be your head that is nodding in slumber? Ah. I thought not. Forgive me. Well, then, to continue..."

Yes, we have settled in, all of us, friend and foe alike, back into the rhythm of the Lawson Peabody School for Young Girls. Classes did begin again and I turned myself to my studies, while January turned to February, and February turned to March.

Most things are as they were when I left—all the teachers are back, and all the same courses: French, Art, History, Geography, the Classics, Math, Science, and Music. Yes, and Embroidery and Household Management are still there, too.

I know most of the girls, and everybody certainly knows me, or *of* me, anyway, because of Amy's book. There are some who have moved away—none have died, thank God— and there are a few new ones. One of these is Elspeth Goodwin, who has just moved to the city with her family, from

Philadelphia. She's a bright, cheerful, pretty girl, who quickly attached herself to me, which was all right. I liked her, and accepted her early invitation to spend a weekend at her house. We had a gay time of it and it was good to get out of the school, at least for a short time. Her parents could not have been nicer to me and they are certainly proud of their daughter, her going off to a fine school and all. She is the very apple of their eye, and she plainly loves them very much, too. Amy finds her a bit flighty, a bit shallow, all ribbons and bows, but what the hell, Amy, not everybody can be as deep as you, and Elspeth's girlish, bubbly enthusiasm gives me cheer.

Another of the new ones is Hepzibah Van Pelt, from New York, who came to the school expressly to study with Maestro Fracelli. She is totally devoted to music and quickly becomes Signor Fracelli's trusted assistant. I am in a string quartet with Hepzibah, she being first violin, and me being second. That makes my Lady Gay mad, but not me and I tell her, *You be a lady now, Gay, and we'll follow these little bugs on the page,* and we do it. It is very satisfying to play in this group, seated in a circle, to come in at the right time, and to hear the Lady Gay's sound blend and meld with the others, her single sound mixing to make something different, something more than the sum of the parts. Christina King, a quiet, decent, modest girl, is on cello, and Caroline Thwackham is on viola—and, yes, she is the granddaughter of that very same Judge Thwackham who sentenced me to be publicly whipped for indecent behavior, but who, thanks to Ezra Pickering's excellent lawyering skills, suspended the sentence, conditioned on me not getting in trouble again. The sentence still hangs over my head, though, should I mess up, which is always possible. We work on Herr Mozart's String Quartet in B Flat, the *Hunt Quartet,* and some of Herr Haydn's stuff, too. There sure are a lot of Germans in this business, I'm thinking as I grimly saw away on poor Lady Gay, but, hey, they seem to be good at it, so why not? But what are we Brits especially good at? Architecture? No, the French have it all over us on that. Art? No, we ain't a patch on the Italian artists when it comes to painting and sculpture and stuff. What, then? *Ah,* I conclude glumly, *it's war, bloody war, and mostly war at sea, at that.*

"...in the theater at Athens, the chorus would be located..." Mr. Yale drones on and on, and I try to keep my forehead from hitting the desk again. It's not that I find the classics deadly dull—actually I like all that stuff about those fighting Greeks. We are going to put on one of the ancient plays. We'll get all dressed up in white robes and stuff and wear laurel wreaths around our brows and I know I'll like that. It's just that we've had a few almost warm days and I've got the urge to be out and about so bad I can hardly stand it. I can hear Lady Gay, in her fiddle case up under my bed, calling out to me: *Jackeee...Jackeee...Let us be away to the merry dance...There are taverns down below where we haven't yet played, where we haven't yet sung, where you haven't yet danced. Come take me up, Jacky, pick up your bow and let us fly...Jackeeeeeee...*

You be good, Gay, and I'll sit here and try to be good, myself. Cheer up; Art is next.

And speaking of being good, or at least making a show of being good, we all go to church every Sunday morning, and prayer meeting on Wednesday evenings. Since it is not far, we march in two columns along Beacon Street and then down Center Street to the Old South Church, where the girls of the Lawson Peabody now go to get their souls scrubbed clean, their last church having burned, and—*ahem*—the less said about that the better. Since all thirty of us attend this church, there are plenty of young men who have suddenly decided that this is the very congregation where they wish to do their praising of God. So, eyeing the boys, and them eyeing us, makes church almost fun. When I'm not looking over a particularly fine stretch of britches over a well-turned male tail—*Look at that one over there...Coo, he's a fine one, pretending to be reading his prayer book while he's cutting his eyes over here. Hah! Caught you, you dog! Here's a wink for you, lad*—when I'm not doing that, I look about the interior of the place. Amy tells me there was a lot of revolutionary stuff that went on in here before their revolution from us awful Brits—fiery speeches and raucous meetings and such. This is the place where a bunch of Bostonians dressed up as Indians and went out *halloo*ing into the night to dump a lot of perfectly good tea in the harbor, all over a silly tax. I notice that they dumped the tea and not the rum, and I am sure there was a tax on that, too. I said this to Amy and she didn't say anything to that. The place is plain, but pleasing in its proportions: high windows, big raised dais for the preacher to lecture at us from. There's lots of fine, polished wood in the pews, like what's under my hands right now, smooth as butter. It sure ain't a lot like Saint Paul's Cathedral back in London, with its stained-glass windows and huge high dome. Me and the gang weren't allowed in that place, 'cause they thought we'd rob the poor box, and they were right in thinking that. We did get in, but not during regular hours, oh, no. It was hard getting into Saint Paul's. It would be easy getting in here. Already I've spotted a couple of ways—cellar windows easily cracked open; hell, our Hugh the Grand could've ripped that door off its hinges with one hand—and we probably could have gotten in through that belfry up there, for the Lord knows we weren't afraid of heights...and there's the poor box over by the door and it looks full...Now, now, that was then and this is now. Be good.

Ah, my poor, good, simple Hughie, where are you now? When I was back in London I found out what happened to some of the old Rooster Charlie Gang, but not you...only that you had been taken by a naval press gang. Well, I've been taken by a press gang, too, so I know what it's like, Hughie, and I hope things worked out for you. Are you out at sea, where I wish I was right now instead of sitting here listening to some old preacher yell at me for sins I ain't committed yet? Are you happy? I hope so.

It was on one such Sunday that Amy took my arm as we came out of the church and said, "Look down that street there. See where those streets come together?" I replied that yes, I did see that. So what? "That is where the massacre took place, right there in front of that building. Before the Revolution, some patriots had assembled to protest acts of the British government and a squad of Regulars was called out to put down the demonstration. Snowballs were thrown at the soldiers and the order was given to fire on the crowd. Five men were killed, and six wounded..."

"I, myself, have always found it a good policy not to throw things at men in uniform who are carrying guns."

"That is *not* my point," she said, giving me a poke. "My point is that the first one to fall in the Boston Massacre, the first man to die in the American Revolution, was a *black* man. A black man named Crispus Attucks. Now look over there."

I followed her gaze, and over there stood Clarissa Howe with her slave. She had brought the girl with her that day to wait outside the church till services were over.

"I take your point, Sister." I sighed and thought, *What I can't understand is why Mistress Pimm would allow this to go on in her school.* Well, it was not my place to ask, and so I didn't.

I grow ever more restless. I cannot go to The Pig. I cannot go and act in Mr. Fennel's and Mr. Bean's theatrical company, even though they have asked for me. I cannot go anywhere without a suitable male escort. Me, who's had upwards of two hundred men under my command. I cannot go pulling traps with Jim, for there have not been any more school holidays that would allow Amy and me to escape back to Dovecote for a spell. Randall, of course, could serve as escort as far as I'm concerned, but not for Mistress, as she is not stupid and knows Randall for what he is—a straight-out rake.

Yes, I chafe under the confinement. While it is true that Little Mary, orphan of the streets, is glad of a safe, warm bed and good food, to be sure, and it is also true that Jacky Faber, student, apprentice lady, and sometime sailor is glad of the fine instruction and warm companions, Tonda-lay-o, Queen of the Jungle and the Ocean Sea, ah, that one, she is not happy at all.

But then, one morning, all three of me find my problem solved.

It is at breakfast on the first Monday in March, and all of the girls at our table are chattering away—Elspeth about the fun she had the past weekend at home, Rebecca about the new kitten that's been adopted downstairs, and me about this and that—when Betsey appears at my elbow.

"Your pardon, Miss, but there's a gentleman to see you. Mistress is with him in the foyer."

What?

"It's an English gentleman, I believe," says Betsey. "From the way he talks, I mean."

My heart takes a leap. *Could it be Jaimy? Oh, dear God, please!*

I put my hand on Betsey's arm. "Betsey! Is he in a Navy uniform? Is he wearing a blue jacket?"

"No, Miss. He's a very large man, and dressed very fine."

My heart returns to its normal position, but still thumping.

"Is it your young man come to carry you off?" gushes Elspeth, delightedly. Rebecca, also, is wide-eyed with curiosity.

I shake my head sadly. "No, dear. Jaimy is tall but rather slight of build. No one would ever call him large. Pity."

I tap my lips with my napkin, put it beside my plate, and rise.

Eyes follow me as I get up and go out. The circle of friends about Amy and me has grown, and the girls who gather about Dolley Frazier are friendly and good to me and mine, but there are some who have absolutely no use for me at all, and it ain't just Clarissa and her crew. I lock eyes with Constance Howell, as I brush past, and see nothing but contempt in her gaze. I had known her slightly from before, a very religious girl, given much to outspoken prayer, who has, if anything, gotten even more pious since I have been away. It's plain that she, too, has read about my wild and wanton ways in Amy's little book. I reflect as I leave the dining hall that having one's life laid out for all to see sometimes ain't the most comfortable thing in the world. *Ah, well. "Them what's don't like me can leave me alone," as the song goes.* I put on the Look and exit the room.

I'm puzzled as I go down the hall toward the foyer. Mistress knows that the British authorities are looking for me, she certainly wouldn't...would she?

I peek cautiously into the foyer, ready to bolt if the caller looks suspicious, but standing there, gloves and hat in hand, is a most glorious sight...

"*Higgins!* Oh, dear, dear Higgins!" I shout as I leap upon him and throw my arms around his neck and rain kisses upon his face. "You could not be more welcome!"

"It is good to see you, too, Miss," he says, as cool as if we had just parted yesterday, instead of in the aftermath of a horrific battle. "However, I do have to breathe."

I relax my grip on his neck a bit, but I can't be stopped. "Higgins! What has happened? What about Jaimy? The Home? My crew? Our friends—"

"*Ahem...*"

This from Mistress, who, I now notice, is standing off to the side and not at all approving of this display of affection.

"You will calm yourself, Miss Faber," she says, her tone severe, "and you will explain this to me."

I reluctantly let go of Higgins's neck and slide back down to the floor.

"Mistress Pimm, may I present my great good friend and protector, Mr. John Higgins," I say, dipping down. "Higgins, Mistress Pimm, Headmistress of the Lawson Peabody."

Mistress acknowledges this with a slight nod, her arms crossed on her chest.

Higgins bows deeply and says, "I am delighted to make your acquaintance, Mistress Pimm. I have heard many good things about you and your fine school from our mutual friend here. But may I point out that while I rejoice in having Miss Faber name me as her friend, I am also proud to announce that I am in her service, as her personal servant, as well."

The eyebrows of Mistress Pimm go up. "A manservant? For a young girl? Is that not somewhat irregular?"

"That may be so, Madame," says Higgins in his smoothest voice, "but the experience, I believe, has been beneficial to both of us."

"*Hmmm,*" says Mistress. She glances at me standing there quivering. "I thought I had noticed a slight improvement in her deportment since her return."

She thinks for a moment and then comes to a decision. "Very well, let us go to the drawing room, where we may converse. Betsey, tea, please, for three."

When we have settled into the easy chairs in the drawing room, and Betsey has brought the tea service, Higgins reaches into a side pocket and pulls out a letter and says, "May I give it to her, Mistress? It is from her young man, a lieutenant in the Royal Navy, and the son of a very respected London family. I will vouch for his character."

My knees go weak and I almost swoon away. *Oh, my joy!*

Mistress considers this. Even with my heart in my mouth at this news, I can see that Higgins is playing the part of an English gentleman to the hilt—impeccable manners, beautifully tailored gray suit, gold-headed walking stick, fine carriage, ankles crossed just right—and I could see that Mistress was buying it. She may have no use for the British Empire, and I have heard that she was a fiery patriot in her day, but she knows class when she sees it, and Higgins is certainly that.

"Very well," she says, and Higgins hands me the letter.

"Slowly, Miss Faber," she cautions as I grab the letter and start to rip it open. "Head up. Affect disinterest. That's it." She turns to talk to Higgins as I break the wax seal and open the letter and begin to read.

Dimly, I hear her say, "Mr. Higgins, would you like for me to show you our school?"

"I would be delighted," says Higgins, rising to join her, leaving me to my letter.

Lieutenant James Emerson Fletcher
c/o The London Home for Little Wanderers
Brideshead Street, London
January 14, 1806

My Dearest Jacky,

    It is my most fervent hope that this letter finds you well. It was with the greatest joy and relief that I received word through your Home that you were well and back in the safety of your school in Boston. Just how you accomplished that feat shall have to be a mystery to me for now, my last glimpse of you having been of a distant, forlorn figure signaling in a small lifeboat amidst the wreckage of the Great Battle.

You may rest assured that all at the Home, your grandfather Vicar Alsop, the delightful Mairead, and all the children were equally joyful at the news of your deliverance.

Upon my return to England, I immediately set about, with the able help of my brother George, who has become a skillful lawyer, to see about setting aside the charges that are against you. I expected it to be a relatively simple matter of making reparations for the ship under dispute, but I was wrong. The Admiralty is being obstinate to the extreme and will hear of nothing except your return to face trial. Even the usual bribes are ineffectual. I truly cannot understand what they want with such a small, insignificant female.

Efforts in this regard will still be made, but I say to hell with it. There is to be a hearing on this matter next month, and I will book passage for the States immediately afterward, no matter the outcome. If we are to live out our lives in the United States, well, so be it. After we are wed and we have you set up in a small cottage, I shall seek employment as a mate on a merchantman. There are very few openings for a junior lieutenant right now, anyway, the threat from Napoléon's navy being over. That suits me fine, as I am sick of war.

In that regard, it is now my painful duty to give you an account of what happened to your friends during the Battle. I will be brief, as I am sending this letter with your man Higgins, and I know he will fill you in on the details. I will only state the following: Gunner's Mates Harkness and Shaughnessy were killed, and I believe you already know that, since I saw you down there with them in the midst of the melee on that day. The Wolverine *also lost Yonkers, Bronson, Turner,*

Magill, Dermott, and Gill, and from your Emerald *crew I have heard of an Allan Kirby killed. Many more were wounded, but most are expected to live. Midshipman Piggott is among their number and is recovering at his home. I know from Higgins that you were already apprised of the death of Midshipman Ned Barrows. I know that his passing causes you the greatest of pain, but if it is any consolation, I did speak with those men who were by his side when he fell, and they report that his end was quick and clean. He did not suffer.*

I, too, grieve with you over the loss of our mates.

Counting the days till I again see your sweet face,
I am Your most Devoted, etc.,

Jaimy

It is all too much. I am hunched over the letter, rocking back and forth, my eyes squeezed shut against a rush of tears, as Higgins and Mistress come back into the room.

Higgins, alarmed at seeing me so distressed, comes quickly over to lay his hand on my shaking shoulders, saying, "I am so sorry, Miss. I thought the letter would bring you the greatest joy."

"I can't get it out of my head, Higgins, I just can't. All their faces, I keep seeing all their faces and I can't...I see everybody coming down to the London docks to welcome the sailors home and Ned's parents come down there, too, and they look for him to come down that gangway but their boy doesn't come, no, he doesn't. He won't ever come, and they'll never again see his face or hear his voice. Not even a body to bury, no, not even that. I see that scene over and over again, with all the other parents and wives and sweet-hearts crowding about and fearfully reading the cold butcher's bill tacked to the side of the Admiralty that re-counts the honored dead. *The honored dead*...And Shaugh-nessy and Harkness and all the others and the blood, *all that blood.* And Kirby, poor young Kirby...if I had never set foot in Ireland with my wild schemes, he'd still be alive, he'd..."

"You cannot know where he'd be. You cannot blame yourself. I know Kirby loved being a member of your crew. He was a volunteer, we all were, remember that. It was all out of your control. Please, here, dry your eyes..."

But it doesn't do any good. The Black Cloud has rolled in to shroud my mind, and I just sit there, rocking back and forth, and keen. Through my grief and pain I hear Mistress say, "Mr. Higgins, we will say good day to you now. I will take care of her. You may feel free to call on her tomorrow. You will see yourself out? Good."

Mistress comes over and sits by my side and says noth-ing, she just lets me cry, my face in my hands. I suspect that curious faces must have appeared at the door—it was, after all, approaching tea time—but a furious glance from Mis-tress would have sent them quickly away.

At last I subside, straighten up, and wipe my nose.

"I am sorry, Mistress. I am all right now."

"Good. You will follow me to my office so that the room can be set for tea."

I follow her out and down the hall. When we reach her office, she sits down at her desk and I go up and put my toes on the white line and wait, still sniffling.

She regards me standing there all miserable for a while. Then she says, "I have noticed, Miss Faber, that since you have been back, you have at times sunk into moods so despairingly black I could not put them down to the usual female vapors."

"I am sorry, Mistress, I did not think anyone had noticed."

"I notice everything about my girls."

"Yes, Mistress. It's just that…that I've seen a lot of my friends die, and it weighs heavily on me. And today, seeing Higgins, the letter from Jaimy, the news…it was all too much." I take a deep, shuddering breath. "It won't happen again."

Again she regards me in silence.

"The year before you first arrived, I lost three of my girls. Two to yellow fever. One to influenza."

I nod my head.

"It happens, Miss Faber."

"Yes, Mistress."

"Many things in this world are not in our hands."

"I know, Mistress."

"God's will, Miss Faber."

"Yes, Mistress, I know. God's will."

Chapter 12

Jacky Faber
The Lawson Peabody School for Young Girls
Boston, Massachusetts, USA
May 19, 1806

Lieutenant James Emerson Fletcher
c/o The London Home for Little Wanderers
Brideshead Street, London, England

My Dearest, Dearest Jaimy, know that I send this with all my
love...

It has been a busy spring here at the Lawson Peabody since
last I wrote to you, and I will now tell you of things, but you
know that I am not good at this so you must forgive me. While
I count myself handy with a brush, I am clumsy with a pen.
I think it's that I am too eager to get things down quickly.
Oops...see, there's another blot.

Anyway, as I told you in my last letter, our Higgins, upon his
arrival, took lodgings down at The Pig. That was true at the
time, but it was not long before he had worked his way fully into

the life of the school, first by acting as butler for some affairs when we had a large number of visitors, then gradually, ever so gradually, he began to take over some of the housekeeping management of the place until such time as he was in full-time employ, skillfully supervising the staff when they were upstairs. Higgins does have his ways, as you know. The serving girls took to him right from the start, of course, and Peg was glad to be rid of the upstairs chores and thankful to be left to her kitchen. In no time at all, Higgins was set up in a downstairs room of his own.

The really big thing for me, Jaimy, is that Mistress quickly figured out Higgins's true nature, and so has come to realize that he is no threat to the young females in his charge, and is, in fact, most protective of his brood, and so she lets him act as escort to us when out of the school. This has allowed me to get out of this place on weekends—not to play The Pig or anything like that, for that's too dangerous, considering, but at least I can get out to visit with Annie and Betsey Byrnes and Sylvie Rossio and the other girls, and to check in with Ezra and Jim...

I put down my quill and look off into the gloom of the drawing room. It's not long till prayers, then lights-out, but I sit back and think of a conversation I had with Higgins just as he was moving into his new quarters.

"Won't you find it rather tame, Higgins, after all you have been through, to be a butler in a girls' school?" I asked, perched on the edge of his bed as he moved his things into the wardrobe.

"Not at all, Miss. While the girls of the Lawson Peabody are delightful, my duties here end after the evening meal, and then I can be off to sample the pleasures of this charming town, and its pleasures are many, I can tell you. For one thing, I have met with your Mr. Fennel and Mr. Bean and have entered into some of their theatricals, and they are priming me for bigger parts. Look at my profile—do you not think I would make a fine King Lear? *Hmmm?* You agree? Yes, I do, too." He flicks a speck of dust off the wardrobe. "All in all, it is a most charming town."

Then it was my turn to be stuffy and I said, "*Ummm.* Well, you had best be careful, Higgins." And he allowed that he always was. Careful, that is.

"And, besides, Miss, who else is going to keep you neat and tidy, if not for me?"

If not for you, indeed, Higgins, for not only do you keep me as neat and tidy as is possible with one such as me, you also keep me from trouble when you can. I recollect the day Higgins arrived with Jaimy's letter and how the Black Cloud came and how I launched into uncontrollable crying there in the drawing room. I also recollect how the very next day I began hearing whispered the lines of that cruel, taunting children's rhyme:

> *Crybaby, cripsie,*
> *Your mother was a gypsy...*
> *Boo-hoo, boo-hoo,*
> *Cry, baby, cry!*

I heard it whenever I got near a certain group of girls or, more likely, when I was walking away from them so that it was said behind my back. It was always from those who cluster themselves about Clarissa and I knew for certain that her hand was in this, even though I could never catch her at it. She must have been one of those who peeked in the drawing room when I was having my bawling session with

Mistress. *Well,* I thought after I had heard this chanted a few times, *I have in the past been called* the little fairy *and* the Captain's whore *and I stood all that.* I reckoned I could stand this, too. *I am a crybaby and always have been and probably always will be and I freely admit it, but if you girls had seen what I have seen, you would know why I was crying and you would cry, too. But since you cannot know, I forgive you for what you are doing to me.*

I had put up with this hazing for about a week, figuring it had to die down sooner or later, when I was coming down the hall on my way to French class and I heard it again, from inside a near classroom. They must have had someone posted with their head out in the hall to see when I was coming. I think I recognized Caroline Thwackham's voice...

> *Crybaby, cripsie,*
> *Your mother was a gypsy...*

But she did not finish the verse, for Clarissa's slow drawl broke in with, "Oh, no, Caroline dear, you shouldn't say that..." She pauses for a beat, then says, "For we all know, poor Jacky's mother was a pros-ti-tute, don't we? That's why she ended up on the street when she was a little bitty child. That's how all those orphans get there, their mothers havin' been harlots who died of those nasty diseases that run through those brothels..."

My books and slate hit the floor as I raced around the corner and into the room in a blind rage, seeking only to rip Clarissa's lying tongue from her throat with my bare hands.

"My mother was a lady!" I snarled as I lunged toward her, claws extended. She stood there calmly, with her cronies gathered about her, as I closed the distance between us. "You miserable piece of—"

But that's as far as I got. A strong, gray-clad arm came around my waist and carried me kicking and squalling from the room.

"Higgins, put me down! I-I'm gonna kill her! I'm gonna—"

"What we are going to do, Miss, is wash your hair. I believe you would benefit by it," says Higgins, putting his free hand over my lower face, stifling my cries of outrage. "There now, Miss, we don't want to arouse and trouble Mistress with your bootless cries, now do we?"

I'm carried, still kicking, along the hall and down the stairway to the servants' area. "A bucket of water, if you would, Mrs. Moody," Higgins asks of Peg, "a bucket of very cold water."

The water is put in the bucket and then my head is put in the water. I gasp at the coldness of it. "But, Higgins," I plead, pulling my head back out, "she called my mother a—"

Higgins's hand gently but firmly pushes my head back down into the frigid water. "Sometimes, Miss, you act your age and sometimes you do not. You know who your mother was and you know what she was. Which was a fine, spirited young lady. What Miss Howe says should make absolutely no difference to you. You know that."

"But—"

"But, Miss, if you continue to play her game, she will win, count on it. Did you notice how she stood there, her hands at her sides when you charged in righteous fury?"

I thought on that and had to admit it was true. It was very unlike Clarissa not to fight back.

"I believe she had every intention," Higgins continued, "to stand there and let you beat upon her unresisting person in front of witnesses until you were pulled away and certainly expelled from the school. Or at the least, made serving girl again."

With the water dripping from my face, I had to realize the wisdom of his words. With a sigh I gave up the struggle, then said, "All right, Higgins. I'll be good now. I promise. I'll let her alone."

"Oh, you do not have to leave her alone, Miss," said Higgins with a slight smile, "just you play your own game, and not hers. Now let's get you towelled off and back to class."

And so it was that I went to Music with my wet hair stuffed up under a maid's mobcap to stand at my place next to the smug Clarissa and I was good. I can't remember what it was we sang that day, but I think it had something to do with the brotherhood of all mankind.

I smile grimly at the memory of that day, and my quill goes back into the inkwell...

Having Higgins back with me has been such a godsend, Jaimy, I cannot tell you just how much. I had been sinking into the slough of despond over the loss of so many of our friends, but he has brought me back to cheerfulness. His spirited telling of little Georgie Piggott's recovery amidst adoring young females who have named him Our Hero and the Lion of Trafalgar and crowned him with laurels did much to restore my spirits. Our departed friends? I must hark back to Liam's advice on the Dolphin *when we lost Benjy—you grieve for a proper time for your mates, then you've got to let them go. And so I have. Amen.*

And then there's the Lawson Peabody Girls Chorus. After having ourselves whipped into fine musical shape by both Signor Fracelli and Hepzibah Van Pelt, we have been going about and giving concerts in various places round the town, only the finest and most proper of houses, to be sure—the Saltonstalls', the Lowells', a few Cabot mansions here and there, the Thwackhams', the de Lises'...

Ah, yes, the house of the de Lise...again my quill lifts from the paper...That was something when we performed at Lissette's place and were treated to tea and cakes after we sang in the comte's elegant hall, with Clarissa acting like she owned the place, she having stayed there *so* many weekends. Yes, and then Lissette's father, the Comte de Lise, himself, French consul to New England, singled me out and introduced himself to me. Startled, I dropped into a curtsy, the elegance of which I am sure was ruined by me having half a piece of cake in my hand and the other half in my mouth. I managed to sputter out an *enchanté*, probably spewing crumbs on the poor man as I said it. I held out my hand, the one that didn't have the cake in it, and he bowed over my hand and kissed the back of it and said, "Pardon, Mademoiselle, but the most amazing coincidence. I have received word from France of a female pirate captain named the same as you, Jac-kee Fay-bear...*La belle jeune fille sans merci*, she is called..." I choked down the cake and replied, "But, Monsieur, how could that be? A woman as captain of a ship, *mais non, jamais*...never...," but he continued to look me over carefully and then said, "My Lissette, she has talked often of you...she has said you have had many adventures...ah, pardon, you seem to have a speck above your eye…," and before I could jerk back, he had put out his hand and rubbed his thumb over my right eyebrow and then looked at the faint brown smudge on his finger and smiled. He then bowed and said, "*Eh, bien*. The speck is gone now…but it was most interesting meeting you. *Au revoir.*" I was taken aback and worried for days that the French might mount an assault on the school and take me, but nothing came of it. Higgins was of the opinion that the Frenchman, though intrigued, wanted to do nothing that would bring joy to the British government. I hoped so.

I pick up the quill again.

Yes, the Chorus is getting quite famous. I suggested that we do a few nights at The Pig, but that was met with stony silence. Ah, well…

I keep thinking back to what you said in your last letter. I was so glad to hear that you might leave the military to enter into the merchant fleet. Oh, Jaimy, we could do it, we really could. I have already started on that course by outfitting my little boat for the setting and tending of lobster and fish traps. I had early on hired a boy, a Jim Tanner, and he has proven to be a very good lad, and the traps have been producing. I have made arrangements for Anzivino's Fish Market to take what we catch, and now we have some money coming in. And if I could get back to singing and dancing in the taverns and maybe get some portrait commissions, we might make enough money to buy a small coaster and carry rum down to New York and Philadelphia. I was shocked to learn that there are over a hundred rum distilleries within a day's ride of Boston. Ships loaded down with molasses for the making of spirits dock every day. Bluenosed New England Puritans, indeed! More like red-nosed ones. Actually, we could start off doing that right now with my Morning Star. *Wouldn't that be glorious— Jim up at the helm, you and me all snugged down in the cabin, the* Star *rolling gracefully over the waves? And then maybe we could buy a small bark like my* Emerald *and we could sail down to the Caribbean? Ah, dear boy, there are some places I could show you there, believe me on that, and I already know a great many fine seamen here, who we could make up into a great crew, and then... Well, I'm getting ahead of myself... If I can never go back to my own country, well, so be it. It ain't so bad here, Jaimy, you'll see. Oh, I just can't wait!*

But, then, I'm rattling on again. Foolish dreams...

Back to the here and now: Wonder of wonders, there is talk of a science field trip next week to one of the islands in Boston Harbor! Oh, how good it will be to get out of here for a day! Our science teacher, Mr. Sackett, has set it up through one of the excursion companies that take the quality folk out on excursions where they may picnic on the grass and pretend they are poor, simple peasants for a day. It is all the thing to do—Amy tells me that the unfortunate Queen Marie Antoinette of France used to spend days at one of her country estates pretending to be a simple milkmaid. It would have been far better for her had she actually been one, I'm thinking, and I'm sure she would agree, if she still wore her head upon her shoulders.

Ain't I getting good at commas?

But that's next week—tomorrow we go to sing across the river at the boys' college, which promises to be fun. All the girls are in an absolute tizzy about it. Not me, of course, for there is nothing of interest for me there as I am promised to another, that being you, dear boy.

Well, this has certainly turned out to be a long letter. Please forgive me, Jaimy, as the evenings here are long and there is not much for me to do, except study and dream of you.

Safe journey, Jaimy.

All my love always,

Jacky

Chapter 13

"Would you come sit over here, Miss? It appears you could use a comb-out, and today is a big day."

"Higgins, why do you make that sound like I am nothing but an unruly pony?"

"There are certain similarities, Miss. The coltish high spirits, the occasional burrs in the unruly mane, the dirty hooves…"

"All right, Higgins, brush away. And it is not such a big night, as we are merely going over to sing for those silly boys at the college."

"I do not think the rest of your fellow students share in your opinion as to the silliness of this evening's event, Miss, considering the uproar in this place," says Higgins. "And what is this, may I ask?" He pulls something out of my hair and holds it before my eyes.

"It is a cocklebur. I was out riding yesterday, and after a while, I dismounted to lie down in the high grass, looking at the sky. It was a glorious fine day."

"Of course. Now I am sure we shall have to check you out for ticks."

"*Ummm*," I purr, as the brush goes through my hair. "Maybe I'll let Randall Trevelyne do that very job later tonight, *ummm…*" I had heard from Amy that Randall has been readmitted to the college.

"If I did not know you were joking, or that Mistress Pimm will be keeping a *very* tight watch on all of you tonight, I might take alarm at that."

Now, Higgins, you wouldn't go telling tales on me, would you? Ah, no, not you…

I lean back and let Higgins do his magic with his brush. I almost doze off, but…

"Isn't this just the most exciting thing! Real boys!" This from Elspeth, who's next to me, having her hair done up by Annie. "I have never been to a ball with real boys!"

"This ain't exactly a ball, Elspeth," I say, lazily. "It's more like a high tea—we sing, everybody claps, we come down and simper as the boys lead us about and give us some tea and cakes, and then we're loaded back in the coaches and hauled back here. That ain't a ball by my way of thinking."

"Yes, but you've been off and had adventures and stuff," she gushes. "Oh, if only I could have had such adventures!"

"Be careful what you wish for, dear. I've found that most adventures are better in the telling of than in the living through."

"What I can't believe is," says Rebecca—whom Higgins has already put up in a high-on-head hairstyle to make her appear older than her thirteen years, as he knew she would want, and she is pleased with it and cannot stop looking at herself in the mirror—"why Mistress is allowing us to go."

I snort. "Mistress always says that her girls make good

110

matches and that college is where the good matches are to be found, in this town, anyway…and no rouge, you, you're not old enough." Rebecca pouts and puts down the rouge pad. "Besides, you couldn't look any lovelier than you do right now without the paint." She has always been "Little" Rebecca to us, her being the youngest, but she has recently put her foot down, demanding that we stop. *After all, I will be fourteen soon and I am* not *so little, so there!*

"Mistress knows where the money is, too," says the ever cynical Amy, who's waiting her turn under the brush. "What *I* cannot believe is that she is letting us go on that field trip. Out on the water and all."

"Come, Sister, the water will hardly be over our heads, and it's always calm in the sheltered harbor, so you needn't worry about that," I say. I know that Amy has never liked the water—the last time back at Dovecote, I took her and Randall out for a sail on the *Star,* but she didn't take to it. She does put up with going back and forth on the *Star* to her farm on the rare weekends when we can get away, because it is so much quicker than the coach. Now that it's warmer, I've brought Jim and the boat back to its mooring in Boston, so it is always ready for us when we need it. Haven't had any more trouble from British Intelligence, so I have become more bold.

"We will get wet from the spray, and when we get to the island, there will be bugs. It will be horrid." She sniffs a profound sniff and returns to her book.

I look over at Annie and ask, "Who's going from downstairs?"

"Me, Miss. And Katy and Sylvie. We're wicked excited to go."

"Me, too, Annie. A full day away from this place and part of it out on the briney. But how will poor Henry Hoffman stand it, not to see his pretty Sylvie for a whole day?"

She laughs but says nothing. We are easy together, for we all well remember when I was one of their number downstairs and was comforted during a time of trial by their openhearted love and affection. Annie, though she knows she'll probably never see the rogue again, was most glad to hear that Davy was not listed among the Honored Dead after the Great Battle.

"Dorothea probably had something to do with it," says Rebecca, "the field trip, I mean." I have to grunt in agreement.

Dorothea Baxter is another new girl, and a very studious girl she is. She is plain, though not unattractive, but I don't think she cares about that sort of thing at all—what she cares about is knowledge, and especially science knowledge. As Hepzibah has become Signor Fracelli's disciple, so Dorothea has become Mr. Sackett's. She is forever in the laboratory, mixing things and making smoke and foul odors, and she is better than anyone at mathematics. My foolish pride tells me that at least I am the best at art, and I tell myself to be content with that.

"That Dorothea, always with her nose in a book," exclaims Elspeth, whose own pert little nose is seldom found in such a place. I reflect that she is a pretty little thing and will turn many male heads this day.

"There are worse ways to spend one's time," says Amy, looking up from her book. "But it is true. I am sure she and Mr. Sackett have been joyously preparing their specimen kits in which they anticipate putting the most disgusting things, whilst dancing about the lab, waving their butterfly nets in wild abandon."

This gets a laugh from all around, then Higgins announces, "There, I believe that's all that can be done with this one," and I get up, give him a mock scowl, and head upstairs to dress.

Back in the dormitory, I find that someone, probably Betsey, has laid out on my bed my freshly brushed and cleaned black school dress. I silently thank her and pull on the garment. I do it with some regret, thinking how much I'd rather wear one of my racier dresses to this affair, but, no, Mistress wants us to look like a proper chorus when we go out to perform, and so the black dress it is. *Plus*, early on, she had made up a wide, pleated white collar for each of us to wear, which covers our chests and extends out over our shoulders, and we all, to a girl, hate them. Annie, fixing mine around my neck the first time, whispered in my ear, "*Aye, Jacky, ye look like a proper flock o' nuns, ye do,*" and I had to agree.

Clarissa is there, two beds from me, being dressed by her slave. When I was on my *Emerald*, I was always dressed by Higgins, but that was by his choice. This girl has no choice, none whatsoever. I turn away in disgust and look to my own things, and calm myself down. I have found that I have something of an uncontrollable temper and Clarissa Howe brings out the absolute worst in me, for sure. *You be good, now.*

I look down with some sorrow on my Naval lieutenant's jacket lying there in the drawer, with my medal laid upon it. Higgins, soon after he arrived, had presented me with that same medal. I examined it and was mystified. On one side was a profile of Lord Nelson and the words ENGLAND EXPECTS EVERY MAN TO DO HIS DUTY and on the other side the word TRAFALGAR and the date of the battle. "But, what is it?" I had asked and Higgins replied, "A medal has been struck commemorating the battle that saved England. See, here's mine," and he had pulled out his and put it about his neck, a gold medal suspended on a red-white-and-blue ribbon, while I, stupefied, held my silver one in my hand. "The captains and admirals received gold ones, the regular officers silver, petty officers bronze, and the seamen pewter," said Higgins. I asked, "But how came I by this?" and he replied, "Captain Trumbull handed in the log of the *Wolverine* and there upon it was your name—Acting Lieutenant Jack Faber—just as Scroggs had entered it, and so you received a silver medal. I, of course, immediately took my common pewter one to a goldsmith to have it gilded." I then gazed at mine for a while, thinking back to Tremendous McKenzie, a ship's boy on the *Wolverine,* who proudly wore a medal commemorating the Battle of the Glorious Fourth, for having been born a male baby on board HMS *Tremendous* on that day. "I am astounded, Higgins," I said, after which Higgins explained, "Well, Captain Trumbull gave it to me, knowing that I would seek you out. The good Captain chuckled as he handed it over and said, 'Tell her she owes me a neat two hundred and fifty pounds, and someday, I mean to collect.'"

Ah, how I would like to wear my lieutenant's jacket this day, in all its navy blue glory, with the gold buttons and piping and all, and to put the medal on my breast and put *that* under Lord Randall Trevelyne's nose tonight...Ah yes, that would be a fine thing…But it is not to be. I sigh and close the drawer. Perhaps on the next trip to Dovecote…

I think about all that as we gather in the foyer to be off. Higgins has called for the coaches, and as we are about to board, he comes up to give me a final brush.

"Higgins, you know you could have gone back to Lady Hollingsworth's employ. You could have stayed with Captain Trumbull. Why did you come back to me?"

He laughs. "The truth is, Miss, I have become used to a life of luxury, and poor Captain Trumbull, although a fine man, is a junior captain without a command, so he could not possibly hope to afford me. And as for the Hollingsworths, well, they are excellent people, to be sure, but I find I also have become used to a life of adventure, and adventure seems to swirl about you, Miss, for better or for worse. As for the money and riches, well, you shall bounce back, I know."

"Huh, some high adventure—escorting a gaggle of girls across a river to sing at a backwater college," I say, as he helps me into my cloak.

"Ah, yes, to a school full of beautiful young men, how boring…Well, enough of that…but then, who knows what adventure the night might bring? Here's the coach, now up with you."

Chapter 14

But the performance is not the biggest part of that day, oh, no, not by a long shot.

We return in the early evening, full of high spirits, each of the girls—well, those who yearn for that sort of thing—sure that she has captured the heart of her perfect boy. We, the older and more seasoned types, who have neared the ripe old age of sixteen, are more blasé about the whole thing and pretend that it is just another concert, don'cha know.

But that is not totally true. What *is* true is that perhaps I shouldn't have let Randall Trevelyne spend so much time with me, and perhaps I shouldn't have danced every dance with him—surprise! The boys had hired a chamber orchestra, so there was dancing after we girls stepped down from the stage, having just performed a set of songs, all of which were chosen to highlight our pure and wholesome natures, and ending with the *Sanctus*. Perhaps I shouldn't have cast my eyes covertly at Clarissa to catch her reaction to me dancing with her former beau—*former fiancé, till I arrived on the scene,* I say to myself smugly—and, oh, I did catch her narrow-eyed gaze directed at me. *Take that, Clarissa, you*—

As we prepare for bed, I swear there is an absolute steam of female rapture hovering just above the heads of the girls in the dormitory.

"Wasn't he just the cutest thing?" exults Elspeth as we are washing up. "Oh, and he was *ever* so attentive to me! Did you know that we held hands the entire time?"

It was hard to miss, the two of them making silly cow-eyes at each other throughout the evening, but still, it was sweet to see and I am of a generous nature when it comes to that sort of thing. "He was that, Elspeth, and I wish you the joy of your first encounter with our trouser-wearing opposites," say I, as I towel off my face. Actually, he *was* a Cabot, so she could do a lot worse than that, when it comes down to it, in the future when she must marry.

We all go back into the dorm and stand by our beds—the right side of each bed, directly in the middle—and wait for Mistress. She arrives, taps her rod on the floor twice, and says, "Prayers," and thirty sets of knees hit the floor in unison. There is much muffled mumbling, and a lot of it, I am sure, is sincere, and then Mistress's cane hits the floor again and we tumble into bed. The lights will be quickly snuffed.

But not extinguished quite fast enough. As I pull back the covers, I see there is something lying there on my clean sheets, something that looks in the flickering light like a slab of raw beef, but it is not that, oh, no—it is a petticoat, in my size and probably one of my very own, taken from my drawer, and it is dyed bright red. I am not the only one who sees the thing—I hear titters from some of the nearby beds.

There are many symbols in our culture: The color blue stands for loyalty and truth, the color white for purity. There are flowers that stand for things, too. If you send a girl roses, that means love. If daisies are presented, the girl knows it means friendship. But red petticoats mean only one thing: a girl of low morals...a slut.

I reach down and touch the thing. It is clumsily dyed and still damp, but not wet. She must have planned this. *Well, I can plan, too, Clarissa...*

I know I cannot sleep in this bed. I throw the covers back over it and stride toward the door. Amy, who did not see what the bed contained, asks, "Jacky, what...?" Elspeth looks mystified by my sudden departure, too, but I just say, "Never mind. I know I will never be truly welcome here, and I don't care."

I don't know if either of them tried to follow me out, but I do know that they would have expected me to go downstairs to be with Peg, or the girl Katy Deere, who I know has a room down there, too. *Water seeks its own level,* at least half the girls would say, and I agree with them. *To hell with the snotty little bitches.*

But I don't go downstairs. Instead, I go up, up to my old room in the attic, where I was put before, when I was first cast out from this company. Beds are kept up there for the servants that some of the girls occasionally bring with them from the country, so the room is not often used. After I get to the top of the stairs, I throw open the door and head for my old bed, and—

I am startled to see the upturned face of the slave girl in the lamplight. She is dressed in her nightshirt and is seated on her bed—*my* old bed—and she is sewing.

I gasp and then manage to say, "I am so sorry. I did not know you were up here."

"It is all right," she says in a soft voice. I detect a French accent.

"Do you mind if I take that bed over there, next to you? I am not welcome down below right now."

"It is not my place to mind. But yes, you are welcome here. I-I know you for one of the kinder ones."

"Thank you," I say and walk around the end of her bed to the next one in line. I pull back the covers and climb in, but I am so furious that I know sleep will not come to me soon. I stare up at the ceiling.

"Here, I will turn off the lamp," says the girl.

"No, no, please, leave it on. I won't be able to sleep, anyway." I get up on one elbow and I face her. "What is your name and how do you come to be here?"

She does not reply for a moment, her head down, seemingly intent on her sewing. Then she lifts her head and looks off into the darkness of the attic.

"My name is Angelique Marie Therese du Toussaint. I was born on the island of Martinique, in the town of La Trinite. One day, about eight years ago, I was playing on the beach with my little brother, Edouard. My father was out on the sea, in his boat, fishing, and our *maman* was up at the house, when the pirates came raiding. When she saw what was happening, Maman came running down to the beach to try to save us, but she could not. She was captured, too, along with many others, both black and white." Angelique pauses, then says, "The whites were ransomed. Us, they sold."

I don't say anything to that, I just look at her. I have seen her many times about, and though she is a slave and follows

Clarissa's snappish orders, she conducts herself with a quiet dignity.

"But why don't you just run away?" I ask, mystified, sitting up now. "Just run out the door. There's nothing she could do, as slavery's outlawed in Boston. I'll help you. I know people who will take you in until we can get you passage back to Martinique. Why don't you do that?"

She looks down at her hands. "I cannot do that, Mademoiselle. You see, my maman and Edouard are still down at the plantation. I have been told that if I run away, it will go very hard for them. So I do not run away."

"Damn that Clarissa!" I say through clenched teeth. "How can you stand it?"

"Stand it? I stand it because I have to stand it." She turns back to her sewing, but in a moment puts up her needle. "Shall I tell you of my life with Miss Clarissa after we were captured?" she asks, with a wan smile on her face. For the first time she looks directly into my eyes.

I nod.

"Eh, *bien*. I was about seven years old when we were herded off the ship at Norfolk and put up for sale at the slave pens. Along with about twenty others, we were bought by Clarissa's father, General Howe. He bought me, especially, to be a companion to his little girl, for she had no playmates, the plantation being far out in the country and she having no sisters. We were the same age. The fact that he did not separate us, Maman and Edouard and me, that he bought all three of us, when he did not need my mother or my brother, was considered to be very kind of him. We were allowed to continue as a family."

She pauses and looks off, lost in the memory. "I was

bought to be her toy, but we quickly became friends. We were inseparable. We played constantly together. We slept in the same room, and sometimes, when it was stormy and the thunder crashed, in the same bed. We wore the same clothes, ate the same food. And, sometimes, as children will, we fought."

Another pause, then a deep breath. "One day we were arguing over a doll and she slapped my hand and I slapped hers back, something we had done many times before, but this time something was different: Clarissa's mother had come into our room with another servant and both of them saw me do it."

Angelique gets to her feet and goes to the window and looks out into the night.

"Clarissa and I were taken to the Great Hall. The Howe family was assembled and the entire household summoned to witness what was to happen. I was made to kneel before Clarissa and she was forced to slap my face, back and forth, over and over, till finally I fell to the floor, unable to rise. She did not want to do it. She stood over me, crying just like I was."

She stops and comes back to face me. "They were teaching me my place, you see. They were also teaching her."

She sits back down and resumes her sewing. "Things were never the same after that. Things became as you see them now. I was taken out to the slave quarters, and instead of being her friend, I became her slave, something, I then realized, I had always been and had simply forgotten."

She turns off the lamp, and I lie there in the dark, eyes wide open, and steaming. And thinking. And plotting.

Chapter 15

"Higgins, can we afford five dollars for a worthy cause?" It is a Saturday and I'm up for an outing and I've got something in mind. *Play my own game, indeed.*

"I believe we can, Miss."

"Good. I want to deliver it personally. You'll need your gear. We can go quietly out the back." Higgins's eyebrows go up at this and I say, "Don't worry, we shan't be gone long." I already have my cloak slung over my arm.

"Very well, Miss."

We go down to his room and Higgins takes off his butler jacket, puts his two small pistols into the pockets of his waistcoat, and then puts on his out-on-the-town jacket. He had purchased these handguns before he left London, and fine pieces they are, being of the very latest invention—they use percussion caps and no longer depend upon the clumsy and often misfiring flintlock. He bought them expressly as protection for me, and I appreciate it. He offered to buy one for me, to keep in my purse, but I would have none of it, as I have seen what guns and cannons can do to the bodies of men. I told him that from now on, it's Peaceable Jack, Honest Mariner. *I have laid down my sword and shield, down by the riverside,* as the song goes, and *I will study war no more.* Higgins did not express an opinion on that.

Higgins takes my cloak from me and holds it open. I step into it and he folds it around my shoulders. I wrap the mantilla around my face and pull the hood over my head. I am well disguised.

"Good. Now, let's go." Then it's out the back and down toward town. Ah, freedom!

As we walk along, I ask Higgins about something that has puzzled me for a while. "Why do they want me so badly that they plastered these WANTED posters all over the place? I'm just one girl. That was just one little ship."

Higgins does not reply but instead tips his hat to a passing man and woman. The man touches his hat and moves on. Then Higgins collects himself and replies, "I've done some thinking on this very thing. It has perplexed me, too, and I've come to the following conclusion: It is not that they care one whit about all that. It is that you know how to speak French, and with an American accent. You have shown yourself to be of an adventurous spirit. You have extricated yourself from many tenuous situations. Need I recite them? No? I thought not. You are not shy about donning various disguises, no matter how scandalous. In short…"

"In short, what?" I can't see what he's getting at.

"In short, you would make the perfect spy."

I gasp at the thought. Higgins continues.

"The new First Lord is very keen on espionage, so I hear. Why, think of it—the Admiralty could put you anywhere— female spies of your knowledge and background would have to be very rare, if they exist at all. So what is the cost of some printed paper in the light of that? Or even the fact that the Navy is putting itself up for some ridicule in this matter by keeping your name in the public eye. The story of a fifteen-year-old girl actually being in command of a Royal Navy ship is being circulated about the fleet, about England itself, making them a laughingstock. To think they are putting up with that to get you back..."

"They ain't gonna get me back," I say, pulling my mantilla tighter about my face. A coach full of men rumbles past and I turn my head away.

"That is to be devoutly hoped, Miss. However, if they do get you back alive, and bend you to their will, well, then it will have been well worth those silly pieces of paper. But suppose you are killed instead of captured and they get back your head in a sack? Well, so be it—what's lost? The cost of printing those posters and the reward they would have to pay to whatever blackguard did you in? At least there would be no more ridicule. But if they get you back alive, ah, then it might well be worth all the cost. They could place you right in Napoléon's own court with very little trouble. You are able to act as both the humble chambermaid and the highborn lady. You could even be the very one serving Boney his snails. Which are very good, by the way."

"I will never be a spy and I will never eat a snail!" I say, rearing back in indignation.

"Never say *never*. Is that not one of your numerous mottos, Miss? Besides, they could force you to do it. By threatening harm to those you love. The practice of statecraft can be very brutal, especially when they are weighing the fate of one girl and her loved ones against that of millions."

I walk along and fume and don't say anything. *Spy, indeed!*

A half hour later we turn into Cornhull Street, and there it is, three houses up. A bronze plaque on the side, next to the door, proclaims it to be the home of the Greater New England Society for the Abolition of Slavery. Higgins opens the door for me and we enter and go up to a desk where a well-dressed and handsome young black man is sitting. I am wearing my maroon riding habit, an outfit that I think gives me an air of aristocratic authority.

"May I help you, Miss?" he says, rising. A *very* handsome young black man.

"Yes," I say languidly. "I would like to make a donation to your cause. A donation in the amount of five dollars."

That gets his attention, as it's probably what he gets in three weeks of pay. He rises and says, "That is very generous of you, Miss. Will you come this way?"

He gestures toward an open door and I sweep in and see an older woman also at a desk. She stands up and says, "Yes?"

I take out a small cloth bag and lay it on her desk. "I wish to donate these five dollars to the antislavery cause," I say.

She smiles and bows and says, "How good of you. It happens that we are having a fund drive and this donation will be very welcome. We are taking gifts from such as yourself and publishing the names of the donors in newspapers all through the United States, in hopes of encouraging other like-minded, good people to join our crusade. We thank you, and the legions of the cruelly oppressed thank you."

"No thanks are necessary," I say, letting my voice grow soft and languid. I already knew about this sort of thing from my friend Amy, she being highly political *and* a staunch abolitionist. "Ah thank *you* for carrying on this holy work." I open the purse that hangs at my waist. "Heah," I say, "is anothah five dollahs to ensure that an advertisement is taken out in mah name in the Richmond paper."

"How kind. We shall see to it. As a matter of fact, there is a dispatch going down to our southern office this very day, and it will appear within the week," she says with a smile. "And who may we put down as the kind benefactor?"

"Mah name is Clarissa Howe," I say. "That is Miss Clarissa Worthington Howe of the Virginia Howes."

Just wait'll Guv'nor Howe gets a load of that! Him owning at least five hundred slaves, and his own darlin' daughter... oh, how I hope it will be hot for her!

About a week later, at Chorus, Mistress appears at the doorway with a large, well-dressed, and obviously very angry man at her side.

Clarissa, who is right next to me, exclaims in delight, "Why, Daddy! What a surprise! What—"

But that's as far as she gets. General Howe speaks not a word as he strides across the room, grabs his daughter by the wrist, and drags her out of the room, out of the school.

We do not see Clarissa for two whole days, and when we do, I make sure I smile sweetly as I give her one of my best curtsies and welcome her back into our company. Just so's there's no mistake. She glares at me with pure and open hatred. She knows, yes, she knows...

Oh, was ten dollars ever better spent?

Chapter 16

"Whoa! Look at the size of that brute!" I exult as the trap breaks the surface. I reach in and pull out the luckless lobster. "He must be three pounds if he's an ounce!"

"Careful of his claws, Missy," says Jim.

"Disgusting bug," says Amy.

"Phylum Arthropoda, class Crustacea, genus and species *Homarus americanus,*" says Dorothea.

"Don't you let that thing splash me," says Elspeth.

"Ah, and for sure he'll decorate some gentleman's table tonight," says I, tossing the beast into the live box and wiping my hands on my skirt.

"Did you know, Sister," intones the ever-cheerful Amy, "that in the early days in Massachusetts it was against the law to feed lobster to the slaves and indentured servants more than thrice a week? Yes, more often than that was considered cruelty."

"I had heard that, Sister, as you have told me about it more than once, but I chalk it up to the early settlers not knowing that *everything* tastes better when it is dipped in melted butter. And maybe with a squeeze of lemon, if you can find one. Ah, yes, that is the secret, and that is why *this* American Homer will be loudly acclaimed by all the dinner guests as he, and a few of his fellows, are brought red and steaming into the banquet!"

I sit myself back down and say to Jim, "That's the last of the traps. Let's take a bit of a cruise about Spectacle Island over there before we head back in." He nods and puts the tiller over.

"Isn't this just the most wonderful day? And tomorrow is the field trip!" exults little Rebecca. "With that nice Mr. Harrison and that funny Jerome!"

I hold my tongue on the wonderfulness of those two. Mr. Harrison is the man who runs the excursion company that will take us out to Peddocks Island tomorrow, and he has been by the school several times to make the final arrangements. Hell, I could take everybody over in two trips with the *Star*, but that proposal falls on deaf ears. On each of his visits, Mr. Harrison has brought with him his Negro slave, Jerome, and many of the girls are much taken with his antics. Jerome has a permanent silly grin on his face and he frolics about in an out-of-date fancy jacket that is at least two sizes too big for him, and he wears a white powdered wig that is always comically askew. He is an accomplished juggler and amazes the girls with several magic tricks, too. But he doesn't amaze me. "We had many black men on the ships on which I served and they knew their seamanship and were respected for it," I say to Amy, who shares my opinion in this matter...*and they didn't have to act like clowns.* This Jerome has cast some japing, rolling-eyed glances in the direction of Angelique, but I see nothing but disgust in her composed face at his amorous displays.

Well, to hell with them, I think and stretch out and look up at the sky and my perfectly trimmed white sail. The sun is shining and it is warm and I am content. The five of us had checked out of the school, to stay the night at Elspeth's house, Higgins having escorted us over there yesterday and then returned to the school...or wherever else he was going for the weekend. As before, Elspeth's parents treated us like we were royalty and we had a grand time. I know that Dorothea agreed to come only because of a promised cruise in the *Star* whereupon she might peer at many of the birds of the bay, and Amy came only to keep an eye on me, but all had fun at the Goodwins' in spite of themselves. Little Rebecca, of course, is always up for a good time, wherever she can find it, poor thing. She has grown used to her parents being off on diplomatic duty and does not cry about it anymore.

"Hah! There's a guillemot! A *Cepphus grylle*! They don't always come down this far. Wait till I tell Mr. Sackett! He will be ever so envious." I look out over the water and see a stubby-winged black bird with white patches on its wings barely making it over the crests of the waves, little as those waves are. Beat on, little bird...

Dorothea has become entranced with my long glass this day and trains it on any hapless bird that might cross her line of sight. Though some make fun of her and her studiousness, I have never heard her say a bad word against anyone, so she is all right with me. I had Elspeth invite her, because I knew she would enjoy this. I look over at her, her eye glued to the glass. She is a pleasant-looking girl of medium height with unruly brown hair that she does not make a great deal of effort to keep neat. As a matter of fact, she has a habit, when deep in study of some tome, of taking a tendril of that hair into her mouth to suck and chew upon. Mistress has told her that she will be switched if she catches her doing it again, but I don't know if that has stopped her in the practice. She also has a pair of spectacles with round-shaped lenses that she wears sometimes when reading. The lenses are tinted blue and I think she wears them in imitation of Dr. Franklin. These Americans do like their Dr. Franklin. From what I've read, he was a bit of a rake—Old Lightning Rod, he was sometimes called—but what the hell.

I've decided to stop later today at Gardner's Chandlery, on our way back to the school, so as to get Dorothea a glass of her own, as I know she will get great joy from it. She will protest that she has no money on her, and none of these rich girls ever do, but I will tell her we will charge it to Faber Shipping, Worldwide, and she can pay me back when next she can wheedle some money out of Daddy. Course I know that once I show her the way up to the widow's walk, we may never see her again 'cause she'll be so busy peering through her long glass at all of the birds, stars, and who knows what all.

"I believe I shall marry that charming Mr. Beauchamp I met at Harvard College that day." Elspeth sighs, beating her eyelashes. "He was ever so attentive to me." We have gotten to the other side of Spectacle Island and are on a gentle beam reach in the light breeze. It is a perfect day and the talk is as light as the air.

"As that Mr. Trevelyne was to you, Jacky," teases Rebecca, entering into the game.

"If by *attentive* you mean his having his hands all over

her when Mistress wasn't looking, then he was that," grumbles Amy.

"Now, now, Sister," simpers I, "Brother Randall was merely being friendly, and you know I am not particularly shy in that way."

"That is certainly the truth. I had to put myself in the way of Constance Howell, who was on her way to tell Mistress on you. If I had not done that, you would have had some serious excuses to make, believe me."

I did not know this. "Why, thank you for that, Amy," I say, and mean it. "I didn't think I was being that bad at the time."

Amy sniffs. "You never think you are being bad."

"So you agree I deserved the red petticoat, then, Sister?" I say, miffed.

"No. That was rude. But if anyone gives people like Constance reason to vent their prudish spleen, it is you, Jacky."

"Them that don't like me can leave me alone, that's what I say."

"If ever I will marry," says Dorothea, the glass still held to her eye, "it will have to be to a man of great learning, who will love me enough to let me pursue my own interests. Otherwise, I shall stay single."

"And what about you, young Jim? Who will you marry?" I ask of my stout coxswain.

"*Whom* will you marry," corrects Amy.

Grrr...

"A sturdy lass who knows how to swing a clam hook and what can bring in two bushels between the tides, that's *whom* I will marry," says my practical Jim, but I don't believe him.

"What about sweet little Claire, who worships the ground you walk upon?" I tease.

He reddens and pretends to check the trim of the sail. "She's a farm girl, and being a seaman, I don't have no truck with such as that."

"Ah, yes, well we shall see. Farm girls do have their charms, you know. They know how to make butter and cheese, and how to put up preserves, and all sorts of things that don't have to do with fishy stuff. Here's a song for you, lad, that you might take to heart." I pull my whistle from my sleeve and tootle a bit of the melody, then sing...

> Now do you ken my bonnie Jean,
> She's every fisher laddie's dream,
> She guts the herring down by the sea
> And saves her kisses just for me!

"How would you like to kiss a girl who's been guttin' herring all day? She'd be smellin' pretty ripe, I'd think." Cries of *eeeeuuwww!* all around.

"I ain't gonna marry nobody, then," swears Jim, upon consideration of the choices offered him.

As we come around the south end of the island, I see an opportunity for some fun with Amy. There is a pack of seals lying about the ledge rock there. I motion for Jim to bring the *Star* in closer to the seals, and he does.

"That is all well for you, Elspeth, and I hope you and your Beauchamp have many fine fat babies, and, Dorothea, I hope you find your kind scientist, but I am afraid that for poor Amy and me, well, we are doomed to live single all of our lives." I heave a great, theatrical sigh.

"Oh?" says Elspeth, her mouth making an open O of disbelief. "But what about your Jaimy, and Amy, your Mr. Pickering?"

"Ah, it's sad, that," I say, shaking my head and affecting a tone of deep melancholy. "My Jaimy is a world away and may never return, and Amy will not give poor Ezra Pickering the time of day."

"I am not ready for that sort of thing," says Amy primly, as I knew she would for she has said it at least a thousand times.

"Nay, for us it will be a lifetime of quiet spinsterhood, taking only Great Silkies for lovers." I nod in solemn affirmation of what I have just said as if I hold it to be the gospel truth. We are getting really close to the seals now. They have seen us and now regard our approach with their big round eyes. Amy is seated on the other side of the *Star* and so does not see them yet.

"I suppose you will now tell us what a Silkie is." She sighs, looking wary.

"Oh, Sister, how can you not know of Silkies? Why, they fairly abound in places like this!" I put on my teaching voice. "Well, then, Silkies are strange mystical beings that are seals in the daytime but can change into half men at night, and when they do, they stand on great strong legs and have huge hairy chests and great beards all twined with seaweed, and sometimes one of them takes it into his mind to suddenly appear in the middle of the night at the foot of the bed of a comely maiden, and when he leaves, she ain't a maiden no more, oh, no, she ain't. Before he gets down to business, he sings her a song and it goes like this..."

I am a man upon the land,
I am a Silkie under the sea
I come from a far, far distant strand
And I have come to get a babe by thee.

And then he has his way with her and then leaves and nine
months later, out pops the wee one. Always a boy, by the
way—there ain't no girl Silkies, otherwise why would Silkies
bother with land girls, it bein' inconvenient, like." I pause to
catch my breath.

"I swear you are a living, breathing scandal," says Amy,
not at all charmed by my little tale.

But I go on. "Of course, it all ends sadly, for the Silkie always comes back to claim his son after he's been weaned, as
he had sung to her before...

And it shall come to pass on a summer's day,
When the sun shines bright on every stone,
I shall come and fetch my little young son,
And teach him how to swim the foam.

And so she never sees the little fellow again, 'cause he's become a Silkie now, too. Unless, of course, she wants to row
out to the ledge rock to look at him lyin' around sunnin'
himself next to his dad."

"How sad," says Rebecca, mock serious.

"Ah, no, lass, it's just the way of the world. Course now
a lot of people say that these stories are just ways of girls ex-
plaining away a sudden swellin' of the belly, but I'm a seaman and I know that Silkies are real 'cause I've seen 'em. I
just barely escaped from one myself, on Malta it was, and it

was a close thing I can tell you and...*Oh, my God!*" I shout and jump to my feet. "Look, Amy! I'll bet that's one right there!" I point over Amy's head and she turns around and gasps to see that the crowd of seals on the rocks is now a scant twenty feet away.

"Look at the rogue! The cheek of the rascal! Oh, Amy! He's looking at you in a real husbandly way, he is! Look at him! Cheek! Damned cheek, it is! You leave our Amy alone now, you hear!"

"You stop that now, you!" cries Amy, looking distressed.

The biggest seal of the lot rolls over and slips into the water.

"Uh-oh," I say with concern, "you've done it now, Amy. Here he comes. I am sure that is a true Silkie and you are sure to have a visit tonight!"

"Tonight? In the *dormitory*?" exclaims Elspeth, delighted.

"Aye," says I. "And won't that be something to watch?"

"I'm sure that Mistress will object," says Rebecca, equally delighted.

"And I am sure you are all being just horrid. Stop it now," warns Amy, steaming.

"Mistress might try to object, but her rod against an eight-foot-tall Silkie? Nay, it wouldn't serve." I put on a resigned tone. "No, nothing can be done. I shall have to travel down to Dovecote and tell Colonel Trevelyne that the Great Silkie of Boston Bay has come and got a babe to his daughter, Amy. And, oh, the good Colonel will cry and rend his clothes and pull his hair, but in the end he will accept it as fathers have since time began. 'Ah, Silkies...what are you going to do?' he'll say and sigh, at last, and I'll sigh, then say, 'There's nothing that can be done, Sir. It's just like when them elfin knights come at you with milk-white cheeks and all clad in the red silk. I mean, what's a poor girl to do?'"

Just then, the seal that had slipped himself into the water chooses this moment to poke his whiskered head up next to the boat and to fix Amy with that big-eyed stare that seals have. She lets out a screech and tumbles to the other side of the boat, and I catch her and throw my arms around her and hold her.

"Oh, you bad thing, you!" she scolds, red-faced. "I do not think you are even a bit of a Christian with all your heathen stories of elves and seal-men and mermaids and spirits!"

I bury my face in the fabric of her dress and let her pound my shoulders with her fists while I roar with laughter.

After we have subsided and Amy has been mollified somewhat, but before we round the point to head back in, something out toward the open sea catches my eye. *Hmmm.* A black-painted ship...about the size of a bark...has pulled up behind Lovell Island.

"Dorothea dear, may I borrow the glass for a moment?" I ask. She hands it over and I put it to my eye, then train it on the black ship. I see the sails slacken and the anchor and its chain spill out over its bow to plunge into the water. I look back over my shoulder at the harbor—there's plenty of room at the docks, and the wind is fair. *Why ain't they going on in? Maybe the cargo will be rowed out to them?* I'll bet they're up to something illegal. Maybe they're smuggling in contraband. I can certainly relate to that, considering my past history. Well, it ain't my ship and it ain't my business, so I return the long glass to the eager hands of Dorothea.

I lie back against the gunwale, let the warm spring sun shine on my face, and think on my station in life. I am back at my school in the company of friends, mostly. My little enterprise with Jim and the *Star* is prospering. The heat seems to be off for a bit on the WANTED posters. Jaimy will be over within a month to claim me, and we can begin our life together.

And tomorrow is a field trip, out on the water again. I bask like a seal in the sun and revel in these thoughts.

I am content.

Chapter 17

The day of the outing dawns glorious—clear and bright, with not a cloud in the sky. The morning is already turning warm, and the spring breezes are light and mild—in short, a perfect day for a picnic.

When I hear the wake-up chimes, I spring up out of bed with a *whoop* and wash and comb and dress, then skip down the stairs, taking two at a time, to breakfast.

Upon entering the dining hall, I wave to Higgins, who's managing the serving, assisted by Betsey and Ruthie. Annie and Sylvie and Katy are to come with us today to help Higgins and Mistress in setting out a proper picnic and are undoubtedly down below in the kitchen with Peg, making up the provisions needed for the day. I slide into my usual chair, where I am soon joined by Elspeth, Dorothea, Rebecca, and, eventually, Amy. Amy is not in the same high spirits as the rest of us, that's for sure, and I know it's because she doesn't really relish going out on the water again. Leave it to me to come up with a best friend who's afraid of the sea, while I am happiest there. Plus, I know she's still smarting a bit over being the butt of my Silkie joke yesterday. I decide I shall make it up to her today.

"Come on, Amy, it'll be fun," I say, giving her a big fat kiss on the cheek before I begin shoveling in my eggs and bacon with my usual gusto. "We'll explore, we'll collect specimens of the seashore life, we'll play fox-and-geese and crack-the-whip, and dance and sing songs and...just get out of here for a change."

"Amen," says Elspeth, and Amy nods but still looks doubtful. Then we all tuck into our breakfasts. A bit later we all get up and scatter, to get ready to go.

"Amy must have gotten on one of the other coaches," I say, craning my neck out the window to look at the line of coaches pulling out and heading for the docks. We are the last in line. Higgins is not atop any of the other coaches, so he must be on top of this one. On the first coach there's that Jerome, acting like a clownish footman, his foolish-looking wig bouncing up and down with the jostling of the carriage. He's waving and grinning widely at all about him and seems to be enjoying himself hugely.

"Amy isn't coming," says Elspeth, sitting across from me.

"What?"

"I thought you knew. Mistress has fallen ill and Amy decided to stay with her."

"No, I didn't know," I say, wondering at this. Mistress is letting us go on this excursion without her being there to watch over us, her helpless charges—a duty I know she takes *very* seriously? "Are you sure?" I ask. "It's not like Mistress to let us go without her."

"Well," says Elspeth, looking about gaily, "apparently she took sick but told Dobbs that we should go, anyway. Why not? That nice Mr. Harrison is in charge of everything, and with that funny Jerome to help him...Actually, I'm glad she's not coming—more time for sport, and less for study. *Hooray!*"

Hmmmm. I'm thinking this seems a bit strange, but maybe Mistress figures that with Higgins and Mr. Sackett along, everything will be on the up-and-up. I decide to enjoy the ride. I rest my elbows on my seabag, which sits securely in my lap. I'd been laughed at and asked why I was bringing that "big old thing," and I said that Jacky Faber doesn't go out on the salt without her seabag and that's that. *Too much can happen out there and all you landlubbers should know that.* Dorothea sits next to Elspeth and she has her new long glass firmly in hand.

The coaches traveled down Common Street and then they turned onto West Street, and now we plunge onto Newbury Street. It seems we are headed toward the lower docks, down at the south end of the city—I guess that's because we'll be closer to our island destination. Newbury becomes Orange Street, and then we turn off on a side street, little more than an alley, really, which does not have a name, or at least not one with a sign.

We pull onto a wharf that appears to be completely deserted. Looking out I see only the single mast of a launch lying alongside the south side of the pier, a launch that I suppose is to be our conveyance. I see no other people about. *Hmmmm...* That Jerome has jumped down and is handing girls down to a man in the boat. He is wearing white gloves and is bowing extravagantly to each girl in turn, smiling all the while, and the girls are setting up a merry chatter. It truly is a glorious day, but a growing worry is starting to gnaw at my mind. *Why so far out of the way? Why a deserted pier?*

I don't wait for Jerome to come open our door, but instead pop it open myself and hop outside, seabag under my arm. The rest of the girls in the carriage tumble out and head for the boat, but I hang back and ask, "Higgins, why didn't you tell me...," as I lift my head to look up at him.

But Higgins isn't there. There's no one on top of the carriage. *What? Where's Higgins? And where's Mr. Sackett? What is going on here? I don't like this...*

I run out on the pier and look sharply about. All the girls are now down in the launch, sitting on a bench that runs entirely around the inside of the gunwales. In the center is a tarpaulin that I suppose covers up the supplies needed for the day. Jerome stands and waves me to come over to the ladder and extends one white-gloved hand.

I don't take his hand. "Where's Mr. Harrison?" I demand of him. "We're not going anywhere, not without Mistress or Higgins, we're not—"

"Oh yes, you are, my dear," I hear Mr. Harrison say behind me, and then I feel something hard pushed into the small of my back, something I know to be the barrel of a pistol. I suck in my breath. "You will get into the boat and you will not say a word or I will put a bullet in your spine. The others will not be able to see this gun, as it is beneath my jacket, and so will not be alarmed. I do not wish them to be alarmed just yet." He is saying this very conversationally into my ear and I'm sure no one in the boat has noticed anything amiss. "And I have another pistol in my other pocket and if you so much as move a muscle in the wrong direction, my second bullet will go into the brain of that little girl right there."

I know he means Rebecca, who is sitting there in the stern of the boat, looking up at me and patting the seat next to her, impatient for me to come join her. Full of fear and dismay, I go down the ladder and sit down beside the girl, my seabag on my lap. We are on the rear seat and there is room for the coxswain and Mr. Harrison to stand behind us. Dobbs is back there, too, but small comfort in that—I can't see him in the role of bold rescuer. The pressure of the metal on my back does not relent.

"Let us cast off, Jerome," says Mr. Harrison.

"Yassuh, Mistuh Harrison. We do dat right now," says Jerome, and he throws off the bowline. The coxswain throws off the stern line, then the sail is raised and we pull away from the pier.

"Isn't it just the most beautiful day, ladies?" asks Mr. Harrison from behind me, and though I can't see his face, I am sure he is beaming out his benevolence on his trusting charges.

We are soon into open water and we take a little spray over the bow. The girls squeal in delight at the coolness on their cheeks and feign dismay over their clothes. The coxswain turns the bow a bit to take the waves in an easier way and the spray stops.

I can see Lovell Island up ahead and getting closer. I suspect we will be going around it to the other side, the sea side, where whatever is going to happen to us will happen out of sight of any on the coast who might be watching. It's sure to be a lot rougher on that side, I figure. I wonder...

"And why is our beloved little Brit being so quiet today?" asks Clarissa, who is seated in about the middle of the starboard seat and is looking at me in her mocking way. I know she has been thinking of ways to get back at me for the abolitionist-newspaper thing—*Oh, Clarissa, if only you knew just how little all that means right now*—and she goes on. "Why, you'd think the dear little thing would be chattering away like the sweet little magpie she is, being on the sea she says she *so* dearly loves."

The pistol is then removed from my back and brought around to press against my temple. The gun is now in plain sight. "I've got other things on my mind right now, Clarissa," I manage to say. I hear Rebecca gasp.

Clarissa's mouth drops open, as does the mouth of anyone watching me for a reply to Clarissa's sally, which is, of course, everyone. They don't have much time to wonder whether this is all a joke or not, for just then the coxswain puts the tiller over and we slip behind Lovell Island and Mr. Harrison says, "All right, men," and the tarpaulin is thrown back and men are revealed crouching there, men holding pistols and pointing them directly into the shocked faces of the ladies of the Lawson Peabody School for Young Girls.

While the ladies are looking down the barrels of the pistols, I'm looking at a ship, a good-sized one, sitting at anchor several hundred yards off shore of the island. It is the black ship I had spied and wondered about yesterday. It is a trim and fast-looking brig, and I gaze at it with a sinking heart. The closer we approach, the more I despair.

We reach the ship and pull around it to where a gangway has been put down. The launch swings in under it and drops its sail. Rough-looking men watch us from behind the railing above as the boat is quickly secured and Harrison barks out, "Up the ladder with you, now! Quickly!"

The still stunned girls of the Lawson Peabody are taken up the gangway, roughly prodded along with hard hands and pistol barrels. We are hurried and cursed, and there are no white-gloved helping hands now. Jerome has disappeared. Rebecca clings to my right side, trembling, as does Elspeth to my left.

After we gain the deck, men force us into a huddle. Our purses are taken and some of them thrown overboard. A man strips the bonnet from Elspeth, and in a moment I feel mine torn away as well. The bonnets, too, are tossed over the side. Dorothea's new spyglass is wrenched from her hands while she looks on in shocked disbelief.

While most of the girls are wailing in horror and dismay, I look about to see where we are and what we will have to contend with. The ship is about one hundred and fifty feet in length, forty feet broad in the beam. I can see six guns, three on either side. There are about forty men altogether, on deck or in the rigging. There is an open hatch near to me, and from the stench coming up from below, I know this ship to be a slaver.

Mr. Harrison stands with crossed arms and smug expression, gazing upon our confused huddle. Incredibly, Dobbs goes over to stand with him. He stands there looking at us with a very satisfied look on his vile face. *You son of a bitch,* I'm thinking, *you sold us out.* I drop my seabag to the deck near the open hatch.

Dolley Frazier, her normally placid and composed face flushed with fury, pushes forward and confronts Harrison.

"Mr. Harrison! What do you mean to gain by this? Are you crazy? Are you mad? You will put us ashore immediately!"

"Oh, no, Miss, beggin' your pardon, but we will not do that," says Harrison, removing his hat and making a mock bow. "Permit me to reintroduce myself, as I am a man of some renown in certain circles. My real name is Colonel Bartholomew Simon, and *you* are at *my* service. Welcome to the *Bloodhound*. It shall be your new home for the immediate future. I do hope you will find it comfortable."

While attention is centered on this exchange of pleasantries, I use my foot to slide my seabag sideways, over to the open hatch. The bag tips over, and I hear the muffled sound of its fall, way down below. I'm thinking that that's where they're probably going to keep us and maybe I'll be able to get it later. If I left it on deck, they would surely take it from me.

"I know who you are now—you're the slaver Blackman Bart. That's who you are, and you are no colonel! You are nothin' but a common slave peddler." This is from Clarissa, who has come up next to Dolley to add her bit. I keep quiet 'cause I know all this talk ain't gonna do no good, no good at all.

"Well, Miss Howe, I may be a slave dealer, but I assure you I am not a common one. Are you surprised I know your name? It is very simple, really. I have sold many, many slaves to your father, and in the course of our last transaction for twenty good strong bucks and twelve young females—half of them already heavy with child, I might add—a very good collection of black flesh, muscle, and bone, not to mention womb, we entered into conversation and he spoke proudly of his daughter and the fine finishing school she attends in Boston. What a perfect opportunity, I thought, thirty certifiably virtuous females just ripe for the plucking." He smiles and nods happily at his own cunning.

Although we are out of sight around the lee of the deserted island and cannot be seen from the shore, still, were I him, I would have hustled us below. But I think he's enjoying this too much to do that.

Also enjoying himself hugely over all this is a boy of about fifteen years. He is cavorting about behind Simon and the rest. He is thin, with big hands and feet and curly blond hair. Suspenders hold up his pants and he wears no shirt. The boy grins at us, showing greenish teeth, and in his excitement, he jumps about like a demented monkey.

"So you would hold us for ransom, then?" asks Dolley, her chin in the air, her Look resolutely in place.

"I am deeply sorry, Miss, but no. In kidnappings there is always the problem of the transfer of the money, and you already know my name. How could I possibly let you go? You do see the problem, don't you, dear?" He shakes his head sadly as if he were a kindly old uncle telling a crestfallen child that she couldn't have any more candy.

"Then what..."

"What, indeed? Well, I will tell you." He clasps his hands behind him and begins to walk back and forth before us. I was right—he *is* enjoying this. "Everyone knows that the transatlantic shipment of slaves will be outlawed here within the next few years," he says with a wistful sigh, as if bemoaning the loss of a hallowed tradition, "and measures must be taken to maximize profit now, while we can. This ship is built to carry four hundred and eighty slaves. We take on six hundred at the barracoons in West Africa, but generally it's only four hundred and fifty or so that survive the crossing. Upon landing, I can get nine hundred dollars for a good strong buck, five hundred for a young woman, more if she's pregnant, and two hundred for a child. So you see, if you have studied your math at the dear Lawson Peabody, my partners and I make a gross profit, before our considerable expenses, of course, of at the very least, three hundred thousand dollars a trip. We figure our actual profit margin at fifty percent. Well worth the risk, wouldn't you say?"

He smiles and pauses, plainly pleased with his own eloquence—this man does like to talk. I notice some sailors are getting fidgety, anxious to be under way and tired of this man's blather. But he is the boss and so goes on.

"But for the lot of you, *ah,* I shall get that amount and then some when we get you to the Arab slave markets in North Africa and you are put up on the auction block and sold."

There is a common gasp from the girls. *Sold into slavery! Not us, surely not us!* Several clutch each other in horror. Elspeth and Rebecca are both clamped to me, on either side, whimpering. *This can't be happening, oh dear God, no!* I had already figured out what our fate was to be and continued my casing of the ship. There's a hatch up forward—that's got to lead down to the crew's quarters, storerooms, and galley. The Captain's and Mates' berths would be at the rear of the ship. All available space would be given over to the massive hold in the middle, the better to, again, maximize profit.

"You would eat at a man's table and then turn around and sell his daughter into a life of debauchery?" asks

Clarissa with all the contempt she can muster, which is considerable—I should know, since I am generally the object of that contempt.

The man who now calls himself Colonel Bartholomew Simon goes over and stands before her. He puts the end of his riding crop under her chin and forces her face up even higher than she was holding it. I must say that, along with Dolley, Clarissa is one of the few who has maintained the Look in this situation.

"You *are* a pretty one. They said that you were. The price on you just went up a thousand dollars," he says. "Eat at his table? Oh no. Do you think that the Grand Lord Howe would have such as me to dinner? No, no, my dear, not that insufferably arrogant ass. Very recently, he did refuse to shake my hand when I held it out to him. In public, no less. My hand was left hanging out in the air, unshaken, for all to see. Which is why this is all the more delicious, don't you see?"

What *he* didn't see was Clarissa working up a gob of spit, which she then rears back and puts straight into his eye. "You pig! Ah will see you hang for this!" Clarissa is a very accurate spitter—I know this from experience.

Colonel Bartholomew Simon puts two fingers into his vest pocket and slowly pulls out a handkerchief. He then carefully wipes the spittle from his face. He is not smiling now.

"No, Miss, you will not. You will never see me again. But you will learn to obey your master. Whoever he turns out to be." And with that he reaches out his hand and slaps her hard across her face, rocking her head back. More gasps from the girls, but not from Clarissa—the red imprint of his hand flares on her cheek but she still maintains the Look.

Well, a version of it, anyway—the languid, half-closed eyes have been replaced by a cold, level gaze of pure hatred.

"Shall we get on with this, then, Colonel Simon?" asks a man, obviously the Captain and just as obviously impatient to be on his way.

Simon turns from Clarissa and goes over to Dobbs, who has been grinning and bobbing his head up and down in his joy at what's been happening here. "Yes, we shall, Captain Blodgett, we shall, indeed. Mr. Dobbs, our thanks to you, Sir, for your fine service in this endeavor!" With that, he pulls a bag from the side pocket of his coat and presents it to the grinning Dobbs. "Your reward, Sir, for a job well done!"

"Thankee, Sir," says the vile Dobbs, clutching the purse and leering at us. "Ain't so high-and-mighty now, are ye, dearies? No more 'Dobbs, fetch this' or 'Dobbs, do that.' No, no. Havin' this money means old Dobbs ain't never gonna have to listen to the likes o' you no more—not that old witch Pimm, neither!"

I speak up for the first time. "Did you kill Mistress?" I ask of Bartholomew Simon. "And Higgins? And Mr. Sackett?"

Simon regards me. "No," he says, and I let out a slow breath of relief. "No, that would have cast too much suspicion on this enterprise. They were made sick, but they will recover. It will be blamed on bad fish or something, not on the mild poison our Mr. Dobbs put in their coffees. But how kind of you to think of someone other than yourself, considering your current situation." He makes a mock bow in my direction. I do not return the courtesy.

"This is preposterous. No one will believe this stupid scheme." This is from Dolley. "We are not common girls. A great hue and cry will be raised. You will be pursued and caught and surely brought to justice." She says this with great conviction.

"Let them hue and let them cry. We will be long gone," says Simon. "Besides, they will think you dead. Drowned, poor things, every one. They will find the wreckage—look, even as we speak, the launch is being swamped."

It was true. Sailors had tied a line to the top of the launch's mast and pulled it over till the side of the boat was underwater and the sea poured in. The launch was soon wallowing on its side. About it bobbed the bonnets and purses taken from the girls. Even as I watched, several of them sank out of sight.

"That will drift in, to the rocks over there, and be wrecked. They will find that and various of your personal belongings—and they will find a body—but your dear bodies will never be found. All will surmise that your heavy dresses dragged you down and you were pulled out to sea. How sad."

I think about toeing off my shoes and making a break for the side and diving over, hoping to make it to the shore of that island and so raise the alarm, but the sailors are standing too close about us for me to break through, and there's no telling what these dogs would do if they saw me making good my escape. They might just throw the girls overboard and then get the hell out of here. And then the girls would drown for real. I'm sure there's not a one of them who can swim. No, I'll have to stick around to see how this plays out.

"Well, if you're gonna make a dead body outta one of 'em," says Dobbs, "I'd say you kill that one there, as she's a real troublemaker, she is." He says this and points directly at my forehead.

"Thank you for the suggestion," says Simon. "We shall act upon it. Bo'sun Chubbuck, if you would be so good?"

A man, a very solid-looking man with a short, thick neck, black brows, and scarred face, has been hanging back by the ship's rail, behind the crowd. He now comes forward and he has a massive club in his right hand.

"Elspeth! Rebecca! Stand away from me!" I hiss, but they only clutch me tighter. "Give me room!"

But I will not be able to fight for my life, for a hand comes from behind me and grabs my neck and holds me fast. *And he'll hold me thus till the club comes down and smashes my skull, oh, Lord, no!*

The Bo'sun takes his club in both hands and swings it like a batsman swinging at a cricket ball and brings it down…But not on me, oh no, not on me, but on the back of Dobbs's head, and it hits with a great, squishy thud. Dobbs looks surprised for a moment, then his eyes roll back in his head and he crumples to the deck.

Simon leans down and picks up the bag of coins. "Fool," he says. "Throw him overboard."

A man takes what's left of handyman Dobbs by the wrists and another by the ankles and they swing him over the rail. There is a splash and it is over. I'm sure he was dead before he hit the water. The man holding my neck lets go and the thumping of my heart begins to slow back down.

The girls are quiet now, as they have just seen a man killed and it was not a pretty thing. It's true that Dobbs was vile and he had it coming, but still, it was an awful sight to see.

Blackman Bart, the self-styled Colonel Bartholomew Simon, now raises his voice and addresses the crew of the *Bloodhound:* "You men listen to me! I am leaving now and I direct you to set sail to make this delivery. You will deliver this cargo intact in all ways, *all ways,* do you mark me on that? Captain Blodgett here has orders to shoot any man who so much as touches one of these girls. They are worth a great deal of money in their current condition and I will not have money lost as a result of your lust! Do you hear?"

There is a low murmur of assent, but one sailor speaks up. It is plain that discipline here is nothing like that of a warship. "What about them three servin' girls?" he says, and points at Annie and Sylvie and Katy, who stand together. "They ain't ladies. Surely we can have our sport with them?" The boy I had seen jumping about before is avidly nodding his head up and down in support of the sailor's proposal.

Both Annie and Sylvie cross themselves and put their hands together in prayer, but their faces are without hope. The girl Katy doesn't do anything except just stand there, her face totally without expression.

"Colonel Simon, Sir," I call out. He turns to look at me. "I know these girls personally. I know them and I know their families. They are all good girls and I can vouch for them as to their character and virtue. They will bring as good a price as any of us."

Simon smiles upon me. "Now, there's a good, practical one. I like that in a girl, and I like that even better in a captive." He turns again to the crew. "So be it. Those three shall be treated as the others are treated. And think on this, you dogs: You are getting *twice* the pay on this voyage. When you're through, you'll be able to buy all the women you could possibly want for months on end. Think on that."

Shuddering, Annie and Sylvie relax a little. The crew is not pleased.

"Besides, in two months, this bunch will be off and sold and a whole new cargo of black women will be brought on board and you can have all the sport you want with them! Are we agreed?"

This time the sounds of agreement are louder.

"Good, then. I'll be off. Godspeed to you all!" Simon goes to the side, where a small boat is waiting to take him ashore, probably somewhere on the south shore, where he'll take a coach back to Virginia. As he goes over the side, he tips his broad-brimmed hat to us and says, "And ladies, I *do* hope you'll enjoy the extraordinary adventure I have so meticulously planned for you!"

"Awright, get 'em below!" bellows Captain Blodgett, and down below we go, the very minute Simon leaves. After the few remaining bonnets and shawls are taken from us and thrown overboard, we are shoved roughly down the hatch—very roughly, with rude hands pushing us between our shoulder blades, down the hatchway stairs, through a barred door, and into the very belly of the *Bloodhound*, down into the very pit of Hell, itself.

Chapter 18

To the horrified young ladies of the Lawson Peabody, the darkness and the vastness of the Hold are not the most fearsome things, nor is the suddenness of their abduction or the hopelessness of their condition. No, it is the stench that is the worst—the stench of a slaver, the stench from too many human beings packed over and over again into too small a space and denied even the most basic of human needs: the need for fresh air, the need for movement, the need even to turn over on the shelf on which you are confined, and the need to care for and protect your family.

The girls of the Lawson Peabody find, upon entry into this Hell, this nether world, a broad and empty Hold, so broad and so empty as to echo even the smallest, most timorous sound the girls make.

I am about the last one thrown down and it takes my eyes a while to accustom themselves to the gloom. As my vision clears, I am able to see that, in addition to the great hold, there are shelves built around the perimeter of the space, one being about eight feet wide, made of open wood slatting on which we all now stand. This shelf gets much wider, maybe by ten more feet, up where it meets the front part of the ship.

Probably that's where they cram the women and children on a regular run. Above us, at shoulder height, is another shelf, about six foot deep, made of the same open slatting. I know why it is made in such a way and I know the girls are going to find out the why of it for themselves real soon—the *Bloodhound* has heeled over and is heading for open water, and the ship is starting to rock and reel. It will not be long, as the smell is enough to get them gagging already.

The great Hold is like a huge theater, really, with the wide shelf area in the middle being the stage, its narrower portion going around the sides being like the regular seats, the shelf above that being like the balcony, and the dark massive hold below, the pit. There are ladders—stairs, actually—on either side of this stage, leading up to the balcony, and from the center of this stage, a larger, single set of stairs goes down into the pit. Light is coming from somewhere above the balcony and my eyes have adjusted enough for me to see that the great Hold is absolutely empty, except for two large cone-shaped containers that are about four foot in diameter at the bottom and have a hole at top, about ten inches across. I know what they are for and I know they are made that way so they won't tip over in rough seas.

And everywhere, everywhere—on every shelf, on every bulkhead, on every deck—hang chains, all of them clinking and clanking with each roll of the ship.

There are some chains that do not clank. They lie there on the bottom, stretched straight out along the sides of the hull. They're simple long chains with an iron neck collar every three or four feet. Even in my despair, I know what they're for—they're the chain train—they are for leading the captives in a line from the African slave pens to the ship, and eventually from the ship to the American auction blocks. I can stand no more, and I look away.

Down there and to the right is my seabag. *Good.* My kick must have sent it flying down the stairs to roll across the "Stage" and over its edge and into the "Pit." I'll have to go down and stow it someplace safe soon. But for now, I stand on the Stage and gather my wits, which are a bit hard to collect since, not only have I been kidnapped, I have also been twice personally threatened with violent death—first with a pistol, then with a club. Even for me, that is not an easy thing. And even for me, one who is used to cruel Fate sneaking up behind me and giving me a whack every time things seem calm and settled, the suddenness of the day's events is shocking, and I have to sit down and put my head in my hands.

For a while I let myself wallow in deep despair like the rest of the girls, and I add my wails and cries to theirs... *and Jaimy was gonna come over soon and get me and now, oh, God, now... the Black Cloud...*

I sit there, stunned, my head hanging, and my soul bereft of all hope for what seems like a long, long while. But, eventually, I force the Black Cloud back to the far side of my mind and rouse myself. I slap my face twice, once on each side, and say to the timid mouse that really is my innermost self, *Ah, well, best get things going, girl, and first things first.*

"Elspeth. Rebecca. Let me go. Move away from me for a while. I've got to go do some things. Here, cling to each other." They do it, very reluctantly, and I rise and go to the steps that lead to the bottom of the Hold and I descend into the gloom below.

I search about and my eyes pick out my seabag lying there in the shadows, but I do not move toward it till I scan the lit bars high above me to make sure none of the crew is peering down. None appears to be doing that, so, picking my way across the long neck chains lying on the deck, I make my way to my bag. I lay my hands upon it and haul it back under the platform that presently holds the very unhappy girls of the Lawson Peabody School for Young Girls.

I am grateful that my seabag is made of deep navy blue canvas, instead of the white duck that contains many a sailor's worldly goods. It is therefore not easily spotted in this dim light, as I hurry it to a place next to one of the heavy, thick oak knees that hold the planks of the hull together. It is the knee closest to the forward wall of the Hold and so it forms a bit of a cave between itself and the bulkhead. It is there that I tuck in my seabag.

There, I think with a small bit of satisfaction. Someone would have to actually come down here under the platform to spot it, and even then it might escape notice. I think about taking my shiv from the bag and sliding it into my sleeve, but then I think better of it: We might well be strip searched tomorrow and I can't afford the loss of that knife.

Now to plan. I sit myself down on the rough boards of this lower deck and make myself think. *Think, dammit! This is a profound mess we find ourselves in, and I'm afraid it's up to you and to no other to figure a way out. Let's see... well, we've got to get organized first... there's thirty-one, no, thirty-two girls, divide roughly by three, yes, three divisions, that's it, and...*

After I've thought and plotted and planned for maybe an hour, I get to my feet, find the ladder back up, and go stand straight before the weeping and recumbent throng, and raise my voice.

"Listen to me, oh you, my sisters." My words echo through the Hold and crying eyes open and look to me. "We must begin to take control of ourselves here. We do ourselves no good by sinking into mindless panic. We have to organize. We must take things one thing at a time. It is about to get very rough and we must be ready for it. We need to get through one day at a time. Right now, we should plan to get through this afternoon and the coming night." I'm keeping the sentences short and simple on purpose, so they get it.

They quiet down some at this, and then Abigail Pierce steps forward and asks, "But what should we do?" She moves her hands nervously in a helpless way.

"Some of you know I have been to sea and thus know how things go out here. By dint of my experience, I think we should divide into three groups, so that we can be organized into fighting units and not be just a jumble of frightened girls, easy for those lousy bastards to push around and manage as they like."

I find I have their full attention and I go on. "I have thought about it and think it should be thus: Division One will be led by Clarissa Howe and will consist of Lissette, Hermione, Abigail, Helen, Judith, Caroline, Hepzibah, Ruth, Christina, and Cloris."

I look out over their upturned faces as I pick out the particular girls. "Dolley Frazier will lead Division Two. In her group will be Minerva, Priscilla, Dorothea, Constance, Martha, Barbara, Catherine, Wilhelmina, and Julia." I hear no complaints, so I continue.

"In the Third Division, with me at the head, will be Rebecca, Elspeth, Annie, Sylvie, Katy, Frances, Sally, Rose, Beatrice, and Hyacinth."

I pause for breath and look about to see how this is taken. I really wanted to stand up and say that I was in charge of everything and this was the way things were going to be, but I knew that Clarissa and her crew would never follow me. So, putting Clarissa at the head of a division was the best way I could see to get things in some sort of order. And with Dolley as a counterbalance twixt Clarissa and me, well...so far, so good, so I go on.

"I have tried to group particular friends together in these divisions, but that does not really matter—you do not have to group together in these divisions all the time, only when we muster to give out information or to take action. Is that understood?" Not only did I put girls I knew to be friends together, I also tried to balance out who I felt to be the strong and the weak across the divisions.

There are general murmurs of agreement. Then Clarissa steps forward and puts her fists on her hips and her face in mine and says, "What I don't understand is who made you boss? I know I sure as hell didn't!"

"I'm only the leader of my Division Three, Clarissa, should they choose to follow me. The same with your Division One, and the same with Dolley's," I say, knowing that we are all going to come together as a team right now, or else divide up into suspicious and powerless little cliques, which will be the end of us as freeborn girls. It's really up to Clarissa and she sure ain't helping.

"How convenient for you," she says. "All the servants in your division, and none for us?" She looks about in mock perplexity. "No one to do our wash? No one to comb our hair? No one to—"

"We are all in this together," I say right back at her. *Count on you to think that way, Clarissa, in the midst of all this! Concern about who will serve you on your way into slavery.* "There are no more ladies and no more serving girls here. Everyone will tend to their own selves. Right now we are all, lady or girl, just meat to be sold on the auction block. Do you understand that?" I put that as crudely as I could to drive the point home, and I guess the point was made, for there are more murmurs of assent.

"All right. Now listen to this. This level we are standing on will be called the Stage. The upper shelves there will be called the Balconies—the port Balcony on the left there, and the starboard Balcony there on the right. That space down there will be called the Pit. You will see, if you look down there, two large containers. They are called the necessary tubs. That is where you will relieve yourselves when you feel the need. I'm sorry that all the privacy you will have right now is your skirts lowered about you, but we will arrange for some sort of curtains to be—"

"But this is all so...so *foul!*" wails Elspeth, her eyes wild. "I can't do it...I can't..." Others join in the lament and I know I must stop it, right now.

"Oh yes, you will, Elspeth," I say, as gently as I can. "You will get used to it."

"No...no...this is all so wrong! I've got to get back! My parents will be missing me, they'll be wondering where I am...Really, I've got to get back, I'm sorry, I can't stay, I'd really like to, but I really must..."

It is plain she is on the edge of hysteria. I go over and

take her by the shoulders and give her a bit of a shake. "You must not worry about what your parents think now, Elspeth. You must concern yourself with what is best for you, and what is best for you now is to control yourself. Here, Annie, Sylvie, take her, hold her."

And they do, and they manage to soothe her, and she quiets. Again I address the girls.

"All right. Let us muster the divisions. Division Two on the starboard side of the Stage...that's it...and Division One in the center." I've got to give Clarissa's division that position—she'd never let me take center stage. "And Division Three over here on the port side of the Stage, by me. Come on, now, let's do it."

The girls are quieter now, as I knew they would be, having been given some direction and the feeling of belonging to a group. When they are all separated into divisions, I say, "Now your division officers will meet. Make yourselves as comfortable as you can. Those that need to use the tubs should do so now, for soon it will be dark and you won't be able to see your way down there. Oh, and another thing: This setting up of divisions is a secret from *them*. Everything we say or do is a secret from them. Understood?" There are murmurs of assent.

Dolley and Clarissa come up to me as a line of girls files down the ladder into the Pit. I know a natural protocol will be set up—all will look away as each one approaches a tub. Skirts will be lifted, then lowered, and all will be right, in that matter, at least.

"So," says Clarissa, "you've got everyone all divided up. Now what's the point of it? We're still trapped."

"It will give them some comfort, especially the weaker ones, to know that someone is taking charge and looking out for them," says I. "Now, let's go up on the Balcony and see what's up and make some plans."

With that, I lead the way up the stairway to the port-side Balcony. As I noticed before, this shelf is about six feet deep, and in spite of the overall smell in the Hold, it seems there was some effort made to clean it up after the last load. We are able to stand here and actually look out on to the deck of the ship. There's about three feet of wall, and above that are iron bars about six inches apart, the entire length of the Balcony. The bottom of the bars is on the same level as the main deck outside, so if a man were to walk by us, our eyes would be level with his knees. Looking across to the starboard side, I see that it's the same there, and across the aft side of the Hold, as well—I can see the helmsman at his wheel back there, and other men here and there about the deck. It's from these open bars that we will get our light. Above the bars is the flat hatch top that looms overhead and covers the entire Hold. Below the bars are the neck chains, hanging fourteen inches apart.

A breeze blows through the bars and all three of us suck it deep in our lungs, gratefully. At least we shall have some fresh air. I peek out and look up, and sure enough, there're wooden flaps on hinges that will be lowered in the event of rough seas or foul weather.

"What plans can we possibly make?" asks Dolley. "We are helpless."

"Helpless now, true, but it will not always be so," I say. "What we can do now is see how things lie, maybe do some exploring, and get the girls settled in for the night. Tomorrow we must—"

EEEEEEEEEEEEEUUUUUUUWWWWWWWWWWWWW!

There is a scream from below and we look down over the edge of the Balcony. There is a flurry of excitement among the girls waiting their turn at the tubs, and it isn't hard to figure out the cause—rats, scared back into their hidey-holes by our sudden entrance into the Hold, have become bolder and are scurrying around the edges of the Pit. There are a *lot* of them.

There are more screams and cries of *Oh my God, no!* and *Please, God! Save us!* and such from the girls in the Pit. I lean over and say, "Don't worry about them. They won't hurt you. We'll deal with them later. Calmness, now."

They do calm down some, but the ever pious Constance Howell sinks to her knees and stretches her arms upward and laments, "Oh, we have truly died and gone to Hell! Oh Lord, what sins did I commit to be sent to this place? What sins, oh Lord, could I have done that I deserved *this*?"

"Now, Connie, there's no use blaming ourselves, nor God, neither," I say down to her. "The fault lies entirely with those who have taken us, and many others before us, into bondage. They will pay for that with the loss of their souls, and we all know there is no greater loss than that."

That seems to mollify them a bit, though there still are assorted cries of *"Eeeek,"* and one of *"Shoo! Shoo! Get back there, you!"* from Rose Crawford, of my Division Three. *That's the spirit, girl.*

"Anyway," I say, turning back and looking out on the deck again, "tomorrow we'll know better how things are going to be, and we will make more solid plans then. I don't think they'll feed us or have anything more to do with us today. They'll probably want to soften us up a bit with the isolation and all. They'll—"

From the quarterdeck comes the ringing of six bells. *Hmmm…these curs at least keep that practice going. Good. It will help us to know the time, later on.*

"They'll be by to see us in the morning, count on it," I say, continuing my casing of the deck. Through the tangle of rigging, I can see a large lifeboat swung out over the side, hanging from davits. *I wonder why they keep it there…On a regular ship, the small boats are stowed on the deck, upside down…Ah, I bet it's to catch water when it rains. There're probably canvas collectors rigged inside the boats—'cause a slaver needs a lot of fresh water, much more than a regular ship. That's got to be it.* "And that was six bells in the afternoon watch, which means it's three o'clock. My, my, it's been a long four hours since last we left the land."

"And all that we held dear," says Dolley, wistfully, but dry-eyed.

"Well, we hold each other dear, and we still have that," I say firmly, and that gets me a snort from Clarissa. "Now we should get the girls settled because soon things will get rough and many of them will be sick. We'll have them sleep up here on the Balcony, heads to the bulkhead, feet pointed to the Pit, so they don't roll over and fall off the edge. The air is better up here and it will be good for them. Dolley, why don't you announce that, and Clarissa, you address them and say that plans are being made and tomorrow we see about making demands to improve our conditions, and then I'll—"

"What I still don't get is why we should listen to anything you say, Little Miss Pushy!" says Clarissa. She comes up in front of me, her eyes drilling into mine. "Come on, *Boss Lady*, you tell me why."

"I ain't the boss, Clarissa," I say, my own eyes narrowing as

I gaze back into hers. "That's why we are setting up this three-way thing. We share the power...and the responsibility."

"Power?" She snorts, and I feel her breath on my face but I don't pull back. "What *power*? Power over some thirty-odd helpless girls? Some *power*."

"They are what we have to work with and work with them we will. They are all we have in the way of an army, and I think they may well surprise you, Miss Clarissa Crappington Howe."

Dolley pushes between us and says, "All right, stop it. Let's go down and speak to them. I'm...I'm starting to not feel so...good." Dolley then swallows hard.

We go back down to the Stage, where all the girls have regathered—and into their divisions, I'm pleased to see. Nothing like a few rats skittering around your skirts to speed things up down at the tubs.

Dolley and Clarissa make their announcements as planned, and then I speak up:

"I think it best we take off our dresses at night to keep them fresh. Things are filthy here, as you can see, but soon we'll get things shaped up. We'll want to look our best when we hit the slave markets. The more they pay for us, the better we'll be treated, I figure." I say this for the benefit of anyone who might be outside listening, so they'll think we're getting resigned to our fate. "Stockings, too. If you leave them on, your feet will start to stink in a few days. Doff your petticoats, too. It's going to be hot where we're going. Roll them up with your stockings and stuff them inside your dresses and fold the dress into a pad for a pillow at night. I suspect none of you has ever before slept on hard planking and you will welcome the small comfort of the pillow, believe me."

With that I unbutton my dress and slide it off. I hop up on the edge of the Balcony, kick off my shoes and roll down my stockings, and put both stockings and shoes inside my dress and roll it up. I know that three-quarters of the girls will be deathly ill within the hour. Some are already turning a bit green about the gills.

"How…how can you be so cold and matter-of-fact about this?" asks Martha Hawthorne, standing below on the Stage and looking up to me in wonder.

"Because what is, is, and what is not, is not. Believe it or not, I've been in worse fixes than this. We will talk and plan tomorrow when we know more about the way of things around here. It's plain they ain't gonna feed us tonight, so I suggest we all get some sleep, even though it is early. Or some rest, at least. Night will fall shortly. Be sure to say your prayers."

And I am sure many, many heartfelt prayers are said, as the *Bloodhound* takes a slow, deep, and stomach-churning roll. The hanging chains on the port side swing out from the bulkhead, while those on the starboard side crash against the ship's inner hull. The rattling of the chains sets up a hellish symphony, one composed by soulless men without pity or remorse, and one that I know we will hear again and again before this is over.

With that, I turn and walk a little ways along the length of the Balcony, lie down, put my bundle 'neath my head, and close my eyes. Rebecca and Elspeth are up in an instant, and I gather them to me. Annie and Sylvie settle not far away and I reach out my hand to them and their touch gives me comfort and I hope the touch of my hand gives them the same.

Chapter 19

But that was not the end of our first day on the *Bloodhound*. Not for me, anyway. Yesterday, before dark but after the girls had gotten into sleeping position and had settled down somewhat, I got Rebecca and Elspeth to cling to each other rather than to me, then I crawled to the edge of the Balcony and lay there with my head over, looking down into the Pit for a long time. After a while I heard a rustle beside me and turned and saw that it was Clarissa.

"What are you looking at?" she demands as she lies down next to me.

"The rats," I say. "I'm watching the rats."

"Friends of yours, no doubt, and certainly on your social level." She sniffs. "But why are you watching them?"

"To see how they get in and out of the Hold. Look, there…" I point to a particularly large rascal who comes out of a hole in the deck. "See how that one runs across the open space and then ducks around that hull support there? Now we see him, now we don't, so he must have gotten through there, somewhere. See, they live in the bilges, the space below that bottom deck, but there ain't no food down there—it's all forward, up in the galley and storerooms—so they've got to find their way to it. And they do, count on it, they always do."

"Why do you want to know that?"

"Because maybe they can show us the way out of here. I'm pretty sure we can't escape through the hatchway where we were brought in. You noticed the lock on the outer door of the hatch when we were put down here? And the lock on the barred inner gate there? Now, maybe I could pick that lock, if I had the tools, but I can't open the lock on the upper one 'cause it's on the outside of the door. No, if we're to get out of here, we'll have to find our way out down there in the Pit somewhere."

"But what will we do if we do get out, what...?"

"First things first. There's lots we can do if we get out, but we'll plan for that later. For now I'm going down to see what's there." Saying that, I get up and head for the stairs. I'm surprised to hear her following me.

We go down the stairs from the Balcony, onto the Stage level, and then down more steps and into the Pit. The light filtering in from the barred windows is a lot dimmer here, but there is enough of it for us to see our way along the forward bulkhead to the spot where we saw the rat go through.

"Here it is," I say. There was a split in one of the bulkhead boards and the rats, with their teeth, had widened it out at the bottom, where it met the Pit decking, to a hole about four inches across. I get down on my knees and look in, and on my face I feel a draft coming through—it smells of cooking fires and food. *Good.*

"What do you see?" asks Clarissa, crouched beside me.

"Nothing yet, but maybe...I think I see a dim glow up ahead and I do smell food." I sit back up and put my hand carefully into the hole—I don't want to get bit—and I judge the thickness of the board. It is about two inches thick and the wood seems pretty soft. "We'll have to widen this out."

"But how?"

"Maybe with our teeth, like the rats," I say. "I recall you being pretty good with yours."

Actually, though, I'm thinking of my shiv tucked safely away in my seabag. I consider telling Clarissa, but, no, not yet.

"Listen, you—"

"Good night, ladies!" shouts someone from high above, and the shutters come slamming down over the bars to be battened down tight for the night. *Damn!* In an instant we are in pitch darkness.

"Well, this certainly complicates things," I growl. "If they're going to do that every evening, then our operating time down here just got cut by half. We'll have to—"

"God help me!" gasps Clarissa, and I hear her frantically groping in the dark for me. She does find me and I feel her arms tight around my waist. Well, well, that's the first time I've ever heard Clarissa call on anyone for help, let alone God himself.

"Could it be that Lady Miss Clarissa Worthington Howe is afraid of the dark?" purr I, enjoying the moment in spite of everything.

Just then, the rat horde, having been denied access to the rat hole by us being there in the light, chooses that moment to swarm over our feet and into the hole.

"*Oh, pleeeeease,*" whimpers Clarissa, and I relent and find her hand and hold it. I had lived in close quarters with rats before, when I lived with Charlie and Hughie and the gang under Blackfriars Bridge, so they don't scare me like they scare Clarissa, but still, I can't say as I like 'em.

"It's all right, Clarissa. Come, take my hand. We'll just go thisaway till we find the stairs. We'll feel our way along the bulkhead. Ah, here they are. Up we go."

When we gain the Stage, enough dim rays of light come in around the edges of the shutters, so that we can make out the stairs up to the Balcony. Then, and only then, does Clarissa release my hand from the death grip in which she had held it, flinging my hand down and stalking off to return to her place on the Balcony.

There being nothing else to do, I follow her and lie down between Elspeth and Rebecca and try not to again give in to dark despair, but it is hard. To be so close to being reunited with Jaimy and then to have this happen... *Well, at least I'm not being taken back to England to be hanged.* There's that, but it is small comfort. *All right, that's enough of that—we'll see what tomorrow brings.* I pull out my ring, which hangs from a ribbon and rests on my breast, and I clutch it in my fist and close my eyes.

Good night, Jaimy. I hope you are safe and well. Know that you are in my heart and in my thoughts always. Know, too, that your girl's back at sea again, and with a new crew—and all girls, this time.

Yo, ho, ho...

Chapter 20

A new day is announced to the girls in the belly of the *Bloodhound* by the flaps being lifted off the bars at eight bells in the Morning Watch, letting light flood into the Hold. Blinking girls rise up to sitting positions and groan—some of the moaning comes from aching bodies unaccustomed to sleeping on hard wood, some from seasickness, but most, I know, from waking up and realizing that it wasn't all just a bad dream, that we are still here. Many awaken moaning and crying.

There are not so many sounds of retching now, the seasick ones having already lost the contents of their bellies—the vomit draining down through the open wooden slatting of the Balcony to the Pit below. There would ordinarily be a sour smell from it, but it goes unnoticed in the overall stench of the Hold.

I, myself, feel pretty achy, too. *You've gotten soft, girl, from all that easy living.* I get myself in a sitting position and rub the sleep out of my eyes. Then I stumble to my feet and step over girl after girl, all dressed as I am dressed, in white chemise and drawers, and bare of calf, ankle, and foot, till I reach the stairs and go down onto the Stage. In a moment Clarissa comes down, followed by some of the others.

"Dolley's too sick to move. A lot of them are. I don't think we'll muster Divisions this morning," I say to her. "Are you all right?"

"Of course I am," Clarissa snaps. "And I'm hungry, too. When am I gonna get something to eat?"

"I expect we'll get a visit from somebody real soon. Then we'll find out about a lot of things."

Clarissa just grunts in reply to that, crossing her arms over her chest and looking grumpy. We wait. The tubs are visited. The girls who can, put on their dresses. I do the same.

Then something above catches my eye. It is the face of the scurvy-looking boy I had seen scampering about the deck yesterday when we were taken. His face is pressed against the bars, looking down at us.

"Hey, you! Boy!" I shout up at him. "Didn't you hear what your captain said? He said we weren't to be bothered! So sod off, you!"

"Captain's my friend," says the boy, in a thin whispery voice, but nevertheless one that carries throughout the Hold. "Captain's my good friend, he's—"

"Nettles! Get away from there!" This is from somebody out on the deck. The boy Nettles takes one last gawk at the bare lower legs stretched out below him and reluctantly disappears from sight. I am quite sure he'll be back.

"That one seems to be quite the specimen," says Dorothea, ever the scientist. It seems she's another one who is neither seasick nor completely cowed by this situation. She's probably already thought of the wondrous birds and other beasts she might see in North Africa, however ravished by sheiks she might be. And the crew of this ship might yet regret taking her new long glass from her. She did not give it up easily.

"Right," I agree. "Clarissa, we're going to have to set up a watch rotation—four girls, one in each corner of the Balcony—to report on what's happening on the deck. We have to know what they are doing and how they go about things. The more we know about them and the less they know about us, the better. Do you agree?"

I don't give a tinker's damn whether she agrees or not—it's going to be done. It's good that the girls around us see us, well, as *officers*, discussing these things, but it's also good that they come to know who's really the boss among us three.

Clarissa knows what's going on, but she doesn't protest. She nods and we both notice that Dolley has somehow found the strength to dress and join us. The motion of the ship has calmed somewhat—more of a gentle up-and-down now, rather than the rolling and yawing of last night— but Dolley is still pale and it must have taken an enormous strength of will for her to get up. *Good Dolley, you always were the best of us.*

There is a clatter from the hatchway behind us. We turn to see that the upper door has been opened and someone is coming down. Through the bars of the inner door we see that it is—

"Jerome!" says Constance Howell, who is standing closest to the doorway. "Oh, thanks be to God, you've come to help us!"

Jerome takes a key and opens the lock and swings the door in and enters the Hold. "Yes, my dear, I've come to help you. I've come to help you adjust to your new life. But…"

Jerome no longer wears the ill-fitting wig, nor the clownish general's red coat and breeches, and he is no longer smiling. He wears a finely cut suit of the deepest purple and he looks us over with a benign, almost fatherly expression. He has a notebook under one arm.

"But I must tell you my name is not Jerome. It is Sin-Kay. *Mister* Sin-Kay to you. I am not Mr. Simon's slave; I am his business partner, and I am here to inspect my cargo. You will all line up here now." He opens his notebook and takes out a pencil.

The girls are shocked beyond words, but I'm not. "You're a goddamned dirty slaver!" I blurt out, unable to stop myself.

"*Tsk, tsk.* Such language from such a sweet little schoolgirl," he says, bringing his gaze upon me. "Damned by your god, maybe. Dirty, no. But a slaver? Yes, it is true that I am a slaver, and, I might add, a very valuable member of Mr. Simon's company, as well. You see, the white men do not go ashore in Africa, as they are afraid of diseases, like the malaria, the dengue fever, the sleeping sickness, and well they should be afraid, for they are susceptible while I am not. I go to the barracoons and gather the cargo while this ship lies safely offshore, and then I bring the cargo aboard in small boats and then we are off, for yet another profitable voyage." His eyes no longer roll about but have become hooded, secretive, sly.

"How could you sell your own people?" I ask with deep and evident disgust. I know I should hang back, be quiet, and watch, but I can't help it.

"My own people? My dear, I am not Bantu. I am not Mali. Nor am I Watusi." He lifts the pink palms of his hands upward as if asking for understanding. "Do I look Dahomey? Do I look—"

"You look like nothin' but a jumped-up nigra to me, for all your fine and fancy clothes!" snarls Clarissa. "And Ah won't have it, yuh heah? Now you get the hell out of heah! There are ladies present!"

It seems that Clarissa lapses back into a more countrified way of speaking when she gets angry or excited, just as I go back to my Cheapside way of talking sometimes in similar circumstances. It is also becoming plain to me that our Clarissa did not learn a large part of her vocabulary at the Lawson Peabody School for Young Girls, but rather in a barnyard.

Sin-Kay's eyes narrow to slits as he goes over to Clarissa, draws up to his full height so that he towers over her, and snarls back, "It will be a great pleasure seeing you up on the block, Miss Howe. A great pleasure."

Clarissa's face is white with fury. "Get away from me, nigra!"

Sin-Kay turns slowly from her and faces the rest of us. "I told you to line up! Do it!" Some of the girls on the Stage begin to form a line.

"Many are too seasick to stand," I say to him. "You can't..."

He turns on me. "You again. Let me tell you what I can do and what I can't. I can as easily sell you to a brothel as to a rich Arab, Missy, so you had best watch your mouth. The whorehouses pay well, too, and I know of several especially low and nasty ones. I may yet do that with your scrawny self in particular, as the sultans prefer their harems stocked with items a bit more fleshy than you." He pauses to let that sink in and then continues, "What I can't do is put up with any more of this back talk. Dummy! Come here!"

There is a noise up the hatchway and someone, or some *thing*, lumbers down the stairs and lurches into the room. It is a huge man, hunched over, with great arms that swing by his side. He has a large scar that runs from his forehead and down one cheek, and he looks around at us, confused and fearful. He is obviously simple. The girls near him recoil in horror.

Sin-Kay smiles. "This is my Dummy. Aside from me, and sometimes the boy Nettles, he will be your sole contact with the outside world until we reach our destination." He notes with satisfaction that we are suitably impressed. "Dummy, go up on the shelf and bring down any girls up there."

The Dummy shuffles off to do it, saying, with a deep rumbling in his barrel chest, "Bring...down...girls."

"No, wait," I say. "No, we'll do it. Rose, Constance, help me."

Sin-Kay smiles and recalls his Dummy, who stands weaving behind his master.

We go up on the Balcony and rouse the others. Rebecca has to be carried down, she is so weak and sick. I pull Elspeth to her feet and she manages to make it down by herself. Constance and Rose get the rest down and we assemble everyone in some sort of line.

"Very well," says Sin-Kay, with satisfaction. "I will now call the roll. You will answer when your name is pronounced." He opens his book. "Rebecca Adams."

"She's here. At my feet. Too sick to stand," I say. "She's just a little girl."

"Well, she won't be one for very long," says Sin-Kay, and he writes something in his book.

You dirty bastard...

"Ruth Alden."

"H-here," stammers Ruth, a slight girl, in Clarissa's Division One. Sin-Kay looks her up and down and makes another note.

"Sally Anderson."

Sally answers, and it's the same routine—name, glance up and down, note, and so on down the line—Applegate, Bailey, Baxter, Cabot...and on and on till...

"Jacky Faber."

"Here," I say, and come to Parade Rest for the scrutiny I know is to come.

"Ah, it's you. Does the Jacky stand for Jacqueline?"

"Whatever you wish."

"I so wish. It will sound better at auction," he says, and then gives me the once-over. "Best gain some weight, girl, or..."

He lets that trail off, then goes on.

"Dolley Frazier."

"Here," says Dolley, as best she can.

"Elspeth Goodwin."

"Here, Sir," she gulps, "and I know you're going to let me go back, 'cause I got to go back, you know, 'cause..." A note is pencilled and he moves on.

Then he summons Martha Hawthorne, writes a quick note, then moves on to call out, "Clarissa Howe."

Clarissa spits out an obscenity I wouldn't have thought she'd known...and she delivers it with such force and familiarity that it speaks of some prior extensive use on her part. It is the usual curse, the *F* variation of *Sod off!*, which trips so easily off *my* tongue, wherein she invites Sin-Kay to go do something both unnatural and, I think, actually impossible to himself.

Sin-Kay does not reply but writes many, many notes next to her name. *Cheer up, Clarissa,* I'm thinking, *if he sends you to a whorehouse, you'll end up owning it within the year, I'll wager.*

Then on and on…Howell…Johnson…King…Leavitt… then…

"Lissette de Lise."

"Present."

"Ah, our French maiden," says our overseer, looming over her slight form. *Come on, Lissette, remember how your Queen Marie conducted herself when she stood next to the guillotine, hearing the mob howling for her head.*

To her credit, Lissette lifts her quivering chin and says nothing.

"I think you shall be bound for the slave pens of Morocco. They speak French there, you know. Yes, there are many a sultan or bey who will pay well to relish the idea of having a female French aristocrat tucked in his bed whilst he negotiates treaties with that same girl's own kinfolk. They are funny that way, you see. They like to pay insult for insult, humiliation for humiliation. And they have suffered some at the hands of you French."

Sin-Kay moves on. Though she trembles, Lissette has not changed expression. *Good girl!*

Finally, he nears the end of his list…Saltonstall… Samuelson…Thwackham…

"Amy Trevelyne."

"She stayed behind to tend to Mistress," I say.

"Ah. A pity." He makes a note. He logs in Hepzibah Van Pelt, Frances Wallace, and Julia Winslow, and then turns to Annie. "Well, the loss of Miss Trevelyne is more than made up by the addition of the three fine serving girls. Your name?"

"Annie...Annie Byrnes," she says.

"And yours?"

"Sylvia Rossio," says Sylvie, hardly above a whisper.

"Ah. An Italian to spice up the mix. Good!" he says heartily and pencils them in. "And, lastly, you."

Katy doesn't say anything, she just stares straight ahead, her eyes dead.

"Come on, what's your name, girl?"

"Katy Deere," she says at last, her voice flat and as dead as her eyes.

Sin-Kay looks her tall and graceless form up and down and shakes his head and makes a note. "All right. If you three have been good girls, then I think I can place you as nicely as the others. If not, then you'll have to go to less charming...establishments."

He snaps the notebook shut and addresses all the girls:

"Very well, the cargo manifest is complete. Now you will have something to eat. From now on you will receive two meals a day—one in the morning a half hour after the shutters are raised and once again a half hour before they are lowered. Bowls and spoons will be issued at each meal, then collected and counted afterward." He stops and turns to his man standing next to him looking confused. "Dummy, go get their food. Have Nettles bring down the bowls." The Dummy nods and leaves, lumbering up the hatchway, intent on his mission.

"You will each be given a cup, which you will keep for the duration of the voyage. You will receive a quart of fresh water a day, one pint in the morning and one in the evening.

179

Each day we will have a roll call and inspection similar to what we did today. We expect to get you to market within thirty days, if the wind holds. Till then, enjoy your voyage. Ah, here's your breakfast."

The Dummy has come back carrying a steaming cauldron in one massive hand and a bucket of water in the other. He puts both down in the entrance to the hatchway. That boy Nettles is right behind him with a stack of bowls and a fistful of spoons clutched in his grubby fingers. A leering smirk is fixed on his face as he looks about at us.

"Put them down, Sammy, and go fetch the cups. We'll need thirty-two," says Sin-Kay.

Sammy Nettles drops his burden to the floor with a clatter and runs back up the hatchway, anxious to get the cups and return to the show, I suppose. Sin-Kay goes into the hatchway and swings the barred door shut behind himself. He then takes his key out and locks it. Everything—cauldron, bucket, utensils, Dummy, and now Nettles again—is behind the door.

"You will get in a line and one by one go up to the door, and the Dummy will hand out your food and water. When you are done, pass your bowls and spoons back to him. He will take them out to the galley and then he will return. He will be your almost constant companion from now on. He may be stupid, but he's smart enough to watch for attempted suicides or any other troublesome things. Believe me, any misbehavior will be dealt with *most* harshly. Now, if there are no questions, I'll bid you good day. Enjoy your breakfast, enjoy your cruise."

Before he can leave, I speak up. "*Mister* Sin-Kay, surely we must have water for washing ourselves and our undergarments. What kind of price do you think you'll get for us if we arrive at the Barbary Coast all filthy and squalid? We must have combs and soap and basins and washcloths and towels, and, furthermore, we need some sheets of canvas to set up a proper privy and..."

"You shall have none of those things," says Sin-Kay. "Ah, but you are the one who said that I was what—*dirty*...?—a bit earlier, did you not, girl? Well, let us see just how dirty *you* become during your stay down here, *hmm?* But don't worry, ladies, we'll see that you are cleaned up before you are put on the auction block. Are there any other questions? Good. I bid you good day, then. Come along, Sammy."

Sin-Kay leaves, with Nettles tagging reluctantly behind him. When they exit up top, I listen for the sound of the outer door being locked, but I don't hear it. So...they don't think it necessary to lock that door when the Dummy is down here below? *Ah, yes, the Dummy—that glorious, wonderful Dummy—God must love me after all.*

We line up for our food, and expressions of profound disgust issue from the first girls to receive theirs: *"Eeeuuww!"* and "What *is* this stuff?" and "They expect us to eat *this?*" I get up to the door and stand before the Dummy and watch him slowly ladle out the ration and then slowly put the spoon in it and then slowly hand it out through the bars, all so very carefully as if he had practiced diligently to get it down right, as I'm sure he did. Finally it's my turn. I take the bowl and the tin cup of water he hands out.

I take a sip of the water—not too foul, and that's good—and then look down into the bowl. Sure enough, it's burgoo. I lift my voice: "It's called burgoo. It's oatmeal boiled in water with whatever they have around to toss in with it. I think this batch has a few peas and maybe some crumbled-up biscuit in it. There's some pork grease floating on the top. You've got to eat it, as it's all you're going to get, and it's probably what you're going to get for every meal." This is met with groans of disgust, but I hear the spoons rattling against the bowls, so I guess they're going to eat it.

I go to the edge of the Stage and sit down with my legs dangling over the edge. I'm joined by other members of my Division Three. I put down my cup and dig into the burgoo. It's thin and not very good. They must think we need less than the sailors. We'll have to work on this later. This and the laundry and wash-water needs that will have to be addressed. If Sin-Kay thinks I'm done with that, he's sadly mistaken.

While the girls are choking down this stuff, I whisper to some of those around me: "Annie. Katy. Sylvie. Bea. When the Dummy goes back out with the dirty bowls, I want you four to fly up to the four corners of the Balcony and look out to see if anyone is listening or spying on us. Annie, starboard-side forward. Katy, port. Sylvie, aft starboard; Bea, port." I point to each spot as I say it, in case they haven't got *port* and *starboard* down yet. They nod in agreement.

I gulp down the rest of my burgoo, stash my still-full cup of water up on the back edge of the Balcony, where I'll be able to get it later, and go to the door.

"I need a bowl to take to that girl over there," I say, pointing to Rebecca's still form lying on the deck. The Dummy looks down at the several bowls and cups left unclaimed. "They're too sick to come get their own and we have to help them." He thinks deeply, puts two and two together, and nods. He ladles the burgoo into the bowl and dips the cup

182

into the water bucket. I say, "Thank you," then carry them over to Rebecca and sit down cross-legged beside her.

I lift her head and cradle it in the crook of my left arm. "Come, Rebecca, you must eat something or else you will die, and we don't want that." Her eyelids flicker as she looks up at me. I take a spoonful of the gruel and put it between her lips and she gulps and swallows. Then she bucks and gags and I turn her to the side so the sick comes out of her mouth and slips down through the slattings.

I put the burgoo aside and lift her head higher and put her cup of water to her lips. "At least you must have water. You lost everything in your belly last night and you must have water or you'll die."

I put my lips to her ear. "Come on, Rebecca Adams, we need you with us in this." Her eyes open again and she sips at the water and then lies back down. I watch her and she keeps the water in. That is good.

I look over at Division One. Clarissa and Lissette are together, seated on the Stage, their backs against the port hull, eating their burgoo. I see that Ruth Alden and Judith Leavitt, both of Clarissa's division, are down, in a state similar to Rebecca's.

I say nothing to Clarissa. Instead, I say to Martha Hawthorne, of Division Two and Dolley Frazier's dearest friend, "Martha. You might look to Catherine and Wilhelmina. Dolley's too sick to take command just yet. Try to get some water down them, at least." Catherine Lowell and Wilhelmina Johnson are both inert forms lying motionless on the deck.

Martha upends her bowl into her mouth, hands it to Dorothea, and goes over to minister to the two down girls. I look over significantly at Clarissa and then at Ruth and

Judith. I catch Clarissa's eye and she catches my meaning—*with the advantages of command also come responsibilities*—and she says, "Christina, Cloris, see what you can do about Ruth and what's-her-name. See if they will drink some water, at least."

Well, delegation of task is a part of command, I suppose, so I have no quarrel with Clarissa's method. I do notice, however, that after I have stopped looking at her, she does crawl over to Ruth and speaks to her, after Christina and Cloris had gotten food and water and were trying to minister to the sick girls.

"Here, Rebecca, try another sip, it'll..."

There is a tug at my sleeve and I see that it's Elspeth, looking plaintively into my eyes.

"Jacky...please...I've got to...my parents..."

Christ! She's still on about that!

"Elspeth, your parents think you are dead. You are not dead and you should take consolation in that. *Now take hold and be quiet!*" I hiss at her. I've got to be cruel—she's just got to stop that nonsense.

Her mouth drops open and her lower lip quivers. I would have thought those eyes had no more tears in them, but they do, and tears stream down her face. Then she bows her head and buries her face in her hands and sobs.

I turn my attention back to Rebecca and pay Elspeth no more mind. In a while she crawls off and curls up in a ball over by the hull to wallow in her misery.

Eventually, all who can eat have eaten and the bowls and spoons are put back through the bars, where the Dummy pours any uneaten burgoo back into the cauldron. He then takes it and the utensils and tromps up the stairs and out through the upper door.

"Now!" I say to my four designated lookouts and they hurry to their positions and peer through the bars. "Report!" I say when they've had a chance to scan the decks.

"No one near," says Beatrice Cooper. She's from a farm north of Boston and seems to be a capable girl. "There are men back there on that raised-up part where the wheel is."

"The quarterdeck," I say. They might as well learn the names of things—it will make things easier, later.

"And I think that's the Captain there...the one with the crossed belts on his chest and the sword by his side."

"That's him all right," I say. "Anything else? Annie?"

"No. Nobody's about."

"It's plain that the crew takes the Captain's orders to heart, else they would be three deep at the bars, gawking at us," I tell the girls around me.

"Nothin' over here, neither," says Katy from port forward. "Just some men over there messin' with them ropes."

"The same," says Sylvie. "I can see the...the quarterdeck from here, too. The Captain's pointing up at the sails and talking to another man."

Probably the First Mate, I'm thinking. "All right, keep a sharp lookout and sing out if you see anyone getting near." With that, I turn and face the other girls on the Stage.

"Listen to me, all of you. Some things need to be said. Elspeth, you sit up and listen!" I pause, and when I'm sure I have everyone's attention, I go on. "Our greatest enemy right now is not those men out there. Our greatest enemy is hopelessness and despair. We cannot allow ourselves to sink into the slough of despond. What Sin-Kay said about suicide sent a chill up my spine, for I know that all of us will at some point feel it is useless to resist and it would be easiest to just give up and end it all—all the misery and pain and the promise of a life spent in shameful slavery." I pause for breath and for effect.

"But not all is hopeless, for I tell you that we *will* get out of this, that we *will* go back home, but to do that we must stick together and be strong and banish all thoughts of gloom and doom from our minds."

"But, Jacky, how *can* we have any hope, in all…in all this?" blurts out Helen Bailey, gesturing with her hands at the Hold in all its grimness.

"Because, Helen, plans are being made. We can't tell you what they are, for they are not firm enough yet. I will tell you that Clarissa and I did some exploring last night and discovered some very interesting things, things that give us great hope." Many heads turn to look at Clarissa, wondering at the strange fact of she and I doing anything together except trying to strangle each other.

"And we have resources our captors do not even know about."

"Resources? What resources?" This from Caroline Thwackham, granddaughter of Judge Thwackham of the People's Court of Boston, with whom I had a passing and not very pleasant acquaintance. I still live under the threat of his sentence of an even dozen lashes should I ever appear in his court again.

"Caroline, are we all not 'Pimm's Girls' and therefore the finest and fiercest of our sex? Are we not?" I pause for a moment for that to take hold. "Yes, we are and *that* is our greatest resource and *that* is what will bring us through this. And mark me on this: Those evil men will yet live to regret the taking of the girls of the Lawson Peabody. And know this, too: It is a long way from here to the coast of Africa, and anything can happen, *anything!*"

There are other resources, but I ain't gonna tell them about those just yet.

Then, all is silence. *Is that the stiffening of backbones I sense?*

"Good. Now let us start conducting ourselves in a manner in which Mistress would approve. There are many ways we can improve our condition. Let us get started." This is, for me, a long speech, but I press on:

"First of all, everything we say or do *must* be kept secret from our captors. And that's *everything*—the fact that we have organized into divisions, the fact that we are talking like this, the fact that plans are being made. They must know nothing of us and what we are doing, yet we must know everything about them. That is why we are going to set daylight watches up there where the lookouts are now, and we are starting that watch rotation *right now.* There are enough of us such that you will each stand a one-hour watch once every day or so. Priscilla, will you set up the schedule?"

Priscilla Cabot, who is a precise, fussy sort, nods. This sort of task is right up her alley.

"We must stay sharp in all the ways we can. Lissette, if you could conduct a class in the French language each day for, say, an hour, I know it would be most appreciated. Hepzibah, a choral group would lift spirits—a song each evening before we go to sleep. I have a suggestion for this evening's—"

"Jacky! Two men coming!" warns Annie. "They're swinging something over here!"

"It's a lifting thing. Like we had to get hay in the barn," says Katy, who also can see out forward.

"All right. Hush, everybody." And we all watch to see what is going to happen. Presently a square of light opens up in the hatch cover that is our ceiling. It is a small hatch that has been thrown open, a small hatch that I hadn't noticed before because of the gloom up there.

"All of yiz. Against the back wall. Quick now, Captain's orders," snaps a man's voice, and two hooks on cables come snaking down into the Hold. "Two of yiz go down there and put the hooks on one o' them tubs."

Hmmm... Cockney, from the sound of him.

"Rose, come with me," I say, and we head down to the Pit. We cross the Pit deck and stand by the tubs and watch as the hooks come slowly down.

"What will you do with 'em, then, Jock?" I ask up at the unseen man who had spoken.

"Dump 'em, you ninny, what the 'ell did you think we'd do wi' 'em? But we ain't supposed to talk to yiz, so shut yer gob."

A real friendly type, I can tell.

"I know that, Jocko," I says back at him, keeping in the Cockney way of talking to maybe get a little familiar with him. "But when you put them over the side, will you give 'em a bit of a rinse?" The tubs are made of shiny tin, so they would rinse right clean.

"Nay. Just dump. Now put on them hooks," says the man. I can see the outline of his head up there silhouetted against the light.

"Here, Rose. Take your hook and put it through the eye there. That's it. Now hold it there till they take up the slack. Good. All right, Jocko, haul away!"

I hear the sound of a winch being ratcheted up on deck and the strain is taken on the cable and the tub rises up and through the hatch. It is then swung to the side and disappears. While waiting for the empty tub to return, I notice for the first time a metal eye on the edge of the bottom of the other tub. Ah. So that is how the job is done—the tub is swung outboard, another line is attached to that bottom eyelet, a strain is taken on that line, the tub is lowered and so upends itself and empties into the sea. Neat. I like to know how things are done.

The first tub swings back in and comes down fast. It has not been rinsed. Damn. It would be such a simple thing for them to do, too.

"Oow, Jocko, you didn't rinse it, and you seem like such a nice cove, you do."

"Stoof it and hook up the other one or we'll send the Dummy down to do it."

"Now, ducks, is that any way to speak to a lady? No, it ain't. Now be a luv and rinse out this one. There you go, mate, hooks on—haul away."

Again the tub rises and again it disappears through the hatch and again returns, unrinsed. The hooks are withdrawn and the hatch slams shut without another word from the men. *We'll see next time, Jocko...*

Later, we have our first French lesson from Lissette, it being mostly call-and-response, of course, having no blackboard and no books, but Lissette does a pretty good job of it, even providing a clear explanation of the future subjunctive case, which I've always found rather baffling. After that is done, I take one of my petticoats and make a great show of tearing part of it into small rags. We each wear two petticoats under our dress, Mistress having been very strict in the matter of the uniformity of our costume, but we sure don't need either one of them here.

"I think we should each claim a sleeping spot, so we can have a place to keep our cups and our dresses when we're not wearing them," I say when I see that I have their attention. "You could mark your place by folding up one of your petticoats and putting it there." All of our underclothes have our initials on them in ink. I keep on ripping and talking. "I think we should spread out equally on each side of the Balcony, not sleep all on one side like we did last night."

Saying that, I take my ripped strips of cloth and my cup of water and go up the stairs to the port Balcony, walk a few steps along it, then stop. I want to be close to the stairs so I can get up unobserved in the night. I put down my cup, which still is half full, and I reach up under my dress and pull down my other petticoat, fold all but one of my strips in it, and arrange it so that the *J. F.* mark shows and put it up next to the hull wall.

Then I go to the edge of the Balcony and sit down. I know they're all still watching me as I dip my rag in my cup enough to moisten it and then I proceed to wash my face— it's not much of a wash, with only a damp rag, but it's something and it feels good. I close my eyes and revel in this small pleasure, and when I open them, I see the girls arranging themselves on the Balcony, and I hear the ripping of fabric.

We'll see who gets dirty, Sin-Kay.

After I've gotten the still-helpless Rebecca and the still-distraught Elspeth arranged in place on either side of my

190

pillow, I use my cloth to clean Rebecca's face, and the coolness of it revives her a bit, so she's able to sit up and lean her back against the wall. That's a good sign.

Leaving them there, I go back to the Stage and announce, "Officers' Call," the traditional signal for the officers to gather for a conference. When Dolley and Clarissa look at me, I motion with my head for them to follow me down into the Pit. Clarissa, who has, of course, taken up residence on the opposite part of the Balcony from me, arranges her bundle to her liking and then follows, as does Dolley.

"We've got to talk," I say to the two of them in a low voice so I can't be overheard by the other girls. "First, let's show Dolley the Rat Hole."

We do it, and when she sees it she says, "But what's the plan? We certainly can't get through that. I certainly can't," she says, looking down at her rather ample chest. Dolley carries a considerable bit of tail, too, but it is all arranged in a pleasing way—she certainly didn't lack for gentlemen callers back at the school. Thinking of the school gives me a sharp pang of homesickness, but I push it down.

"We are going to widen it out."

"But how?"

"Yes, *how*, Commander Know-it-all?" echoes Clarissa, her voice heavy with scorn.

"With this." And with that, I pull my shiv out of my sleeve. Even in the dim light down here, the blade shines, its edge sharp as a razor and the cock's head I had carved on the handle, so long ago, grinning evilly.

"Where did you get that?" asks Dolley, her eyes wide in wonder. I believe she has forgotten her seasickness.

"I had it stashed in my seabag, which I managed to kick

down into the Hold when all eyes were on you two while you were talking with that evil Simon," I say. I had taken the blade out this morning when no one was looking and had decided then to hide it separate from the bag, in case the bag was discovered. There's a lot of stuff in that bag that'll come in handy, but without the knife, we are lost.

"We can set up shifts of two girls each—one carves away while the other rests, and they pass the knife back and forth. If we do it throughout each day when we have light, we'll have it wide enough in no time. We're under the Stage here and can't be spotted from above." At that, we all look up at the light coming through the slats of the Stage. Dolley nods in agreement.

"But what then?" asks the ever-doubtful Clarissa.

"We see what's on the other side, is what. We know the galley is over there, and so we know we can steal fire. We can steal other things we'll need, too," I whisper urgently. "And we know there's a powder magazine over there, too. Did you notice the six guns on deck when we were brought aboard? There's got to be powder for them."

"We're going to shoot them?" asks Dolley. "I don't know if the girls are—"

"No. Here's the plan as I have roughed it out: We get through to the other side. We find the powder magazine. We make a fuse. On the day of our escape, we create a diversion, get all the men on deck and all the girls through the Rat Hole and into one of those lifeboats hanging outboard. We light the fuse, lower the boat, and get away from the ship. We will have already disabled the other lifeboat so it can't be launched to chase us down. I know how to sail that boat—hell, I could sail this one, but I don't think we've got enough strength to overpower the crew, as they're a grim, mean bunch. So anyway, the powder blows, the wretched *Bloodhound* sinks, and we sail away to the shipping lanes to the north. If we have good weather, we're sure to be picked up shortly by a passing warship or merchantman, and back we go to Boston."

It is wonderful to see the glimmer of hope, however slight, shine in their faces—the chance, though right now very slim, of going home.

"Course, there's lots to be done between now and then, and I ain't figured out everything yet, but—"

"But it's a chance!" says Clarissa, pounding one fist into the palm of the other. "It's a real chance! Let's start right now! Give me that knife!"

"Not just yet. Let's give the girls some time to settle in and get used to things. I don't want them to know anything about this at all—not the knife, not the plan, not anything. If we are betrayed, we are lost, and we don't know how strong some of the girls would be in the face of temptation. No, let's wait, we have time—this is only the second day and it will take at least a month to get us over to wherever they're planning to sell us. In a little while we'll know better how things lie. Agreed?"

They both nod.

"Good. Now let's get the girls settled in their routines. It will give them some comfort. I, myself, am looking forward to Hepzibah's choral practice this afternoon."

And this evening later, much, much later, I'm looking forward to visiting an old and very dear friend...

Chapter 21

I lie here in the dark and I wait. And while I wait, I think back on the events of this evening.

The early-evening choral practice went wonderfully, with Hepzibah placing us in ranks on the Stage in a similar manner to where we once stood before Signor Fracelli—sopranos in the middle, altos to either side. We did Bach's "Sheep May Safely Graze," which went over well, in spite of the fact that we didn't have a written score in front of us. We ran over some rough spots several times, but memory served and we eventually got it right. I wonder what the scum up above thought of the sounds of music coming from the helpless captives below. *Could this be how the quality acts in times of trouble, scum?*

Then the shutters came slamming down again at six in the evening, right between the two dogwatches, and we were thrown again into darkness, but not before we all got back to our kips and settled in before it happened. The girls are beginning to live according to the bells of the various watches.

I lie here and think, and I know the others are doing the same. It's plenty light out and too early to go to sleep just yet. There's no reason to shut us down this early. We'll have to bring it up with Sin-Kay in the morning, and I think we should have some of the other girls speak up to Sin-Kay so he doesn't get the idea that me and Dolley and Clarissa are the leaders, 'cause then he might—

"Jacky...," a voice says from the dark—whose voice, I don't know.

"What?"

"How do you think they managed to capture us like this? How did they get away with it? It all seems so bizarre..."

I sit up and collect my thoughts on that, then I say, "I think it probably went something like this: Simon and Jerome come up to Boston, probably on some other business—runaway slave or something like that. Simon, smarting over some slight from Clarissa's dad and looking for an easy score, cases out the school. They find the surly Dobbs, plainly dissatisfied with his station in life. They get him drunk and talking, and then they present him with what he thinks is the offer of a lifetime—turned out to be just so, though the lifetime turned out to be shorter than he expected. So Simon has cards printed up that say 'Harrison's Tours—See the Beautiful Massachusetts Bay in all its splendor—scientific day tours.' Dobbs shows it to Mr. Sackett, who has a fine inquisitive mind and loves fieldwork and is a lover of birds, too. And he's thinking, *Oh, who knows what species we might see out there on a far island?*"

"He said exactly that," says a voice that is plainly Dorothea's, she having been Mr. Sackett's special student. "He said that on that very morning."

"Mr. Sackett then enthusiastically presents the idea to Mistress, and she is skeptical, of course, but Simon arranges to meet her, and, as the suave Mr. Harrison, shows her he knows how to act the perfect gentleman, and he presents her with seemingly solid letters of reference. Sin-Kay, as Jerome, is around playing the clown to endear himself to the girls and to show how happy and harmless everything is, and Mistress agrees—after all, she's going along, too, as well as Higgins and Mr. Sackett. Don't forget, it's springtime for Mistress, too, and she thinks she'd probably enjoy the day. That's how the job was done. Dobbs poisoned the three of them the next day, and we all got in the coaches as meek as mice. It was nicely done, I must say. I don't think I could have come up with a better plan, myself."

Silence.

Then another, smaller voice comes out of the dark. "I know you said we'd get out of this, Jacky. But what if we don't? What will happen if they get us to Africa?"

Ah, the night dreads. During the day you are able to be strong, face things a little more bravely, but then comes the night...

"Well, I imagine we'll be taken ashore, cleaned up, examined as to the state of our virtue, and then one by one, or maybe in small groups sometimes, we'll be put up on the auction block, which is rather like a small stage, and sold to the highest bidder." I decide to be frank in this matter, to strengthen their resolve to escape that fate. "I've heard that you are stripped naked when you are on the block, but I don't know for sure..." There are gasps of shock from all around me. "Let's ask Clarissa. Clarissa, was it like that when you bought Angelique?"

"I don't know. I wasn't there!" hisses Clarissa through teeth I know to be clenched in a snarl. "She was bought *for* me, not *by* me."

"Ah. So that makes it all right, then."

"Shut up, you."

"Be quiet, both of you," warns wise Dolley, trying to keep order among the so-called officers. She's right, of course. I shouldn't have said that.

"But I don't want to be sold to anyone!" This is a wail from Elspeth, next to me.

"I'm sure that many who sailed in the opposite direction had *exactly* the same wish, dear," I say, patting her shoulder.

"But they are being so *cruel* to us! So cruel!"

I think for a bit before replying.

"You know, I have sailed with seamen who had signed on to slavers before and they described to me the horrors of those voyages—how over five hundred men, women, and children would be packed into a hold like this, the men held by these neck chains here behind us, stretched out fourteen inches apart so they could not even turn over, packed together on all these shelves, on every inch of space. If a person on the upper shelf was sick, then his sickness would rain down on the ones below. If there's dysentery, then that goes down, too. Sometimes as many as half of them would die on the way over. Other times, if they were spotted by a British patrol, in order to avoid getting seized as a slaver, they threw everyone overboard to drown. Men, women, and children."

I pause to let them think on this, then I go on. "Is it any wonder that when women were sometimes allowed on deck for an airing, they would throw their babies overboard and jump in after them, to drown rather than remain with these incomprehensibly cruel fiends who subjected them to such horror? Remember, these people were taken from their villages in the interior of Africa. Since they didn't speak any of the languages spoken in the slave pens on the coast, they had no idea what was going to happen to them, or where these monsters with their big strange boat were taking them. At least *we* know what they plan for us. Us being treated badly? Nay, my sisters, we are being treated like queens compared to that!"

Another long silence. There is the sound of weeping again. Perhaps I shouldn't have...

"Jacky." I recognize Dolley's voice again. "You must know that we've all read Amy's book about your early life. Will you tell us about what happened to you after you left the school the night it burned? Amy said she had received a letter, soon after that, saying you had signed on to a whaler. It sounds wondrously exciting. Will you tell us about it?"

Good Dolley, she's always right there when she's needed to be, to soothe tempers, to calm fears, or, in this case, to change the subject.

"Sure, I will," I say, and I'm about to give them a quick account of my doings since I left the Lawson Peabody the first time, when I reconsider. Why not stretch it out over several days, maybe even a week? I am a natural show-off, after all, and these evenings are long, and it might cheer them. I decide to do it and then lift my voice:

"*'Ishmael!' I called out as I skipped down the gangplank of the* Pequod, *my seabag on my shoulder. 'Good sailing to you!'*"

"*'And to thee, Jacky...'*"

In a short while, I've crawled off the Balcony and felt my way to the center of the Stage, and I continue with the story, complete with embellishments and gestures, to my invisible audience listening in the dark.

"*'Thee are sure thee will not marry me?'*"

————

Later, much later, after I had finished my story for the night and all about me breathed deep and regular in sleep, I again leave my kip and go down to the Stage. I feel my way along the wall till my hands touch the bars of the doorway, the doorway behind which sleeps the snoring Dummy.

"*Hughie!*" I hiss. "*Wake up!*"

He snorts in his sleep and then awakens. "Huh? What you want? You leave me be now, gonna tell Mister..."

"No, no, Hughie, don't tell Mister. Just listen...," I say urgently. I don't want him flying off for Sin-Kay. "It's me, Hughie, it's me, Little Mary from Rooster Charlie's gang. Don't you remember?" *Come on, Hughie, remember, please remember...*

It is not so much of a coincidence that Hugh the Grand should end up here. Taken by a press gang, as the girl Joannie said he was, he would surely have proved too stupid to be a seaman on a warship, or even a merchantman, and would naturally have drifted to a slaver, which'd take just about anyone who lacks a conscience. Not that Hughie lacks one; it's just that he doesn't know, he being simple and all. Of course, I recognized him the instant I laid eyes on him, and rejoiced. There's lots that girls can do, but there's some things they just can't, and I know that—like have the strength to lower a lifeboat into the water when it has to go down.

"We was mates, Hughie, you and me," I say, hoping that slipping back into my old way of talking would give his memory a jog. I sense him in there shaking his great big head in confusion. "Remember how we all lived under Black-friars Bridge, you and me and Polly and Nan and Judy and Charlie? How I used to ride on your shoulders and I'd read

199

the newspapers posted on the printers' walls to see if we could get a penny? Remember how—"

"Charlie...loved Charlie. Charlie went away."

Hallelujah!

"We all loved Charlie, Hughie, we did."

"Little Mary?" he says, and seems to be wondering at the notion. "Little Mary went away, too. Toby come."

"That's right, Hughie, and now I've come back and we can be mates again."

"Was happy then...Mary."

"Aye, Hughie, we was a good bunch, but we got some good ones here, and we can have a new gang and you can be in it."

"I can be in the gang?"

"Sure you can, Hughie, but just one thing," I say, and reach in through the bars and find his hand. "Do you know how to keep a secret, Hughie? Like when you don't tell about somethin'?"

"Uh-huh."

"Well, you can't tell anyone that you know me and that you're in our gang now. Don't tell Nettles. Don't tell Mister."

"Hate Sammy. Hate Mister. Won't tell."

"Good, Hughie, that's real good." I give his hand a squeeze. "I've got to go back to my kip now. I'll see you in the morning and I'll wink at you so's you'll know which one I am, 'cause I've changed some since last we was mates. And remember, *mum*'s the word, Hughie, all right?"

"Mum."

"Good night, Hughie. You was always just the best boy."

Chapter 22

"Here he comes," reports Wilhelmina Johnson up on starboard aft lookout. "Got Nettles with him."

Earlier, when the flaps went up, I had gone to the hatchway and winked broadly at Hughie. He blushed and grinned his big foolish grin, and I put my finger to my lips and whispered, *"Shush now,"* and he nodded and kept on smiling, his big head lolling back and forth in joy.

Again there's the sound of the upper locks being opened, and Sin-Kay comes down the stairs. Hughie, his smile now gone, presses himself against the bulkhead to let his master pass. The bottom door is opened, and Sin-Kay enters the Hold, with Nettles following, being his usual awful, smirking self. With them also is Chubbuck, the Bo'sun, who takes a position next to the doorway and leans against the bulkhead in a posture of complete brutish indifference to the proceedings. I take note that his club swings on a lanyard by his side and that he wears a cutlass in a leather sheath on his other side.

"Good morning, ladies," says our jailer, "I trust you slept well? No? Ah, well, soon you'll be reclining on silk sheets, eating pomegranates, and awaiting the arrival of your Sheik of Araby. Some of you, anyway." It appears our Mister Sin-Kay is in a fine mood.

He opens his notebook and calls out, "Rebecca Adams."

"Here."

"Good. Go stand over there, girl." He gestures to the port side. "We are going to line you up alphabetically. Ruth Alden."

Ruth goes over to stand next to Rebecca.

"Sally Anderson, then Hermione Applegate. Once we get all this done, I want you to remember the person to the right and left of you so you can re-form this line every time I enter. You will do that without being told. Is that clear?"

He waits for some reply, but he gets none. "All right... Bailey...Baxter...Byrnes..."

And so on till we're all lined up proper, to his way of thinking at least. I have Katy Deere on my right and Dolley Frazier on my left.

"Very well, we will now have inspection," says Sin-Kay, and he goes to the end of the line and confronts Julia Winslow, a delicate, cheerful girl, who was given much to ribbons and bows and frilly things back at the school. She is not cheerful now, as Sin-Kay says to her, "Open your mouth."

"Wha-what?" asks Julia, taken aback by the order.

"Show me your teeth, girl. The condition of your teeth affects your salability and hence your price, so open your mouth such that I might look."

"I...I won't," quavers Julia, putting her hands to her mouth.

"Bo'sun Chubbuck, if you would be so good," says Sin-Kay, taking one step backward so that the brutish Chubbuck can come up, take the terrified girl by the neck with one hairy hand, and with the thumb and forefinger of the other, push in on her back teeth, forcing her mouth open.

"Very good, Bo'sun Chubbuck. You may step back now."

Chubbuck releases Julia and moves back to his place by the door and resumes his former stance. Shaking, Julia stands with her mouth open.

Sin-Kay peers in her mouth and then says, "Bare your front teeth," and Julia pulls back her lips in a grim parody of a smile. Tears of shame trickle from her eyes.

"Good," he says. He makes a note in his book and then moves on to Frances Wallace. He has no more trouble with the rest of the girls obeying his order. Better to do it than to be touched by the awful Chubbuck.

When he reaches Clarissa, four girls down from me, her baring of teeth is not some gruesome parody of a smile, oh no. It is the snarl of an animal that would like nothing better than to lunge forward and rip out Sin-Kay's throat.

A minute later he is up to me. "Ah, we meet again our little Miss English Smart-mouth from yesterday. I trust you passed a pleasant night, Your Highness?"

"Another delightful evening at the elegant Hotel Bloodhound, to be sure. The staff has been ever so attentive to our needs," I say, without expression. I case my eyes and look over his shoulder.

That gets a short bark of a laugh from our innkeeper. He then orders me to open up and I do it without question. I grimace, he checks my tusks, and then moves on down the line.

In a while he is done with this exercise in humiliation and orders Hughie and Nettles to start the feeding, then prepares to leave.

"Your pardon, Sir," pipes up Judy Leavitt, as she has been coached. "Some of us girls had needle and thread in our purses that were taken from us. Combs, too. If we could have them—"

"The answer is no," says Sin-Kay, simply.

We had picked three girls to do the asking today, so Clarissa, Dolley, and I don't get to be seen as the leaders. If there's any trouble—and I *do* plan for there to be much trouble—all they would need to do is merely separate us from the others, and all would be lost. Frances Wallace is next.

"I beg your pardon, Sir," she says, "but why cannot the shutters stay up till dark? We know there are a good four hours of daylight after you have them put down. It makes the night so very long and our spirits are suffering."

"Again, no."

Then Sally Anderson, who is near the head of the line, asks, "If... if we could have some water with which to wash ourselves... even salt water would help. Please, Sir, we are ladies, you know."

"The answer to that is, also, *no,*" says Sin-Kay. His face is without expression, his voice level, but I think he is becoming impatient.

"Please, Sir, the salt water is nothing to you," says Martha, who stands next to Clarissa. "There's a whole ocean of it out there—"

"I told you the answer is *no!*" shouts Sin-Kay, advancing on Martha. She shrinks back in fear.

"Don't worry, Martha, honey. He won't touch you," purrs Clarissa. "You saw how he had to get that ape Up-chuck, or whatevah the hell his name is, to assault dear Julia that way and pry open her poor jaws. And you know why?"

She pauses, then charges on. "'Cause for all his fancy clothes and fine mannahs, he is nothin' but a low-down dirty field nigra who don't know his place, and he knows that if he so much as lays a finger on you, his so-called ass-so-ci-ates would get a rope and string his black ass up faster than you can sing 'nigra in the woodpile, do-si-do,' business partners or not!"

Sin-Kay nods and smiles, as if savoring a private joke, turns, then goes over to stand before Clarissa. He puts his hands behind his back and regards her.

"Did you know, Miss Howe," he finally says, "that I made arrangements for my *ass-so-ci-ate* Colonel Bartholomew Simon to purchase your girl Angelique for me? No? But then, how could you know, for you have been my honored guest here at the Hotel Bloodhound, as your Lady Miss Faber would have it. Yes, it is true, though. Your father's household would have no further use for her, since you are considered dead and gone, and Colonel Simon's offer will have been most generous. The shy, demure, and most beautiful Angelique will *definitely* be waiting for me upon my return."

I've noticed that when Clarissa Worthington Howe is enraged beyond words, her cheeks go even more pale than they usually are and a red spot appears on each cheek. I know that, because that rage has so often been directed at me. The red spots appear now, and though shaking with rage, she says nothing.

"You see, Miss Howe, the fact is, I have no desire for gray women, women such as yourselves," he goes on, giving us all a significant look. "But I will find Miss Angelique most enjoyable, you can count on that."

———

"Officers' Call. Lookouts up and report," I say after Sin-Kay disappears up the hatchway. Helen, Martha, Frances, and Sylvie leave the line and dash up to their posts. As Dolley and Clarissa and I come together, the calls of "All clear" come from above.

Clarissa is seething with fury, and out of her mouth comes a stream of curses that would even put some of mine to shame. "You give me that knife you got and I'll take care of that black bastard!" she hisses at me. "I'll cut him so bad that—"

"Shush, you! That would gain us nothing, Clarissa, and you know it!" I hiss back at her. "Hush, now! You calm down or you'll ruin everything." Her chest gradually stops heaving, but her eyes still blaze with pure fury.

"There. That's better," I say, soothingly. "And don't worry. We're going to do something about this and we're going to start right now."

"But what can we do?" asks Dolley. "We have no control over anything."

"We have control over something that is very valuable to him, and that something is our very bodies themselves. He looks on us as cargo? All right, the cargo will refuse to eat. Our bodies will thus become less valuable, become, in fact, skin and bones. He meets our demands or we starve ourselves to death, simple as that. What do you say?" I wait for their answer.

"I'll do anything to get at that rotten son of a bitch!" Clarissa spits out, clenching and unclenching her fists.

Hughie and Nettles are bringing down the food and water, and the girls are beginning to line up. "Wait a minute, girls," Dolley calls out to them, "don't take anything just yet." She turns back to me. "Do you think they can do it? The girls, I mean."

"Well, it will be a good test of their mettle, whether or not they can hold together in something like this. We have to know that before we start on the escape plan. They've had almost two days now to settle in. I say we try it."

"All right, if they'll all agree to go along with it."

"Right, we can't have any holdouts. I'll speak to them now."

I turn to the girls, who, though stunned and astounded by Sin-Kay's heartless responses, are naturally curious as to what we three have been talking about.

I don't speak out right away. Instead I take Wilhelmina by the arm and say to her in a low voice, "Willa, have the girls crowd about the doorway and then have them turn and face me. That way Nettles won't be able to see who's talking." She nods and then sets about quietly herding the girls to the door.

When the view from the doorway is blocked and the girls are looking at me expectantly, I put on my American accent voice and say, "Listen to me, my sisters. You are standing there confused, wondering why that man treats us so cruelly, so heartlessly, for no reason at all. Well, the truth of it is that he *does* have a reason: By denying us even the most basic things of life, he means to break us down, girl by girl, till we have not a shred of self-respect left. He seeks to mold us, to make us pliable, to bend us to his will, so that when we mount the auction block, we will be as docile as a herd of cows. Are we going to let him do that? Oh, my sisters, are we going to let him break us?"

There is a low mutter of *no*s and *no-we-won't*s that is truly not very bold, but it's a start.

"Good for you. Now, we have come up with a plan of action and here it is: First we present Sin-Kay with a list of demands. They will be for more water, better food, and shutters up till dark. Then we refuse to eat until those demands are met. It is as simple as that. We will be messing with the one thing about us he holds dear: our healthy bodies and the price they will bring. It is the only thing we can do right now, as our bodies are the only thing we have power over. What do you think?"

There is an instant buzz of chatter. *Let's do it* and *the food is awful anyway* and *I'm for it.* I let them talk on for a bit and then I call the vote.

"We must have you all with us on this, every one of you. If you are not wholeheartedly with us on this, say so now, for we *must* have *everyone* committed to this or the plan will not work." No one says anything. "All right, all those who say we go on a hunger strike, raise your right hand."

The right hands of about half the girls shoot into the air. A few seconds later some more, who are somewhat less enthusiastic, raise their hands. Then the rest haltingly come up.

"All right. Lower your hands. Now, all opposed." There is silence and no hand goes up.

"We are officially on strike. Let's have a cheer, now; sisterhood forever!"

Sisterhood forever! comes back the roar from the girls of the Lawson Peabody. *Hooray! Hooray!*

When they quiet down some, I call out in a voice I make lower than my usual, so as to disguise it: "Nettles! Go tell Sin-Kay that we are all on a hunger strike and that we'll eat no more of your slop till we get more water, better food, and have the flaps open till dark!"

"You all are really gonna git it and I'm gonna git to watch. Oh boy, oh boy! Hee-hee." Nettles exits, giggling, to go to Sin-Kay with his news.

When he is gone, I say urgently, "Quick! We got to get our chant down so Sin-Kay can't single out any one of us as a leader. Now, when you hear me clap my hands three times, we'll all chant *'More water, better food, flaps open till dark!'* Each time you hear the three claps, you'll repeat the refrain five times—count them off on the fingers of one hand—and then stop. That way we'll start together and stop together. Let's try it now. I think you'll find that it's got a nice bit of a rhythm to it. Here we go…" *Clap-clap-clap.*

> *More water!*
> *Better food!*
> *Flaps open till dark!*

Good. I think they've got it. Nice clean start. I nod my approval.

> *More water!*
> *Better food!*
> *Flaps open till dark…*

…and so on till the five refrains are done and end neatly and together.

"Well done, ladies! For today, we will chant that any time Sin-Kay tries to talk to us. If I'm being watched by him, either Dolley or Clarissa will do the claps. Tomorrow, we'll up the ante. As for now, here's a bit of a treat. I have here a comb."

I reach up my sleeve and pull out my large tortoiseshell comb, one that Higgins had picked up for me in London, and I hold it up. There is a general gasp. *A comb! We can comb our hair! Oh, joy!* Ah, the small comforts and pleasures of life.

"I had it stuck up my sleeve when we were taken," I say, lying. Actually, I had it in my seabag, but I don't want them all to know about that yet. Let's first see how they all do in this strike. "Use it to comb each other's hair. Keep an eye out for lice—we'll have to keep close watch on that—put your hair up in pigtails, braids, or buns, something that will stay neat, for it will be a long time till you will be able to wash it."

I hand the comb to Cloris. "Don't let that slimy Nettles see it—he'd peach on us for sure and we'd lose it. Now let's get our water and get on with our day."

Cups are retrieved from kips and held through the bars for Hughie to fill. When I step up with mine, I see him sitting there, looking befuddled. I reach in and give his curly head a pet. "No food for us today, Hughie, luv. You can take the pot back out after everyone's got their water."

He looks even more confused, but he nods and ladles out the water.

I go up on the Balcony and sit next to Katy, who is on watch. "Notice anything, Katy?"

"Nope, nobody around." Katy keeps mostly to herself, sitting alone up in the Balcony, whether on watch or not. Annie and Sylvie have each other, and they've gotten tight with Rose. All three also have started watching out for Rebecca now that I'm so busy all the time.

"I mean, notice anything in general, like."

She ponders this a bit, then says, "Only men on this ship who've got weapons is the Captain, the Mate, and Chubbuck. That black man might have sumthin' in the way of pistols under his coat. Don't know. Prolly does. Ain't got no friends, though…never see no one talkin' to him when he comes out on deck."

She pauses and thinks some more. "That crazy boy Nettles goes in the Captain's room anytime the man calls for him. When that happens, the men out on deck wiggle their hands and hips and snicker, but they don't do that if the Mate or Chubbuck is there to see 'em do it."

Another pause, but I am patient.

"At night, I think the boy goes in the Captain's room and don't come out till mornin'. Course, can't see at night, but I can in the mornin'."

I put my hand on her shoulder and give it a squeeze. "You're a good soldier, Katy, and we…"

"He's a-comin' back," says Katy. She is looking out and nodding. I don't have to turn to look to know who she means.

I hop back down to the Stage and join the crowd of girls just as the lock rattles and Sin-Kay comes back into the Hold. He looks amused.

"So. A hunger strike, is it? Well, I can tell you this…"

I put my hands behind me and clap palm of left hand against back of right hand three times and we all burst out:

More water!
Better food!
Flaps open till dark!

We don't pause after the first refrain but swing right into the next.

> *More water!*
> *Better food!*
> *Flaps open till dark!*

Sin-Kay puts his hands behind his back and leaves them clasped there as he wanders about our midst, watching our mouths move with the chant.

> *More water!*
> *Better food!*
> *Flaps open till dark!*

Sin-Kay stops in front of our nervous Abigail Pierce, and he glares down at her. She stops chanting and trembles before him, but we all keep chanting all the louder and Abby starts chanting again when he moves on. *Good girl.*

> *More water!*
> *Better food!*
> *Flaps open till dark!*

Knowing it's the last refrain, we raise our voices loud and really lay into it.

> *More water!*
> *Better food!*
> *Flaps open till dark!*

Then we snap our jaws shut, ending perfectly together.

Sin-Kay nods in appreciation. "Very well, conduct your hunger strike. It will avail you nothing, you will see. Dinner will be served at the usual time," he says, as he turns and goes to the door where the leering Nettles waits. "It's a pity, though. Tonight you were going to be given a nice hot biscuit with your burgoo." He lets that sink in and then adds, "I want you to think about that biscuit. Good day to—"

Clap-clap-clap.

More water!
Better food!
Flaps open till dark...

And we chant him out of the place. We complete the five and then erupt in a cheer of self-congratulation for our bravery. *Sisterhood forever! Hooray! Hooray! Hooray!*

"We've got to keep them busy, keep their minds off their bellies," I say to Clarissa and Dolley after things have calmed down. We're sitting cross-legged in conference at the edge of the Stage. "For one thing, I want to start teaching everybody how to step dance—"

"That Irish stuff?" Clarissa sniffs, ever the snob.

"You can call it that. I'll do them by divisions. You'll see that it will give them some good exercise, as we get none down here and that is not good for us. It will—"

"Captain's going below," reports the lookout above.

"It will give them cheer when they get good at it. *And* the sound of their hooves rattling on the Stage will hide the sound of whatever we are doing below, when we start the Plan."

Dolley nods, and then so does Clarissa.

"So with that and Lissette's French class and Hepzibah's choral practice," says Dolley, "and your storytelling in the evening, we have the days somewhat planned out. Good."

"Yes. There's nothing like a good routine to soothe the troubled soul. I think I'll get started on the dancing now and—"

"Here comes the hooks again!" comes the call from a lookout. We get to our feet.

Hmm...I'm thinking there's more than one way to get some water.

I reach back my hand and unbutton my dress. I step out of it and hand it to Hyacinth, who is standing nearby. "Will you fold this and put it up in my kip? Thanks."

All of us wear the same sort of undershirt—it is a soft cotton chemise with a scooped neck tied at the front with a bit of string, and it has short sleeves that go down just over the upper arms. I take the sleeves on my shirt and slide each of them just a bit over my shoulders.

The small hatch cover is pulled back and a shaft of light shines down to a spot on the lower deck next to the tubs.

"Connie, will you help me this time?" I ask and head down toward the spotlight. Constance Howell follows. I swear I hear her mumbling prayers behind me. Does she ever stop badgering God with her constant prayers?

I step into the shaft of light and look up as the hooks are being lowered.

"Ahoy, Jocko! Good to see you again, mate!" I call out.

"Shaddap, you. I ain't yer mate and me name's not Jocko—it's Mick."

"Well, 'ello, Mick!" I says, flashing him one of my brightest smiles. I can see his face in the light up there—he's got a bit of a pug nose, hair low on his forehead, a wide mouth, and lips that are rather large for a man. "I'm Jacky, and who's yer friend?"

"His name's Keefe, if it was any of your business, which it ain't." Keefe has a long, thin face so deeply tanned and grooved from being out in the elements that it's like a slab of old, weathered wood.

"I like you, Mick, I really do. I think it's your sunny nature that's made me take a shine to you," I say as I reach out and catch the hooks and pass one over to Constance. "Now, Mick, about what we was talkin' about the last time I 'ad the pleasure of your company—all us girls would be mighty grateful if you'd give this tub a rinse after you empty it, and that other tub a double rinse *and* fill it with salt water 'fore you drop it back down here. You'll do that, won't you, luv?" I put my hands behind my back and bounce up and down on my toes.

"We ain't gonna do nothin' like that at all. Now shut yer gob."

"Will ye do it if I give you a look at me bare bum?"

"*Wot?*" Both heads pop over the side of the hatch and stare down at me. I think they're noticing for the first time that I ain't got my dress on.

"If you do it, I'll pull down me knickers and give you a look at me bare bum," I say, repeating the offer. These two ain't the brightest lights in the world, that's for sure.

The two heads disappear. I can hear a hurried conversation twixt the two. Then the heads pop over the edge again, looking down while casting furtive glances to the side.

"All right, let's see it, then."

A deep breath. *Well, a girl's gotta do what a girl's gotta do.* Careful about the tattoo, though. If that's ever known, I'm a dead duck—wouldn't get no price at all in Algiers, no, I wouldn't, and it'd be straight to the fo'c'sle for me, prolly wi' a detour under that Sammy Nettles.

I turn, undo the string, and let slip my drawers so that the waist slides down to just under my butt cheeks. I put my weight on my right leg, count to three, then shift it to the left, count to three, then I pull my drawers back up. "There. That's all you'll get for now, lads, so go do your job like good fellows."

"Ooooow, Missy, that was prime it was, but no, Missy, ye've got to do it again, and turn around, too, or we ain't gonna do nothin'."

"No, I don't gotta do it again, Mick, or turn around even," says I, tying up the string on my drawers. "All I got to do is yell for the Captain and tell 'im you've been a-peekin' at me bare bum and he'll tie you both t' the gratin' and flog yer sorry asses till y' die. You know he will."

The two men look sharply at each other and realize the wisdom of what I'm saying.

"Oow, but don't take it so hard, luvs…Maybe next time I'll drop me knickers again…maybe give you a little bit more…every other day, is it? Maybe in a few weeks we'll be such good friends, I'll even give you a peek at the rest of me parts. Wouldn't that be somethin', now? See, it's favor fer favor, like…"

The tub is jerked out of sight. In minutes, it comes back in, dripping salt water, freshly rinsed. We hook up the second tub, and it comes back in rinsed, dripping, and full of fresh salt water. The hatch is closed and I turn and give the thumbs-up sign to my crew. Many look aghast, but many look glad to see the tub of water, however salty it may be.

"That was disgraceful!" says Constance Howell, glaring at me and shaking with righteous shock. I had heard her beside me, gasping in disbelief throughout the whole episode. She is plainly outraged by my behavior.

"We got the water, didn't we?" I snap back at her. I've been getting a little irritated with Miss Holiness lately. I turn my attention back to the other girls, who are clustered on the Stage. "Division Three! Come help me move these tubs under the Balcony. Everybody, come help."

The girls tumble off the Stage as I begin to organize the moving, but our Constance is not yet through chastising me.

"How could you have done that?" she hisses. "You shameless hussy!"

I have had enough and I turn and light into her. "Listen, Miss Prissy," I snarl, "I don't know if you know anything about my past, and I don't care if you do or not, but do know this: I lived as a beggar on the streets of London for five years with nothing on but a shift to hide my nakedness. You know what a shift is? It's like this here undershirt 'cept it ain't got no sleeves and it's a little longer but not by much. Five years and *nothing* else. Do you catch my meaning? No shoes, no stockings, no coat, no drawers, no nothing—and now you stand there and scold me and expect *me* to be *shy*?"

I lift my hand and point my finger between her eyes. "No, Connie, I ain't shy about what I just did, and I ain't shy about doing *anything* that will get us out of this goddamn mess. *Anything.* Do you understand that? Good." I take my finger from her face and point it at the water tub. "Now you put your shoulder to that tub and help us get it under the Balcony. Now, *move!*"

I turn my back on her and address the others, who have clustered around. "It's time we set up a proper privy. We'll move the tubs over here and drape petticoats around for privacy. Rebecca, be a love and go get my petticoat out of my kip."

"Aye, aye, Sir!" says Rebecca, saluting and scooting off on her mission. She is over her seasickness and is most glad of it. It is good to see her feeling better, and it calms my seething temper.

Moving the empty tub is easy, the full one much harder, but we get it done, and Rebecca is right back with my remaining unripped slip.

I take the petticoat and rip it down its center seam so as to double its area. "See, we'll use tiny strips to tie up the corners like this," and I show them how we'll make sort of a U around the tubs by tying the corners of the torn petticoats to the slats of the Balcony.

"Ruth, you're good with a needle, and I sure wish we had one, 'cause it'd make the job a lot easier. But we don't, so what you'll have to do is knot the edges of the petticoats together. Will you do it? Good. Now, we'll need about six more petticoats to do the job, so offer 'em up, ladies, and you shall have a private bathhouse!"

The slips are retrieved and ripped, and Ruth Alden directs the job, and it is soon done.

"As fine a piece of work as ever I have seen," I say, surveying our new privy. "Now, as to who will be first to wash up...I'll close my eyes, spin around with my finger pointing out, and when I open my eyes, the person I'm pointing at will be first and we'll continue down Sin-Kay's alphabetical line to the end and then around to the other end. All right? Here goes."

I spin around a few times and when I open my eyes, I'm pointing at Cathy Lowell. She wastes no time in going back to her kip and getting her washcloths and disappearing behind the curtain.

"On the beat now. One, two, three, and four! Left foot up, down toes, and now *hard* on the heel!" Obediently, the ten left feet of the girls of my division, Division Three, lift and hit the floor, as the girls begin to learn the dance. Except for Katy, Sylvie, and Annie, these girls are more used to the stately movements of the minuet and gavotte, but this will be good for them, as it is more active and will get the blood flowing. We cannot allow ourselves to get too soft here in the bowels of the *Bloodhound*.

I started them off on learning this Irish dancing as soon as I had my turn in the washroom. It was not much, being able to strip off one's clothes for a few moments and dip a washcloth into the vat and wash oneself off, but it was something, salt water or no. I have several bars of soap in my seabag, and I will bring them out, but I still don't wish for them to know about that yet, so I keep quiet and the soap stays in my bag.

The girls, having completed their toilette, as Mademoiselle Lissette would have it, have hung their washrags to dry from slats all around the Balcony, so that the Hold is festooned with little white flags. It's almost festive.

Then I have Division One up for Dance. Clarissa hates to do anything under my instruction, of course, and chafes at the indignity of it all, but her dear friend Lissette lifts her elegant hoof and so the fuming Clarissa has to do it, too. It warms my heart to see it.

"Again. All together now. One, two, three, and *four...*"

French class, then Chorus, and then Clarissa, Dolley, and I have a strike meeting and decide what we're going to do tomorrow. As we are breaking up, Hughie and Nettles bring in the dinner—it is the usual kettle of steaming burgoo, but this time there is a basket of hot biscuits. I know Sin-Kay served them up as a way to torture us, and torture us they do. It's been a full twenty-four hours now since we've eaten and the smell of the biscuits hits us like a hammer.

"Oh, Jacky," pleads Elspeth, "couldn't we just have the biscuit?"

"No, Elspeth, not even the biscuit. Be strong now."

Nettles is grinning and holding out a biscuit through the bars, waving it around, trying to tempt us.

"Hey, girlies, watch this," he says as he dips the biscuit, the wonderfully golden brown and probably not-very-weevilly biscuit, into the pot of burgoo and then pops it into his mouth. "*Mmmmmmmmmm,*" he moans in satisfaction.

There are moans from several of the girls, too.

I turn my back to the doorway and clap my hands three times.

More water!
Better food!
Flaps open till dark!

We chanted till they took the food away and the flaps came slamming down. Sudden darkness filled the Hold, as well as an oppressive silence.

I know that doubts about the strike are now worming their way into some minds. "I've got an idea!" I pipe up all cheery in the dark, figuring I've got to get their minds off food somehow. "Let's play Grandmother's Trunk! Everybody feel around and join hands and get in a circle. Come on, now. That's it."

Hands reach around in the dark and encounter other hands, and the circle is made.

"Since I thought of it, I'll go first, and we'll go around to the right," I say. Then I recite, "I took a trip to my grandmother's house and in my trunk I put...a paper of pins!" I squeeze the hand of the girl on my right, who turns out to be Hermione.

"I took a trip to my grandmother's house, and in my trunk I put a paper of pins...and a hairbrush."

"I took a trip to my grandmother's house, and in my trunk I put a paper of pins, a hairbrush...and my doll," says Rebecca, and that gets some snorts.

"I took a trip to my grandmother's house, and in my trunk I packed a paper of pins, a hairbrush, my doll," says Constance, "...and my prayer book." *Of course...*

Then Clarissa's lazy drawl comes out of the darkness. "I took a trip to my grandmomma's house, and just why I would do that I do not know, she bein' a horrid old person, but anyway, I packed my trunk, and in it I put that silly paper of pins, a hairbrush, my doll Sally Ann, my prayer book...if I could find the damned thing, that is, and...a big ole juicy Virginia ham, glistenin', positively *glistenin'* with a deep honey glaze and studded with those lovely little brown cloves."

Uh-oh...

Before I can protest, the next girl in line, Barbara Samuelson, jumps in and says rapidly, "I took a trip to my grandmother's house, and in my trunk I packed a paper of pins, hairbrush, my doll Agnes, prayer book, ham, and..." Here she slows down and I can almost sense the spit pooling in her mouth as she says, "...and a whole roasted goose! With crackly skin, just right, oh, God!"

By the time it gets to three more girls, they drop the memory part of the game and merely state their deep-down favorite thing that they want to eat right here, right now. Curiously, though, they pick up on Clarissa's lead and name their dolls. *Hmm...imagine that, Clarissa with a doll named Sally Ann.*

It's Annie's turn. "My dolly Colleen...and a big slice of colcannon, hot off the stove!"

I think about stopping this, that this is not good for them, but no, let them go. They're having a good time, and I probably couldn't stop it anyway, even if I tried. And I know they consider me pushy enough already without me barging in now and ruining their fun.

Rose Crawford comes up with "My doll Judy...and fried groundhog with cornmeal batter, the ribs just so crunchy and good, oh." Rose is one of the girls from the country. I thought that this would ordinarily have brought *yucks* from some, but now it does not. It's amazing what twenty-four hours and a growling belly can do to a girl's outlook.

Then Sylvie says, "My doll Gabriella...and *maccharruni con pesto Trapenese* for sure, yes." We don't have to know what that is, but from the quiet passion in her voice, we know it is very, very good and we would like to have some, too, whatever it is.

Around it goes. Turkeys, roast beef, chops—everything gets a heartfelt mention. Even possum gets a nod, from another country girl.

Now it's Elspeth, stammering, "My d-doll Tatters... and...and the glass of warm milk and honey my mommy brings me at buh-bedtime."

Oh, come on, Elspeth...please.

Some of the girls choose side dishes—*my doll Janey Mae...and a bowl of mashed potatoes*—or desserts, like *my doll Felicity...and a cherry pie,* as if we were putting together a grand banquet. Well, the dinner table is groaning and ready to break with all we are putting on it, that's for certain.

When it's her turn, Dorothea Baxter up and says, "My doll Olivia Galileo...and Newton's *Principia Mathematica.*" There is silence. Then a titter. Some snickering. Then outright full-scale laughter fills the Hold. Only Dorothea, in the midst of this orgy of food wishes, would wish for a *book*. "Well, and maybe a watercress sandwich," she adds, when the laughter has died down. I reflect that this is the first time since we were put down here that we have laughed as a group, and I hope *they* hear it out there.

When it comes to Katy, she simply says, "Dollbaby... and a brace o' squirrels. Cooked like Mama cooked 'em. With gravy."

The game continues all around till, finally, Cloris Minton says, "My doll Henrietta...and a huge plum pudding!" and she squeezes my left hand.

"It's come back to me," I say, "and now that we have had our fill, ladies, it's Storytime!" With hoots and laughter and a round of applause, the girls head for the Balcony and I head for the center of the Stage.

"Now you'll remember from yesterday how I took the coach from Peter's Head to London, went to Jaimy's house, met his mum, and got tossed out on my ear. All right, then...

"A tousled head popped up from under the pile of rags and straw that is the old Blackfriars Bridge kip. It belongs to a boy of about eight years..."

After I have finished my bit, and all the doings of the day are done, I sit with Hughie for a while, telling him about the pretty horses back at the Lawson Peabody School for Young Girls in Boston, and I ask if he would like to see them someday. "I know you would, Hughie, 'cause I remember back under the Blackfriars Bridge, when we kids would dream about what we wanted to be when we grew up and you said you wanted to be a hostler, 'cause you liked horses. You remember that, Hughie? Sure, you do. Hey, you wanna join our new gang? Why, this gang right here, Hughie. All these girls, and you, Hugh the Grand, bein' a member, too. Remember how Rooster Charlie used to call you Our Muscle? Well, you can be Our Muscle again, with this gang. What do you say? Good, Hughie, good. Welcome to the gang, but remember, this is a secret gang and you can't tell anybody about it. Good night now, Hughie. You're a good boy."

And so to bed.

Good evening, Jaimy. I hope you are safe and well. You probably haven't got word yet on what has happened to us, and that's just as well, but I am fine, or as well as can be expected. We are in a nice routine now and the girls are gaining in confidence with this hunger strike. I got us some wash water this morning and just how I got it I may tell you about sometime after we've been married for fifty years or so, or I may not. This morning, after everyone had washed, we had Dance Instruction and then French and then Chorus—Hepzibah led us in Mr. Mozart's "Laudate Dominum," and it was lovely—you should have heard it. Then we held a meeting and told the girls what we're going to do tomorrow with the strike, and they are ready to go. We had a game and then we had Storytime. Jaimy, I hope you don't mind that I've been telling them of our adventures of late, knowing how proper you are, having been brought up right as you were, but the girls seem to enjoy it so... so I know you'll forgive me. I'm up to the part where I threw my ring down at your feet and ran off. When I think how different my life would have been had I not done that... Ah, well. We had "Praise God from Whom All Blessings Flow" as the evening's hymn and that was nice—I've always liked that one. When we all stretched out to sleep, that Connie Howell said we should all recite one prayer together and I said she could pray out loud if she wanted, and if she kept it short, but that I would pray to myself. And this right here is my prayer.

G'night, luv.

Chapter 23

John Higgins
The Lawson Peabody School for Young Girls
Beacon Street, Boston, Massachusetts, USA
May 28, 1806

Lieutenant James Fletcher
Bartleby's Inn
West Street
London, England

My Dear Mister Fletcher,

It is with a heavy heart that I must tell you some disquieting news. Our Miss Faber has gone missing and is presumed dead.

A boating party carrying the young ladies of the Lawson Peabody School on an outing apparently foundered on the rocks of an island shore. The presumption here is that the boat was swamped and the girls drowned. Personal articles have washed up and one body has been found.

Now that I have given you the worst of the news, I will tell you of some events that I feel might give you some hope.

Upon my receiving the dreadful news of the accident, I went directly down to the courthouse, where I had been told evidence of the disaster was being collected. Many soaked bonnets, shawls, purses were spread out on a bench in an anteroom and the body of Dobbs, the school handyman who went on the excursion, ostensibly to act as guardian to the girls, was laid out on a table in a side room. I must say I breathed a sigh of relief to find that the one body that had so far been found had been his and was not the corporeal remains of one of the girls. This anteroom had been set up as a morgue to receive the bodies of the girls as they are found, but none, in fact, had as yet been discovered. I found that passing strange, but said nothing. Some others present in the room in their official capacities were of the opinion that the young ladies' lighter forms simply had been carried out to sea, but I was not of that mind. At least one or two should have been found out of the thirty-two girls missing—twenty-nine of the young ladies of the school and three of the servant girls. Miss Amy Trevelyne, Miss Faber's dearest friend, elected not to go on the ill-fated excursion, choosing to stay behind to tend to Mistress Pimm, who had suddenly fallen ill. I met Miss Trevelyne at the courthouse in the company of Ezra Pickering, Miss Faber's American lawyer and very dear friend. Stricken with grief as he was, he was attempting to give comfort to Miss Trevelyne, who, though clearly in great anguish, still demanded to see the evidence of her dearest friend's demise.

We looked over the collection of sodden clothing, and I asked permission to view the body of Mr. Dobbs, which permission was granted, I believe, mainly because of the presence of Lawyer Pickering. He and I entered the makeshift morgue and went to the body. The deceased was lying faceup with his hands crossed on his chest, wearing an expression of what seemed to be mild surprise, but then, I suppose many of us exit this world with just such a look on our faces. I asked if an autopsy was going to be performed and was told that none was planned since it was plain that the man had drowned.

I asked that the body be stripped, and at Mr. Pickering's insistence, it was done. Clumsily and churlishly done, to be sure, by two disgruntled courthouse workers, but done, nonetheless. I then commenced my examination.

There were, of course, many contusions on the man's arms, legs, and body, entirely consistent with the body being tossed about in the surf and against the rocks of the shore. Still, to me, it seemed peculiar that the contusions did not have the purplish hue that occurs with bruises to a person who still has blood flowing in his veins. Putting on my gloves and raising the corpse's head as the body lay supine on the table, I felt a curious softness in the back of the skull and I drew Mr. Pickering's attention to it.

"I believe the man was hit on the back of the head before entering the water," I stated, and Mr. Pickering, upon making his own examination, concurred. "Hit very hard," he said, nodding, obviously thinking of the implications of this fact.

We then went back out into the hall with the intention of finding the attending physician. We sent one of the men off to look for him, and as he hurried off, we saw that Mistress Pimm had entered the building. She was plainly still shaky from her recent illness, but yet she stood erect, and, upon seeing Miss Trevelyne, nodded. Miss Trevelyne nodded back. There were *no tears, no wails of grief and despair. Even in my own distress, I could not help but admire the stoical nature of these New England Yankee women, one of whom was sure she had lost her beloved classmates and her dearest friend, and the other who had lost virtually her entire school and all the girls who had been entrusted to her care.*

I will now digress to the subject of Mistress Pimm's illness and a very important fact that pertains to it: The school mistress was not the only one suddenly stricken by sickness on that fateful day. You see, the plan for the outing was to include both me and Mistress Pimm, as well as Mr. Sackett, the Science and Math teacher. Mistress Pimm and myself were to instruct the girls on how to set out a proper picnic on the grass, and Mr. Sackett would instruct them, before and after the luncheon, on the nature of the flora and fauna of the seashore and help them collect specimens for future study. Such was not to be.

On the morning of the excursion, Miss Faber, bouncing up and down and off the walls in her usual enthusiasm over an outing or, for that matter, anything out of the ordinary, left me downstairs to continue packing the provisions as she returned to her friends upstairs. While I did so, assisted ably by the girls Annie and Sylvie, Mr. Dobbs did come upon me and insist that I try a cup of a new brew of coffee lately brought up from South America and said to be the finest thing of its kind. Although I had never particularly liked the company of handyman Dobbs, I could not, as Head of Staff, decently refuse. I took the cup and Dobbs hurried off with another cup for Mr. Sackett. It was, actually, quite good and I drank it down gratefully...a tinge of bitterness in it, though...and twenty minutes later I was in bed, barely conscious, with the worst case of the grippe I had ever experienced. I have never been of a sickly nature and this came as a complete surprise to me. I assumed, in my near delirium, that the outing would be called off, with me unable to attend and lend my protection, but such was not to be. Neither Mistress Pimm nor I knew of the other's distress and incapacity, and so the day went on as planned, but not as planned by us, oh no, but as planned by the kidnappers, as kidnappers I now believe them to be.

Upon seeing me there in the courthouse, Mistress Pimm approached and demanded what I knew. I informed her that, aside from the articles of clothing and other personal items, nothing of the girls has been found. I told her of my examination of Dobbs and the following conversation ensued:

"Where is he?" she asked, looking about.

"In this room here, Mistress," said Mr. Pickering, "but he is…"

She brushed by him and opened the door and entered the room. She did not shrink from the sight of the naked body, but went right up to it and waited for me to lift the head to show her the concussion.

"So you surmise he was dead before he went into the water?"

"Yes, Mistress," I said. It was then that the physician, a bald and fussy little man, entered the room, muttering, "My, my, what a thing, what a thing…"

"How can we know for sure?" she asked.

"We should look to see if there is water in his lungs," I replied. "That will tell us."

"Oh, that won't be necessary," said the doctor, shaking his head. "This man obviously drowned and this is certainly no place for a lady, Madame, no place…"

Mistress Pimm turned to regard the little man and brought the full force of her steely gaze upon him.

"Open him up," she said, calmly and levelly, and the doctor tut-tutted and fussed, but he did go get his bag of tools, and the autopsy was performed.

There was no water in the corpse's lungs. Mistress Pimm was in attendance the entire time and she viewed the results, with, I believe, some satisfaction.

It has now been several days since the girls' disappearance and the following facts stand:

1. No bodies have yet been found.

2. No demand for ransom has been received.

3. A larger ship was seen in the area on that day. An old, long-since retired sea captain, who spends his lonely days in his room looking out through the window with his telescope at the ships entering and leaving the harbor, reported spying a two-masted ship lying off behind Lovell Island for a short time. Although he could not read her name, he was sure, because of his knowledge of ship configuration and rigging, that the craft did not come into Boston Harbor, either before or after the day of the tragedy, a fact he found rather strange. Strange enough, indeed, that he felt compelled to hobble down to the courthouse to report it.

Taking the preceding facts into account, we could only come to the conclusion that the ship was a slaver and that the girls are being taken to the slave markets, most likely in North Africa, to be sold.

After we convinced the local authorities and the bereaved families of our conclusion, several small, fast cutters were dispatched from Boston to search for the mystery ship, and word was sent down to Virginia to General Howe, father of one of the missing girls, so that search ships can be sent out from there, too. He is a man of great means and can bear the cost of doing so. But it is a very large ocean...

So, there is plenty of room for hope, Sir. For even discounting the other evidence, I cannot believe that Miss Jacky Faber would be capable of drowning on a clear, calm day in smooth waters close to land. I have seen her in action—Sir, I was on the Wolverine on that very day when she jumped overboard and swam for the shore, very nearly making it before she was recaptured. The girl who could swim like that did not drown on a warm day in the calm waters of Massachusetts Bay, I assure you. As for being captured, well, she has been in worse predicaments, and she is a very clever and resourceful girl, as I am sure you know quite well.

I hope I have not been tedious, as I wanted only to lay the facts before you in as plain a manner as I could. I will end with the following: I cannot believe that such a spirit as hers has been quenched, or that her light, a light that has shone so brightly, has been so cruelly snuffed.

I will wait for further developments before informing the Reverend Alsop and Jacky's other friends at the Home, as I do not want to cause them needless distress just yet.

Wishing that this letter brought you better news, and trusting that you know we are doing all we can from here, I am your most obedient servant,

John Higgins

Chapter 24

The next morning, we are ready. Everyone is up and in their dresses and crouched at even intervals all around the Balcony, holding their cups and facing the lowered flaps. When the first one is lifted, I clap three times and...

> *More water!*
> *Better food!*
> *Flaps open till dark!*

"Wot the hell?" The outburst startles some of the men so much that they drop the flaps back down, but they recover and the shutters are raised and we continue our assault on their ears.

> *More water!*
> *Better food!*
> *Flaps open till dark!*

We are relentless. Over and over we chant it. We hit the bars with our cups on *more*, *better*, and *flaps* and it sets up a nice rhythm and a grand clatter. Looking out across the deck, we see the Captain burst out of his cabin, followed quickly by a yawning Nettles. A few of the men we can see out there act puzzled, but most are amused—they know what's good for them, however, so they look away and hide their faces from their captain's anger.

"Sin-Kay! Get up here!" bellows the Captain, and Sin-Kay comes up through the forward hatch, smoothing his deep purple jacket. Immediately upon gaining the deck, Sin-Kay is buttonholed by the Captain, who is pointing at us there pounding and chanting at the bars. We cannot hear the Captain's earnest words, but we can imagine what they are.

Sin-Kay makes mollifying gestures, like he'll take care of everything. *Don't worry, just wait, they are only hysterical females, they will tire, you will see...*

The Captain turns from him abruptly and goes up on his quarterdeck, crosses his arms, and glares at the set of the sails. Sin-Kay, with murder in his eyes, heads for us.

He comes down the hatchway, just as Hughie is bringing down the pot of burgoo.

"I do not know what you hope to accomplish with this, but..."

> *More water!*
> *Better food!*
> *Flaps open till dark!*

"...but you cannot possibly win. And when I find out who's behind this," and here he glares at Clarissa, "it will go *very* hard for them."

More water!
Better food!
Flaps open till dark!

"Pah!" He spits. "I have had enough of this! You shall break, depend upon it!" He goes back out, leaving a confused Hughie holding his ladle over his steaming pot, not knowing what to do. Seeing that Nettles is not with him, I jump down from the Balcony and go to the hatchway. I reach in through the bars and run my hand through Hughie's tousled hair.

"No food yet, Hughie, but we'll be all right, you'll see," I say, 'cause he looks worried. It's been thirty-six hours now since food has crossed our lips.

"Gotta eat, Mary," he mumbles. He dips his ladle in the burgoo and fills a bowl and goes to pass it to me.

"Not yet, Hughie," I say, backing away from the steaming bowl of the now delicious-looking gruel. The girls have come to the end of another cycle of chants, and I say, just loud enough for them to hear and no one else, "All of you are doing just fine. Division One, down for water. Divisions Two and Three, back at 'em." *Clap, clap, clap.*

As the other two divisions swing back into it, Clarissa and her Division One climb down off the Balcony and have their water cups filled. After they have refreshed themselves, the other divisions will be called down in turn, and the first division will go back up. That way we'll always have at least twenty girls up at the bars at all times, chanting, with one division resting—we don't want anyone's voice to give out.

Clarissa comes over to confer, her nose in her cup. As the

water hits her belly, it gives off a threatening growl, demanding more than mere water.

"After they've all drunk their water, we'll go to the second phase of the Plan, all right?"

She grunts in reply. "Right. Do you think they'll hold?"

"They're all right so far. We can only wait and see," I say, and then go back up to my division. A peek out shows that the Captain still stands glowering on his quarterdeck. I slam my cup extra hard against the iron bars and join in the chant.

More water!
Better food!
Flaps open till dark!

When we're done with the last five chant repetitions, I hold up my hand and all fall silent. I count to six, then drop my arm. The girls take a common deep breath and Phase Two begins:

Ninety-nine bottles of wine on the wall,
Ninety-nine bottles of wine!
Take one down
And pass it around,
Ninety-eight bottles of wine on the wall!
Ninety-eight bottles of wine on the wall...

And so on and so on, in the classic drive-your-parents-mad ditty. We keep it going, pausing every ten bottles to do five of the regular chant, and then back to those never-ending bottles of wine. The Captain is now pacing back and forth on the deck, right out in front of us. As we get down to fifty bottles of wine, he rushes the cage and kicks at a hand clutching a bar. Minerva barely gets her fingers back in time. He goes back to the quarterdeck, mumbling curses under his breath. His pacing grows more and more agitated as we work our way down through the numbers.

Finally we get to the end.

> *One bottle of wine on the wall,*
> *One bottle of wine!*
> *Take one down*
> *And pass it around,*
> *No bottles of wine on the wall!*

There is a ringing silence.

I count to six, raise my hand, then bring it down. Another common deep breath is taken and...

> *Ninety-nine bottles of wine on the wall,*
> *Ninety-nine bottles of wine...*

That cuts it. The Captain is off the quarterdeck, bellowing, "Chubbuck! Dunphy! To me!" and he charges to the hatchway and plunges down the stairs, followed quickly by his henchmen. Hughie, scared, shrinks back against the wall.

"Open this goddamn door!" he roars, and Sin-Kay, who has heard the commotion and come down as well into the now quite crowded hatchway, pulls out his key and opens the cage door. The enraged Captain Blodgett strides to the center of the Stage.

"All of you, get down here!" he shouts up at us. Nobody moves.

I think of doing the three claps to get them started again, but don't. Let's see what he has to say first, I'm thinking. I catch Clarissa's attention, across from me, on the other Balcony, and nudge Sylvie, beside me. Sylvie looks at me, I nod, and she leads the way. And so we all follow her down to the Stage. Clarissa elbows Cloris and they all follow her.

When we are all assembled on the Stage, we are addressed by the seething Captain.

"Who put you up to this? Who's your leader?" he spits out. "Who? Tell me now, or it will go hard for you."

Silence.

"Captain, it is probably the blon—," says Sin-Kay from the Captain's side.

"*Mister* Sin-Kay, when I want your damned advice, I'll ask for it. Now take yourself and your Dummy and get back to your cabin! Now!"

Sin-Kay jerks as if slapped. "I must protest," he says, furious at this turn. "I was under the impression that *I* was in charge of the cargo and I—"

"And you have been doing a damn poor job of it! I will remind you that I am the Captain of this ship and in charge of everything and everyone in it! Now get the hell out of here and take your Dummy with you!"

Sin-Kay holds the Captain's eyes for a moment and then turns abruptly away and goes up the gangway, cuffing Hughie behind the head to show him he is to follow. Hughie looks back at me in confusion and fear as he follows his master out.

After they are gone, the Captain forces himself to take several deep breaths before going on. His fury abates a bit, and a look of sly cunning comes over his face. "It could go very, very well for the one of you who tells me. Very well, indeed."

He goes over and stands before Constance. "How about you? You will tell me, won't you?" Connie shakes her head and the Captain whips out his knife. He grabs her by the neck and puts the point of the knife against her throat. "Tell me or I'll kill you."

Connie, her eyes filled with terror, puts her hands together and says, "The Lord is my shepherd, I shall not want. He leadeth me—"

The Captain releases her neck and backhands her to the deck of the Stage. He looks about for his next victim. It turns out he doesn't have to choose.

"W-will you send me home if I tell you?" comes a quavering voice from on his right.

Oh, Elspeth, no!

A smile comes over the Captain's face and he turns to her. "Of course, my dear, I will send you home if you tell me. On my word of honor."

Elspeth's eyes are wild as she holds her supplicating hands up to the Captain. Then she blurts it out.

"Jacky's the one you want! Right there!" she cries, pointing her finger at me. "She's the leader! She's the one who's been a pirate and everything! She put everyone up to this. Oh, I can't stand it here! Take her, take all of them! Just let me go! You'll let me go now, won't you? Now that I've told you? You will, won't you? Oh, you promised you would, you—"

"Take her up on deck!" roars Blodgett, and he ain't talking about Elspeth. He charges back up the hatchway as Chubbuck and Dunphy each grab one of my arms and I am dragged out the gate. I manage one look back at Elspeth's face. She looks at the retreating Captain and then at me.

"I'm sorry, Jacky, I'm sorry. But I just can't be here any longer, I just can't...," she blubbers, and then I'm up the stairs and on the top deck, blinking against the light.

The Captain stands by the mast and I am shoved in front of him. "That Dobbs fellow said you was a troublemaker and I guess he was right. Take off your dress!" he bellows in my face. I try to keep my legs from shaking as I reach back and unfasten the button at the back of my neck. The Captain turns from me and... *Good Lord, he's taken the Cat-of-nine-tails from its hook on the mast!*

I stand there trembling for real now and staring only at the Cat. *Could it be that I am to be flogged?*

"Take off the dress. I won't tell you again," he says through clenched teeth.

Despairing, I reach up with my right hand and slip my left sleeve over my shoulder and then with my left hand I slip off the right sleeve and my dress falls off me to the deck. I step out of it.

"Tie her to the mast. Face-first," says the Captain, matter-of-factly now.

Chubbuck barks out two names, and two brutes take me to the mast and roughly shove me up against it. One holds me to it, while the other ties a rope to my right wrist and loops it around the mast and then ties my other wrist. I am left hugging the mast tightly, so tightly that I won't slip down when my legs fail to hold me up.

It's really going to happen, oh, Lord help me...

"Get the rest of them up here. I want them to see this. And watch them! I want no one jumping over the side!"

The girls are brought up on deck, and they stand there, tremulously waiting.

"Now you listen to me, all of you! I ain't gonna stand for any more of your horseshit, you hear me? Do you?" snarls the Captain, waving the Cat at them, its nine blood-crusted strands of knotted rope snaking and twining about under their noses. "Well, you'd better listen to me, 'cause this is what you're gonna get if you don't!"

I hear him come up next to me. He wraps his fingers around a big shank of my hair and snaps back my head to make me look at the foul thing in his hand. Then he puts the Cat back on its hook. *Maybe he was just bluffing, maybe... oh, please...*

"I'm not going to scar you, girl, you're worth too much for that," he says in a low growl, "but I promise you this: You will never, *ever,* forget this day." With that, he lets go of my hair and grabs my undershirt at the nape of my neck in both his hands and rips it down the back to my waist, then pulls the ragged remnants down over my shoulders.

He steps back, picks up the Cat again, and in a moment I hear it hissing through the air on its way to my naked back.

Chapter 25

 The hunger strike is over and we are back down in the belly of the *Bloodhound*.

After the Captain had finished whipping me and my bonds were cut from my wrists and I had collapsed barely conscious to the deck, it was Sylvie and Annie and Dolley, I think, who picked me up and carried me down the stairs of the hatchway. I was handed up to my kip on the Balcony, my chest heaving with great, wracking sobs. *The pain, good Lord, the awful, searing pain...*

I had sense enough to realize that the Captain had followed us into the Hold and stood regarding his cargo. Most were grouped about me, but not all—a trembling Elspeth stood to the side and looked at the Captain expectantly, her eyes blinking rapidly in hope. A hope that I, even in my confusion and misery, knew to be a vain one.

"Captain...please...you said...oh, send me home, please," she bleated. She wrung her hands and looked at him with imploring eyes. "I told you what you wanted to know, now—"

"Oh, I will send you home, girl, oh yes, I will be true to

my word. But it will be to your *new* home in North Africa that I will send you," said Captain Blodgett. He reached into his pocket and pulled out a piece of blue ribbon. He threw it at Elspeth's feet and she looked at it in confusion. "However, I will give you this. That is for your hair. And for your information. Good day to you, good day to you all. I trust you will be *much* better behaved in the future."

With that, he turned and went back up the ladder and out the hatch.

Elspeth looks after him, unbelieving, then she looks around at the girls standing about and feels their accusing eyes fixed on hers, and then she falls to her knees next to the cheap piece of ribbon and cries out her despair in a long, wordless wail of utter hopelessness. Before the hatch above is closed and locked, a jar is thrown down. It hits, bounces, and then rolls about on the deck and comes to rest at Rose's feet. She bends and picks it up.

"What is this, then?" she asks, opening the lid and sniffing at it.

I gulp and swallow and force myself to stop crying. "It— it is salve...for my back," I manage to wheeze out. Rose looks at my back and then swallows and has to look away. Then she straightens up and comes to me to apply the medicine.

"No...wait...," I say. My chest is still heaving, but I try to calm down, and when I get settled a bit, I say, "Bring her here...bring her to me," and I'm looking down the rows of girls straight into the tormented eyes of Elspeth Goodwin.

"No, no," she says, desperately looking about like a hunted animal, cornered and without hope. "No, please, I'm sorry, I'm sorry..."

"*Sorry* ain't gonna do it, you snivelin' toad," says Clarissa, lunging toward her. Elspeth shrinks back, but Clarissa's hand lashes out and backhands her hard across the face. Elspeth cries out and buries her face in her hands, but she can't hide there, for Clarissa grabs a fistful of the girl's hair and drags her roughly forward, then forces her to kneel before me.

"Please don't hurt me! *Please! Please! Don't hurt meeeeeee...,*" Elspeth keens, tears streaming out of her eyes, her face turned upward, her features distorted into a crazed mask of pain and shame. Sadly, I remember just how merry and bright those features once were.

"Give me your hand, Elspeth," I say, and reach my left hand out toward her. I wince a bit at having to move. She looks at my hand, uncomprehending. "Give me your hand," I say again. "I will not hurt you."

She shakily puts out her hand, as if presenting it to a coiled snake, fully expecting to be struck. I take her hand in mine.

"I forgive you, Elspeth, I do," I say. The girl whimpers and hangs her head. "I forgive you because you have grown up in a world where all was goodness and sweetness and light and you had no understanding of the vileness and evilness that exists in the world. You were not ready for it when it came at you so hard, and so it is not your fault. I forgive you."

She whimpers and clasps my hand.

"Now, Elspeth, you may put the salve on my back."

Rose hands her the jar. She nods and takes it and dips into it and gets some on her fingers and looks down at my back. "It's horrible...so horrible." She shudders. "Everything is just so...*horrible I can't stand it!*"

"Yes, you can. Now just do it."

She sniffles and nods and reaches out and starts putting the salve on the welts on my shoulders. I stiffen and cry out at the touch...*It burns, oh sweet Jesus, it burns*...and she jerks back.

"No, no, it's...all right. Just do it," I say and grit my teeth and steel myself for the ordeal. The Captain was true to his word—he did not scar me. He made sure that none of the Cat's claw marks overlapped any of the others. His first stroke took me high on the shoulders, and while I did gasp in shock, I did not cry out. His second was lower and I groaned and writhed in agony, but it was his third, the one that caught me around the waist when the Cat's tails snaked around and stung my belly, that's when I lost all control and shrieked out my anguish and pain. The other strokes I don't remember too well. I know I begged for mercy and got none. I know my legs went out on the fourth and I thereafter hung limp, held up only by the ropes around my wrists. I think there were six lashes in all, but I don't know. I was beyond knowing anything by then.

Now I'm lying down here in the gloom, with the weeping and choking Elspeth rubbing the salve over the rows of red and swollen welts on my back with all the girls looking on. Eventually, she gets it covered with the greasy medicine, and it does feel better, and I am able to sink down and rest my face on the backs of my hands and reflect on things.

The first thought that rages through my mind is *I will see thee in Hell for what you did to me, Captain Blodgett, you may count on that!* Secondly, I realize the good that has come of this: All of the girls now see *exactly* what treachery will bring them—a tiny bit of blue ribbon and an ocean of shame.

The strike is broken, but we will not be. I lift my head and speak.

"I, Jacky Faber, swear on my very life that I will never betray you, my sisters, and I will bend every fiber of my being to gaining our release from this prison, even if I myself do not live to see it." I look to Clarissa.

She looks back at me and says, "I, Clarissa Worthington Howe, do swear on my very life that I will not betray you, my sisters, and I will bend every fiber of my being to gaining our release from this hellhole, even if I do not live to see it."

Dolley steps up and takes my hand in hers. "I, Dorothy Frazier, do so swear on my life that I will never betray you, my sisters, in any way and will strive with every fiber of my being to gain our freedom from this hell, even if I do not live to see it."

Then Beatrice Cooper and Hermione Applegate, and then Annie Byrnes and Sylvie Rossio, and then girl after girl till all have made their testament. Lissette stumbles on the English but gets the sense of it right, and then plainspoken Rose Crawford says, "So say you all, and so says I." The last was Martha Hawthorne who simply said, "Martha Livingston Hawthorne, the daughter of patriots and on their names, so sworn."

When all are done and Elspeth still stands sobbing by my side, Clarissa stoops to the deck and snatches the scrap of blue ribbon. She comes up next to Elspeth and again grabs a fistful of her hair and forces her to her knees. Elspeth looks up at her, her eyes wild with fear and despair. "She may have forgiven you, El*spiss,* but I have not," hisses Clarissa into her ear. "You shall wear this mark of shame until the day you die, and I hope that day is soon!" With that, she wraps the ribbon around the clump of hair she holds and ties it tight, cruelly tight. Then she shoves Elspeth back into the shadows, where the whimpering girl goes down, curls into a ball of misery, and says nothing. And she will say nothing for days and days and days.

Chapter 26

"Zee hooks are coming," reports Lissette up on lookout. I lift my head and watch the upper hatch being opened. It is the day after the flogging, and I cannot yet put on my shirt. I must lie facedown and not move.

Yesterday, about an hour after the spectacle of my whipping was over, the burgoo was brought down by a highly agitated Hughie… *"Mary hurt? Captain hurt Mary? Mister hurt Mary? Mary? Where are you? Mary?"* He was looking wildly about, the burgoo sloshing out of the pot and over his feet. *"Nothin' better happen to Mary…"* Hughie's dim, but not so dim as he can't tell that something has happened.

"No, Hughie, I ain't hurt. Ain't no one hurt me," I managed to gasp, motioning for some of the girls to get in front of me so he couldn't see. We don't need him going berserk, not yet, anyway. "I'm just a bit sick is all. A little tummy ache. I'll be fine. Just you dish out that burgoo now, Hughie, 'cause we'll all sure eat it now." *Now that all have seen what Captain Blodgett is capable of doing.*

Frances Wallace and Helen Bailey caught my eye and my meaning and reached through the bars to pet Hughie and say soothing things to him, and he calmed down and started handing out the suddenly delicious burgoo to the hungry girls.

It was dear Sylvie who spooned my ration into my mouth before she had hers. In spite of my pain, the burgoo tasted wondrous good, as did the biscuit.

Not long after that, Sammy Nettles came down into the hatchway with a spool of thread and a needle attached and shoved it through the bars.

"Captain says use this to sew up Smart-mouth's shirt. Can't have her runnin' round half nekkid, he says." Nettles giggled. "All right with me, though. Oh, yes." He craned his head around, trying to look up at me on the Balcony, but the angle ain't right and he couldn't. Good.

Annie, who was near the door, went to get the needle and thread, but Nettles jerked his hand back as she reached out her own.

"Now, now," he said, "not so fast there, girly. You're a pretty one, you are. How's about a little kiss first?"

"Kiss you?" retorted Annie in disgust. "I'd rather kiss a pig! Now, give me that or I'll tell the Captain you ain't obeying his orders."

Nettles flung the spool in with a curse and left, needlessly giving Hughie a cuff on the head as he went out. When they were sure he was gone, Annie and Caroline and Sylvie came over to me and gently raised my upper body enough to peel off the remnants of my undershirt. I gritted my teeth and tried not to cry out as this was being done, and it was done most tenderly, but still I could not stifle a groan—any move ment of the skin back there brought me the greatest agony.

Four or five unripped petticoats were laid out beneath me after I was lifted, so that when I was laid back down, I did not have my bare chest lying against the rough slatting. *Thank you, Sisters.*

Thinking of my sisters and the bond we have made, I looked out to the Stage and saw Elspeth's huddled form lying there, curled into a ball. I reflected that once again a bargain had been made, sealed with blood and pain, and that not all the pain was mine.

"Saw you out there, this mornin', Smart-mouth, yes I did. When you got your ass whipped. *Ahhh,* that was some fine it was…"

Damn. We had thought that Sammy Nettles had left, but the louse had merely gone on deck and had crouched at the bars under the lifted flap so that he could gaze down at me, while not being seen by those on the quarterdeck.

"I ain't had such a good time since we started on this trip, no, I sure ain't." He had his hands wrapped around the bars with his face in between, shining with sweat. "Girl, you twisted and screamed, oh, man, it was so fine—"

"Whyn't you go back and sit on the Captain's lap and leave me alone," said I, noticing that Clarissa was slipping along the bulkhead behind me.

"Wot? Wot do you mean by that?" demanded Sammy, his pleasure in my pain suddenly gone.

And that's when Clarissa swung around and, with all her might, hit Sammy hard on the knuckles with her cup.

"Yeeow!" he howled, recoiling backward.

"You git the hell outta here, you dirty thing," hissed Clarissa as Nettles slunk away, whining over his bashed hand.

"Thanks, Clarissa," I said, and I lowered my face to the backs of my hands again and closed my eyes. I expected Clarissa to flounce off again but she didn't. I sensed her still standing there and looking down upon me. I opened my eyes. "What?" I asked.

For a while she didn't say anything, just looked at me. Then, finally, "After Blodgett whipped you three times with that awful thing, he pulled your head back and asked you if anyone else was in on the strike...any other leaders...and said he'd stop whippin' you if you told...You shook your head no and so he kept on whippin' on you..."

Hmmm...I did dimly remember something like that happening, but the searing pain was such that I'm sure I didn't even know what he was saying, let alone being sensible enough to reply. If I did shake my head no it was in begging him to stop.

"...and...and I don't know...if he had been doin' that to me...if I would have told on you and Dolley. I don't know."

I worked up a chuckle and said, "Come on, Clarissa, if it was you he was asking that question of, you would've lunged up and bitten off his ear, you know that. Now stop doubting yourself. We don't need that." I closed my eyes again and said no more, but I sensed that she stood there for a while before moving off.

There was no Storytime last night, and there will be none tonight.

I bring myself back to the present and watch the top hatch open and the light pour in once again. As the hooks come in, Abby Pierce comes to me with her petticoat.

"Do...do you want me to put this over you so they won't see you like this?" she asks. She's as quivery nervous as ever, but she's holding up. Just goes to show, you never can tell who's going to stand steady and who ain't.

"No, thanks, Abby. Just leave it be. And, everybody, play along with this," I say, and scootch myself—*ouch ouch ouch!*—over to the edge of the Balcony so I can look up at the hatch. And so Mick and Keefe can look down at me. Then I start in to crying.

And it's full-scale, openmouthed, no-holds-barred bawling—tears pour out of my eyes, I buck, I hiccup, I wail, I moan. It ain't hard to do, as I've got plenty to cry about and my back still hurts like hell. When I see the sailors' heads appear at the edge of the open hatch, I pause long enough to look up at them through my teary eyelashes and whimper, "Sorry, lads, this is all the show you'll get today, lads... *boo hoo hoo gasp whimper*...and if you're enjoyin' lookin' at what he done to me, then shame on you...*hoo hoo hoo*... shame on you both, shame on all of yiz! I thought you was me mates, I did...*snivel, aaaarrrgh, cry, cry, cry*..."

Then I lay my head back down on my hands and weep more quietly and wait. Dolley and Barbara go down to handle the hooks. As the first tub is raised, I can hear Mick and Keefe mumbling as they do the job.

...filthy bastard...there's lots better things to do with a piece like that than flog it half t'death...and 'e 'ad to pick our game little Cockney girl to beat on...couldn't pick one of the stuck-up types, no...'e messed up our fun, 'e did...'tain't right.

And wonder of wonders, when the tubs come back in,

the one is rinsed and the other is rinsed and filled with clean salt water.

Hmmm...

I think on this for a while and then I think on other things, then what I think is, *The girls are ready.* I lift my head and announce, "Officers' Call," and Dolley and Clarissa are soon by my side.

Chapter 27

James Fletcher
The Pig and Whistle
Boston, Massachusetts, USA
June 3, 1806

Miss Jacky Faber
Somewhere in the World, God Willing

My Dearest Jacky,

Once again I write letters to a phantom. While I despair of ever seeing you again, I rejoice in the possibility that you might still be alive. I shall recount the events since last I wrote in the faint but fervent hope that someday you might read these lines.

The attempts to clear your name did not go well—the Admiralty remains obstinate in their demands for your return to their custody and I have washed my hands of the whole affair. So be it, I declared, if she and I have to spend our lives in the outer reaches of the world, then that is how it will be. I am sure the Colonies have their charms.

I booked passage for New York the next day, choosing that

port instead of Boston in case Admiralty Intelligence was keeping an eye on me and my travels, the better to find you. My father and brother came down to the pier to see me off, and many tears were shed, for we assumed that I might never come back that way again. My mother, also, came down that day, but I sent word that I would not receive her. So from where I stood, I observed her only dimly as a huddled, hunched figure seated alone in the coach.

The voyage itself was a joy—fair winds, gentle seas, good company at the Captain's table, I could not have wished for more—that combined with the anticipated joy of once more holding you in my arms, and this time for good and ever.

That, of course, was not to be. I arrived in New York, made sure I was not being followed, and took a coach, under an assumed name, for Boston. Foolishly, I made plans for our future on the way: I would first see that you were well set up in good lodging, and I would then seek gainful employment before presuming to ask you to wed. After all, how could I ask you to enter such a state without being in a position to keep and care for you in at least a modest manner? I planned first to see if the American Navy had any use for junior lieutenants, and failing that, I would seek a berth on a merchantman.

Arriving in Boston, full of hope, I looked up your attorney, Mr. Pickering, to ascertain your whereabouts, and received the devastating news. Mr. Pickering was most soothing and kind and immediately put me in touch with your man Higgins. I cannot tell you, Jacky, what an invaluable man Higgins is—he put my storming mind to some rest with his calm, concise, and careful telling of the events and his solid suspicions that the disappearance of the girls of the Lawson Peabody was an abduction and not a simple seaborne tragedy. He reported that he had written to me of these happenings, but I did not receive his letter, having already sailed.

Higgins set me up at the Pig and Whistle, where I met many of your friends who could not be more concerned over your welfare. He then took me to the courthouse and showed me the remaining evidence of the crime—the bonnets, the purses, the shawls that came ashore following that awful day.

I have been introduced to your dear friend Miss Amy Trevelyne, and though she is devastated by recent events, she continues to hold up her head, her love for you quite evident.

I have met Mistress Pimm, your headmistress, and found her as formidable as any Bo'sun's Mate. She certainly gave me the once-over. I hope she did not find me wanting as a possible match for one of "her girls." She is steadfast in her belief as to your ultimate deliverance.

I have also met your bold Mr. Randall Trevelyne, brother of Miss Amy, mentioned above. Hmmm. You know, Jacky—it is interesting to note that as I travel this world, I keep encountering boys, yes, and men, too, all of whom have been left in your wake, and yet all of whom continue to feel they have some sort of claim upon your affections.

Even though I know you are foresworn to me, and the fact that I am once again in your heart is a constant comfort to me, this frequent meeting of young males who have had some congress with you—relatively innocent congress, I am sure—causes me to wonder. But then, these are idle jealousies, worthy of neither me nor my memories of you.

Enough of that. Here is what we are doing to resolve the situation: General Howe, father to your classmate Clarissa, has taken over the southern strategy and has ships out combing the southern sea-lanes. Henry Hoffman, beside himself with grief over the loss of his betrothed, Sylvia Rossio, has been dispatched to comb the seamen's dives in the ports from Boston to Philadelphia for any news. He is a superb horseman and can cover a lot of ground. Your coxswain Jim Tanner has been a great help to me in finding my way around these unfamiliar surroundings. He, too, is steadfast in his belief that you will eventually be found safe, and he had to be restrained from setting out in your Morning Star to look for you. Denied that, he continues to haul your traps.

Upon Ezra Pickering's urging, the Honorable Caleb Strong, Governor of Massachusetts, has by diplomatic pouch sent word of this abduction to various embassies in North Africa as we feel this is your most likely destination.

I have met with the parents of many of the girls and have given them some comfort, I believe, in relating your proven competence in dire straits such as these. Those girls could not have a better companion than you in their time of trial.

Hoping that you are at least alive and reasonably well,

I am, your most devoted etc.,

Jaimy

Chapter 28

My back is better. It just feels like a bad sunburn, like those I used to get in the early days on the *Dolphin*, when we sailed down to the Mediterranean and, as things got warm, off went my shirt like the rest of the boys, me not having become a woman yet, and so just like them up top. I got scorched really bad, but eventually I tanned up and didn't burn anymore. Till now.

I can now put on the shirt that Ruth Alden had sewed up so nicely for me. When she had taken the shirt for mending, I told her not to give the needle and thread back and to be very thrifty with the thread as we may need it later, and if they should ask, to tell 'em she dropped them and they fell down into the lower Hold with the rats and they could go get them if they wanted.

Following Sin-Kay's curt morning inspection—he's still smarting from his humiliation by the Captain—and after our breakfast burgoo, we start on the Plan in earnest.

Yesterday, I'd met with Dolley and Clarissa and we agreed that we could tell the rest of the girls everything about what we planned. We brought them up to us by division so we could talk low, and we told them about the Rat Hole, my shiv, and the Plan. All were excited and ready to go, all except one—Elspeth has retreated into herself and has to be made to do the simplest of things, like eating and washing and the rest. She is shunned by the others, even though I tell them not to do that, and she spends her days curled up in a corner. Dolley Frazier and Martha Hawthorne, who are on either side of her in Sin-Kay's line, must pull her to her feet and hold her there till the inspection is over.

"See? You just take out one little chip at a time. Cut down, and when you've got a splinter, cut across to free it," I say, working at the side of the Rat Hole, way back underneath the Stage, with Division Two looking on. "Don't hurry it, as we've got plenty of time—see, like that." A little chip falls free. "Since we'll be working at this constantlike, those little chips will add up and we'll be through in no time. Whatever you do, don't twist the blade. We *can't* have it broken. Do you see?"

The girls nod. Up over our heads, Division Three is pounding out the dance rhythm, setting up a grand clatter to cover up any sounds we might make.

"What's on the other side, Jacky?" asks Julia.

"I don't know. It's too dark in there. We'll have to wait till we have the Hole big enough to stick our heads in." I did spend some time down here after the flaps had closed, peering through the Hole, and I thought I could see a faint light, maybe like the glow that would filter in at the bottom of a door. I don't know. We'll just have to wait.

I get back to my feet and dust off my underclothes, which is what I am wearing.

"I for one am going to start leaving my dress off after

inspection 'cause the work is going to get close and dirty. But, wait, here's a treat." I go over to the niche where my seabag is hidden, pull it out, and open it. I take the bar of soap I knew to be in it and hold it up, and there are exclamations of wonder. "I don't know how much good it will do with the salt water, but it will do some. Make it last, ladies." I give the bar to Minerva, who takes it eagerly.

"Priscilla, since you did such a fine job setting up the lookout rotation, will you set up the work details, two girls to a section, one carving, the other resting? Thanks. I know that's all too much to keep in your head, so I will give you a piece of paper so you can write it down."

I reach in my bag and find my precious little pad of paper. I give her a sheet and a writing implement. She looks at it curiously. "It's called a pencil, a new invention just lately come out of Germany. Much neater than a pen, and see, you can carry it up in your hair. But don't let Sin-Kay see it."

"I won't and I'll get right on this."

"Good. Now send Division One down here."

There was much done today. The Rat Hole rotation was set up in half-hour sections of two girls each, and the chipping away started. By the time the flaps came down and it was too dark to work, we had gained a good three inches upward and one inch to the side. At this rate, I should be able to poke my head through in three or four more days.

Tonight, I resume my story.

"...and then as I lay sprawled on the deck, my hands still bound behind me, the man leaned over me and smiled and *made a mock bow. 'Welcome to His Majesty's ship* Wolverine, *girl. I know you're going to enjoy your stay,' he says, looking me up and down. His teeth are worn gray stubs, and his puffy face bristles with several days' growth of beard. 'But if you ever again call your captain a fool, I will hang you from that yardarm there. Do you understand, girl?'*

"*Captain? Surely this creature could not be the Captain....*"

Much later, when all is quiet, I creep back down to sit with Hughie for a while and hold his hand and tell him about the pretty little horses again.

Chapter 29

"Elspeth, open," I order, holding the spoonful of gruel to her lips. I am sitting on the Balcony and I have her head cradled in the crook of my arm. "Open your mouth."

"No...let me alone."

"You must eat, Elspeth."

"Just let me die," she whispers. "Just let me go."

"Now what am I going to tell your parents when we get back home? That everybody was saved 'cept you? That won't be a very pleasant duty, Elspeth, and I don't want to have to do it. Now open up." I push the spoon against her lips.

A tear comes out of her eye at the mention of her parents.

"Come on, Elspeth, do it for them if not for yourself."

She opens her mouth and I spoon in the burgoo. When I have gotten it down her, I lay her head back down and leave her in her misery. I go to the Stage, past my Division Three, which is at dance practice, and down into the Pit to check the progress.

Lissette is lying facedown, doing her stint at the Rat Hole. All the girls have taken my advice about wearing our dresses only during Sin-Kay's inspection, so all of us are ghostly white in the gloom. Over our heads the rattle of dancing feet continues, a scarce foot above my head—and rattle they do, as we have decided to put our shoes back on when doing that exercise, to make even more noise so we'll be certain that our actions down here are covered up. I figure that anyone down below on the other side who might hear our carving would reckon that it was just rats doing their ceaseless gnawing. None of the girls, when at their work, has ever reported hearing anything close on the other side, nor has a light ever been seen.

"Let me see, Lissette," I say and she rolls over, out of the way. I get down on my belly and put my head to the Rat Hole. The top of my head fits, but I hang up when I get to my ears. I pull back out and say to the girls gathered about, "A few more days and then maybe we'll get to see what's in there. No sense in getting my head stuck by trying to push it through too quick. After all, the Hole's got to be made big enough to get the largest of us through when we finally go." Dolley coughs, "Ahem!" a not-so-subtle way of reminding us of her physical endowments.

I shift a bit so as to be able to shove my arm through the Hole all the way to my shoulder, then I feel around. There is something to the right that feels like a...what? A post, a support? I run my hand up the post and encounter a flat surface. *Aha!* It is a shelf, which is very good, as the overhang of that shelf will hide the ever-widening hole beneath it from whomever might enter. I hope that, anyway.

My hand continues to explore. I next encounter what seems to be a keg—a heavy one, too, because I cannot make it budge when I grunt and push hard on it. My fingers run down the side of it and they hit some things I recognize immediately as nails. *Hmmm.*

My roaming hand hits nothing else, so I pull it out and look at it. It's dusty, but I see nothing more, no flour or—I sniff my fingers—gunpowder, either.

I get back up and Lissette rolls over again to resume her whittling.

"Not much," I report to those standing about, "just some shelves and kegs...of nails, probably. I think it must be a storeroom of some kind—one that's not used much. We can only hope that it ain't locked on the other side, but if it is, we'll deal with it once I can get through the Hole." There are murmurs of agreement.

I dust off my hands and go over to the niche where my seabag is hidden. I reach in, take it out, and open it, intending to get another piece of paper for Priscilla Cabot, who says she needs it for the watch rotation. *Hmmm...* I shall have to advise her to be more thrifty, to write smaller. When I pull out the pad, with it comes my packet of letters from Jaimy, and on top of them, the miniature portrait I had done of him. I look at it in the gloom and I see a fragment of writing on a letter—*My Dearest Jacky...* My eyes mist over. I knew these things were in my bag, but I didn't let myself look at them because the other girls had nothing in this regard to comfort them, and...and I feel breath on my cheek and I look to the side and see a blond tendril of hair falling over my shoulder.

"Why don't you read some of those letters during your charming little Storytime, Jacky dear. I'm sure we'd all enjoy a good laugh."

"Don't you start, Clarissa," I say, with warning in my tone. Her face is a mere inch from mine.

"Oh. Ah won't say a mumblin' word about your little sailor boy," she says, unfazed. "But you know, when we get back to Boston, I just may give that Mr. Fletcher of yours leave to call on me. He seems like a halfway decent-lookin' fellow. It might be amusin' to show him what the company of a *real* lady is like."

A red steam of rage envelops me and my hands hook into claws, but Clarissa moves away, humming a tune, and I subside, snarling only, "One of these days, Clarissa..."

I hear a short laugh near my right side and I see that it is from Lissette de Lise, taking a break from her stint at carving at the Rat Hole. Her partner, Hermione Applegate, has taken the knife from her and is stretched out, working away. Lissette is seated, cross-legged, on the deck of the Pit.

It strikes me that, while Clarissa always manages to look beautiful no matter the circumstance, Lissette always manages to look, well, elegant—that long thin neck, long thin nose with flared nostrils, head held just right—maybe there is something to aristocratic breeding, after all.

"You are so very smart, Jac-kee Fay-bear, I did not know that before, but I do know it now. So very clever," she says, smiling to herself. "But you do not know everything, especially about my friend Clarissa. For instance, you did not know why Clarissa brought the black girl Angelique back to the school with her. *Non?* As a personal servant? *Mais non,* she needed none; there were plenty at the school and we have many at our home, too. If she had wanted one, I would have given her two."

Lissette pauses to brush back a curl from her face. "No,

265

no, she brought her to Boston because she did not want the girl to be 'breeded'—is that right? What do you say when a girl animal is put with a man animal to make her have babies—ah, *bred*, right? Just like the 'bread' we eat, right? You English and your crazy language. Eh, *bien*, when General Howe saw the thing in the paper about slavery, he go insane. He takes Clarissa and says, 'Why am I sending you to that school? To learn the ways of damned Yankees? No! I am going to send your slave Angelique back to Belvedere so you cannot give her back her time!' Huh! Only time I ever see Clarissa beg. She begs that the girl not be sent back. She says it was only a cruel joke played by a classmate. Finally the General, he relents and goes home." Lissette cocks an eye at me. "If the girl had been sent back to Virginia and that breeding thing had been done to her because of your little trick with the newspaper ad, that would have been— what is the word? Ah, the 'irony.' Yes, that's it. The irony. *Excusez-moi, s'il vous plaît,* I must get back to the carving now."

Damn...

Up in our kip, as my closest sisters and I now call our spot on the Balcony, I lean my back against the hull and think about what Lissette had said about Clarissa.

Back at the Lawson Peabody, Angelique had told me about that business about "giving them back their time." Sometimes I would go up to the attic to visit with her and she seemed glad of the company. I showed her how to get up on the widow's walk so she could get some fresh air, and we would stand there and look out over the city and talk.

"*Oui*," she said one day when I asked her about the phrase. "They do not say 'set free' because they like to make it sound as if a simple bargain was made—that we would willingly give up our time on this earth in return for being brought into the light of Christianity and their civilization. You see, they were doing us the greatest of favors, and so they feel no guilt."

I remember that as I look at the rows upon rows of hanging neck chains clanging back and forth in rhythm with the pitch and roll of the ship. There is one swinging on either side of me as I sit thinking of the *willing* captives they so recently held. We hardly notice the chains or the constant sound they make anymore, they have become so much a part of our daily lives. Horrible things, yet we take them as normal, now. Strange, what you can grow used to in this life.

Angelique told me of other practices of the slaveholders—how they would lie with the black girls they owned when they got old enough to get with child, and when the babies were born and grew up a bit, they would be sold. I shook my head in disbelief—imagine, selling your own children—what a world this is.

I'm shaken out of my reverie by the call, "Hooks coming!" from the lookout. I get to my feet and head down to the Pit.

It's showtime.

After the day's performance, my first show for the men since the flogging, I bid good day to Mick and Keefe and I cinch up my pants and start toward the Balcony, intending to sit and look out with Katy, but before I get there, Constance comes up to me on the Stage, shaking with outrage.

"I think you enjoy doing that awful thing, I really do!"

"Well, Connie, I do like to give an audience its money's worth. But if you'd like to take over for me, I'd be glad to step aside." I look around at her back. "You've got a nice trim tail. I think the boys would enjoy a peek. Shall I put you on the docket for the day after tomorrow? Yes? Well, consider yourself on it!"

There is laughter at this from several girls who are lying on the Balcony, their heads over the side. Constance gapes at all this, her mouth open. Then she snaps it shut, turns, and stalks off.

"Don't you pay that one any mind, Jacky," says Rose Crawford, sitting up in our kip with Annie and Sylvie. "We all know what you do for us."

"Thanks, Sister," I say, going up and settling myself among them. Once again I lift Elspeth's head and place it in my lap and stroke her hair, and again she does not respond but only looks off into the space of the Hold. Katy Deere is over at the bars, looking out.

"What do you see, Katy?" I ask.

She is silent for a bit and then sits back on her haunches, her eyes always on what's happening on the other side of the bars. "Them two ain't the only ones watchin' you prance around down there."

Trust Katy to be watching what's happening on the edges when everyone else is watching the main show.

"No, there's another—back there on the port-side aft is where he peeks in. He's the same one what dumps food slops over the side. I know it's food slops and not the other, 'cause the birds come around every time."

Hmmm. I think to myself, *That's gotta be the cook, or at least his helper. And I bet there's sharks gathering under us, too, for those selfsame slops.*

"Do you hear what Mick and Keefe call him?"

"They call him Cookie," she says, letting out a rare chuckle. Well, I reckon that clears that up. So he's the cook...very good information to have.

I'm thinking of the cook and looking down into the Pit at some of the rats skittering around the edges. The girls have gotten used to the rats and the rats have gotten used to us, but not so familiar with us that we can get near enough to catch them. They have found new ways to get into the rest of the ship and so leave us alone at the Rat Hole.

"Sure wish we could get some of those millers," I say, wistfully.

"What are millers?" asks Annie, beside me.

"Sailors call rats 'millers' when they catch them to eat them." *"EE-eeeeuuuwww...,"* from the girls gathered about. "After they've been at sea awhile, all the fresh meat runs out, and so they turn to the millers. It's generally the Bo'sun who runs the business—catching and selling them to the officer's mess, and to crew members who can afford to buy them," I say. "I've eaten them many times. They're pretty good."

"Yuck," says Rebecca, who has been listening in. Some others, too, express disgust.

"But why 'millers'?" asks Annie.

"Because the rats generally live on the ship's supply of flour. 'Millers,' 'flour,' get it? And since they live on good, wholesome stuff, it's all right to eat 'em in return."

"I won't eat one," says Sylvie, firmly.

"What's the difference between a rat and a squirrel? A

bushy tail, is all," I say. "But who cares? We can't catch 'em, anyway."

Katy turns and looks down at me. "Come up here," she says.

Wondering, I go up next to her.

"See that sail right there?" She points at a low, scudding sail. I nod. "See that it's got pieces of wood stuck in it?"

"Right. Those are called 'battens.' They keep the edges of the fore- and aft-sails stiff, so they don't flap in the wind." The battens are about four or five feet long and slip into sleeves sewn in the sails. They are thin and whippy so that they bend with the curve of the sail.

"Well," says Katy, "you git me some o' them battens and some cord and I'll git you all them critters you want, whatever you wanna call 'em."

I take the matter under serious advisement, as Katy Deere is of a very serious nature and does not spend her time in idle chatter.

But now it's off to French class, and then it's my turn at the Rat Hole, for no one is excused from that duty.

That night, after the hymn, and when everybody is settled in and I hear regular breathing all about me, I again creep down to sit with Hughie for a while. I reach out to him and ruffle his hair because I know he likes it, and then I run my hand down the side of his face and feel the deep scar that furrows his cheek.

"Who give you that, Hughie?"

"Mister."

"Why?"

"'Cause I was bad."

"How were you bad, Hughie?"

"There was this girl...last time...one of them dark ones...she had this little baby an' she made signs to show me that the little baby needed more food...good food. So I snuck and got it for her. Mister catched me at it. Said I was bein' bad...hit me with his stick and blood come out."

I sense that he is rocking slowly back and forth at the memory of this.

"Didn't matter none, though...Little baby died couple days later...so did the girl. Mister made me put 'em over the side...said they was dead 'cause I was bad."

I take several shuddering breaths to calm myself, then say, "Don't you *ever* think that you were bad, Hughie, 'cause you never, ever was. You was always just the best boy and that's the truth of it. Now you think about the pretty horses and ponies and fillies back at the Lawson Peabody stables when you and me and the rest of the gang get back there, Hughie," I say, resting my head against the bars, my hand now in his, my voice going on in a singsong way. "First, there's my little mare Lily; she's such a sweet thing, you won't have any trouble with her at all. But Brinker—now there's one you'll have to have a firm hand with as he is a bit wild." I sense Hughie's head bobbing up and down in solemn agreement. "And then there's Molly, the hot-running bay—you'll have to make special sure that she's cooled down after a run—and Jupiter, Clarissa's horse; now, there's a handful, I can tell you..."

He falls asleep after a while, dreaming, I'm sure, of horses and saddles and meadows and hay, and I put his hand gently down and go back to my kip.

Good night, Hughie. You just sleep now and dream of the pretty little horses.

Chapter 30

"Oh, please, God, in your mercy, please let him catch us!" prays Constance Howell.

We are all standing on the rear Balcony watching the ship that was spotted early this morning and which has been getting closer by the hour. The men on deck have been frantically making as much sail as they can to draw away, but the ship just gets nearer. We watch from the Balcony, our hearts pounding. There is a shout, "It's an American!" and sure enough, we can now see the colors of the flag at the top of the mast.

Elspeth is suddenly by my side, the dirty blue ribbon dangling in front of her now hopeful face. She clutches my arm, saying, "Oh, I just know my papa has sent that ship to rescue me! I just know it."

There are cheers from other girls, too, and cries of despair from the men outside. I know that the rest of the girls hope for rescue by this ship, but I do not. I am sick with dread.

"It's the good old *Constitution*!" joyously shouts some girl, and another cheer goes up. Sure enough, it is that ship—I know, because I had seen her when we were patrolling the Barbary Coast back in '04. *But what's she doing here?* I wonder in spite of my fear.

The *Constitution* looks like it's now about three miles away, on our port quarter. At this rate they'll be alongside of us in two or three hours. There are flags raised on the American frigate, no doubt signalling Captain Blodgett to heave to and back his sails so that the *Bloodhound* can be boarded and inspected, but the Captain, himself at the wheel, just shakes his fist at the approaching ship and shouts curses.

Several of the girls have joined hands and are dancing in a circle, singing. Hepzibah is lining up other girls, saying, "Oh, we just must have Mr. Handel's 'Hallelujah Chorus' from the *Messiah,* as we are truly delivered." And then Clarissa is at my left hand, smirking. "See," she says, "we didn't need you after all." Now Constance is at my right hand, saying smugly, "That's right, you know. God delivered us, not Jacky Faber. You ought to be ashamed for the way you've behaved."

There is a low *booommm,* and a puff of smoke drifts away from the bow of the *Constitution.* They have fired a warning shot across our bow.

"Shut the flaps," shouts Captain Blodgett, and down they come, plunging us into darkness in the middle of the day. The girls' former joy has been considerably dampened. We sit there in the dark and wait. A hand goes into mine, and I know that it's Rebecca's. I give it a hopeful squeeze.

There is another *boom.* Then the flaps on the starboard side suddenly go back up and light pours into the Hold. *Oh, no!* I realize in despair, *the side that can't be seen from the* Constitution*! And these men can't be caught with the evidence that is us!*

There is a rattling of keys in locks, and Sin-Kay and Chubbuck and the Mate Dunphy hurry in and onto the Stage. They are followed by Mick and Keefe and two other sailors, all of whom rush down into the Pit.

"Get in the line!" orders Sin-Kay. "Now!"

The girls, shocked, start to do it.

"No, no!" I shout. "Don't do it! They're going to kill us! Fight! Fight!"

Dunphy rushes up to me and sticks his pistol into my mouth and grinds the barrel hard against the back of my throat and snarls, "One more word and I'll blow your brains out!" I gag and choke and can say nothing. The line forms up raggedly with much moaning and crying. I hear Clarissa putting up resistance: *"God damn you to hell! Get your filthy hands—"* then a *thud* and then no more from her.

As I knew they were going to, the sailors bring up that horror: the *marching chain*. Rebecca is the first in line and she shrinks back in terror as a man reaches for her. But he takes her roughly by the arm and puts the first neck manacle in the chain around her thin little neck and snaps it shut. Then he takes the next in line, Ruth Alden, and does the same to her, and so on down the line. Piteous pleas for mercy fall on uncaring ears as the grim work proceeds. Sally, then Hermione, then Helen, Dorothea, and my poor Annie, then Priscilla and on and on till Katy Deere, and then it's Mick himself who clamps the cold hard thing around my own neck and says, *"Sorry, kid,"* and then does the same to Dolley, and then Elspeth, who is already dead in the eyes, and then Martha, and Clarissa, groggy from Chubbuck's blow, then Connie, her hands up in prayer, then Wilhelmina, and Chrissy and Judy and Lissette, and on down the line to Sylvie, then Hyacinth, Barbara, Caroline, Hepzibah, Frances, and finally, Julia Winslow.

When they are done, there is still a length of chain with neck manacles hanging from it leading out from the one on poor Julia's neck. Chubbuck picks up that length of chain and pulls Julia toward the hatchway. She has no choice but to follow, as do all the others in her wake—those who resist are hit and kicked till they move along.

The light blinds us as we are led on deck. Chubbuck takes his end of the chain over to an opening in the rail where a gangway might ordinarily be put, but as my eyes become used to the light, I see that an anchor, a big one, weighing maybe a hundred pounds, sits there, instead. It is poised right on the edge.

"Hurry up!" yells the Captain from the quarterdeck. "They're almost upon us!"

Chubbuck hastily secures the anchor to the end of the chain—the last neck manacle snapped shut around the shaft of the anchor does the job. He then wastes no time in kicking the anchor over the side.

The chain plays out and suddenly Julia—dear delicate little Julia Winslow—is jerked over the side to follow the anchor down, Julia, who hardly makes a splash when she hits the water. Then it's Frances who follows her in, then Hepzibah, then Caroline, then Barbara, Hyacinth, and *good-bye Sylvie!* and then Abby, Cloris, and splash by dismal splash, they each go over, dragged down by the relentless weight of the anchor. We are pulled forward, step by step. I try to hold on to the rail to slow down that awful pull, but Dunphy hits my hand with his club and I can't do nothin' but let go and be dragged—*oh God*—dragged along with the rest. Splash by splash, now Cathy, then Lissette, who holds her head high all the way to the edge, but her neck, too, is jerked violently sideways and she goes over and down with the rest. Now Judy, now Chrissy, now Wilhelmina, then Connie, her hands staying together in prayer as she goes headfirst into the sea. Clarissa is next and the last thing she does on this earth is spit in Chubbuck's eye, and then she's over, too, in spite of all the life that was in her. I'm getting closer now, closer to my own end, close enough to see those ahead of me disappear into the depths...*Good-bye, Martha,* and then Elspeth's pathetic splash. I hold Dolley's hand in mine till it's wrenched from my grip and then it's my turn to feel the awful weight and I am pulled over and into the water and Katy and the rest are dragged in after me.

I futilely hold my breath as long as I can as I go down and down. I can see those who have gone before me, their dresses looking like black orchids floating in the dark blueness, their white legs and feet twinkling like the middle parts of the flowers before they wink out of sight, down into the depths, one by one.

I can't hold my breath any longer and I close my eyes and I open my mouth and my lungs fill and I choke—*oh God*—I choke, and then I start screaming and a part of my dying self wonders how I could be screaming underwater, but still I scream and scream and...

...and I open my eyes again and I find myself not hurtling down to the blackness at the bottom of the sea but instead in the darkness of the belly of the *Bloodhound*, being comforted by Annie and Sylvie and Rebecca, who are holding my screaming, choking, and shaking self and pleading with me to *wake up, Jacky! Oh, please wake up!*

Chapter 31

The work continues. On this afternoon, after Chorus and burgoo, I gather Clarissa and Dolley to talk about long-range plans. We sit on the Stage, cross-legged, knees touching, in a circle of three.

"We've turned east," I say, "and that means we're heading over to Africa. From what I can see of the sun, and judging from the heat, I suspect we were well off the coast of Florida when they put the helm over."

"Which means?" asks Dolley, eyebrows up.

"Which means they intend to stay below the sea-lanes and out of sight as much as possible. It also means that our time is growing shorter."

Dolley and Clarissa are considering this when Constance Howell walks up next to us and says, "I am planning on forming a prayer group. Do I need *your* permission for that?" she asks, looking down her nose. Of all the girls, she has resisted the three-division, three-officer setup the most.

"That will be all right, as long as it doesn't interfere with your other duties," I say. Clarissa and Dolley nod in agreement.

"Good," replies Constance. "We shall pray for our deliverance," she says smugly. "And for your salvation," she adds, looking pointedly at me. "You are all invited to join us."

Clarissa snorts and waves her off contemptuously, but I don't let it go. "Pray for deliverance? Don't you think God would like us to get out of this ourselves? He must get awful annoyed with those prayers coming up at Him all the time."

"Do not blaspheme, Miss," says Connie, sternly.

I sigh and think, *Did anyone ever have less use for me?* "I am not being disrespectful, I am just thinking."

"If we are to be saved, it is God who will deliver us, not you, Miss Faber, and don't let your pride make you think otherwise." She's really getting hot now. Christina King, Catherine Lowell, and Minerva Corbett are lurking in the shadows behind her. That must be the prayer group.

"Well, He might help," I say, in a musing way. "But then again, He might not. Maybe He is testing *you*, Constance Howell, to see how much you can take and still remain devoted to Him. Think of poor Job, in the Bible—sores all over his body, his crops fail, his wife and sons and daughters die, and still he remains faithful to his God. Hey, Connie, maybe God hasn't even started on you yet. Maybe He'd like to see how you hold up spiritually when you're on the auction block? Ever think of that?"

She spins on her heels and goes off in a huff.

"All right. Back to business," says Dolley.

"Right," says I. "Anyway, we've got to get moving on things."

"But what else can we do, besides the carving?"

"Well, I've been thinking. The lookouts report that this is not a happy ship: There's the Captain, Mate, and Chubbuck...they've got no use for Sin-Kay, who doesn't like them any more than they like him. And then there's the crew...they ain't exactly a gang of good friends, either—there's little groups of 'em who hang together and don't mix much with the others."

"So?" asks Clarissa, idly chewing on a fingernail.

"So I say we turn 'em against each other even more—get 'em distrustful, nervouslike...make 'em think they're on an unlucky ship. There's nothing more superstitious than a sailor, I can tell you that. Katy tells me some of the crew have been listening to our singing and storytelling at night—we might be able to use that. And if we get 'em turned against each other, they won't fight as a group when we make our break. See?"

Both Dolley and Clarissa nod, so I continue. "I'll work on the crew, first through Mick and Keefe. Then, well, we'll see what develops. Clarissa, keep needling Sin-Kay, but be careful, you don't want to push him too far."

Clarissa grins. "It'll be an absolute pleasure," she purrs.

"How are your divisions?" I ask. We report on the divisions every day.

"Mine's all right," answers Dolley. "Wilhelmina had the sniffles, but she's better now. A few of them are down in the dumps, but you know how that goes."

"Well I know," I say. "I still can't get Elspeth to come back around."

"Let her die," says Clarissa. "The dirty little snitch."

"Now, Clarissa," I begin, but I'm interrupted by the sight of Judy Leavitt's head appearing at the edge of the Stage. She wipes sweat off her brow with the back of her hand. It's plain she's been working down below at the Rat Hole.

279

"Jacky, come look. We got past that big knot and are into some really soft wood now. A big chunk just came out."

We leap down into the Pit to go under the Stage to the Hole. Caroline, who has continued to work the edge with the knife, stops when I lay my hand on her shoulder and whisper, "Caroline, get up and let me look."

I gasp in delight. They have made amazing progress. There's easily enough room now for me to poke my head through. *"Beautiful work!"* I whisper. As the Hole has gotten bigger, we have made a rule that only whispers can be spoken down at the work site, so that anyone who chances to be outside of that room beyond the Rat Hole doesn't pick up our voices. Everyone knows that if the Hole is discovered, we are lost.

I go down on my belly and stick my head through and wait for my eyes to adjust to the darkness. I give it a good five minutes, but all that swims out of the gloom is a faint strip of light at floor level off to the right. My suspicion that it's the crack under a door is confirmed when the light flutters, as if someone had just walked past. *Please don't come in, not yet!* But they walk on, and all is well. I let out my breath and slide back out.

"I can't see anything," I say to the waiting girls as I get to my feet. "I'll have to get light. Keep carving in that direction there. At this rate I'll be able to get all of me through soon."

Caroline drops down and I look at her for a moment. I've noticed that some of these girls are getting right fit, what with the short rations and the dance exercise and all, which is good. When we make the final break, we'll need all the strength we can muster, because even if everything goes right, it still ain't gonna be easy.

I go over to the hidey-hole that holds my seabag and I thrust my arm down into the bag and pull out one of my two candles and my flint striker. I usually kept the striker on board the *Star* for lighting my spirit stove, but on the day of the picnic I had brought it with me, thinking we might have a jolly campfire on the island. Well, we didn't have that, but I am damned glad to have this here with me now.

The girls have been told to keep the chips from the Rat Hole work in a pile off to the side, and from that pile I separate the tiniest shavings and form them into their own little pile. Squeezing the striker, I send a spark down into the tinder. It glows, but then winks out. I try again, and this time the spark stays and smoulders. I blow on it and it flutters into flame and I quickly stick the wick of my candle into it, and when it catches, just as quickly do I snuff out the tinder blaze with my cupped hand. Can't have anybody smelling smoke—fire on board is the one thing that sailors fear above all other things... 'cept maybe ghosts.

Taking the lit candle back to the work site, I again crouch down in front of the Rat Hole, and after a quick check to make sure no one has come into that dark outer room, I stick the candle as far into the Hole as I can. It is a squat candle and I put it down without fear of it tipping. I do have other fears, though.

"I am quite sure that the room next to us is not the powder magazine, but I cannot be sure. If it is, and the candle ignites it, then I hope to see you all in Heaven." There are some nods, and not a few hands go into the prayer position, as I duck down again and stick my head in the Hole.

It is not the powder magazine. It seems to be the carpenter's storeroom, and we could not have hoped for a better find. It is full of lumber and spars for repairing the ship, but if nothing befalls this voyage, then the place would be seldom used. I turn my head and see a wall of tools, like saws and augers and such…There's a hammer, and there's plenty of nails of all sorts about…*Ah, and Katy, there is a pile of brand-new battens, just like you asked for.*

I pull back out, then reach in and retrieve the candle. I blow it out and tell them what I saw. Then I go meet with Clarissa and Dolley, and when I do, we decide to go to round-the-clock work on the Rat Hole. We each present it to our divisions, and the girls, even though they know they will be working by feel in the pitch dark among the rats and their own private fears, agree. I could not be prouder of them. As if on cue, the bells are rung and the flaps come down.

I stay on the Stage as the girls feel their way by me on the way to their kips. Everyone's getting real good at blind-man's bluff.

I glance up in the direction of the starboard-side flaps, and even though I can't see them up there listening, I know they are there. And have I got a dandy for them tonight. When all are settled, I clear my throat and begin…

"*'Be gentle with me, Robin. Treat me like a lady,' said I, as I reached for him. He ripped off his jacket and was fumbling with the laces on his shirt when there came a furious pounding on the door.*

"*'Lieutenant Faber! The Captain wants you in his cabin right now!' I recognized the voice as…yes, well, I recognized the voice as belonging to Private Rodgers, one of the ship's two Marines.*

"*I rose from the bed and put my hands on Robin's sagging*

shoulders. 'I'm sorry, Robin, I really am,' I whispered, so the Marine outside couldn't hear. 'Kiss me one more time and then I must dress and go...'"

"Now, that is the last straw!" shouts Constance Howell, from somewhere on the starboard Balcony. "This is completely obscene! You were...were *unclothed* in front of that boy and yet you would stand and *kiss* him?"

"Do you want me to tell what happened, or shall I lie, Connie?" I ask quietly. "If everybody wants me to stop, I will." I wait for a reply and hear none. "Fine, I'll stop," I say, heading back to my kip. "I don't need this."

Now there are murmurs of "No...no..."

Then, out of the dark comes Clarissa's slow drawl, "Whyn't you jus' hush up, Sister Constance, and let her tell her lies? They are mildly entertainin', you'll have to agree, even though I don't believe even half of 'em. I mean, what boy in his right mind would want to kiss *her*, even if she *was* butt naked?" She waits a beat before continuing, "*Especially* if she was butt naked."

That gets a real laugh, and then there are cries of "Hear, hear!" and "Press on, Jacky!" and I swear I hear a guttural male voice from outside the flaps say, "Aye, let 'er tell it. It's just gettin' good."

"And you don't have to listen, Connie dear," Clarissa continues. "You can go far enough forward so you won't hear her scandalous little ol' story. Try sayin' the Lord's Prayer over and over again. That should do it. But jus' you say it to yourself, if you please."

There is heard a disgusted *oh!* from Connie's direction and the sound of someone turning over and probably clapping of hands over her ears.

"Go on, Jacky," I hear Dolley say, and I go back out to my spot and lift my voice again.

"*I dressed myself and went out, and the Marines collected me and took me to the Captain's cabin.*

"*Captain Scroggs was seated at his table, with a bottle and two glasses in front of him. It was plain he had already been into the spirits, as his face was even more puffed and florid than it was before. 'Sit down, girl, and have a drink,' he said, shoving the glass in front of me.*

"*From outside I could hear a deep humming... 'Hmmmm'... coming from the throats of the men in the rigging... my friends, who were giving the Captain a warning, a warning that mutiny was imminent if he didn't change his ways.* Thanks, lads, *I thought,* but too late for me...

"*'Hmmmmmm...'*"

Chapter 32

"You will be cheered to know, ladies," says Sin-Kay with some satisfaction, "that we have completed a good third of our journey. Soon you will be secure in your new homes, with your new masters, your new life. Adams!"

"Here."

"Alden!"

"Here."

And so on down the line, past me, to...

"Goodwin!"

No answer. Dolley and Martha have her propped up between them.

"She's here," says Martha for her.

Sin-Kay looks at the listless Elspeth. He puts his pencil under her chin and lifts her face. "You'd better get this one back on the line soon, or it's the fleshpots for her. Or over the side, one or the other."

"We'll take care of her," says I. "She'll get better."

He slides his eyes over to me. "Ah. Smart-mouth. Well, I expect to see some improvement soon, or else. Hawthorne!"

"Here," says Martha.

"Howe!"

"Here Ah is, Massa Sinkey."

He brings his gaze to rest on Clarissa. Using little strips of petticoat cloth, she had tied up her hair in little pigtails sprouting all over her head. She also wears an idiot's silly grin.

"What is this, then?" he asks, not amused.

"Why, Massa Sinkey, Ah thought you'd like me this way, gettin' ready to be a nice little ol' pickaninny fo' some big bad sultan!"

There are side-glances and snickers from the girls in the line. And I think I hear a laugh from out on the deck.

"Have your fun then, Blondie," says Sin-Kay, "but the end will be the same. Howell!"

He goes on down the list. When he is done, he snaps the notebook shut and leaves. "No ration for Blondie today," he says to Nettles before the cage door locks behind him.

"Don't want yo' slops, no how, Massa Stinkey," says Clarissa, sticking out her tongue. "You knows where you can shove 'em? Someplace where the sun don't shine, dat's where."

Later, I get with Clarissa and tell her she did good in needling Sin-Kay that way, but cautioned her not to go too far, recalling the Cat. She nods, but I don't know if she took what I said to heart, because she is such a proud thing.

After breakfast, we're back down on the job. Teams of girls had worked through the night, each pair knowing the ones to be awakened next, timed by the bells of the watch. They had to feel their way through the pitch dark, but they did it. We have gained much on the Rat Hole, and I get down now to try to wiggle through. The candle and tinder are close at hand, ready to light.

"If I wiggle my toes, grab my ankles and pull me back fast," I whisper to those gathered about me. Then I kneel down and stick my hands in first, arms straight out before me. Then I drop to my belly and put my head through. It goes in easily enough and I pull with my hands and just manage to get my shoulders, then chest, through. Up on my elbows, I strain to pull my bottom after me, but I know it ain't gonna serve. No sense in getting stuck this early in the game. I wiggle my toes and feel hands on my legs, then I am pulled back out. And none too gently, either—my under-shirt pulls up as I am dragged and raked across the raw, splintery wood of the Hole.

"*Damn*," I whisper, sitting up and pulling down the chemise. "I wanted to get to those battens today. Well, keep at it and—"

"Let me try, Jacky," comes a whisper from Rebecca, who has knelt next to me.

I look over at her...*Hmmm*...She is the only one smaller than me.

"All right," I say, "but you've got to be very quiet and careful."

She nods, all big-eyed in the gloom.

"It will be very dark in there, but we'll light the candle if you get through and I'll reach in with it and you'll be able to see. But if you hear anyone coming down the passageway, you've got to get back quick. Got it?"

"Got it."

"Now, when you get through there, you will see off to

the right a stack of battens—thin whippy pieces of wood. Take…how many, Katy?"

"Three, for now, and check for cord," whispers Katy Deere.

"Right. Here we go." I strike the flint and light the tinder and then the candle. Rebecca goes to the Rat Hole.

She has no trouble at all getting her small self through. *Note to self: Stop eating that layer of grease on top of the burgoo.* As I see the soles of her feet disappear, I get down and put arm, candle, and head through.

I see that she is standing already by the battens. She stoops down, picks up three, and slides them over next to me.

"See any cord? Any twine?"

"No. Not yet…"

"Don't worry about it…wait." I feel a tapping on my rump and I pull back out, leaving the candle in place. "What?"

"Here. Let me look," says Katy, then her head and one arm go through the hole.

In a moment I hear some muffled whispering. Then an eternity of worry goes by, and finally, Katy slides back out and in her hand is a chisel. She puts it to the side and reaches back in and this time pulls out a mallet. Then the three battens are taken through—one long, two short. Then the snuffed candle, then Rebecca's face, then the rest of her. She sits up cross-legged, quivering with excitement.

"You done good, girl," says Katy. "Good as any Injun."

Rebecca beams under the praise. She knows that words are rare from Katy Deere and that Katy means what she says when she does speak.

It seems that Katy looked at the tools arrayed on the wall and directed the girl to the things she would need, then Rebecca went over and got them and passed them down.

"No string, though," says Rebecca, sorrowfully.

"Don't worry, dear," says I. "I have string."

"Good," says Katy Deere, and she reaches back into the Rat Hole and comes back with four of the nails I had discovered before, lying scattered on the floor of the beautiful, and most bountiful, storeroom. "These'll do for starters. I'll need the knife sometimes, so I'll work on these battens right here next to the big job."

I go back to get my seabag and stick my arm in and rummage around deep in the bottom, for I know that what I am looking for has been there a long time. *Ha! Got it.*

It is a packet of oiled paper that holds the fish lures that Professor Tilden, back on the *Dolphin,* had taught us to make and urged us to keep. *Thanks, Tilly, for all you done.*

There are three lures, each of them brightly painted wood with a strong hook, and each of them attached to about twenty-five feet of strong, waxed cord. I choose one, untie the lure, and hand the cord to Katy.

She takes it and chuckles. "What else you got in that thing, Jacky? Two, three hardware stores?"

It is the first bit of humor I have ever heard from her. First time I've heard anything like a laugh, too.

"Just the essentials, Katy, that's all I ever carry."

Katy had set up her project well to the side of the business at the Rat Hole, so that the sounds of her work would not be heard by any of our captors on the other side. Fascinated, I sit down to watch her.

First, she chooses one of the short battens, the one with the straightest grain—one whose lines went right up parallel, from top to bottom—and lays it flat on the deck. Then she draws a line about half an inch away from the long edge of the batten, using the pencil I had given Priscilla to draw up the duty roster. Taking up the chisel, she commences to place the business edge on that line and give its butt a bit of a hit with the mallet. The sound is not loud, but still she times the hit to occur when the chains clash against the side with the ship's rhythmic roll. *I'll have to remember that little trick,* I say to myself. She taps carefully along the whole length of the pencilled line till, finally, a nice long, straight strip pops off. Borrowing the knife for a moment, she splits one end and notches the other. While she has the knife, she takes up the long batten and puts a notch on each end and carves down the sides at the ends, making a graceful curve of the whole thing. Handing the knife back to the Rat Hole workers, she sets aside the long batten and turns again to the strip. She takes up one of the nails and puts it in the split end. These nails are about three inches long and are flat, since they are pounded out by a blacksmith and then cut to size. Katy takes a small length of the cord and separates the three strands, then takes one and wraps it around the wood that holds the nail and ties it down tight.

"Too bad we ain't got feathers," she says.

"We got feathers," I say, and dive back into my seabag. I pull out my writing quills. The girls look at me in wonder. *Well, of course I would have those in there, wouldn't you?*

Katy takes a quill and splits it down the center.

"Too bad we ain't got glue," I say.

"Don't need no glue," says Katy.

She takes three pieces of half quill, strips a bit of the feathery part off each end, exposing the bare center spine, and uses more of the cord strands to lash them down sort of opposite each other on the notched end of the stick.

"Injun kids showed me how to do that. They didn't have no glue, neither. Can you light that candle for a bit?"

I do it and she drips the hot wax over the lashed parts of the arrow and smoothes it over with her finger and then hands it to me.

I hold it up and admire it while she strings the bow.

"Now, let's see about them millers," says Katy Deere.

Rats ain't the only creatures this thing could kill, I'm thinking with some satisfaction.

Later in the day, I'm sitting on the Stage, listening to Dorothea give a lecture on the life of Galileo, but I'm watching Katy. She's down in the Pit, crouched under the starboard Balcony, way back under so she can't be seen by anyone looking through the bars. She lies down there in the Pit for hours, it seems, the bow pulled back and an arrow nocked in place and trained on a hole where we know the rats come out.

Suddenly there is a *twang* and a high squeak, and I know that we have our first miller, and when Dorothea is finished, I go station myself next to the lookout up on the forward port Balcony and wait. It's Sylvie who's got the watch there, and I sit with her in silence. Looking at her sitting there, scanning the deck with her dark eyes, intent on her duty, I think of poor Henry Hoffman and what he must be going through, with his dear girl gone. Does he think her dead? Kidnapped? I don't know what any of them are thinking back there, and I shake my head to stop thinking about that.

Ah. There's Keefe, walking by on some errand. "Keefe," I hiss, "c'mere!"

He looks around guardedly and comes near, but not too near, and asks, "Wot you want?"

"Tell Cookie I wants to see him. About makin' a deal for some millers."

He looks dubious but I put my face to the bars and flutter my eyes and look piteous. "C'mon, Keefie, you'll do it for me, won't you?" I've been giving the boys a tiny bit more with each of my special performances down by the tubs, just to keep their interest up.

"Awright," he says.

"Tell 'im to meet me here, where he won't be seen from the quarterdeck. Sometime when it's convenient to him. We're always home."

By the time Cookie comes to call, Katy has bagged three more millers. I'm down at the work site when I get the call from the lookout that he's coming, and I'm up there in a flash, holding the four rats by their tails.

Cookie looks warily about, but squats down next to the bars. "So what's the deal?" he asks.

"Look, Cookie," I say, "we got millers, lots o' them, and you ain't. You know they all live over here and only go forward to raid your stores."

"Little blighters," he grumbles in agreement.

"So, we give you four millers and you cook 'em up nice and give us back three, and you get to keep the fourth to sell or enjoy yourself," I say, all reasonable.

"One for you, three for me," he says, as I knew he would.

"Fifty-fifty," says I, "or no deal…and no more show and no more stories." I know from my lookout reports that he's been enjoying both forms of entertainment.

"Awright. Deal. Hand 'em over."

I swing the carcasses through the bars and he gathers them up.

"You'll get yours tomorrow. 'Bout noon."

"Good enough, Cookie, and thanks."

Chapter 33

We line up for inspection, and by now no one, not even Constance, is bothering to put on her dress—most of the time it's just too damned hot and what's the point, anyway? Sin-Kay has not commented on this—he probably thinks it's a good sign of us being broken and not caring anymore and all. Fine. Let him think that.

He has taken to carrying a riding crop under his arm during these inspections—I guess to make us scared. I reflect that it was probably that very thing that put the scar on poor Hughie's cheek. *Bastard.*

Clarissa does not mock him outright today. No, she just hums a little tune when he stands in front of her, and then she bursts out laughing, as if at some little private joke—at Sin-Kay's expense, of course. He doesn't let it go.

"All of you are too skinny. You will notice today that your rations are being improved." He takes his riding crop in hand and with it he lifts up the front of Clarissa's undershirt, enough to show her lower ribs. "We cannot have this when we arrive at the slave pens. Weight must be gained."

"Yassuh, Mistah Stinkey, we be fattenin' right on up, you'll see," pipes up Clarissa. "Jes' like a bunch o' happy little ol' cows in yo' feedlot. Yum, yum, jes' let me at that fine, *fine* burgooooooo!"

Several of us, up and down the line, echo Clarissa's lowing…*Mmmmmoooooo*…Another great sound, I'm thinking, that you can make without moving your lips.

There are several stifled snorts of laughter.

Sin-Kay glares at Clarissa and then turns abruptly away. He knows this bit of fun will be reported to the rest of the crew—some of them are always lurking and listening—and he doesn't like it. We continue to grow in stature in the crew's eyes, and he continues to be diminished.

"Fine. Have your fun. Sammy, report to me any of them who do not eat their full bowl, and they shall be force-fed like geese. Dismissed!"

We do not move on his command, just as we had planned, but only come to attention and stay that way until he leaves the Hold.

We go forward and get our rations from Hughie under Sammy's watchful eye. When I look in my bowl, I nod toward Wilhelmina and she does her usual trick—she groups girls around the hatchway so that Nettles can't see in.

"Dolley, Clarissa," I say, and they come over, looking into their bowls. "Just an extra thick layer of pork grease on top, that's all," I say, as I put my nose down and sniff. "Rancid, too. Let's pass the word, quietly, for them not to eat it."

"Some 'improved rations,'" says Dolley, looking disgustedly at the greenish fat swirling around in her bowl.

"Right," says Clarissa, equally revolted. "But what can we do with it? That creepy boy Nettles'll tell on us, sure as hell."

"Let's get the word to the girls and then we'll figure that out," says I, and we three scatter to warn our divisions.

It's Katy Deere who has the solution. "Let's get us a coupla pieces of cloth and have each girl spoon her pig fat in it. It'll harden up when it cools and then we'll use it to draw them millers outta their holes. They're sure to get more wary as I keep nailin' 'em. I'm bettin' they'll like this stuff enough to come out and take a chance to get some of it."

We line up and do it so our bellies are not assaulted by that awful stuff. And when the grease cools, Katy will have a fine, if disgusting, ball of pork fat. Even without that bait, she had killed six more millers since yesterday's hunt—they wait in a pile at the port-side forward Balcony watch station, the rendezvous point for the exchange.

I go down to the work site to check on things and am much encouraged. The round-the-clock schedule has really sped up things, and I know just by looking at the Rat Hole that I'll be able to get through it. Before I go, though, I return to my seabag and change clothes. I reach in and pull out a small bundle and open it up.

"What is that?" whispers Rebecca, always fascinated with what I am up to.

"My burglar outfit," I whisper back. "If I'm surprised over there, I'll be better able to hide in this rig than I would in white drawers and undershirt." It is the same outfit I used to haunt the not-so-very-Reverend Mather back at the school when I found out what he had done to that poor Janey Porter.

"Trust *you* to have a thief's costume," says Constance Howell, whose turn it is at the Hole and who has overheard the whispered talk between Rebecca and me.

"Just tend to your duty, Connie, and leave me to mine,"

I say in a low voice, a voice with a good deal of warning in it.

I whip off my drawers and hear a firm *tsk!* from Connie, but who cares? I climb into my tight black britches—actually the same britches I stripped off Charlie Rooster's body all those years ago and had later dyed black. Then it's on with my serving-girl black stockings and off with my white chemise so I can pull on my tight jersey sweater and black leather gloves. My knit wool watch cap completes the outfit—and, when I pull the watch cap down over my face, there ain't a white bit of me showin' 'cept for the whites of my eyes peering through the slits cut in the cap.

"Ooohh," breathes Rebecca, "you look like a proper imp from down below, you do."

Constance sniffs loudly but reserves judgement on the impishness of my character, which is lucky, 'cause I'm just about ready to smack her a good one.

The candle is lit and I go through the Hole. I still scrape a bit at my hips, so I know it'll be a while before Dolley could get through, but hey, chip by chip, we'll get there.

Standing up on the other side and holding the candle, I look about me. I see a worktable, and there are kegs and boxes stacked about on shelves and on the deck. There's some boards of various lengths, and...a coil of rope, and, *aha!* there's a spool of twine beside it. But first things first.

I go to the door to check it out. I can tell from the hinges that the door swings in and to starboard. I hold the candle to the latch, but I can't tell anything about it from this side, and I don't want to stick a blade through and jiggle it about in the daytime because someone might hear and wonder at the noise. I put my ear to the door crack and listen but hear nothing except faraway sounds. Course, it's not likely I would, since I'm down in the bottom of the ship, just above the bilges, and the sleeping quarters and the galley would be up on higher decks. *Hmmm.* Thinking about the kitchen makes me wonder if that's the smell of our millers roasting. Hope so. Maybe later tonight, when all are sleeping, I'll give the latch a try with my shiv. But for now, it's back to business.

I crouch down and choose eight more battens and slide them back through the Rat Hole. Waiting hands take them immediately. Katy's going to make up some more bows and then we'll see which of the girls turn out to be handy with them.

Then I go back and get the spool of cording and put it through, whispering, "Cut off about twenty yards of that and then pass it back." I wait there, crouched, until its return. I know that some girl is measuring it out, nose to extended arm, nose to extended arm, repeated twenty times. A hand appears below me, holding the spool, and I take it and put it back where it was and then continue my exploration.

If the ship's carpenter is in charge of this space, he sure ain't a neat custodian—there's piles of odd pieces of metal angles, and while some tools are hung on pegs on the bulkhead, others are just strewn about on the worktable top. There's about five brace-and-augers, tools for drilling holes—that's good, we might need those—and there's mallets and files...*Good, good*...And everything being a mess, nothing will be missed if we borrow some tools for a while. I take up a file and pass that through—Katy needs it to round off the arrows—and then I spy stacked buckets and...What's in this box? *Glory!* It's cakes of laundry soap!

I take one big cake and one bucket and put them through the Hole, hoping that the girls on the other side don't shout out loud over *that* prize. They don't, though I know that much linen will be scrubbed and hung out to dry under the Stage this day and...

Then I freeze. *Oh, my God! Someone's coming!* There's a clatter of boot heels on the outside ladder and then footsteps outside the door. The latch rattles.

I snuff out the candle and suck the acrid smoke into my mouth so it won't be smelled. No time to get back to the Hole. I leap back against the passageway bulkhead and flatten myself as the door swings open and covers me.

One man enters the room, muttering to himself, "Goddamn Chubbuck, whyn't he get his own goddamn spikes, the sod..." The much put-upon man rummages about on the worktable, as far as I can figure out, me being out of sight behind the door. Then...*Horrors!*...The ship has taken a more pronounced roll and the door starts to swing closed! If he turns, he'll see me! *Quick.* I reach up and grab the top of the door and swing it back toward me. Then I hear, "There. This should serve, and the filthy bugger can go to hell if it don't." Then I hear his footsteps, and the door is pulled from my lightly restraining fingers and slammed shut. The sound of his boots gets fainter and fainter. Then silence.

I let out my breath and waste no time in feeling my way back to the Rat Hole and out.

Damn! That was close. *Note to self: We can't be surprised like that again.*

I praise the girls gathered about the Hole for not crying out and giving us away during that time of peril. They are certainly turning into a coolheaded bunch, by and large, and I rejoice in it.

"All right, light the candle again," I say.

"But surely you're not going back in there again!" whimpers one of the girls. "You were almost caught!"

"Only for a moment, Rose," I say. "And you shall see that we will be the safer for it."

The candle is lit and I slide through to the storeroom once more. I jump up, grab from the wall a brace-and-bit with a small drill I had spotted before, and am back down and through the Hole in an instant.

After all have calmed back down and are again at work on widening the Hole, I make yet another visit to my seabag. I reach in and pull out one of my door wedges, one of the ones I had used when I was touring Cape Cod, to keep unwanted visitors out of my rooms at various inns. As wondering eyes watch me, I squat down and clamp the wedge with my toes and put the bit to the thicker end and start drilling. In a matter of minutes, I finish, then I squirm through the Rat Hole once again and return the brace-and-bit to its place on the workbench. This time I do it by feel, without the candle, as I am becoming quite familiar with our dear storeroom.

Taking about fifteen feet of the twine, I slip the end through the newly drilled hole in the wedge and tie it down tight, whipping the end for neatness.

"See, the next time someone goes through, the first thing she does is put this wedge under the door. If someone surprises us and tries to open the door, he won't be able to—he'll rattle the door thinkin' it's stuck 'cause of the dampness or something. Then the girl out there scampers back through here and yanks the cord, pulling the wedge back here, too. If the intruder hears it skitter across the floor, he'll think it's merely a rat. Got it?"

As I wriggle out of my burglar gear and back into my usual undershirt and drawers, I talk to Dolley and Clarissa, who both have come down to the work site. "We had a big scare there. It shows us we've got to cover our tracks better. There's some planking and saws over there, and I say the next thing we must do is make a hatch cover for the Rat Hole in case we are ever really inspected. We *must* do that, for if the Hole is discovered, we are lost."

"Good. We will do it. But won't they hear us sawing?" asks Dolley.

"We'll wait till we have a good rockin' blow, when the chains are really clashing against the sides, and then we'll time our saw cuts to that. *Clang!* Cut! *Clang!* Cut! We won't be heard. Every sailor is busy during a blow, be it a King's ship or a slaver. They won't be thinking much of us, I can tell you.

"And nobody is to go through the Hole to the storeroom for the time being, unless we three say so. Is that clear?" I ask, reaching over and placing my stern finger on the nose of the ever more adventurous Rebecca. All around us nod, including her, but I know I shall have to watch our Rebecca. She crosses her eyes comically, looking down at my finger on her nose, then giggles, curls up in a ball, and rolls away. *Hmmm...*

"Jacky," comes the soft call from high above, "bag down."

Bag?... Ha! It's gotta be our millers!

I jump to my feet and fly out of the Pit and up to the port-side forward watch station. Ruth Alden sits there, on watch, with an oilskin bag at her feet. A line from the neck of the bag extends out through the bars and beyond.

I pull open the top of the bag and a wondrous smell hits my nose. The spit pools in my mouth and threatens to spill out over my chin. I swallow hard and attend to business. I reach in and pull out a greasy parchment package. I open it and admire the gloriously roasted millers within. I wrap it back up, lay it aside, and say to Ruth, "Okay, now stuff those other millers in the bag!"

But she shrinks back, horrified at the thought of touching the six dead rats piled in the corner.

"All right, I'll do it," I say, bending to the task. "But I'll wager, Ruth Alden, that within the week you'll be smacking your lips over the arrival of these things!"

She shakes her head and looks greenish about the gills, but we'll see...

I give two tugs on the line when all the millers are stuffed inside the bag, and it jerks up and out of sight. Then I make for under the Stage, the package warm in my hands.

"Pass the word. We've got roast miller. Everybody can have at least a bite."

But it turns out that not everyone wants a bite. In fact, there are only four of us willing to try. The first one to plunk herself down next to me is Lissette. She sees the surprise on my face and says, "You English, you are always making fun of the French for the eating of the escargot and the legs of the frog. Eh, *bien.* Make fun of me for this, too, but I will have some meat."

We are joined by Rose, the farm girl, and by Katy, who crouches down on her haunches in the circle, while the rest of us sit cross-legged. I open the package and the two roasted millers lie glistening and brown in the dim light. There is a crowd of girls standing about us, looking down, fascinated.

"My shiv, please, for a moment." And my knife is passed over from the work site. I take it and cut each miller into six pieces—the two large rear legs, the smaller front ones, the back, and the chest.

Lissette has brought one of her cloth strips with her as a napkin, and this she spreads over her knees. Class always tells, don't it?

I hand a hind leg to Katy and say, "For the Huntress, herself, the first taste."

She takes a bite. "*Mmmm*," she says. "Yep, a lot like squirrel." Then she polishes off the rest of the leg and tosses the bones down on the parchment.

I give a leg each to Rose and Lissette. I take one of the small legs for myself and waste no time in getting one into my mouth.

"*Mmmmmmmm...,*" I moan. I strip the meat off with my teeth, chew slowly so as to savor it, and then swallow. I crunch the end of the bone where it is soft and suck on it. It is wondrous good. I can tell that Cookie had soaked the millers in vinegar overnight to take out the gamey wild taste, and he even put some salt and pepper on them. *Good for you, Cookie.* I don't forget kindnesses, no matter how small they are or who they come from.

"Like groundhog, too," says Rose, running her tongue over her now-greasy lips.

"Nobody else?" I ask of the crowd. No one says anything. "Very well, maybe next time."

There is a thump of knees and Clarissa is there next to me. She cuts a sharp look at Lissette, I guess for consorting with the likes of me. Lissette doesn't seem to notice. "All right, give me a piece," Clarissa orders. Count on her not to be left out of anything, no matter what. I give her the remaining back leg and she sniffs it, then puts it in her mouth. I watch her eyes and they almost cross in ecstasy.

I take up the knife again and cut the chest and back pieces into four small parts each, so we can better divide the remainder among us.

"Here, Lissette, try the ribs—ain't much meat but they crunch up real good."

"*Ummm*," she says in appreciation. In the near silence, we can hear her fine, wellborn teeth crushing the ribs.

"I could see this in some nice gravy," says Katy, chewing on her own bones.

"Some gravy yes, Kay-tee, but maybe also a fine Bordeaux, *non*?" says the French aristocrat to the raw frontier girl crouched next to her. I doubt Katy has ever tasted a fine wine like that, or any wine at all, for that matter, but she nods in reply. I think also that Lissette de Lise has never before eaten a rat, but, hey, I have tasted fine wines, as well as rats, and I, too, nod in agreement.

"We could call it *raton au vin*, eh, Lissette?" I say, and she laughs, then notices Rebecca crawling into the circle on hands and knees, looking at the remaining pieces. "Here, *ma petite*, try this," says Lissette, picking up a chunk of back and holding it under the girl's nose. Rebecca inhales deeply and then opens her mouth.

Well, that's six of us, at least, to divide up the three millers coming tomorrow.

Conversation ends and there is heard only the crunching of bones and smacking of lips and grunts of pleasure. Were it not for the fact that we do not growl and snap, we are like any pack of wild wolves around a kill.

Late that night, long after Storytime—wherein I told them some more about my wild roving in the *Emerald,* which got me some hurrahs from my more adventurous sisters and a muttered *"Not only a tramp but a thief, as well,"* from Constance Howell's direction—yes, late that night I found myself back in the storeroom for the sole purpose of trying that damned latch again. I had left word to be awakened at one thirty in the morning, figuring all sailors not on watch would be dead asleep by then. I felt my way down to the Rat Hole and found Hyacinth and Frances carving away. We lit the candle and in I went, my shiv in my hand. I stood and put the candle on the workbench and shielded the flame with a box between it and the door. Wouldn't want someone outside the door seeing a glow of candlelight around the edges.

I slid the knife through the door crack, next to the latch, and lifted up, hoping that maybe it was a simple up-and-down thing, but no...nothing. I pulled the door inward, and no, nothing. *Damn!...All right, calm down, you...*I next put the point of the knife on what I thought might be the metal slug of a cross-latch and tried to pull it sideways, bit by bit. Still nothing. *Damn!*

What I wouldn't give for a look on the other side!

I give up for now and go back through the Rat Hole. Tomorrow is another day, and I must content myself with that.

I crawl out of the Pit and climb back up into my kip, where I snug up next to Annie and Sylvie and Rebecca and so settle myself to bed.

Good night, Jaimy, I pray that you are well...

Chapter 34

Word of our progress has cheered the girls mightily and it is an eager bunch that gathers for breakfast after we stand down from Sin-Kay's inspection line, but my failure to loosen the latch last night does not cheer me. Ah, well…begone, dull care, I'll try again tonight. I go up and take my bowl of burgoo from Hughie.

"That's a real good story you're tellin', Mary," says Hughie. "I like it a lot."

"Thanks, Hughie," I say, reaching through and ruffling his hair.

"I think it's stupid," sneers Nettles. "Story about some stupid girlie jumpin' around with a pig sticker, thinkin' she's somethin' hot. But she ain't 'cause she's just a stupid girl and girls ain't good for nothing but one thing, and you know what that thing is, don't you, girly?"

"Sod off, Sammy, you stinking little snot-bag," I snarl back at him. I hand off my bowl to Rebecca and thrust my cup through the bars. "Shut up and give me my water."

"Tell me what that thing is, then I'll give you your water, Smart-mouth." He giggles and does not give me the water.

"Give me the water or I'll yell for Sin-Kay."

"All right, here's your water," he says, smiling at me. He dips my cup and hands it to me. "But now *I'll* tell *you* what girls are good for…"

And he proceeds to mouth a string of obscene fantasies starring him and me.

"…and then, after you do that for a while, I'm gonna—"

"You need your mouth washed out, boy!" I shout and dash my cup of water into his face. He rears back shocked, the water dripping down his face and onto his shirt. Then he lunges at the bars, his arms reaching through to grab at me.

"I'll get you, you little bitch!"

I dance just outside his reach. "No, you ain't, Sammy! You ain't gonna get me or anyone like me, ever! You know why? It's 'cause you're a disgustin' little slug what even your mother couldn't love! When did she throw you out? As soon as she saw your ugly face, I bet! And I bet she washed her hands three times when she saw the back of you for good!"

His face is against the bars, twisted with rage, and his fingers strain to get me, but they can't and he knows it. Finally he pulls back his arms and wipes off his face. When he removes his hands, the rage in his face has been replaced with one of low animal cunning.

"Hey, Smart-mouth, you like this here Dummy?" he asks, punching Hughie in the shoulder. He saw me give Hughie that pet before. I shouldn't have done that in his sight, I shouldn't have done it, I realize now with growing dread.

"He's a good boy. Leave him alone," I say, knowin' it ain't gonna do no good. He punches Hughie's shoulder again, hard.

"How do you like it when I hit your Dummy?" This time

he balls up his fist and bashes Hughie full in the face. Hughie cries out, and Nettles hits him again. And again.

I rush up to the bars. "Hit him back, Hughie, hit him!" I cry, furious with Nettles and with myself.

But Hughie does nothing; he just rocks back and forth, saying, "Can't. Mister said can't. Can't." And then he starts crying. He doesn't even hold up his hands to protect his face. Blood begins pouring from his nose.

Nettles keeps hitting him and looking over to watch my anguished, helpless reaction. I know what I have to do.

I turn away and say, "Wilhelmina." I catch her eye and look to the door. She nods and soon all Nettles can see is a wall of girls' backs as they eat their burgoo.

Having no audience, he soon tires of his sport, and with a final taunt of "How's that, Smart-mouth?" he leaves.

I weave my way through the wall of girls to the gateway and reach through and pull Hughie's weeping, bloody head to my chest, as close as I can, what with the bars between us.

"Don't you worry, Hughie. He's gonna get his," I say, and pet his curly hair. "He's really gonna get his, and it's gonna be soon, I promise you that."

Other girls join me in laying on hands and murmuring soothing sounds, and his crying slowly ebbs, then stops.

Later, when Hughie's all calmed down and is, in fact, asleep, I go down to check on the work at the Rat Hole.

All about me, in that space below the Stage, are hanging not only the petticoat strips from before, but now full petticoats and drawers because of the laundry soap I found in the storeroom. I push my way through them, and though dry, mostly, they are stiff as boards from the salt water in which they were washed. Well, better clean than soft, is the general feeling.

"How's it going?" I whisper when I reach the work site.

"Real good," says Annie, handing the shiv to Rose for her turn. "I'm sure everyone could fit through now, and we're squaring it off so it won't be noticeable from either side when we get the boards up."

"*Ummm*," I say, inspecting the job. "Right, the boards. I can't wait to get them up. We could be discovered so easily. The first blow, we do it."

I stand back up. Katy's over setting up the extra bows. There are girls about her, rounding off arrows with the file, then lashing down arrowheads and feathers. *Good.*

"Hooks down!" comes the call from above, and I roll out from under the Stage and into the Pit. The hooks come snaking down. I nod to Clarissa and to Rebecca, and they nod back. They are ready. Rebecca comes down with me to the tubs.

"'Ello, Mick and Kecfe!" I crow. "'Ow good to see your 'andsome, smiling faces!" We fasten the hooks.

"Never mind that," says Mick, "just get on wit' it."

"Now, now Mickey, it never does no good to rush a girl. You should know that, bein' a well-traveled man o' the world and all. First, the tubs, *then* the Main Event."

By way of answer, the tubs are jerked out of sight and return streaming with salt water, and clean. *Good boys.*

I undo the drawstring of my drawers and give them a bit of this...and maybe a little bit of that...I like to think that I'm being artistic-like about this whole thing, swirling about and all, and in a kind of dance—I sure would like to have some musical accompaniment, though, as that would really help the act out a lot. Maybe an *oud* and a *bouzouki* or two, and a *djembe* drum, like that time in Morocco when I...well, never mind. When I'm done and I pull up my drawers and pull down my camisole, I feel that I've given them their money's worth. I have always tried to do that when I am in performance.

That's usually the end of it, but today it ain't. As I'm buttoning up, I follow the gazes of the two men above me and see that they fall on none other than Clarissa Worthington Howe, who has chosen this moment to be sitting on the stairs leading from the Stage down into the Pit, washing her feet and lower legs. She does it very slowly and very carefully. When she gets to washing her upper calves, she rolls her drawers up over her knees...well up over her knees.

"Coo, look at that," breathes Mick.

"Eh, Jacky," says Keefe, "y'think that blondie there would ever do what you do?"

I look over as if surprised to see Clarissa doing her act on the Stage stairs. The act we had, in fact, rehearsed.

"*Wot?* Wot's the matter with me bum, then, that you want to look at others? I thought mine was lookin' 'specially pert and sassy today."

"Aye, it's looking right fine, it is. But...that blondie. Y'think she'd do it?"

"Ah, nay, Mick, she's much too pure and beautiful. If you were to see her bare arse, yer eyes would start out of yer head, and you'd be blind forever by the creamy goodness of it all, you would, and ye'd never be able to speak again. You'll have to make do wi' me scrawny butt," I say, my hands still on my waistband. And then I say, in a musing sort of way, "But y'know, Mick, she has lately been talking about takin' a bath, she has—half out of her mind with it, she is. Y'see, back at her castle—she is a princess, you know—she took a bath every day, twice a day in summer, and once a week in milk, and doing without here on the ship is about to drive her balmy, it is…So stick around, lads, she might give you a show yet."

Clarissa, pretending not to hear all this, gets up, stretches, and languidly goes up the stairs to the Stage, slowly rotating her hips.

"Ooooh, my…," says Mick and Keefe in wonder.

"Nay, nay, put it out of your heads, lads. Stick with a nice, easy lady like me," says I, looking for an opening.

It comes.

"Yer a loony, you are. Talking like that and showing yerself to us that way. You ain't no lady at all. Yer a loony," says Mick, disappointed now that Clarissa has taken her exit.

"Oi'm a loony? Here's a tub hauler what's a dead man callin' *me* a loony," I say, crossing my arms on my chest, apparently miffed by this exchange.

"What do y'mean by that?"

"I don't mind you seein' me bum. And me legs and all the rest. After all, you're dead men and dead men don't tell tales, so me rep-u-ta-tion will be spotless."

"And what do you mean by that?"

"Mick, Mick, Mick," I say, sadly shaking my head. "You poor, dumb bloke, you."

I pause, as if genuinely sorry over his impending fate, and then I press on.

"Y'know, Mick, I'm a Cockney, too, and I've always found that us Cheapside types was, by and large, pretty crafty and cunnin'-like. But you, Mick, you're bein' real dumb, you are. Do you really think you're going to be allowed to go back to America where you might snitch on Colonel Bart Simon about the kidnapping of thirty or so girls from the finest families in the United States? You see this little girl here?" Rebecca is by my side and has a big-eyed woebegone look on her face and her hands are raised as if in prayerful supplication. "She's Rebecca Adams, *President Adams's granddaughter,* for Chris'sake. Pres-i-dent, like, of the U-ni-ted States. Oh, you might have promised not to tell, all solemnlike, but Simon can't trust you not to get drunk sometime and spill the beans and put his neck in a noose, can he now? Nay, after we're all sold and settled and the Captain's got the money, you'll get your pay, you will, and it will be either a bullet in your head or a sword in your belly. And over the side you'll go. Think about what 'appened to Dobbs, now, hey? Aye, the Captain, Mate, Sin-Kay, and Chubbuck will be the only ones livin' through this voyage, that's for sure. And us girls in our harems, of course, eatin' grapes and pomegranates and sweetmeats, and lyin' about in hot, steamin' baths and havin' eunuchs towel us off after our swims."

"That's a load o' malarky," says Mick, sounding a bit worried, nonetheless.

"Malarky? How 'bout this for malarky? You'll notice that only them four coves I just mentioned got weapons? Swords and pistols and such? What've you got? Your little riggin' knives? Ha! It's pathetic, it is. You'll be gathered together and killed like sheep, count on it."

"Huh?"

"And think on this, Mick. The Captain's nasty little fancy boy Sammy'll still be mincin' about up here, whilst poor ol'

Mick will be lying dead down below with the crabs snippin' off his willie. Keefe, too."

"Snippin' off me wot?"

"Yer willie. You know what I'm talking about...yer privates, like."

"I told you not to talk to them bitches!" roars Bo'sun Chubbuck, coming up from behind and giving Mick one behind the ear with his club and then delivering another blow to Keefe. There are howls of pain and the hatch comes slamming shut.

Gotta pay for your pleasures, mates. And I know you'll be thinkin' of what I said.

Back under the Stage, I meet with Dolley and Clarissa to plot and plan. We all fear discovery now that we've come this far, and we cannot wait to get the cover boards cut and in place. At the same time we do the boards, we'll make a hidey-hole out of the niche where my seabag is stowed, so we'll be able to hide the bows and arrows there, too. We'd be in deep trouble if Sin-Kay or the Captain ever decided to do a real thorough inspection. I guess that sometimes it's best to be thought of as just a bunch of helpless, unresourceful girls.

Right now we've got enough laundry hanging down here to keep anybody who glances under the Stage from seeing anything, but if he looked real close...

"Bag down," comes the call from above. *Hooray! Let's eat!*

This time we have two more girls join us in the feast. After we're done and are licking fingers, Katy picks up her bow and goes hunting again. This time she has several girls with her, with bows of their own.

A while later, we have gathered six more millers, with hopes for more.

This evening, after a rousing *"Laudate Dominum,"* I resume my story. I'm getting near the end. I'm at the part where Jaimy and I almost come together as man and wife, there on the *Wolverine* after my capture. Without benefit of clergy, like. I know what's coming, but I tell it, anyway.

"I reached out an arm and pulled in Lieutenant James Emerson Fletcher by his collar and closed the door and threw the latch. Jaimy looked at me and I threw my arms around him and we both fell toward the bed and then we were in it and then..."

And then, sure enough, Constance Howell's enraged voice comes at me.

"She's going to do it *again!* No, no, no! I will not have it, and I will not have one such as her as the leader!"

I sigh and say, "I'm not the leader, Connie, you know that. There are three of us. I'm—"

"How can you stand there and say that you did that without shame?" she asks, outraged at my conduct then, and even more at my willingness to talk about it now.

"You've got to remember, Connie, that at the time, I was almost certainly going to be taken back to England and then, just as surely, hanged. So a little worldly bliss before the big drop, choke, and swing... Well, you may fault me for it, but I don't."

"I certainly do fault you for it and I want no more of your awful story. There are impressionable young girls here and...you...you're nothing but a common tart! You're nothing but a..."

The sound starts somewhere to my left, as a low *hmm-mmm*...first one girl, then another, then some more off to my right. Then more, and louder. The warning sound fills the Hold of the *Bloodhound*, thirty throats thrumming, throbbing, and full of menace, directed toward Constance Howell.

She is silenced. I believe she shall have no more comments on me and my ways.

When the *hmmmmm* dies away, and all is quiet, I start up again.

"*'Fill your eyes with me, Jaimy, and then kiss me, and kiss me hard and long, for it may be the last time.'*

"He does, oh, yes, he does.

"*'Now go, Jaimy.'*

"*And with one last feverish kiss, he does that, too.*"

I end it here for the evening. I do believe I hear more than one deep, heartfelt sigh out there in the dark.

Chapter 35

Another day. Flaps up, Sin-Kay down.

We line up, yawning and stretching.

Sin-Kay starts taking the roll, *Frazier…Goodwin… Hawthorne…Howe…*

Am I imagining it, or does he approach Clarissa's name with a certain dread?

"Heah, Mistah Stinkey!" is all she says, but there is a mischievous light in her eyes.

Sin-Kay moves down the line. *Howell…Johnson…King…*

"Eeny, meeny, miney, moe. Catch a Stinkey by the toe! If he hollers, let him go! Eeny, meeny, miney, moe!" Clarissa bursts out loudly in singsong, gaily bouncing on her toes. I think I hear some snickering out on the deck.

Sin-Kay comes back to face her. "You think that was funny?"

"Yassuh, Mistah Stinkey. I think it's *very* funny. Now, how funny you gonna think it is when my daddy catches you for what you done? Only he goin' to catch you by the neck, not by the toe, and I don't think he's evah, evah gonna let you go. Nope! Not till you're hangin' there dead, and bugs eat out your eyes."

"It is going to be *such* a pleasure seeing you up on the block," says Sin-Kay, then sighing softly. He goes on. *Leavitt... de Lise... Lowell...*

He gets to the end of the line, snaps his notebook shut, and leaves the Hold.

But Clarissa is not done with him this day, oh no, not yet.

After we all have had our breakfast burgoo and are handing our spoons and bowls back in, I'm noticing that Clarissa keeps looking up at Barbara Samuelson, who's on port-side aft watch.

"Clarissa!" she says. "He's back on deck!"

"Good. Caroline, come on!"

Uh-oh, I'm thinking. *What's going on?*

Both Caroline Thwackham and Clarissa Howe race up the stairs to the port-side Balcony and position themselves by the bars.

"You know what I was wonderin', Clarabelle?" asks Clarissa, loudly. Loud enough for anyone on deck to hear.

"What was you wonderin', Annabelle dear?" inquires Caroline, just as loud, back at her. It appears that the two have worked out a skit of sorts.

"I was wondering about our dear Mistah Stinkey..."

I go up on the Balcony and look out and see that Sin-Kay is standing by the rail, his back to us, his hands clasped behind him.

"You were?"

"Yes, I was, Clarabelle," says Clarissa. "I was picturin' him gettin' up in the mornin', jus' before he does his little ol' thing with all us adorin' girls."

"Yes?"

"I was thinkin' how he must get up from his feather bed,

317

from out of the softness of his damask sheets, all refreshed from his night's rest—"

"Havin' been sleepin' the sleep of the just, Annabelle, uh-huh."

"Even so, Clarabelle, I was thinkin' just that. Then I was thinkin' how he must rise up and put on his rare silken undergarments…"

"Uh-huh."

"Then he pulls his fine hose over his legs and then puts on those fine, fine britches."

"Uh-huh, I can see him doin' it," says Caroline, who's turning out to be quite the comic actress here. *Best be careful, both of you. I'm beginning to worry about this. You've pushed him enough, Clarissa. Pull back!* But she won't…

"Then he puts on a crisp, clean, frilly white shirt with all that Italian lace trimmin'…"

"And then?"

"And then he puts on that fine deep purple coat that all us girls admire so much…"

"And then?"

"And then he puts on his fine French cologne…a lot of it, splashin' it all around."

"And then?"

"Maybe a little powder here and there…"

"And then?"

"And *then* he looks in the mirror," says Clarissa, and her voice has grown hard.

I'm keeping my eyes on Sin-Kay's back, and I've been seeing his head sink lower and lower between his bunched shoulders. His neck is swelling over his collar. *Don't do this, Clarissa!*

"And then?"

"Why, Clarabelle," says Clarissa, "he looks in the mirror and his shoulders slump and then he moans, 'For all my finery, still just a nigra...'"

Oh Lord.

Sin-Kay turns and heads for the hatchway. In a moment he is down the stairs and the key is in the lock of the gate. I fly back down to the Stage, just as he bursts into the Hold. I can see that he is enraged beyond all reason. He spies Clarissa on the stairs to the Balcony, lurches toward her, grabs her by the hair, and drags her squealing to the gate.

He pulls back her head and snarls into her face, "That's it! You're going over the side! You will be dead within minutes!"

With that, he drags her up the stairs, yelling to Hughie, "Get out of the way, you idiot!" and Hughie, terrified, stumbles back out of the hatchway.

"Nettles!" shouts Sin-Kay, as he and his screeching burden go out the upper door. "Lock the gate!"

Nettles starts to swing the gate shut, but I'm on a dead run toward him. The gate is two inches from closing and locking when I hit it with my shoulder, rocking Nettles back against the wall.

"Help me!" I shout, and slam him again with the gate. Katy and Rose and Chrissy are at my side. "Get him again!"

We pull back the gate and smash it against him. And then again. He is stunned, but still he manages to struggle out from behind it. I leap in front of him and lift my knee and get him in the crotch. He coughs and doubles over. *That's one for Hughie, you miserable little toad! And here's another!*

Nettles crumples to the floor, gasping.

"He's done! Come on, we've got to help her! Katy, you stay here and watch our stuff." She knows what I mean and nods. "Kill anyone who spots the Rat Hole!" Again she nods, then heads down to the Pit, no doubt to arm herself.

"Everybody else," I shout, "out of the Hold! Scatter about the ship! Make them haul you back! Climb up the rigging, scatter all around the deck, but don't go down below up forward and don't let anyone take you down there! Got it? All right, let's go!"

And the ladies of the Lawson Peabody School for Young Girls pour out of the hatchway, with me and Dolley in the lead.

Bursting out into the light, I see that Sin-Kay intends to do as he says. He's got Clarissa bent over the rail. He has gripped her hair in his left hand, and with his right hand he has grabbed the seat of her drawers and is preparing to pitch her over the side.

Dolley and I both dive at her and grab a leg each.

"Please, Sir," I wail. "Please don't kill her! We'll make her be good from now on, we promise!"

It doesn't seem to be doing any good. Sin-Kay seems intent on throwing Clarissa over the rail and into the sea. I catch a look at her face and she is no longer squalling—she is just staring down at the churning waves below, looking, in fact, at eternity. It is a look I've never before seen on her face.

Dolley and I tighten our grips on Clarissa's legs. *Just hold on, Dolley, just hold on!*

There is the sound of boots near us, and I know it is Captain Blodgett.

"What the hell is going on?" he bellows.

"This one is going over the side! We have to make an example of her!" answers Sin-Kay, his chest heaving with the exertion of trying to heave Clarissa overboard.

"Like hell she is!" roars the Captain. "She's worth at least ten thousand dollars! I ain't seein' *that* go over!"

"We'll take it out of my share! Get over, you! Let go!" He hauls back and gives Dolley, who's on the left leg, a swift kick in her belly. She grunts, but does not let go.

"Your share, hell! Simon wanted this one especially to go up on the block!"

"This is *my* cargo, Captain, and *I* will decide what *I* will do with them."

"Your cargo? *My* ship, Sin-Kay, and never forget it! And now, oh Christ! Damn! They're all out now!"

I look to the side and see white-clad forms scattering everywhere about the ship. *Good girls!*

"This one must be punished!" says Sin-Kay, his furious face in the Captain's equally furious face.

"Punished? You want punished? I'll give you punished!" shouts the Captain. He strides to the mast and snatches the Cat from its hook. Lunging back, he shoves the butt of it in Sin-Kay's face and forces Clarissa out of his grasp. Sin-Kay staggers back to the rail. I nod to Dolley and we both let go our grip.

The Captain drags Clarissa over to the hatchway and stands her up. He swings the Cat and catches Clarissa across her upper legs. She screeches and he lashes her again and yet again and then pushes her down the hatchway. "*That's* punished. Now get the rest of them back in *now*! All hands! Catch them and put them down!"

I watch my sisters *whoop*ing and *halloo*ing about the

ship, and I grab Dolley's hand and say, "Dolley! Go down in the Hold, and as the girls are caught and sent down, line them up in the inspection line so's we can account for all of them. Some sailor may try to spirit one away!"

She nods and heads down, sorry, I think, to be missing the fun, but ever mindful of her duty.

Me? I head for the bow and the hatchway that I know will take me down below to the crew's quarters and beyond. Before I duck in, I take a belaying pin from its rack at the rail and stick the clublike thing in my waistband.

I clatter down the ladder. On the right I see the open area where the men would swing their hammocks at night and on the left is the galley, still not cleaned up from breakfast. Behind me is the chain locker, where the anchor chain rests when not in use. *Ha!* There's another ladder, to the lower level, and I waste no time in clambering down it.

It's a lot darker on this level, but enough light comes through the hatchway that, as my eyes become used to the gloom, I can see well enough to get around. Here's a room to the right. I open the door and see that it's a storeroom... for food, mostly—there's flour spilled on the deck and stacked firkins, which I guess are for lard and such. I close the door and go farther down the passageway. Another storeroom to the left and then—*ah*—then there's a door with heavy leather curtains hanging in front of it: *the powder magazine!* I pull the leather aside and see that the door is secured with a heavy, strong lock. Well, I expected that...I mean, what Captain wouldn't lock up his powder? Especially one who denies weapons to most of his men. Well, there's more than one way into a room, and not just through the door.

What I wasn't looking for was a great piece of luck, but I find it nonetheless: Right next to the magazine I see a door with a latch. I lift the latch and poke my head in and—*Oh, joy!*—it is our own dear storeroom! I close the door and study the latch and find that it is really quite simple—it's got one slug that swings over and down, and another that swings from the other side over on top of that one. I'll need my shiv and another piece of metal of some sort to hold up one lever while I'm lifting the other one. But I'll be able to manage that easily with the tools in the storeroom.

All right, now to trace my way out. Since next time I'll be doing it in the pitch dark, I'd better take careful notice. First, it's out the storeroom door, to go straight for one, two, three, four paces to the ladder. Next it's up the ladder, eight steps, feel the top landing, then twelve paces to the next ladder. *Remember this now, you.* The door to the anchor-chain locker is behind that ladder, another six paces.

I'm about to go back up this ladder into the light to join in the melee, but there's a commotion at the top. I duck back into the galley and peek around the side.

Hmmm...It's a sailor, one I recognize as the scummy cove who asked Blackman Bart Simon for the use of the serving girls on that first day when we were taken. I guess that thought was never far from his mind, 'cause he's sure got one now. He's got Annie Byrnes, with one arm round her waist and the hand of the other arm over her mouth. She is struggling mightily, kicking out with hands and feet, clinging to any handhold to prevent herself from being taken down. But he is twice her size and she is going to lose the fight.

I don't know where he's planning to take her...Ah, he has gone under the ladder, so it is to be the chain locker. *Not a very soft bridal bed for our Annie, you cur,* I think as I come round with the belaying pin and lay it hard on the back of his skull. He pitches forward, clutching his head and groaning. I swing back and hit him again. This time he does nothing but slump down.

Annie crawls out from beneath him, breathing hard.

"Come on!" I say. "Let's get you back in the Hold! You've been handled enough!"

Brushing her hair out of her eyes with the back of her forearm, she follows me down into the bowels of the *Bloodhound.* We reach the storeroom door, I open the latches, and we go in and close it behind us.

"The Rat Hole is over there. On your hands and knees, now, follow me."

I feel her hand on my ankle as I crawl toward the Hole and then through it—and stop cold. I feel a sharp point against my temple and I know it to be an arrowhead.

"Katy!" I hiss. "It's just me, Jacky. And I've got Annie, too."

The arrow is withdrawn and we go out into the gloom below the Stage.

"What's happening?" I ask Katy.

"Dolley's checking 'em in up on the Stage as they're tossed down. About half of 'em are back."

"Good," I say. "And great news, Katy! I've found—"

"Uh," says Katy, "one thing... That girl Elspeth. She went up, too, and she ain't been back."

I suck in my breath. *Damn!*

I can't go back the way I came, 'cause I can't take the time to fiddle with the latch. Straight out of the Pit and across the Stage and up the hatchway is the only answer, and I do it, pushing my way up past the girls who are being shoved back down the stairs. When I reach the top, I see Keefe holding a struggling Barbara Samuelson and I slide past him, avoiding the grip of another sailor who tries to catch me. Momentarily free, I look frantically about me and... *There!* On the port quarter! She's got one leg over and is looking down into the water. She lifts the other leg to bring it over. There is no expression on her face.

I rush to go there, but I am grabbed by a seaman I do not know.

"Keefe!" I shriek. "Drop that one! Go get the girl back there!" I've managed to free one arm from the sailor's grasp to point at Elspeth, teetering on the rail. "She's gonna jump!"

Keefe looks, drops Barbara, and bounds across the deck. He reaches his right arm around Elspeth's waist just as she launches herself off. He swings her back aboard and gathers her up.

He puts her into the hatchway just as I am thrown there by my own guardian sailor. I put my arm on her shoulder and reach up to Keefe and squeeze his hand and say, "Thank you, Keefe! You've just lessened your time in Hell for that!" I strain my neck upward and plant a kiss upon his bristly cheek, and then I am forced down into the Hold with the rest.

The inspection line is still being formed under Dolley's supervision. I put Elspeth in her place and go to find Constance Howell. Sullen and seething, she is standing to the side and brushing off her arms as if they are unclean. "I have never before been handled in such a way, *never!*"

"Well, offer it up, Connie, and consider that you have done your duty," I say, but I ain't done with her yet. I reach over and take her by the arm and pull her along with me, ignoring her protests.

"What are you doing?" she cries, and tries to wriggle free, but my grip is too strong.

"You are being assigned another duty, Constance Howell, and this is it." We have come to stand over Elspeth, who has crumpled to the deck. "I just saw her try to kill herself. We cannot let that happen. You are to counsel this girl. Comfort her. *Pray* over her. You are to teach her that it is a sin in our religion to kill yourself. Will you do that? Will you bring your faith to bear on this matter and save this girl?"

There is tumult all around us. She could jerk her arm away from my hand and go back to her place. But she does not. She merely nods and crouches down and puts her hand on Elspeth's shoulder.

I look to the others. They jabber happily away with, "I have never been pawed in such a disgraceful way before!" or "It took three of the brutes to corner me!" and "I fetched that one a good kick that he won't forget!"

Clarissa lies facedown at the edge of the Stage, the knuckles of her left hand between her teeth. She stares off into the Pit. Whether she is thinking about how close she came to death or whether she is remembering the sting of the lash, I don't know. All I know is her eyes lift and meet mine and an understanding passes between us.

I nod and turn to the others. "All right," I say. "Is everyone all right?"

They all own that they are, yes, all right and have survived their adventure above decks in good order.

"Is everybody back?"

"Everybody except Rebecca Adams," answers Dolley quietly. The place falls silent.

Lord. I head for the hatchway but I know I ain't gonna be able to get back out. *Oh, Rebecca...*

Just then the outer door opens and Rebecca Adams comes tumbling down the stairs to land on her hands and knees at my feet.

"I got all the way to the top of the highest mast before they got me," she exults. "And I was the last one caught! So, there!"

PART III

Chapter 36

It ain't been three days since the breakout, but things are moving right along.

The very night of that riotous day, we were blessed with a spirited gale that set the ship to rocking and the chains to rattling. We worked through the night on the Rat Hole cover, a whole gang of us down there under the Stage, marking off and sawing the boards to fit. As planned, we timed the saw thrusts with the crash of the chains against the sides. *Clash/thrust!* Pause...*Clash/thrust!* and so on through the dark hours. Whilst the work was going on, and it was not my turn at the sawing, I crept over to try the storeroom door. Using my shiv and a thin file, I was able to open it easily. *That's enough for now,* I thought, as I closed it back up. *No sense in rushing things. We must lay some more groundwork in the way of, well... the highly developed sense of the superstitious in the common sailor.*

Being able to figure out the workings of the latch and see the layout of the forepart of the ship from the other side of this door made the indignities suffered on that day well worth it. I get with Dolley and Clarissa and plans are made and we begin to carry them out.

Three boards stacked one on top of the other do the trick for the Rat Hole, with two screws on each board end to hold them in place. A crack in one of the massive knees of the ship is a perfect hiding place for the screwdriver, 'cause we'll need that close at hand when the time comes. The hidey-hole takes more time, since we've got to hide not only my seabag but five longbows and many arrows, as well. We rest much better, though, knowing this has been done.

In the ensuing days, we keep up our strength with a steady supply of freshly roasted millers. Ever since Katy first killed those millers, four more girls—Christina King, Hermione Applegate, Minerva Corbett, and my sturdy Rose Crawford—have shown themselves to be keenly interested in the bows and what they can do, and they are constantly at their new study. We do not lack for freshly killed rats.

I meet once again with Clarissa and Dolley and we talk it over and decide to go directly into the powder magazine from our side rather than through the side of the store-room, which would have been easier because the wood is thinner there, but there would be more risk of discovery. I have a better, quicker way of getting through than with our old carve-with-my-shiv method, now that we've got access to the tools in the storeroom, but we decide to be cautious and make the covering boards before we make a single cut in that direction.

We set a new watch at the edge of the Balcony to alert us if anybody is coming down, so we will have time to get all boards back up should there be a surprise inspection. The girl on watch sits on the stairs to the Stage, keeping an eye on the gate. Should any of the crew unlock that gate and look to be coming through, that girl will loudly wail *"Oh, Lord, save us!"* which would alert the others to start milling about and acting like hysterical females, fainting and falling about and throwing themselves in the way of the approaching intruders. We practice this over and over again till we get it right. It is rather fun, and we get into giggling fits over it. We are getting ready. The time is coming soon.

Last night, after the story, which I'm just about done with, we all settled in, had the hymn of the evening, and those who say 'em said prayers.

Now I give Rebecca a nudge with my foot and she sits up and loudly recites, "Oh, Jacky! I'm just so scared!"

"Scared of what, dear?" I ask in return.

"I...I think I saw a ghost last night...Down in the Pit!"

There is a common gasp from the girls...and a few deeper ones from outside the flaps.

"Come now, Rebecca. We're all Christian girls here and we do not believe in ghosts."

"I know, I know...," she goes on breathlessly. "But I saw it, I really did. It was a little thing, all thin and dark...like a skeleton, only black. It was sitting against the side and it had a chain around its neck and it was moaning...like, 'Oooooooo...,' and it was rocking back and forth and had its face in its hands and kept going, 'Ooooooo...'"

"Stop it, Rebecca," orders Clarissa from across the way. "You're just upsettin' everybody. You didn't see nothin' of the kind. Just your silly imagination."

Rebecca starts crying, and I can feel her shoulders shaking. "Noooooo," she wails. "I'm sure I saw it. It was all black and scary, but it had like a red glow all around it, that's how

I could see it in the dark! And there was a smell...a smell like Hell is supposed to smell! Like sulfur...like brimstone!"

"Now, Rebecca," I say, as if trying to placate the poor girl.

"No, I saw it. And I just know it's the poor lost soul of one of those poor slaves who died on the way over in this awful Hold! This awful, awful Hold!"

I put my lips down next to her ear and whisper, *"All right, Rebecca, you little hambone, that's enough. Don't overdo it."*

But she has one more thing to say. "And...and as I watched it, it got up and walked right through the side of the ship! I know it's trying to find its way back to its home, and it can't, oh God, it can't! It's just so sad!"

There are some cries and whimpers from the other girls, just as we had all planned.

Now, let's see how *that* sets with the crew.

Chapter 37

It's a very subdued Mick and Keefe who come for the tubs the next morning. I'm sure the ghost story has gone through the ship like grain through a goose, and I'm equally sure they've been jumping at the sight of their own shadows, 'cause I know sailors, and right now this ain't a happy bunch of swabs, that's for sure.

"What's the matter, Mick? You ain't your usual jolly self today," I say as the clean water tub hits the deck. I give 'em their bit, thinking that we'd better leave soon, as I ain't got all that much left to show. Clarissa lolls about the Stage in plain view as before and it doesn't escape the crew's notice. We're probably the only bit of joy in their lives right now, I figures.

Mick doesn't say anything to that. Keefe just grunts.

"Cheer up, lads, the voyage will be over in a couple of weeks and you'll be either rich...or dead," chirps I, bouncing on my toes and grinning up at him.

"You stop wi' that, you," growls Mick, and the hooks are jerked up and out and the hatch slammed shut.

Well...that was a bit of all right, I'm thinking with some satisfaction. We had set up Rebecca's ghost story last night for a couple of reasons: One, to further put the crew on edge, and two, to cover for me when I go out into the ship in my burglar rig. I *have* to go out to do some things, and if I am spotted, I want them to think that I'm the Black Ghost. At least that's what I'm hoping, because I've got to go out there tonight.

But that's for later. For now, it's down to the work site.

Measuring the distance from the Rat Hole to the starboard side of the storeroom, we figure out that the back bulkhead of the powder room is centered about eight feet to the right of the Rat Hole. What we are confronted with there is plainly strong, thick slabs of wood set up between massive cross-braces, and it is there that we decide to go through.

After we make the covering boards to cover our mischief, I trace out a two-foot square on the planks with some carpenter's chalk I had found in the storeroom. Then we take a brace-and-auger with about a half-inch bit and drill a hole in the upper left corner. The good thing about the drill is that it doesn't make noise like a saw does. Leaning on the back of the brace and turning the auger, I feel it break through at about two and one-half inches. *Pretty thick,* I think, *but we do have time on our side.* When I pull the bit back out to start the hole in the opposite corner, I notice that there isn't just sawdust in its grooves—no, there is a blackish powder as well. I quick put my tongue on it, and sure enough, that old familiar smell and taste of sulfur and saltpeter—gunpowder! We are into a bag!

"No more candles when we're working around here or we'll all be playing on our harps up in Heaven," I say to the work party on duty. "No, we'll have to do this job in the daytime, but it should be quick—we'll drill a hole in each corner, then halfway between each and then halfway between each of those and so on till we've got a bunch of holes with only little bits of wood connecting them, then we'll run my shiv down and across and that square of wood'll pop out nice as you please. We'll keep the same work rotation as before, but you must switch the brace back and forth a lot—it's easy to get a blister doing this and we don't want that. All right? Let's go!"

While they're drilling, I meet with Clarissa and Dolley and tell them, "I figure we'll be into the powder magazine in a day or two, so I've got to get some things done tonight."

"What is it you have to do out there?" asks Dolley.

"Well, I have to see just how things lie. First, I'd like a look at the stars, to see how far south we are. It's clear out, so I should be able to get a good notion of that from the height of the North Star above the horizon. Then I need to pace off the entire escape route. And I'll want a look into the lifeboat we'll be taking—the one on the starboard side—to see what it's got in the way of food and water. I suspect none, but we've got to know. Also I've got to check out its rigging to see how it will be lowered. Hughie is simple so he's got to be told very plain how to do it when it comes to that. Lastly, we're going to have to disable the other lifeboat, so they won't be able to chase us down in that. I won't disable it now, though, 'cause it might be discovered. It'll be one of the last things we do."

Dolley nods, as does Clarissa. I look over at Clarissa and study her face. She has been quiet in the inspection line lately, as we have encouraged her to be. Sin Kay has run his inspections very quickly, very sullenly, clearly smarting over the treatment he got on the day of the riot. It is now very clear that he, too, wants this voyage to be over. Clarissa doesn't talk much about that day, that day when she, too, felt the bite of the lash. She did not complain, she did not cry that day or night, but I noticed that the next day she cut a three-foot length of the bow cord and tied it loosely around her waist, so that it would always be at her hand.

We break up the meeting and I stand in the Pit and look about me. The drilling proceeds at the work site. A troupe of girls dances on the Stage, both for exercise and to cover any noise we might make below. Katy and the four girls she has chosen as fellow ratters sit below the Stage and work on their equipment before they head back out on the hunt. Dorothea has taken to calling them the Dianas, and soon everybody is. All the watches are at their stations—at the hatchway, on the Stage, and four on the Balcony. All is as it should be, all is in train.

That night, I end my story.

"*. . . and the last I've seen of Jaimy was him standing at the rail of that ship, looking out at me as I steered the lifeboat and myself away from the scene of battle and my recent captivity. A burning hulk of a ship comes between us and I saw Jaimy no more.*

"You all know the rest—how I came back to Boston and to the school. And here I am, as we all are."

I bow in the darkness and am gratified to hear the applause as well as more than a few stifled sobs.

When it dies down, I hear Hughie say behind me, "That was a good story, Mary. Now can you tell me one about how we used to be back with Charlie and the gang?"

Hmmm... I think on this. Storytime has been good for the morale of the girls, and what else can fill the time till we go? The girls all sense that it will be soon and they're getting jumpy. Can't have that.

"All right, Hughie," I say. "We'll do that tomorrow night. For now, let's everyone get some sleep."

Sleep for them, but not for me. Not much, anyway. When I'm awakened by the watch, at two in the morning, I disengage myself from Rebecca and Annie, stand, stretch, and head down to the Rat Hole. I'm already dressed in my burglar gear and have my shiv tucked in my belt. Sally Anderson and Beatrice Cooper were awakened a half hour earlier. They light the candle and open the Rat Hole for me.

"Oh, Jacky, do be careful," whispers Bea, placing her hand on my arm.

"I will be. You just be careful with that candle. Snuff it out as soon as I go through. Leave the screwdriver right next to the bulkhead, so when I get back I can put the boards up by feel. Then go to bed. I'll be all right."

I go through the Rat Hole and the light is snuffed out behind me. I feel my way through the darkness, to the door. There is no crack of light beneath it now, but that is good. I stand and put my shiv through the doorjamb and feel for the lever. When I've got it, I slide the thin file in above it and lift. Then I lift my shiv and the door swings open. I pull my watch cap down over my face.

I put both knife and file back in my waistband and step out into the passageway, turn right, and pace four steps to the ladder, my hands out in front of me. I touch the ladder and go up the eight steps. I stop and listen. So far no light, no sounds. When I reach the next level, I can see a faint glowing from above. That would be moonlight filtering in through the top hatch, it being left open on this calm night for what little air it can bring down to this stifling deck. I start the twelve steps along to the ladder leading out and go by the crew's quarters and hear them in there snoring in the hot, fetid dark. *Worse than the Hold,* I'm thinking, and that place is tough to beat when it comes to stink. I pass the galley on my left and climb the ladder to the blessed outside.

I pause there to take several deep breaths of the pure, clean air, and to look up at the starlit sky, something I have not seen for a long, long time. It is so quiet that I can hear my heart pounding in my chest at the sight of it all. The moon is rising clear and bright in the east. How I did miss seeing the majesty of the heavens wheeling about me in the night...Well, enough of that. On to business.

I creep out of the hatchway and onto the deck and slink over to the cover of the anchor capstan—the huge, horizontal winch that, with the aid of eight big men on the capstan bars, pulls up the anchor when need be. By craning my neck, I can see most of the deck from here.

There's no one up forward, which is surprising to me— on a Royal Navy ship there was always a bow lookout, no matter what the conditions. The fact that I am alone up here gives me courage to pad across the deck and to peer around the hatch that houses us girls in the Hold, and to look back at the quarterdeck. I see three men there, the first being the helmsman, intent on steering his course by the compass and not looking at much else, and two others, sitting on the edge of the quarterdeck. As I am watching, one of the men

340

gets up, stretches, and then heads for the bow, as if to make an inspection. *Hmmmm...*

I hunker down, out of sight, and watch his progress. He goes up to the foot of the bowsprit and sits himself down with a grunt.

I crouch low in the rigging and make myself observe intently for a full half hour to make sure no others are about. The man on the bow sits quiet for a bit and then I see his head slump forward on his chest and deep snores are heard. He's fast asleep, the lazy sod. *Some lookout,* the Royal Navy part of me sneers.

While I sit here, I look up at Polaris and see that it is about thirty degrees off the horizon, like one-third of the way from straight out level to straight above. A look down at the water with its islands of floating seaweed slipping by confirms my suspicions—we are in the Sargasso Sea, that region of the Atlantic above the trade winds and below the prevailing westerlies, that strange sea that is feared above all others by superstitious sailors, and there *is* no other kind of sailor. Stories of ghost ships, and of ghastly apparitions, and of other weird, unexplainable things fill their tales of this place, tales they tell one another in their dark holds at night to feed one another's darkest fears. I suspect the Captain decided to come this way because most ships avoided the Sargasso like the plague, but he would risk it to escape detection. But the sailors don't like it, I know they don't. And that could be good. *Very* good.

I head for the starboard lifeboat.

I first check out the davits—those hooked-over crane things from which the boat is hanging. A hook goes to the bow and another to the stern, and lines run from those hooks up through the davits, to two small winches—the winches that Hughie will have to release to lower the boat. It will take some strength and I will have to drill him on it, over and over.

Now for the boat itself. Staying close to it, I feel around for how the canvas cover is attached. There is a single line, about a half-inch thick, that runs through grommets on the canvas and then around small cleats on the rail of the boat. Grommet, then cleat, grommet, then cleat, and so on along the whole length. It is not lashed all that taut, probably 'cause they want the canvas loose enough to catch as much water as it can when it rains. Good. That means the first girl to the boat—and right now I'm thinking it'll be Dolley—will be able to get the cover off easily, so's the girls can tumble right in.

I pull the line off the cleats to loosen up the canvas enough so's I can throw a leg up and over and climb in the boat. I lie there quiet for a while and then get up on my elbow and look about. Enough moonlight is coming in so I can see that there's three sets of oars. The mast juts up through the canvas cover and the sail boom is attached to it. I can see that it's a simple sloop rig, with a main and a jib. I'd have preferred a gaff or cat rig, but we'll get along with this. From asking around, I've learned that two of the girls, Hyacinth and Cathy, have some sailing experience, them being taught pleasure-sailing by their dads and brothers, so they will be the second and third in the boat so as to get the sail up and the boat ready to steer away. There's the main halyard right there...and the downhaul...and the mainsheet neatly coiled. Somebody on this godforsaken bark knows his job.

I crawl forward. There's a small cuddy up at the bow—more like a cowling, really, since it ain't got a hatch, but it should still prove useful. I feel around some more. Nothing. No tins of biscuits, no skins of water. Well, we'll see what we can do in that regard before we go.

That's all that can be done tonight. I must get back.

I leave the lifeboat and re-lash the canvas. I creep back across the deck to the forward hatchway and I see that the so-called lookout is still asleep. If caught, that snooze would have gotten him an even dozen lashes in the Royal Navy, and that's in peacetime—during a time of war, maybe even a noose. Here, he just slumbers on.

I can't resist.

I pad over to the port-side lifeboat, unsecure the canvas, and crawl inside. Might as well at least start the disabling of this boat, I'm thinking. I feel around and find the boom and the mainsheet coiled beneath it. The mainsheet is a line that goes up to a pulley on the boom, and it is used to trim the sail. Why it's called a *sheet* rather than a line is beyond me, but, hey, a lot of maritime terms don't make any sense. 'Cept to us sailors, of course.

I pull out my shiv and cut off the mainsheet, right at the boom. Then I sit there and tie a special knot in the end—what you do is make two loops in the line near the end and then whip the bitter end around them and end up by pushing the end through the loop that's left and pulling it tight by opening up the opposite loop. If you whip it around three or four times, it's called a slip noose, but if you put eight turns on it, ah, then it becomes Old Jack Hemp—the hangman's knot. I whip it eight times.

I crawl back outside and rerig the canvas. There is no

sound, except the creaking of the rigging and the snoring of the lookout. I check to make sure that no one else is about and then I creep up behind the sleeping man and gently place the noose over his head and softly place it down on his shoulders. He snorts but does not wake up. I don't have to tighten it—this will do fine.

Time to go back to the Hold. I go to the hatch and down the first ladder and along the passageway. There's the galley...and I peek in. There are portholes on the side and enough moonlight comes in that I can make out a teakettle on top of the stove. *Oh, for a cup of tea...*My greed overcomes me and I tiptoe over to it and pull off the lid and stick my nose in. *Ahhh...it's still warm, it's—*

Uh-oh...Someone's coming! Footsteps are coming from the sleeping berth!

I put back the lid, drop to the floor, roll under the stove, and hold my breath.

A man walks in and I hear him strike a flint, then a lamp is lit, flooding the room with light. I see his feet shuffling around not two yards from me. He grumbles and I hear him opening the stove door and shoving in sticks of wood. The fire within starts to crackle. There's more clattering of metal cups and pots and two more sets of feet come into the galley.

"Tea up yet, Cookie?" comes a thick voice.

"Arf a mo', Mick," says Cookie, which in Cockney means *in a minute.*

"Um," says Mick, settling himself down on a bench. I scootch as far back under as I can. "Bloody watches, disturbing a man's sleep for no reason. Out in the middle o' the goddamn ocean."

I can see Mick's legs and knees from under the stove—if he took a mind to bend down, he could see me as well. *Damn! I could have been back in my kip by now if I hadn't—*

"Is that Carruthers up yet?" asks a voice I recognize as Keefe's. "He's s'posed to be on helm."

"I give 'im a shake," says Mick. "That's as close as I'll get to that cove."

"Tea's up."

"Thanks, Cookie."

There is the sound of tea being poured into tin cups and slurped. Then there is a sudden movement and a face bends down under the stove to peer at me. I stiffen, but it is not a human face, no, it is the face of a very curious cat. It comes up to me, nose to nose, and sniffs.

Nice pussy, I mouth silently as I stroke the fur on her back just in front of her tail, that spot where all cats love to be scratched. She purrs...*Not so loud, pussy, please...*

"What's to eat?"

"Just some johnnycake, is all, and don't complain. I do what I can."

"Well, let's have it, then." Sounds of munching. *Oh, what I would do for some johnnycake,* I think, drooling in spite of my precarious position.

Another set of feet enters the room. "Gimme somethin', and be quick about it," the owner of the feet growls, and there is more rattling of mess gear. Keefe's own feet move to the other side of the kitchen. I think I recognize the growling voice. "Damn head still hurts from where that bitch hit me. If I ever find out which one it was, I'll kill 'er, don't care what the Cap'n says, the filthy sod." Yep, Carruthers is the cove who tried to nab Annie, for sure.

Cookie chuckles, then says, "Prolly was that Jacky girl, I'll bet. She's a real pistol, she is." It's plain that Cookie ain't afraid of Carruthers like Mick and Keefe are. Every ship has to have its bully, and I'm thinkin' this bloke is the *Bloodhound*'s very own specimen of the breed.

"She'll be a dead pistol if I get aholt of 'er. I wouldn't even do 'er before I kilt 'er. Just take a club and smash 'er bleedin' head in, see 'ow she likes it done to her," he says.

"Now, now, Eben," says the cook, "then she wouldn't be able to do her little dance now, would she?"

There follows a lively discussion of the charms of my various parts that makes my face flush under the watch cap. *Men, I swear…*

But not all seem to appreciate my essential loveliness.

"I seen 'er do her little act. Warn't worth watchin'… scrawny little midget," says Carruthers, rather uncharitably, I'm thinking. "Now that blondie, if she ever does somethin' like that, you come and tell me quick or I'll kick both yer asses."

"Jacky did say that blondie was itching for a bath on the deck. Coo, wouldn't that be somethin'. Make this damned trip almost worthwhile," says Keefe.

"*Jacky* is it, now?" sneers Carruthers. "Sounds like our Keefie 'as made himself a little friend."

"Jacky ain't so bad," says Mick in my defense. "Just wish she hadn't said that thing about the Captain killin' us all when we get over there. And me poor body in the water and all…I ain't afraid of dyin' 'cause a seaman's a fool if he don't know that 'e might end up down there wi' Davy Jones someday…But when she said that thing about the crabs nippin' off me privates, well, that made it real personal-like...Wrecked me slumbers, it has."

"What thing did she say about the Captain killin' us?" demands Carruthers. I'm surprised he didn't know yet. *Shame on you, Mick, for not planting my little worm of doubt more quickly throughout the crew.*

"She said that the Captain planned on killing us when we got to Africa so's we couldn't blab about taking these high-toned girls and get Simon and the rest of 'em hanged. Said the Captain and Dunphy and Chubbuck was the only ones on board with guns and swords to do the killin' when the time came. That's what she said."

"*Hmmm...,*" says Carruthers.

"And that girl sayin' she saw a black ghost walk through the side o' the ship last night. I ain't had a peaceful moment since, I ain't," whines Keefe. "This is me and Mick's first time on a slaver and we both vow it'll be our last, if we lives through it."

"Yer both a pair o' cowardly scrubs, y'are, afraid o' yer own shadows," says Eben Carruthers, his voice full of scorn. "But the thing about weapons, well, we'll have to see about that."

The cat chooses this time to give out with a loud *meow. Damn!*

"What you got under there, Jezebel?" asks Cookie. "A nice fat rat? Let's see..." He starts to bend down for a look.

"*Yowwwwwweeeee!*"

There is a shriek from outside. 'Tis plain the lookout has awakened to find his special neckwear, and none too soon, neither. Cookie straightens back up and all four men pound out to see what the matter is.

I roll out from under the stove, grab a piece of johnny-cake, and start to head back down to the bottom of the ship and safety. The traitorous Jezebel carefully arranges her paws beneath her and watches me go, without further comment.

Sally and Bea have waited up for me, and together we get the boards back up in no time at all.

"Here," I say, finding their hands and passing each of them a piece of the cake.

"What is it?"

"Johnnycake. Not enough to divide with the rest. Consider it a small reward for your constancy."

"Ummmm."

Chapter 38

Lt. James Emerson Fletcher
The Pig and Whistle
State Street
Boston, Massachusetts, USA
June 17, 1806

Miss Jacky Faber
Somewhere on the Atlantic Ocean

My Dearest Jacky,

I take comfort in writing these words to you in the hope that
you will someday read them and excuse my poor, stiff prose. I
am a seaman and not a man of letters, as you well know.

Here are things as they now stand:

Higgins continues to be the rock upon which we place all
our hopes. He is tireless in his investigations of your disappearance and has actually come up with even further proof
that a kidnapping occurred, as opposed to a tragic accident.
He called upon me one day not long past and bade me to

accompany him again to view the evidence held at the court-house. I shall put it in his words:

"You, see, Sir, most of these purses, which undeniably be-long to some of the girls"—the sad, sodden purses and shawls and other personal items were lined up on a shelf in the base-ment of said courthouse—"have one thing in common. They are open, and they were open when they were found. I know, because I was here when they were brought in. Now, in the past, I have been in service to a number of families, and there is one thing I am sure of: When a woman or a girl finishes re-trieving something from her purse, she snaps the clasp shut. Highborn or low, lady or servant, it does not matter. Almost all of these purses were open—as if rough sailors, ordered to strip them from the girls and throw them overboard as evidence of the young ladies' destruction, could not resist opening them to see if they contained anything of value."

As I have said, Higgins is invaluable. A keener mind I have never before encountered. It is very lucky that he is here in this place, for aside from his investigations and observations so far, he was instrumental in averting a true injustice. I know that it would distress you to know this, and perhaps it is fortunate that you do not—Mistress Pimm was brought up on charges.

She was taken before a Court of Inquiry concerning the loss of virtually her entire student body and placed in the Dock of the Court. Many of the parents of the lost girls are so dis-traught that they felt they must find someone to blame for the tragedy. It is to Mistress Pimm's credit that she stood there, black-clad and silent, her face composed and her back ramrod straight. She then told her story in a firm, unquavering voice, but it was not enough. The parents, led by those of one Elspeth Goodwin, demanded more, and John Higgins ascended to the

Dock and gave it to them. He meticulously stated the case, fact by fact, supporting his certainty that you and your companions were kidnapped by dastardly slavers and were not dead. With Higgins's testimony, Mistress Pimm survived the ordeal, and the parents, I believe, were given some hope.

Higgins has observed me writing these words to you and has asked that I send you his best wishes and hopes that you are keeping yourself safe and not being overly impulsive. I told him I believed the last of his wishes to be a vain hope, and he was forced to concur.

Henry Hoffman is now based in New York. He has established lines of communication to all the mid-Atlantic ports and waits eagerly for news. It is my devout hope that his waiting is not in vain. General Howe continues to scour the southern ports and seas for word of his daughter and the others.

Randall Trevelyne comes often to The Pig to inquire after any news, and we have taken dinner together many times. It is easy to see why you were attracted to him, and believe me, Jacky, I am not stupid. I know you were drawn to him, so do not say nay—he is polished, well-mannered, has an excellent singing voice, and is self-assured in all social settings. Though he is rash and impulsive, he cuts a gallant figure—he is, as the Bard would have it, "the glass of fashion and the mold of form"—in short, everything I am not. He is quick to take offense and has drawn his sword on more than one occasion. But not against me—rest easy, Jacky, as we are friends. He talks of his impatience to get into battle, and I try to disabuse him of this notion, but he is obstinate. He cannot seem to get it out of his head that you, a mere female, have been in combat many times and that he has not. I point out to him that your being in grave danger in those situations was just an unfortunate *string of events, but he feels that this in no way exempts him from the necessity of being tested in battle. It is equally unfortunate on a global scale that things are heating up between our two countries and that Randall and I, who now sit and eat and drink together, could yet end up on opposite sides of a great battle, each trying to kill the other. Why we, the British and the Americans, who share a common language and heritage and who are so much alike, must find reasons to fight each other is astounding to me. Stupid politics is all it is, and beyond my understanding. In any case, as regards Randall Trevelyne, if, indeed, you do make it back to us, I will let you choose and not hold you to your former promise.*

Your Most Affectionate and etc. . . . etc.,

Jaimy

Chapter 39

We are into the powder magazine. All the holes had been drilled, right next to each other on the lines of the traced square, and I took my shiv and cut down through the few splinters that were still holding the wooden square in place, and it fell forward into our hands. Carefully putting it aside, we now look in, but since I have forbidden candles near this spot, all we can make out in the gloom under the Stage are fat bags of powder crowded up next to the newly named Powder Hole. Some of them appear to have been punctured. To the side of the bags is darkness.

Hmmm, I say to myself, *let's see what else is in there.*

First things first, though. "Bea, get me a rag. That's one of mine hanging right there. Thanks."

Of course, there's rags and petticoats and drawers hanging all about down here under the Stage, drying from their last cleaning, but I can't take anyone else's stuff. I gotta say, though, as I sniff the rag that is handed to me, the laundry soap we got from the storeroom has gone a long way in helping us stay neat and tidy.

I rip my rag in little strips and use them to plug up the holes that our drill bit has made in several bags. I get the nearby girls to scoop up the powder that had spilled on our side and then we dump it back into the magazine, as we can't be caught with any of that stuff over here. Cups of salt water are brought up from the clean tub and the residue washed away and down through the slats. Good. All clean, and maybe the rats will like the flavor.

That done, I feel around the bags and find that there is a more open space to the left side. I reach my hand in and freeze. I have touched something smooth. It feels like a metal canister of some kind. Could it be a bomb? An explosive shell? I pick it up very, very carefully and bring it out into the dim light.

It's not metal at all. It is a bottle, and on it is a label. I read it and a grin spreads across my face. "Hey, Mam'selle," I say to Lissette, who is crouched nearby, at my left hand. "Do the words *Côte du Rhône* mean anything to you?"

She comes over on hands and knees to gaze in wonder at the wine bottle. "Ah, *mon amie,* I was born there," she says in wonder and joy.

We take two more bottles from the stash and place them in Lissette's lap for her to lovingly run her fingers over them—it's plain that the Captain chose to store his wine there in the most heavily locked space on the ship, where no one could get at it. *Right…*

We then close the safety boards over the Powder Hole and take down the boards from the Rat Hole. I'm about to go through, when Katy leans down and whispers, *"See if'n there's any glue in there. If there is, get it and bring out five more of them battens."* I nod, knowing Katy well enough not to question her. I go in with a candle and the wedge for the door. I stand up, stick the wedge under the door, and look around. First, I find what I came in for—the smallest auger, to use as a corkscrew—then I look about for glue. On a low shelf, there is a pot with a brush handle sticking out of a slot in its cover. I pick it up and sniff. Sure enough, it's rabbit's-skin glue—and fresh enough, from the smell. I grab five more battens and shove everything through, then take myself out, pull the string to retrieve the wedge, and put the boards back up.

As if on cue from the stage of one of Mr. Fennel's and Mr. Bean's theatrical productions in Boston comes word from above...

"Bag down."

There are eight fat millers in this batch. We whisper the news of the upcoming feast from girl to girl, and thirty-two tin cups are brought down and placed in a row. I pull the first cork and pass it to Lissette. She sniffs it and her eyes roll back and she nods and sticks the red end of it in her mouth and sucks on it. *Ummmm...* Funny how that word is the same in both French and English—or any language, for that matter. I've even heard dogs use it to express joy and contentment.

I pour a bit into each cup till the bottle is empty and then do the next bottle—it's a Burgundy, but I don't think the girls will mind the blend. Finally the last, another Côte du Rhône, and each girl has almost three ounces in her cup.

There is yet another treat: I had gone out last night for just a short run across to the other storeroom in the lower passageway, the one that held the ship's basic foodstuffs. I felt around in the darkness and found what I suspected was a tin of soda crackers and brought it back with me. I was right in my suspicion. We'll take some of these with us in the boat, if we can, so there will be something in the way of food—I hadn't yet figured out a way to carry water, though, and that had worried me, but not anymore.

I retrieve the tin from the hidey-hole and count out two crackers for each girl and place them beside each cup. There are six girls on watch—one at the gate, one at the edge of the Stage, and four lookouts on the Balcony. Their shares are put aside till they are relieved.

I replace the tin in the hiding spot and put the empty bottles there as well. Dolley has my shiv and has cut up the millers into small parts. Many of the girls now partake of the nearly daily feast.

"All right, now," I say, then hands reach out and soon nothing is heard except gasps of ecstasy over the fine wine and the common crackers and the crispy, crackly miller meat.

I take a sip of my wine and let it sit on my tongue for a while before swallowing, my eyes closed. *Oh, joy...* I let out a small moan and have a bite of cracker and another tiny sip. *Ummmm.* I snare a choice miller back leg and make short work of that. I know my sisters would agree with me that this is truly the very finest of feasts.

Pausing in the glory of my gluttony, I notice Constance Howell kneeling and holding her cup and looking in at its contents. I can see that she is struggling with herself.

"Go ahead and drink it, Connie. God hasn't put that wine before you to tempt you. He has given it to you to sustain you," I say to her. "Consider it a sacrament, 'cause that's what it is."

I'm thinkin' of bolstering this argument by reminding her that Jesus, His Own Holy Self, had poured a good deal of the fruit of the vine down His Own Holy Neck during His tour of duty on Earth, and even changed some water into wine to make up for a lack of it one time—at a wedding, I think it was.

But I don't have to. She takes a sip, then gets up, collecting her crackers and the cup and crackers next to hers. I know they are for Elspeth and I thank her for it, silently, of course, for I know that Connie Howell doesn't want to hear anything in the way of moral guidance from Jacky Faber, that's for sure.

The luncheon is finished. We ate and drank in a leisurely way, at the same time knowing, however, that if we heard a *Lord, save us!* from above, we would have had to dump everything in the necessary tub to escape detection, but it didn't happen. We cleaned up, disposed of the few bones not chewed up and swallowed, and got down to the work of the day.

In addition to the ongoing classes in French, Dance, Science, and Chorus, there is now a class in Fundamentals of Sailing, conducted by the Misses Catherine Lowell and Hyacinth Saltonstall, the two girls who have actually sailed a small boat before. I keep my nose out of it, listening only for any dangerous falsehoods, but there are none. The girls come down in groups of six to receive instruction. I have given Cathy and Hyacinth pencils and some pieces of paper and they have faithfully drawn diagrams as to the various "points of sail" and they carefully describe how the sails are set depending on how the wind is coming at the boat. Everybody knows this backing up of skills is in case anyone, me or Cathy or Hyacinth, is knocked out of action, so that others will be able to take over the navigating of the boat. It's not often mentioned, but casualties can be expected when we make our break for freedom.

The only time I interrupt the Sailing sessions is to give some pointers on rough-water sailing, as I know neither Cathy nor Hyacinth has experienced that: *You've got to take the seas on either side of your bow, or either side of your stern, but not direct on. If you go direct on to a wave with your bow, it'll dive down under it and you'll take on water. If you let a high wave take you directly astern, you'll be swamped. If you are swamped, do not panic, as panic is your most fearsome enemy. First, drop the sails... then everybody get out of the boat and cling to the sides—the boat will still float—and start bailing with the cracker tins we will have in the boat till the gunwales come out of the water. It will be discouraging work and you will despair of success, but it can be done. When the water level is down far enough, one by one you can get back in the boat to help bail. Got it?* They have it.

So while the pounding of the heels overhead in the Dance class continues, so does Katy's work with the bows. After today's hunt, she has taken the battens I got the other day and glued one each inside the five bows already made, and set them aside to dry, making them twice as thick as they were before. Twice as thick and twice as strong. "The others were all right for the rats," she says to me, "but for killin' men, we're gonna need stronger." I don't dispute it.

I look back as I leave Katy and her girls at their work, there under the cover of the Stage. Chrissy, Hermione, Minerva, and Rose have bonded into a tight-knit group centered about the solemn Katy. They took my shiv and cut their drawers off short and now roll them up to the tops of their thighs for better ease of movement. They wear headbands of the white cloth, the tied ends of which have been dipped in blood, whether rat's blood or their own is not known. They have taken to keeping to themselves when not on some duty. They squat in a circle and speak low, if at all. Who knows what vows have been taken and sworn.

I gaze about me at all the instruction and industry that is going on and reflect that we have a full curriculum, and I think Mistress would be proud.

Enough of idle speculation. Back to work, you.

With the help of Sylvie and Judy, I take down the safety boards covering the Powder Hole. Again, I reach into the darkness to feel about. There're the bottles, and there are a lot of them—probably piled all the way out to the door that's locked on the other side. That's good, 'cause what we take from this end will not be missed, and if it is, it'll likely be blamed on some hapless sailor. I can't get in any farther.

"Here," I say, "let's take down some of the bags from the top. Maybe I can crawl over them."

We do it, ever mindful of a *Lord, save us!* from above. When four bags are out and stacked, I again try to crawl over the top of the piled bags in the powder magazine, and I manage to do it. But what my questing fingers find is more bags and more bottles, and nothing more—not what I was look-ing for, at any rate. I crawl back out and spy Dorothea Baxter.

Sylvie and Judy put back the boards as I take Dorothea aside.

"Go get Ruthie and meet me back down here." Mystified, she goes and does it. Ruth Alden soon ducks under the Stage with Dorothea by her side.

"There're no fuses in there. We'll have to make our own," I explain. "We'll keep one bag of powder in the hidey-hole. Ruth, you're our best with the needle—we'll need a long, thin tube made of petticoat cloth, tied off at regular inter-vals, like a long sausage, only instead of meat inside, there will be powder. Dorothea, you'll need to experiment to see how fast each segment of our fuse will burn—try to get it to one second each. I figure it'll take one hundred seconds from when the last girl goes through the Rat Hole till we get everyone in the boat and the situation on deck dealt with. Got it?"

Ruth nods, secure in the knowledge of her skill, but Dorothea asks, "What of the smell of the burning powder? What if one of the crew gets a whiff and questions it?"

"That's why we planted that smell-of-brimstone thing in the Black Ghost story. We can blame it on that if anyone says anything."

"Ah," says Dorothea, "we'll get right on it."

"Sylvie," I say to the two at the Powder Hole. "Before you put the top board on, let's pull out a bag."

That set in motion, I go and get my seabag from its berth. I reach in and get my last pencil and my dwindling sheaf of paper and sit down on the deck under the Stage and compose a letter.

REWARD

*A sum of Fifty (50) dollars American will
be Paid to the Person who finds this Bottle and
delivers it and its Contents to:
Mister Ezra Pickering
Union Street, Boston, Massachusetts, USA*

My Dear Ezra:

We of the Lawson Peabody School for Young Girls are not dead of drowning or anything else. We were kidnapped by Bartholomew Simon, known in Boston as Mr. Harrison, and his Cohorts, for the Purpose of selling us in North Africa as Slaves. Those men should be apprehended and punished as soon as possible so they will be able to do no more evil in the world. We do not wish this sale of our Persons to happen, so we have made plans to gain our freedom.

Please do not worry about us, as all of us are well and in Good Spirits and most Hopeful. Your prayers, however, would be most welcome.

Personal notes are enclosed.

*Sincerely,
The Girls of the Lawson Peabody
(Mistress Pimm's Girls)*

I rip up most of my remaining sheets of precious paper into thirty-two small squares. Then I call all who are not on watch down to listen to me read this, and when I am done, I say, "Each of you will be given a scrap of paper to write a note to your families. You have the afternoon to compose your message, but since we have only a few pencils, it's important that you have your note composed before you get the pencil. Although I have quill and ink, I think it best that we write these in pencil, because moisture could seep into the bottle. We will be sending only this one bottle because of the danger in getting it to the water. I, for one, intend on beating it back to Boston."

There is a small cheer, and though I know all will set to work with joy at the prospect of communicating with their people back home, I know also that many a tear will trickle from many an eye and drop off many a nose before this particular job is done.

Well, we've had our treats today—it's about time we gave one to the crew. The lookouts have been alerted to let me know when the Captain, Dunphy, and Chubbuck are out of sight.

"Jacky," comes the call from above and I leap up into the Balcony, accompanied by fellow members of the Royal Bloodhound Theater Company. I look around at the deck and am gratified to see that there are many of the crew about—there's Keefe and Mick and a few I know to see but not to name. *That's enough,* I think, and give Caroline Thwackham the nod, and she starts it out, speaking just loud enough to be heard on deck, without being too obvious.

"You know, Jacky, when I was looking out through the bars yesterday, the ship took a big roll and I was able to see the water, itself..."

"So?" I ask. It's true, we're usually not able to see the surface of the sea close at hand, because we're down so low.

"So, I saw big clumps of seaweed in it. I know you've

been to sea before. Don't you find it strange, us being so far out?" I chose Caroline for this because she did such a good job in Clarissa's little skit on the day of the Great Riot.

Dorothea takes her cue. "Mr. Sackett says there's a place out here called the Sargasso Sea. He showed it to us on his globe. Could that be where we are?"

My turn. "Oh, no, dear, we couldn't be in the Sargasso— no sane Captain would think of bringing his ship and crew through there."

"Why not?" asks Caroline.

"'Cause it's a horrible, haunted place, is why. There're all sorts of sailors' tales of ships getting hopelessly becalmed and entangled in mossy seaweed, to become ghastly derelicts, rotting away in the tropic sun, covered in slime, their crews long dead of thirst and disease and far worse than that, even." I'm noticing out of the corner of my eye that the crew on deck have stopped their work and are listening.

The fourth member of our little cast of players picks it up.

"I don't know if any of you know it, but my family is in the shipping business in Boston," says Julia Winslow. "About six years ago one of my father's captains came back from a voyage with a very strange story. It seems his ship, the *Amazon*, was sailing on the edge of that Sargasso Sea one day, when his lookout spotted a ship on the horizon. As they drew closer, the Captain put his spyglass on the ship and saw that it was one he knew—it was the brig *Marie Celestine*, which had recently sailed out of Boston, bound for the Lesser Antilles with a full cargo of trade goods. On board was Captain James Boggs, his wife, and young daughter, and a crew of twenty-five."

Julia pauses for breath and then goes on.

"Closer and closer the *Amazon* got to the *Marie Celestine,* and the nearer they got, the stranger things became. They saw that the ship's sails were not trimmed, they were just flapping loose in the breeze. Then they saw something that made their blood freeze—*there was no man on the wheel!* The helm just spun around, back and forth, aimlessly."

Again she pauses—the men on deck draw in closer to us. I make a little sign to Julia that she can lower her voice. She does.

"The Captain of the *Amazon,* suspecting that it might be a plague ship, sends a man over in a rowboat to the derelict, that man having survived smallpox once and therefore being immune to the disease. He boards, goes below, and soon reappears, waving for others to follow. They do and this is what they find: The cargo is intact. There is no sign of struggle. The lifeboats are still in their davits. Tables are set in the crew's mess, and food is left on the plates. The captain's table is set for three. The silverware is where it should be. Nothing is awry, but"—now Julia lowers her voice to a harsh whisper—*"there is no one aboard, not one single soul!"*

Caroline and Dorothea gasp, and I think I hear some sharp intakes of breath from outside.

"The only thing out of the ordinary found on the *Marie Celestine,*" Julia concludes, "was a string of seaweed at the door to the crew's berth."

"*Brrrrr…*" Caroline shivers convincingly, despite the heat of the Hold.

"*Brrrr* is right," says I. "It was four years ago when I was on the *Dolphin* and I first heard that story, and I heard lots of others about the Sargasso since, and none of 'em good. Listen to this..." The others lean in to listen, and I believe I have the full attention of the crew as well. "There was one cove on the *Dolphin*, Snag Thompson being his name, who sailed through the Sargasso one time and he told me things, which he swears are all true. He said that sometimes the seaweed gets so thick, a ship can hardly push through the mess, and the weed is this sick, gray-green color, like the skin of a corpse. He said he heard tales of ships brought to a stop, entangled in the stuff and never to come out, their crews sufferin' horrible deaths and never seen again. It's said that the Sargasso weed gets into a man's very blood and takes him over complete, till he ain't a man no more, but a monster."

"Oh my," breathes Julia. She really is just the gentlest thing and is totally believable in her distress.

"That's what he said, and I believe 'im, 'cause he was a good and honest mate of mine. He said he heard that it started with a man's feet—the first sign was if a man's feet started stinkin' real bad—and then the weed would start to grow between his toes, then over his feet and ankles, and then up through the vein on the inside of his leg and by then it was too late. You could try to rip it off or cut it off or shave it off but it warn't no use—the weed was in your blood."

All four of us grab a foot and bring it up to our nose to sniff, and although I have smelled sweeter things, I shake my head in relief, as do the other girls.

"Right, and that ain't all," I say, pressing on. "Snag knew a bloke who saw this with his very own eyes. They were becalmed one night in the Sargasso, and it was dreadful hot and steamy with thick fog all around, and late in the midwatch they heard a scratching at the side of their ship and they got a lantern and held it over the side and the fog blew off for a second and they saw something they knew would stay with them to the end of their days. There, on a wet and soggy seaweed raft, sat this heap of a *thing*—it was no longer a man but plainly had once been one. It was covered, head to toe, with the vile weed, and the only thing left vaguely human about it was its open mouth pleading with the sailors to end its misery. Which act of mercy they could not grant, the fog having enclosed everything once again in its moist and choking embrace."

"Lord...," says Caroline.

We are silent for a moment, and then I speak up again.

"Julia, do you know whatever happened to the *Marie Celestine*? The ship itself, I mean."

"My father says it was towed to some southern port and painted black and renamed, for no sailor would set foot on that brig again...and...Good Lord! You don't think that this ship could..."

We let it go at that, and just then Chubbuck provides for us a curtain to our little play, by roaring up and telling the men to get back to work and being very free with his club.

The Bloodhound Players manage to get down below the Stage before collapsing in fits of muffled laughter.

"Can you imagine," I chortle, lying on my back and pumping my hands and feet in the air for joy, "them down there tonight smelling each other's feet!"

After a while we subside, but it's hard for me, what with visions of Mick and Keefe sitting down in the galley, gravely pulling their toes apart to inspect what might lie between.

"Well played, all," I finally say, getting up and hugging Caroline and Julia and giving Dorothea's hand a squeeze. "Now, back to our duties."

I reflect that someday I may try my hand at playwriting.

The girls are done writing their personal notes now and I gather them up and tightly fold them together in packets and slip them into the bottle. While the eyes of most of the girls are moist as they pass me their notes, Clarissa's are bone dry as she hands me hers, saying, "If you are thinkin' I wrote some sentimental twaddle like the rest of you, you are dead wrong. All I did was kindly ask my daddy not to hang that Bartholomew Simon till I got back as I want to be there for the festive occasion. I plan on packing a picnic lunch and enjoyin' it hugely while watchin' that scum swing." I have no doubt that is exactly what she wrote.

I take up my scrap of paper and sit down to write mine.

Dear Jaimy,

Remember that girl you said you liked and wanted to marry but you thought was drowned in a boat accident? Well, she didn't. I'm still alive and kicking at this time. If you get this without seeing me, though, you'll know that our plan of escape failed and I am either passed on or in some sultan's harem, dressed in veils and baggy pants and smoking a hookah.

Ha. Ha. Just kidding. Really, though, Jaimy, if I don't come back, I hope you have a happy life and will think of me sometimes, fondly. I am, your girl always,

Jacky Faber

With that, I snort back a tear of my own and stuff the note into the bottle. I know that this could just as easily wash up in a Spanish port as an English-speaking one, so I ask around to see if anyone knows any of that language. None do, so I just write the one phrase I know, *"Mucho dinero,"* in the margin of the main letter, with dollar signs next to it and an arrow pointing to Ezra's address. That should do it. I stuff this letter in last, so it will be read first.

I press the cork back in, ram it home, pound it down level, and then light the candle and drip wax over the end of the bottle till it's got a good thick cap of wax. I shall mail it tonight.

The flaps have fallen, Chorus is over, and I stand in the middle of the Stage in the total darkness.

"All right," I say. "Hughie here has requested that I tell some stories about when him and me ran with the Rooster Charlie Gang in London. Some of you know that I grew up there in that gang, and that there were six of us—Rooster Charlie Brewster, the leader, our Hughie here, then there were Polly, Judy, Nancy, and me. I was maybe nine at the time and called Little Mary because of my size, but I was not the youngest one, not by a long shot. That honor fell on the shoulders of Polly, our beautiful little angel, she of the golden locks and big, round blue eyes, eyes as blue as the sky, who had wandered one day into our kip under Blackfriars Bridge, her thumb stuck firmly in her mouth, saying nothing, just standing there waiting. We took her in, as I had been taken in, years before. She was our best beggar."

I clear my throat. "Here goes…"

THE DRUNKARD STUMBLED out of the Admiral Benbow, weaving slowly from left to right. He fell once but got back to his feet, real unsteady-like, and headed down Tudor Street...I'm peekin' round the corner of North Bridge Street, with my good stout Hughie at my side. Charlie's on the other side with Nancy, and he signals to me to hold back. Judy and Polly are in the alley next to them. We have been waiting for hours for one such as him to come out.

The drunkard stops, sways for a moment, then his head goes back and he falls forward on his face. Charlie says, "Now!" and we're all out and on the drunkard in an instant. As follows our usual way of doin' things, Charlie goes straight for the purse, whilst Polly and Judy pulls off the boots. Next Hughie flips him over and I start unbuttoning his coat and vest. Then I undo his pants so's Nancy can pull 'em down and off. "Hughie! Sit 'im up!" I say, and Hughie does it. I strip off his coat, fling it to the waiting Judy, who's collectin' all the stuff. I'm workin' on the vest when I hear Charlie say, "Damn!"

I look up from my labors and see two shadowy figures have joined us. My heart goes into me mouth, but it ain't the police, no, it's two of the Shanky Boys, the gang who owns the turf on the east side of ours.

"This 'ere drunk's ours," says the taller of the two.

"Like 'ell," says Charlie. "He's down on our side o' the line, so 'e's ours. This ain't Shanky turf."

"Our turf's where we says it is and I says this 'ere's our drunkard, so get off him. His hands are lyin' on our side."

I leap up and stand on the back of the fallen drunk and spit out, "You bugger off, Turkle! His purse is on our side, so 'e's ours!" Turkle's this wormy cove with bad teeth and smells a lot like Sammy Nettles of present-day renown.

Charlie whips out his shiv, the blade gleaming in the moonlight. Hughie comes up behind him, growling and ready to do damage. The Shankies retreat.

But before they do, Turkle points his finger at me and says, "One of these days, Little Bleeding Bloody Mary, we're gonna catch you wit'out Fee-Fi-Fo-Fum there, and then you watch out!"

"Eat dirt and die!" I spit at their backs.

We finish the job on the drunk and head back to the kip. We'll certainly eat well tomorrow from what we have earned today.

But that was just the start. The great Street Urchin Turf War was on...

Chapter 40

Clatter, clatter. The keys are rattled and the gates are opened and Sin-Kay enters the Hold, and we climb down off the Balcony, groggy from slumber, to line up in the inspection line once again. The roll is called and we answer and Sin-Kay uses his riding crop to lift a few shirtfronts.

First he does it to Bea Cooper. "*Tsk, tsk!*" he says. "Still too many ribs showing. I see no appreciable weight gain, and that is not a good thing."

Then he skips four girls on the right, including me, to land on Dolley. He raises the front of her shirt, then says, "Ah, now there's a fine one to grace a sultan's bed! Good work!" Dolley stares straight ahead and says nothing. "How about you?" he demands of Martha Hawthorne, two down on the right. "How are you coming along?"

I put the back of my hand in front of my mouth and yawn and say, "If you want to fatten us up, why don't you just give us two good biscuits instead of more of that foul grease? We'd keep it down better. Half of us are throwing up that greasy garbage you give us." We have, of course, been turning the grease into rat—er, *miller*—bait and it has been very effective.

He turns and walks over to stand in front of me.

"Ah, Lady Smart-mouth, I had thought we'd hear no more from you since your experience with the lash."

"It only seems reasonable, Sir, " I say, "if you want us to fatten..."

"Um," he says, "we'll see. How did your back heal, by the way? Turn around and lift your shirt."

I turn around, reach my hands back, and flip up my shirt.

"Good," he says, laying the tip of his riding crop on my back. "No scarring. Captain Blodgett was most skillful in his application of the whip. Just that one little raised welt there. It should not affect your salability. You may cover yourself. Nettles! Calm yourself!" I drop my shirt.

He moves on to leave, but another voice is raised. I look over at Clarissa, but the voice is not hers. We have forbade her to say anything else to Sin-Kay, for her own protection, and she has done her job on that score. It rankles her, and she seethes, but she holds her tongue. I have noticed that when she is at inspection, she tucks the cord that she now wears around her waist down into her drawers so it cannot be seen.

No, it is Constance Howell who says, "Mister Sin-Kay, I would like to request a Holy Bible."

Sin-Kay snorts. "But that is the holy book of the Christians, if I am not mistaken, and you are going to have to learn a whole new religion soon, my dear. Why bother with that nonsense?"

I can see that Connie is struck to the core by that blasphemy, but she collects herself and pushes on.

"I am trying to give help and solace to one of our number who has fallen into deep despair. I believe a Bible would help me in that regard. She will be of little use to you in her current condition."

Sin-Kay walks over and plants himself in front of Elspeth, who stands with head down, her hair hanging over her face. Connie has at least washed Elspeth's hair and neatened her up some, and I have commended her for it. The hated blue ribbon is still in the tangle of her hair, though. Clarissa has demanded that it stay, and no one has said nay to that.

"This is the one, then?" asks Sin-Kay.

"Yes."

"Very well. If such an item as that *Bible* exists on this ship, you shall have it."

He then turns and leaves.

Hmmm, I'm thinkin'...*He sure is in a good mood today. Prolly 'cause he's contemplatin' his upcoming payoff.* Counting his chicks, as it were, before they are sold. *Well, you are right in that,* Jerome, *for your payoff is indeed coming soon.*

We're down below and Dorothea and Ruth have set up their first fuse experiment. They have a three-foot section laid out along the underpart of the Stage, well away from the Powder Hole. It is very like a long, thin sausage, about a half-inch thick, with the links being about eight inches long. Where the links are pinched in, the fuse is only about a quarter-inch wide. That is so all the powder doesn't collect on the end when lifted.

We are ready to light and time it.

"But won't it explode?" asks Rebecca, looking on, wide-eyed.

"No, dear. Gunpowder only explodes if it's contained— like in a pistol barrel or a rifle or a bomb...or in that magazine there," I explain. I ready my flint striker. There is a small pile of loose powder next to the end of the fuse.

"Rebecca. Back up top," I order. She reluctantly goes out and up on the Balcony, but she still keeps an eye on us down below. She is to be there if any of the crew on deck happens to smell the burning powder, in which case she'll go into her *Oh-Lord-I-just-saw-the-Black-Ghost!-Oh-Lord-please-save-me-from-the-demons-of-Hell!* act yet again. We all have our duties.

I strike the flint and the spark lands on the loose pile. It flares up and the end of the fuse catches. Dorothea points her finger to the burning part of the fuse and follows it along as it burns, counting, "*One one hundred, two one hundred, three one hundred, four...*"

When the fuse burns to the end of a link, the burning slows down as it hits the constricted pinch between the links, and then flares up again... *one hundred, five one hundred, six...*

"All right," says Dorothea, and she pours the cup of water she had at hand over the fuse to extinguish it. "It looks like it's burning at a rate of six inches per second, with a slight pause between the links."

"So, it's easy then," I say. "Six-inch links, with a little bit of leeway between 'em. So make a fuse with a hundred links."

"We'll need cloth," says Ruth, looking about at the strips of rag hanging above her.

I get up and go for my seabag. I reach in and pull out a tightly wadded bunch of cloth. Clarissa is seated near the Rat Hole and looks up as I toss it to Ruth.

"Will that do?"

She catches it and opens it up. It is the red petticoat that once was placed on my bed back at the Lawson Peabody.

"It will do just fine," says Ruth, snickering. She and Dorothea set to their work.

Clarissa says nothing, but only smiles to herself and stares off into the distance.

Somewhat later, I sit with Dolley and Clarissa discussing the state of things. I recount to Dolley how I went out last night and dropped the message bottle gently into the water. It went in with a tiny *plop,* not enough to alarm anyone, as it sounded like a small fish jumping. Not that any man of the watch was on the bow. No, they were all huddled back on the quarterdeck, very glad of each other's company in light of all the scary tales that have been told. *Stand by, mates, there's more to come.*

Clarissa already knew about me going out last night, as she insisted on going with me partway. She maintains, and rightly so, that all three of us should know how to get out of the outer storeroom door and up to the next deck. Tomorrow I shall set the wedge and take Dolley, and then Katy, for they will be the first ones out. As time allows, we will show some of the others.

We are discussing these things when we hear the call, "*Lord, save us!*" and we freeze and look about to see that all is concealed. Then we hear, "*Nettles, with a book,*" and we relax.

In a moment Constance Howell comes down to see us, the Bible clutched to her breast.

"Now that we have this precious jewel, I would like to have a time set aside each day for a reading of several passages," she says, breathlessly.

I look at Dolley and Clarissa and they both shrug, and I say, "Of course, Connie. How about at three forty-five, just before the flaps come down? We will have had our dinner and the scriptures shall give us further sustenance. You'll know the time from the bells."

She nods and turns away.

"Bag down!" I hear as she walks away. I smile in anticipation and go to open our wine cellar.

It is fifteen minutes till four in the afternoon and we have had our afternoon burgoo and water. Our water, however, is not totally drunk—no, each of us pours a portion of our water ration into an empty wine bottle and it is recorked and put back into the powder magazine, to wait for our departure, when it will be sorely needed. There will be no more bottles used for messages.

Constance Howell steps out onto the center of the Stage. All the rest of us are arrayed on the Balcony, resting from the day's labors. I sit with my back to the hull, with Annie's and Sylvie's shoulders touching mine on either side. Rebecca is curled up next to me, her head in my lap. There is wine, cracker, miller, and burgoo in my belly and I am as content as I can be, under the circumstances.

"Today will be our first reading from the Holy Gospels. Does anyone have a special chapter or verse that holds particular meaning for her that I might read it now?"

Oh, Connie, you are such a poor and trusting soul, and such an easy target!

Back when I was on the HMS *Dolphin* as a ship's boy, Deacon Dunne, the ship's chaplain, would require us boys to memorize a certain amount of scripture each week, and what we learned would be recited back to him on Sundays after the service. Since I had the time, and much mischief in my soul, I used to delight in gleaning the Bible for passages that seemed to mean nothing in a religious sense, like maybe one of those old Hebrews counting his goats, like—*"Yea, and he did count each of his goats and they did number fifty and five and he did say unto his wife, Wife, I have counted my goats and they are verily five and fifty and she did say, Mighty art thou among shepherds to have goats fifty and five,"* and so on, to get the Deacon steamed...*And then there was the other stuff, like...*

I wriggle away from my friends and stick my head over the edge of the Balcony and say down to her, "Hey, Connie! How about the Song of Solomon, verse 7? That has always given me great comfort in time of need."

She looks up at my head hanging over the edge of the Balcony. "All right," she says, warily. It's plain that she had a different religious upbringing than did I, for it's equally plain that she doesn't know what's coming. She finds the passage and begins.

> *Behold, thou art fair, my love,*
> *behold, thou art fair!*
> *Your rounded thighs are like jewels,*
> *the work of a master hand.*
> *Your n-n-navel is a rounded bowl,*
> *that never lacks for wine.*

Connie falters a bit there, and many other faces have joined mine in hanging over the edge, grinning down at her. There are a few snorts and titters of laughter, but Connie squares her shoulders and soldiers on.

Your belly is a heap of wheat,
encircled with lilies.
Your two b-b-breasts are like…

She closes the book and falls to her knees and starts bawling.

"I just knew you'd mess it up! I just knew you'd ruin it!" she wails. "You have to make everything a joke, oh, you do, you doooo-hoo-hooo-hoo! How could you buh-buh-be so mean, oh, how could you be so meeeeean?"

Uh-oh.

She's got her face turned upward, the tears streaming out of her eyes, plain for all to see. There is no more laughter from the girls. Once again, I've gone too far.

I get up and jump down to the Stage and kneel down next to her and put my arm around her shaking shoulders.

"Come on, Connie…Please, Connie, I'm sorry. Please forgive me. Please stop crying. Please. I won't do it again. I'm sorry, I really, really am."

And it's true. I *am* sorry. I have never before thought of myself as *mean.* Stupidly impulsive, yes; sometimes thoughtless, yes; vindictive and vengeful, oh, yes. But mean, no. Now I realize that I can be mean and petty and hurtful and I have been that to Connie. I resolve to be better.

Connie starts to quiet a bit.

"That's better. Now dry your eyes, Sister, please. Know that Anything-for-a-Laugh-Jacky is truly sorry."

She looks at me through tear-brimming eyes. "Are you really?"

"Yes, I am, Connie. It's just that I wasn't brought up proper like the rest of you. I promise to be better. Now,

378

show that you have found it in your heart to forgive me by reading Psalm 137 before they drop the flaps." I take the Bible and open it to that passage and hand it to her. "Please, Connie. Stand up. Read it. It's not another trick. It speaks to our condition. Please."

She stands and reads.

By the rivers of Babylon, there we sat down,
*   and yes, we wept, when we remembered Zion.*
We hung our harps, our lyres, upon the willows
*   that on the banks there grew.*
For they that carried us away in captivity,
*   required from us a song;*
And they the wicked who hurt us and tortured us,
*   required mirth, saying,*
*   "Sing to us a song of Zion."*
But how can we sing the Lord's song
*   in a strange land?*

The flaps come slamming down, and we assemble for Chorus and raise our own voices in song—there in the Hold of the *Bloodhound*, there in our captivity, there in our own Babylon.

Chapter 41

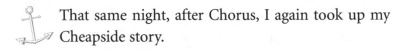 That same night, after Chorus, I again took up my Cheapside story.

IT IS A FINE summer's day and me and Nancy and Charlie and Hughie are lollin' about the kip, waitin' for the others to come back in to report on what they might have come up with in the way of food or coin.

We already have two nice fat pasties that Nancy and I got off a vendor. Nancy distracted him by pulling on his pant leg and whining, "Please give me one, Sir! I'm starvin', I am!" and when he turned to curse her and kick her away, I managed to nip two of the little pies off his tray. Serves the bugger right for bein' a cruel miser, I say.

Things had quieted down between us and the Shanky Boys since our face-off over that unfortunate drunkard. Words had been said, threats had been made, and eventually rocks had been thrown, but peace had generally come back to Cheapside.

Y'see, though we was a small gang and therefore weak, we had some advantages—we were quick and we were mobile and it was known that we never let a wrong against us go unpunished.

"That, and the fact that we had bold Hughie, here, to help with the punishin'. Didn't we, Hughie?"

The Shankies, on the other hand—and there were about thirty of them and not all were kids—had a permanent headquarters, and so were vulnerable to our attacks. They were led by the despicable Pigger O'Toole, and their kip was the bottom floor of a condemned building on Paternoster Lane, the area around Saint Paul's Cathedral bein' their turf. The owner of the property was surely afraid to throw them out and so it became more and more like a stinkin' pigsty and therefore more theirs to keep. As soon as hostilities broke out, we left our kip and headed for the rooftops, which we of the Rooster Charlie Gang knew very, very well. We knew how to get from low shed to one-story house to the roof of a higher building and thence to yet a higher one, and then to the tops of the highest. We'd spent a lot of time up there, sometimes when the peelers was after us, and sometimes during other gang wars, and we knew how to live up there. We had piles of rocks stored in gutters. We watched out for unguarded pies cooling on windowsills down below, pies that would not cool there for very long, you may be sure. We knew how to sleep in those placcs where the roofs come together, so as not to fall off.

When we were up there, sometimes the Shankies would try to get up there, too, and aim to catch us and throw us over, but they were clumsy, while we were quick. Once, a bunch of 'em was chasin' us over a rooftop on Saint Andrew Street and our gang all leaped over to a house on Carter Street, that bein' a jump of only six feet between and hardly worth mentioning 'cept that the drop between was a sheer eight stories. Hughie scooped up little Polly when it come to the jump, like he always did, and so we all got across safe...

"Right, Hughie, you was big, but you was nimble, yes you was..."

Anyway, one of the Shankies, Fast Eddie was his name, thought he could be a hero to his chums and follow us over, but it turned out he didn't quite have the spring in his legs for it, and so he ended up playing a starring role in the renowned anatomist Dr. Richard Graves's presentation to some Royal Academy. I heard that one of his legs was cut off from the rest of his corpse and suspended on this rig while the good doctor would send an electrical charge through it, making the muscles jerk—*galvanization,* I think the term was, proving something or other...

"er...yes, Dorothea, you can explain it to us during your lecture tomorrow..."

And though I didn't have much use for Fast Eddie, ending up on an anatomist's slab was a fate that many of us were doomed for and so we could take no joy in his sad end.

With our rocks, we were able to do much damage on those walking below. We did not have to throw them, no—just lean over the edge of a rooftop, with one of your mates holding on to your shift so you didn't tumble over to your death, to drop the rock at the proper time, trying to figure the distance traveled by your target before the rock you held would meet him in midstep. It was a very satisfying thing to do. Soon the Shankies were afraid to walk the streets, at least in the daytime, but male pride would not let them call a truce, no. Something else would have to give, and finally, it did.

Once, we were peering over the edge of a house on Old Bailey, ready to drop some stones on any Shankies who might amble past, and we see three of them running up the street. One of 'em's got what looks like a lady's purse in his fist, and there's whistles sounding behind them. They turn right and head into the alley next to us, not knowin' it's a blind alley with a high fence at the other end. They stop in horror to watch the two policemen come poundin' in after 'em. It's the noose for them for sure.

"Hit 'em," says Charlie, wingin' a stone, and we pick up ours and are about to wing them, but he says, "The coppers, not the Shanks!"

We wonder at the wisdom of that, but we do it.

The police, amazed at the hail of missiles from above, and having no wish to be brained over the apprehension of a couple of petty thieves, retreat. The Shankies climb over the fence to safety, but before they go, Charlie stands up, so they can see him, and says, "You owe us."

And they do. The truce is negotiated and we move back to the kip. With only one dead and a mere dozen wounded, we all counted it a decent end to a minor war.

The Rooster Charlie Gang was a peaceable bunch, mostly—content to work our own little patch of the city and take what came our way. Toby Oyster's crew had the turf to the west of us, on Tudor, but we was always all right with them—even joined up and shared our turf sometimes when times was good, like when the big fairs came to town—and way to the north was Fagin's crew of pickpockets, but Charlie was tight with the Dodger, Fagin's head boy, so we got along. No, it was Pigger's crew that was the problem, them havin' a prime piece of turf but always greedy for more.

So we're sittin' there in our kip that day, eyein' the two pasties we had stole, our mouths waterin' up and hopin' the other two get back soon so's we can divide 'em up and eat 'em, when Judy comes runnin' in, shoutin', "Pigger O'Toole's stole our Polly!"

I take an invisible bow down there on the dark Stage and say, "I'll continue this little tale tomorrow night. Be sure to get your tickets. The good seats are going fast."

There is the sound of laughter and girls turning over and settling in to sleep. I give Hughie an affectionate ruffle of his hair, and he says, "I like the story, Mary," and I go up and settle between my mates, where I will sleep until two bells into the midwatch. I will be awakened then to take both Dolley and Katy into the storeroom to be taught how to open the outer door, for they will be the first ones through when the time comes.

But I am too keyed up to sleep right off after the performance, so I put my nose in the nape of Annie's neck and throw my arm around her waist and feel her comforting hand on the back of mine, and while I wait for blessed sleep to come claim me, I think on things...

Y'know, Jaimy, as I lie here in the dark of the Hold, it occurs to me that I might be able to take this ship—I mean with the

Dianas and the powder and the crew all divided and ready to jump out of their skins—but still, no... I only know a few of the crew—the rest of them stay well away from us as ordered. And from what I've seen of them, they are a hard-bitten bunch—not like poor stupid Mick and Keefe—no, they are thugs used to cruelty, to pushing poor terrified people down dark passageways to stuff them into cramped holds, to chain them neck-and-foot to bulkheads and let them never see light nor day nor any human kindness for weeks and weeks on end. No, there's forty of them and thirty-some of us, so we've got to go with the original plan, I know that.

Plus, y'know, even if we took the ship and I got control of it, I could never love it like I loved my Emerald...or the Dolphin...and even the Wolverine. Call it wrong, of me, un-Christian of me, even, but deep down inside I believe that things, things that ain't living, can still pick up some of the evil that's been done by people on them, or near them, or by them, or...I don't know what I mean, really...It's like a tree that's been used for a gallows to strangle the life out of some poor sod, or a lonely grave where some demented lover has slain his poor lovin' sweetheart and buried her poor remains...or a slaver that has been the witness of countless deaths, horrible agonies, unspeakable cruelties, cruelties one can scarcely speak without such revulsion that... No, I could never love this ship, as it has become a vile thing, a thing that I think even hates itself. In the creak of the timbers, in the clash of the chains, I hear the moaning, and I would always hear the moaning...

Anyway, I think of you always and of that rose-covered cottage by the sea... But I don't know if you're gonna be able to keep me stuffed down in it. You know how I am, Jaimy, but also know that I am yours forever.

Chapter 42

"Hooks down."

I bounce off the Balcony to head down to do my duty, but I don't have to do it this time. I find my modesty is safe for today, for Mick puts his head over the edge and shakes it and gives me a look. Which is good, 'cause 'bout the only thing I'm still covering up is my tattoo. I take my fingers off my waistband and attend to the hooks. In a minute I see Mick's reason for caution—Dunphy's scowling face also pops up over the edge of the top hatch and looks about for any mischief. I perform the task at hand like a proper seaman and signal for the first tub to go up. It comes back rinsed, and then I hook up the clean-water tub.

While *I* ain't stripping today, Mick and Keefe, and even Dunphy, do get a bit of a treat. We have Clarissa set up on the edge of the Stage, once again, with one leg crossed over the other. Pretending she doesn't know she's being watched, she takes her right hand and drops the left sleeve of her chemise, and with a wet rag she wipes her shoulder, and then she lifts her chin and very slowly cleans her neck. Now she shrugs down the other sleeve and very, *very* slowly runs the rag back and forth, back and forth, from shoulder to shoulder across the now bare top of her chest. Then she pulls the sleeves back up, rises, and undulates out of sight.

"Oh, my...," Mick breathes.

"Back to work, the both of yiz," says Dunphy. I notice that he didn't say that till Clarissa's little show was over, though.

"Tubs down, ladies," I sing out. "Let's get 'em back in the privy."

They swarm down and we get the job done. Several of the girls reach for their hanging washcloths to avail themselves of the fresh salt water, but I say, "Wait. Let's see what luck we have in fishing today."

With that, I pull my sleeve up over my shoulder and stick my arm all the way into the clean-water tub and feel around with my hand.

"Yuck," says Clarissa. "Now it's contaminated."

I pay her no mind and keep swirling my hand around and...*Ha!* I feel something slimy. I grab it and pull it out triumphantly for all to see—a foot-and-a-half piece of gray-green seaweed.

"And now I suppose you'll eat that awful thing, won't you, and disgust us further?" asks Clarissa.

"No, Clarissa, sweet sister of my soul," I say with satisfaction. "Not a treat for me, just another little something for the boys...a little something from the *Marie Celestine.*"

Later, after checking on the progress with the fuse and joining in on the dancing for a while, just to show 'em how it's *really* done, I go up and join Katy, up on starboard-side forward watch.

"Hello, Kate, what's happenin' out there?" I say by way of greeting. I sit down, lean back, and pat my belly in contentment. We had some fine, fine Bordeaux wine with our noon feast today, and it went down real easy. We're emptying four bottles a day now, enjoying their contents, and then filling them back up with water, recorking, and putting them back in the Powder Hole.

"Nothin' much, Jacky," she replies. "Just that the crew's gettin' real jumpy—lookin' around all scared and shifty-eyed. A little while ago one of 'em dropped a bucket behind another man and he 'bout jumped out of his skin. It almost come to a fight."

"Good," I say, and we fall silent, content to just sit together and watch the doin's on deck and the clouds scudding by.

After a while, though, she takes a deep breath and sits up straight and says, "Gotta tell you sumthin'…sumthin' about me, Jacky." She is grimly silent for a while, but I don't rush her.

"'Fore I come to Boston, I lived out on our little farm on the banks of the Allegheny, Armstrong County, way out on the frontier. 'Twas Father and Mama and me, and it was a hard life we had, but we was all right. We had enough to eat and there was some other homesteads about, so we had church on Sundays and sometimes there was barn raisings and play-parties for the kids. Father was strict, but he never laid a hand on me in anger. Mama was a churchwoman, through and through. We said a blessing before every meal and prayers at night. She loved God, but I know she loved me, too."

She stops to tuck a strand of her long, straight brown hair behind her ear. After looking out across the water for another few moments, she continues.

"Late last summer when the corn was ready to be brought in, my uncle came by to help with it. He didn't have no land and he wasn't married and so he worked as a hired hand on the farms thereabouts."

Another pause. I can tell this is hard for her.

"They was bringin' the last of it into the corn crib when it started to rain, but Father didn't want to stop till it was all done and so he got all wet and then caught a chill and then a fever. Three days later he was dead, and people come from the farms around to his funeral. Ever'one said it was Divine Providence that my uncle was there to watch out for Mama and me."

She does not look me in the eye once during this whole thing. Her expression does not change.

"Warn't three days after they put Father in the ground that Uncle come at me and he took me 'round the back of the shed and he threw me to the ground and did me. I cried out but he still did me. Yes, he did, and he did me every day after that."

I feel like I have been punched in the stomach.

"Your mother?" I ask, as soft as I can.

"She knew he was dirtying me, and it kilt her, it did. What with Father dyin' and what Uncle was doin' to me, she lost all her faith. She stopped believin' and then she stopped eatin'. She ate nothing, even refused to drink any water— not even a drop. Lord knows I tried to get her to eat or drink something. I begged her and begged her, but she wouldn't listen. She just stopped wanting to live and she died—just like that. It couldn't have been more than two weeks…"

"How old were you?"

"By my best reckonin' I was 'bout thirteen."

"What happened then?"

"Two days after Ma was put down and everybody left, he come at me again, but this time I was ready for him and I swung 'round and smashed him in the face, smashed him with a shovel as hard as I could hit him and then lit out. Left him there, on his hands and knees, groanin'."

"Then?"

"Took to the road. Kep' goin' on it. Eatin' berries and roots and plants I knew. Some rabbits I kilt. Just went east, 'cause I knew there was nothin' out to the west. Ended up in Boston. Went from big house to big house axin' for work. Didn't find none. Couldn't talk right for 'em. Looked at me funny and closed the doors. Hadn't et for a week when I went to the door of the school and axed for work. Think I passed out on the doorstep from bein' hungry. Peg pulled me in and gave me work."

If it had been anyone else, I would have gathered her to me for comfort and patted her back and said, "There, there," but not Kate. She is too solitary, too alone, and I fear she will ever be. There is a *very* long silence now and I let it hang in the air.

Another deep breath and...

"So you see, when we get where we're goin', they're gonna look me over and they're gonna find me wantin', 'cause I bled all over that day he first took me, and they're gonna sell me to one of those places...I don't even know the names of 'em."

"They're called brothels...whorehouses."

"Maybe. When the preacher come around, he used to point at us and say things like, 'Dens of Iniquity,' and 'Houses of Shame,' and we didn't know what he was talkin' about. And it all seemed so far away then. Don't seem so far away now, though."

More silence, which gives me time to take this whole story in...*Poor Katy, poor girl*...Then she speaks again and this time it is with firmness and this time she turns to look me square in the eye.

"I'm tellin' you all this so's you'll know—I ain't goin' to one of those places to let them dirty on me. Ain't gonna let no man dirty on me ag'in. No, I've been handled rough enough. I'm gonna die in this place, and it's all right. I don't care. Truth be known, I've been as happy here as I been any-where since Mama died."

Her eyes narrow and she goes on.

"And my girls have decided to do the same."

"Your girls?"

"You all call 'em the Dianas. Don't know why. Ain't none of 'em named Diana. It's Chrissy and Minnie and Hermione and Rose."

I sigh and explain. "It was back in the old countries— Greece and Rome and Egypt—the places where things got started up in the old days. They had men gods and boy gods and dwarf gods and such, and they even had girl gods, too, and one of 'em was Diana, Goddess of the Hunt, and she was Goddess of some other things, too, like chastity and the moon, but she was always pictured as havin' a bow and arrow with her. So that's why the girls call you the Dianas," I conclude. "It's a compliment, really."

"They had girl gods?"

"Yes, they did, Katy, and they were fierce ones, too. The Goddess Athena went around hurling lightning bolts and making life hell for men who failed to pay her due respect, and the Goddess Juno was making volcanos spew out, and changing those who had dared cross her into piggies, and the girl-god Ceres was making the crops grow each year but raining death and destruction down on any farmer who dared to be ungrateful, and so on and so forth. It went on like that till some guys got together and came up with the one-god thing—him being God, the *Father,* and male and all that—and things went downhill for girls ever after that, far as I can figure. It was always, 'Get in your dress, girl, your smock, your shift or your burnoose or your veil, but whatever it is, girl, put it on and shut the hell up,' is how I see it."

"Huh!"

"But back to modern times, Katy. Maybe it won't turn out that you have to die here. Maybe things will turn out better for you someday. Now here is the plan and your part in it. Tell me what you think."

I lay it out for her, and she considers it and nods.

"Well, if it don't work out the way you say, at least we'll take a lot of 'em with us."

"Yes, we will. And if it comes to that, I'll be with you all the way to the end. Maybe you don't know it, but I've got a tattoo right here on my hip. That will make me worthless to them awfully picky sultans, too. So I ain't goin', neither."

She again nods and something like a smile comes over her face and she lifts her clenched fist. I lift mine and we knock them together, and that's as close as you get to Katy Deere in this life, I suspect.

My talk with Katy reminds me of my duty, and the one duty in particular that I had not yet gotten to in the press of events, the one concerning that nightmare of nightmares I had not so long ago. I go back down to the fuse-makers and find Ruth and Dorothea hard at work. Ruth stitches and when she has a section done, Dorothea pours in the powder through a funnel she has made of paper rolled into a cone. The section is pinched off at six inches, Ruth sews it tight, and the next link is started. The fuse is laid out across the deck under the Stage, looking like a length of red linked sausages. There are now about fifty of them—halfway there. *Good.*

"Pray, Sisters, cease your labors on this for a short while and make two short, four-second fuses. When you are finished making them, take the top two bags of powder from the Powder Hole, puncture both bags and jam a fuse into each one, then sew the bag up tight around it. Then put the bags back into the Powder Hole." They look mystified. "It's important...for emergencies, like. You'll see."

And they do it.

This night, when Connie does her reading, she announces that it will be John 13:1 to John 13:12. That's the bit where Jesus, at His Last Supper, gets up, takes off His robe, throws it over a chair, wraps a towel around His waist, and gets down and washes His disciples' feet, which I had always thought was pretty humble and downright nice of Him. I thought that, I did, but then, there was always the naggin' suspicion in my head that maybe some of the disciples' feet might have been sendin' something heavenward that wasn't all that sweet-smellin' and maybe Jesus thought He'd have to put an end to it if He was to enjoy His last dinner on this earth. And we all do like to enjoy our dinners, don't we?

After the reading, which was well received by all, we had a lively discussion concerning the meaning of the passage, and the wiser ones settled on cleanliness from sin in the presence of Jesus being the main point, as opposed to simple foot odor. I didn't press the point, and then the flaps came slamming down, ending the debate.

We had Giovannelli's *Jubilate Deo* in Chorus and we shook the very timbers of the *Bloodhound* with it, and then it was time for me to go on with my Cheapside tale.

ON HEARING THE news of our Polly bein' snatched, Charlie tore out of the kip, with Hughie right on his heels. Us girls all picked up rocks and followed them out at a dead run up Water Street to Broad, across Ludgate, and then on to Paternoster and Pigger O'Toole's and the Shanky Boys' kip.

It was a perfect pigsty, the kind of place what gives slums a bad name. Filth and garbage piled up outside, cheeky rats goin' through it all and not carin' who knew it. The door was closed.

"Give 'em one, Nancy," says Charlie. His flushed face is just about as red as his hair.

"Right-o, Chuckie," says Nancy, and pegs one of her rocks at one of the lower windows and it smashes through with a satisfying crash.

That gets their attention. Faces appear at the other windows and the door flies open and angry Shankies pour out to face us. There's about twenty of them to the five of us. They know we got rocks and they see Charlie's shiv in his hand and they see that he's mad enough to kill, and so hang back.

Then their ranks part and Pigger O'Toole himself comes out, holding our Polly by the hand. Seeing us, she tries to jerk her hand out of his grimy paw and come join us, but he just tightens his grip. Polly puts the thumb of her other hand in her mouth and says nothing, just looks down at the ground.

"That warn't nice, Charlie, bustin' our winder like that," says Pigger, calmly. He runs a finger in his ear, twists it around, and then takes it out to examine what it might have found there. Pigger O'Toole could be the ugliest, most unpleasant cove I've ever seen in this world, and I've seen a lot of them that could give him a run for his money in that regard, but, no, I gotta say Pigger was the champ. His close-chopped greasy black hair ran down his low, sloping forehead to about an inch above his horribly pitted nose. He's got a stubble of beard that surrounds the gap-toothed hole of his mouth, and that stubble goes all the way up to his little pig eyes. He's squat and stooped and way beyond filthy. He's probably about twenty-five and it's a real pity he ain't been hanged long ago.

"This ain't right, Pigger! Give 'er back!" yells Charlie, choking with rage. "It's against the Code!"

"To 'ell with the Code and to 'ell wi' you! This girl come here of 'er own free will, she did. Didn't you, darlin'?" Pigger looks down at Polly while scratching the huge belly that hangs over his pants. "Didn't want to live no more wi' the likes of that nasty Rooster Charlie and his big dummy and that dirty bunch o' snot-nosed girls that run with 'im."

"I'm warnin' you for the last time, Pigger, hand 'er over!"

"Aye, the little angel come walkin' right up to me and the boys, askin' to be took in, and as we needed to fill out our beggin' ranks, we decided like good Christians to take the poor thing in and give her our love and affection. Just look at 'er little face—don't it just make y'want to give her a penny?"

Pigger liked to hear himself talk, but I can talk, too. "Let her go, Pigger!" I shouts. "We saved your boys Scut Jetter and Flick Coontz from the peelers last week, and if we hadn't, they'd both be hangin' in gibbets right now with the birds pickin' out their eyes, instead of standin' there next to you droolin' like the morons they are. So you owe us! Let her go!"

Pigger brings his little piggy eyes to rest on me. "Ah, Mary Faber, the little bint what can read but what's got such a wise mouth," he says, smiling a gap-toothed grin. "I'm thinkin' maybe you'll be next to join our family. We'll work on that mouth thing for you. Fix that right up."

"In a pig's eye, Pigger, or *your* filthy eye if a clean and honest pig can't be found," says I in return. "Hughie, up."

Hughie stoops down and I climb up on his shoulders and wrap my legs around his neck, a rock in each hand and get ready.

Scut Jetter, emboldened by the Shankies' superior numbers and seekin' to impress his boss, takes his finger out of his nose long enough to sneer, "Hey, Hughie, sure hope fer yer sake that you wash yer neck real good when you get back to yer kip, little Lady Smart-mouth ridin' you like that, and all."

"Aw, c'mon, Clarissa, settle down—it wasn't that funny. Jeez."

Anyway, Charlie was tired of the wordplay, as was I. "Enough of this," he says. "Ready on."

Ready on—that's our gang's signal for "Get ready to fight," and fight we must, for this outrage cannot go unanswered. If we don't do something, word will get around to the other gangs and we'll be done—we'd just have to split up and each join whatever gang would take us.

"Go!" shouts Charlie, and he leads us into battle.

Judy and Nancy immediately let fly with their rocks and stoop down and pick up more as we charge along. Curses and cries of pain from the Shankies testify to the girls' skill.

I have a rock in either hand, but these rocks are not for throwing, oh, no. These are my special fighting rocks. They are squarish and fit my hands in such a way as to stick out a bit as I grasp them with fingers and thumbs. Y'see, our Hughie here and me had a special way of fighting as a team, and—

"Yes, Hughie, I can hear you back there chortlin' 'cause you know what's comin'..."

And that way was this: We'd charge into the enemy with me on top, and Hughie would grab the first bloke he could get his hands on, lift him up so's his face was about level with mine, then I'd open my arms wide and bring the rocks around and whack the victim on either ear if he was facin' me, or on the nose and back of the head, if he warn't. It was highly effective, either way. I liked to think of us as a strike force, brawn and brains united for the common good.

So it is in that way that Hughie and I wade into the Battle of Paternoster Lane. Hughie grabs the glib but slow-movin' Scut Jetter, lifts him up till he's lookin' with shock into my eyes, and I slam him on both ears with my stones...aye, and with a certain satisfaction. *How's that for insult, hey, Scut?* His eyes cross and I yell, "Drop!" Hughie drops him and grabs the next unfortunate cove. This one is facing to my right as he comes into my view and so he gets it on the nose and back of head. There is blood now on my right-hand rock. "Drop!" He disappears, to crumple onto the stones, and another victim is hoisted into view. This one is facing away and so don't know what hit him when the rocks come against his ears. He'll only know that he'll not be hearin' right for a while. Might even find it a bit difficult to stand up without bein' dizzy, too, but it serves him right. Serves 'em all right, takin' our Polly like that.

While Hughie's looking for another one to grab, I look over and see that Charlie's using his shiv to try to get close to Pigger, but he can't 'cause two of Pigger's boys got regular swords and they're jabbin' at Charlie and keepin' him off Pigger, and Charlie's got some blood showin' on his right leg, so I yell, "Hughie, over there!" When I point toward Charlie and Hughie sees the blood, he roars out his mighty roar and lurches over to Charlie's aid. A rock thrown by Judy catches one of the swordsmen on the side of the head and he goes down moanin', but there's still the other sod. I see Hughie's hands reaching for his neck, and yes, he's got him. Then the bugger raises his sword, but before he can bring it down on Hughie, I smash my rocks on the top of his head and the sword drops, and Charlie sprints after Pigger. But Pigger backs into his doorway and slams the door, and up the street we hear shrill whistles and we know it's the coppers, so we have to run away, leaving the wounded Shankies on the cobblestones.

I jump down so's Hughie can pick up Nancy, who's been hit hard and can't walk, and we all hie back to the kip to lick our wounds and cry over our lost Polly.

I give a full curtsy in the dark and say, "Tomorrow night we shall conclude this tale of war and woe, but till then, good night and peace be with you all. Good night, Hughie, and know that there would not have been any story without you." There is a chorus of agreement from the girls, and I know Hughie revels in the sound.

I crawl back into the kip with my friends for a few hours of sleep before my midnight creep.

I am awakened by the maid of the watch, Helen Bailey, at one thirty in the morning. I shake the cobwebs from my mind and head down to the Rat Hole, but before leaving the Stage, I go over to the other Balcony and shake Clarissa awake.

"Psst! Clarissa. It's time."

She groans and rolls over and then sits up. My hand is still on her shoulder and she picks it up and throws it off.

"All right," she says, groggily, "I'm up."

She puts her feet on the Balcony stairs and follows me down to the Stage and then down beneath it, where we can see the faint glow of a candle and Helen and Cloris on watch. I get out my scabag and pull out my Black Ghost gear and put it on, carefully laying my chemise and drawers neatly off to the side should I need to get to them quick.

They have already taken the screws out of the Rat Hole safety boards, and we pull the boards down and place them to the side. It had been decided amongst Dolley and Clarissa and me that, although the Plan did not include Clarissa going out this way on the day of the escape, she should still know how to open the outer latch on the storeroom and the rest of the escape route, in case things went awry. Besides, as she herself said, she was an officer and should know.

I take the candle and the wedge and crawl through and stand up. I put the wedge under the door and the candle on the bench. Clarissa comes through and stands up.

"Here," I whisper, "take the knife and put it through here and lift up. Yes, that's it. Now take this file, put it through there, and push sideways... right, like that."

The door swings inward.

"All right," I say. "Now stay here till I get back."

"Like hell," she says, and I look at her sharply. In the light of the candle I can see that her eyes are shining with the excitement of being out, being out somewhere she's not supposed to be. I know the tingle that can bring and I know she feels it. "I'm going with you."

"Clarissa," I whisper, "you can't. You're dressed all in white. You'd be seen—"

"I'll take the clothes off."

"You'd still be white," says I, but I know she's going to be obstinate so I relent. "Look, come with me to the bottom of the first ladder. That way you'll see the whole escape route. All right?"

She nods and we slip out.

I go to the ladder and start to climb. When my head clears the next level, I stop and listen and hear only snores and coughs and belches from the crew's quarters. There's some light coming in the open hatch above, and I can see there's no one in the kitchen. Then I feel Clarissa's head butt me in my behind. *Damn!*

I lean back down, grab her hair so's I'll know where her ear is and hiss into it, "You're going to get us caught! Now get back down!"

She doesn't move. "All right. Stay here. I'll be right back," I whisper and climb on to the next level. I pad along the passageway till I'm outside the crew's berth, then I lay down the strand of seaweed I had gotten earlier in the day. I make it so it's stretched out straight into the berth, nice and regular, so it doesn't look accidental. We'd kept it nice and moist so it'll look especially slimy when the crew sees it in the morning. I had thought about arranging it so it made a *C* and an *M*, after that poor, cursed ship, but I figured no one in the crew could read, anyway, so I dropped that idea.

I get back to the ladder and Clarissa's blond head is still popped up, looking around. I shove it back down and together we feel our way back to the storeroom and quietly close the door.

"That was...exciting," she whispers. "Are you going out tomorrow night?"

"Yes," I reply, not liking where this is going. "I have to start disabling the other lifeboat."

"Good," she says. "Wake me up then, too."

She's had a taste and she's gonna be hard to hold back.

Chapter 43

"Ship."

I hear the word uttered by Abby Pierce, up on port quarter lookout. I fly to her side to look out. She points to a sail on the far-off horizon. We can only see the tops of the sails, but it seems to have three masts. And it seems to be headed for us. I see the men on deck putting up more sail.

Damn!

"Everybody down," I say. "Emergency meeting. Down under the Stage. Yes, everybody, even the watches. It's important. Now! Let's do it."

For the first time since we came on board, there is no one on any watch—not on the Balcony, not at the gate, not at the edge of the Stage. The girls crowd into the space and look at me expectantly.

"Sit," I say, and they do.

I stand before them and begin.

"There is a ship out there that looks like it might be headed for us—"

I hear several quiet shouts of *"Hooray!"*

"There are those of you who think this is a good thing.

That the ship we see out there might run us down and rescue us and take those who have taken us into captivity off to justice."

More quiet cries of *"Hear, hear!"*

"But, oh my sisters, I must tell you that it will not happen in that way."

They are quiet now.

"What will happen is this: Before any ship gets close enough to grapple and board and search us, Captain Blodgett will order that we be manacled by our necks on to one of those long chains you see lying down there next to the hull, that we be taken on deck in such a way that we cannot be seen by the other ship, that an anchor be affixed to the chain that binds us, and that we be thrown overboard, like bait on a fish line."

Shocked silence.

"I did not tell you this before because I didn't want to ruin your sleep," I say. *As mine has been ruined*, I think.

"But...but who could do such an awful thing?" asks Cloris.

"Cloris, they know that if they are caught with any of us aboard, each and every one of them will hang for it. There's men on this ship who have done things as evil as what I have described. Don't judge them all by poor simple Mick and Keefe, here on their first journey and regretting it. Or even Cookie. There's men on this ship who have made fifteen, twenty, such voyages—who knows what horrible things they have seen? Who knows what terrible things they have done? Believe me, they will do it."

"They will drown us like helpless kittens," says Julia, her voice trailing off in despair.

"That will not happen," I say, "if we stand and fight."

"And that we will do," says Dolley firmly. "Better they kill us here so they, too, will pay with their lives for what they have done."

I nod and lay out my plan. "Right. Here is what we will do. When you hear the code words 'Plan B' we will do the following: Whoever is on watch at the gate and on the Stage will have a loop of wire about their waists—the wire will be passed from watch to watch—and they will take their wires and twist them around the gate bars and the bars to the side to slow up anyone coming in at us. Everyone will meet down here, and Abby and Helen will take down the boards covering the Rat Hole and the Powder Hole—start doing it now while you're listening to this, as we've got to go in to get the wire. We might well be implementing Plan B this very morning. I know we should have done this before, but I grew complacent because we had seen so few ships, and for that I am sorry. The Dianas will take up positions on the outside, to nail anyone who manages to get through the gate and tries to get at us. Everyone who does not have a weapon will grab a bottle from the Powder Hole and, holding the bottle by the neck, will smash it against the next bottle—it will give you a jagged, sharp, and very effective weapon. Annie and Martha will light two candles and place them on the Balcony. Clarissa and I will then take the two bags of powder, the ones that have the short fuses attached to them, up on the Balcony. We will watch the approaching ship and if it looks like the time is right, we will light our charges and throw them toward the quarterdeck, where they will flare up and, it is to be hoped, ignite the mainsail. At that time we will yell, 'Go! Go!' and all of you will go out the Rat Hole.

Dolley will lead the way because she'll need to open the outer door. The Dianas will follow her to clear the way of any trouble. When you come out onto the deck, try to climb into the rigging where you'll be seen by those on the other ship, who will be watching through long glasses. If a seaman tries to stop you, come up with your broken bottle under his chin, as hard as you can."

I pause to take a breath.

"Any questions?" I ask. There are none. "It will be messy and bloody and many will die, but it would be far better for us to die fighting on deck than to submit to being slaughtered like animals." There are resolute nods all around. When I think of that cowed crowd of scared, whimpering girls who were first thrown down into this Pit, well…

"All right, everyone back on watch. Sally, when they get the boards down, get a candle lit and crawl through and set the wedge. You'll find the spool of wire on the deck to the right. The cutters are sitting on it. Take about six feet, then cut it in half. Now, let's see what that ship is up to." And with that, I spring back up on the Balcony, with Clarissa right behind me.

The ship is still out there and seems to have gained on us a little.

"What do you think it is?" asks Clarissa.

"Don't know. Too far away," I reply. "Could be a merchant, a warship, a pirate, even. Whatever it is, it's trouble, and I wish it would go away. Sure would like to pull out my long glass, but we can't risk that."

"How much do our little bag-bombs weigh?"

"About ten pounds."

She nods. "Yes. I could throw it to just about there. It'd

be fun. Wouldn't those scum do some jumpin' around then?" She grins, picturing it in her mind.

"Yes, they would. But I like Plan A better than Plan B."

"Maybe. Still, I'd like to...wait, what's happening?"

The ship, which had been on our quarter, was now dead astern. The *Bloodhound* had turned.

"Blodgett has come to a new course to see if that ship intends to follow us. We'll know in a minute if he changes course to match ours." I ready myself to yell out "Plan B" and set things in motion.

We watch, and the set of the sails of the other ship does not change. I let out my breath and relax. "He's not going to pursue us."

"Damn. I could have used a good fight," says Clarissa.

"Don't worry, Clarissa, you'll get that fight soon enough. This has been a good lesson for us—we can't just plan and plan and not act. Let's pass the word that we'll be leaving as soon as the fuse is done and the weather is right, and all should prepare themselves for it."

I turn back to the others and raise my voice. "False alarm. That ship is not chasing us. Let's get back to ordinary routine."

Ordinary routine is work continuing on the fuse while the dancers rattle overhead. The fuse work is tedious and slow—the seams have to be sewn very tightly so that the powder doesn't leak out—and Ruth has enlisted the services of Frances Wallace to spell her when her hand cramps up.

"I swear I'll never again touch a needle in this life," grumbles Ruth, flexing her fingers.

"Oh yes, you will," I laugh and pat her shoulder to show that we really appreciate what she's doing. "Soon you'll be back doin' those roses and vines and fancy scrollwork for which you are famous throughout the land."

"*Hmmm,*" she says, unconvinced but happy to think of herself back home doing homely things.

Katy and the Dianas are in a line under the Stage, exercising with their new, stronger bows. *Pull, hold…hold… relax. Pull, hold…hold…hold…relax. Pull, hold…hold… hold* till their arms quiver and shake with the effort of holding the string back…*relax.*

The Dianas now not only roll up their cutoff drawers, but also the sleeves of their undershirts, and when they are in the "hold" position, I notice up-and-down grooves have appeared in their shoulder muscles. Their legs, too…You can see the separate muscles, just like on me…or on me when I've been climbing the rigging for a—

"Hey. Something's up," comes the call from Annie on starboard quarter lookout. I leap up to see what's what.

"It looks like the whole crew is out there," she says, and she is right. There's Mick and Keefe and Cookie and the rest, and that Carruthers is out in front of all of 'em with his arms crossed on his chest, his lower lip jutting out, lookin' seriously surly. He may be a bully and a thug, but he is without a doubt the crew's leader.

"It looks like they want a meeting with the Captain. That Nettles just went into the cabin to tell him."

I think Annie's right—Chubbuck and Dunphy are standing by and lookin' just as serious as Carruthers.

The cabin door opens and Blodgett comes out, wearing both his sword *and* his pistols, which he doesn't ordinarily do. He goes up to confront Carruthers.

"What the devil do you men want?" he demands.

Carruthers pulls off his cap and says, "We got some questions, Captain, and we wants 'em answered."

"So ask them," says the Captain.

"First, how come you and the Mate and the Bo'sun is the only ones aboard with weapons? There's some on board that says you plan to kill the lot of us when we get to Africa, 'cause of the nature of this cargo, which you think we might talk about sometime and get you and your bosses in trouble. What you got to say to that?"

The Captain breaks out in a big smile. "Now, boys, when have you *ever* been on a ship where the crew is armed, unless you've sailed on a pirate? Think back, now, have you?"

The crew thinks on this and mumbles things like, *"Well, maybe not,"* and *"Come to think of it..."*

"And as for killing you? Why, you're the best crew I've ever had. I know you each for a good closemouthed lad who ain't never gonna peach on nobody. Besides, everyone back in the States thinks these girls are dead. Who's gonna be lookin' for 'em? Or news of 'em? Nay, these girls are a dead issue, count on it."

Carruthers thinks on this for a moment and then says, "There's been some strange things happenin' on this ship lately. Ghostly things, and we don't like it. There's talk of a Black Ghost what maybe slipped a noose over Henry Pritchett's head one night. There's seaweed poppin' up where it ain't supposed to be. There's big sharks followin' us. Strange noises..."

The Captain continues to smile. "Now, Carruthers, you know what a superstitious lot sailors are. It's in our very nature. There ain't no ghost, trust me, and sharks always follow a ship, surely you know that."

But Carruthers is not yet through. "Has this ship always been the *Bloodhound*? Or did it have another name in the past, like maybe the *Marie Celestine*?"

The Captain gives out a short bark of a laugh. "Boys, boys, boys! I saw this ship's keel laid in Charleston twelve years ago and I've sailed in her every year since! And so has Mate Dunphy and the Bo'sun. Ain't that right?" Dunphy nods and Chubbuck does, too, after the Mate gives him a jab.

"So you see, lads, there's nothing to worry about. We'll soon be at our destination and you'll all be rich," says the Captain with smug satisfaction writ all over his face. "But I'm glad we had this little talk, I am, to help clear the air, like. I'll even do this to set your minds at ease—Carruthers is your man, so let's fit him out with a fine sword, so he'll be armed, too. All right? Good. Carruthers, come with me into my cabin and we'll set you up."

Carruthers, a bit shocked by this turn, shrugs and follows Blodgett into his cabin.

He swaggers out a full minute later, his face flushed and smiling, and wearing a sabre in a scabbard around his waist.

"Let's have a cheer, lads," shouts the Captain, "and an extra tot for every man jack of you at dinner tonight!"

There is a cheer, but it ain't exactly a full-throated one. No, when the men break up and file past our bars, I see that Mick and Keefe are still looking grim.

I rush over to where they are passing, grab the bars, and hiss out at them, "He's been bought! You know that, boys! He's been bought!"

They look at me but say nothing. I snatch my hands back as Chubbuck's club hits the bars where my fingers have just been.

"Shaddap, you."

Flaps down, Hepzibah's Chorus, Connie's Scriptures, then I get up and finish my Cheapside tale.

CHARLIE'S BEEN real moody lately and I know it's 'cause the Polly thing has been weighing heavy on his mind.

Oh, I know he felt bad for Polly herself, like we all did, but it was his loss of face with the other gangs that galled him the most. He was usually full of fun and jokes, but he wasn't now. Now he had his shiv out a lot, sharpening it against the stones of Blackfriars Bridge. I know he's gonna try to kill Pigger—but that won't solve anything, I know it won't. I try to tell him, they'll just hang you is all and I don't want that, Charlie, I don't— but he don't listen. His pride is on the line, and I've come to know that with males, sometimes there just ain't no use in talkin' to 'em.

It's been about a week since the Paternoster fight, but Pigger don't show himself, prolly figurin' what Charlie's got in mind. Pigger's big, but Charlie's a real hothead, and Pigger knows that and he ain't taking no chances. We ain't seen Polly that whole time, neither...

"No, Julia, we couldn't go to the police and complain. We wouldn't think of doing that, as the police were not our friends. Besides, it would break the Code of the Streets and we'd be seen as snitches and that would be the end of us. And no, Caroline, we couldn't just set fire to their filthy sty and flush 'em out—fire was much feared in London and anyone caught setting one was sure to end up dead very quickly. It's true they didn't hang nine-year-old kids—usually no one younger than fourteen got strung up—but a

copper and his club could get the same job done. Once I got caught trying to pinch something or other and a cop grabbed me by the neck, took me into an alley, lifted me up, and started slamming me back against a stone wall, over and over again. My head went back on the first slam, hard against the stone, and my eyesight got a bit foggy around the edges. The second slam about broke my skull and things got real hazy, and by about the fifth one, everything went dark. I woke up back in the kip, sick with the worst headache I've ever had, before and since. Charlie and the bunch had found me crumpled up in that alley, out cold, and Hughie carried me back. I counted myself lucky to be alive, and lucky to have been found by my mates before Muck the Corpse Seller found me. No, Sisters, the police were not our friends."

But Polly or no Polly, we still had to eat, so we headed up to Fleet Street on this day, to try our luck with the reading-of-the-broadsides bit. When we got there, there was a pretty good crowd, it bein' the day the newspapers came out, and Nancy and Judy slipped right into the people standin' about to see what might present itself, like perhaps a gentleman's fancy handkerchief hanging carelessly out of his pocket, or somesuch. Charlie was about to take up his usual post close to Hughie and me, but I saw something that made me grab his arm and hiss, "Charlie! There's two Shanky Boys over there! Hold back and pretend you don't see them! Trust me!"

Charlie looks over to see Flick and Scut, the same two lowlifes we'd saved from the coppers before—plainly they was here to see if they could pick a few pockets. Charlie's hand goes for his shiv, but I plead,

"Please, Charlie!" and he nods and fades back into an alley to watch and see what I'm up to.

"Hughie!" I say. "Up!" and good Hugh the Grand bends down and puts his two hands together, fingers entwined, for me to put my foot in, and then I am lifted up onto his broad shoulders. I feel the reassuring grip of his hands around my ankles as we make our way through the crowd and up to the newly printed broadsides tacked to the printer's wall. Then I go into my act.

"Ladies and Gents! This here is your own dear Mary Faber reading you the news of the day! Look ye here, we have an account of that nasty Bonaparte kickin' up sand in Egypt, chasin' the poor wogs from one end o' the place to the other and takin' all their stuff . . . and 'ere's a notice that Miss Tessie Briggs and Mr. Asa Smoggs is gettin' wed and they're publishin' the banns right here before your very eyes, and I knows there's gonna be a big weddin' party 'cause I already got me invitation here tucked in me shift, and how about you?" As usual, my extra patter gets me a little laugh, and then I rock back like I seen somethin' that shakes me to my very core. "Coo! Look at this!" I say, pointing to a large bill. "It says here that a reward of five-hundred-pounds sterling is offered for the capture, dead or alive, of the no-tor-i-ous criminal Patrick O'Toole, alias Pigger O'Toole, on a charge of kidnappin' one Polly Von, long-lost granddaughter of Lord Peter Von, peer o' the realm and all that. It seems the little tyke was misplaced on a royal trip and snatched by the a-fore-men-tioned thug, who is known to inhabit various hells in Cheapside, the chief of which is on Paternoster Lane. Anyone wishin' to claim the reward must be careful in the app-re-hen-sion of the fiend, as he is known to be armed and dangerous, and must secure the safety of the child. App-li-ca-tion for the reward may be made at the Royal Huff-ing-ton Manor, London."

Out of the corner of my eye, I see the Shankies lookin' sharp at each other.

Several hard-lookin' types surge forward. "Are ye sure o' that, girl?" says one particularly vile-lookin' cove.

"That I am, Sir, it says so right here, and if it's in print, it's got to be so," I says, eyes round in wonder. "Coo, five hundred pounds...Wouldn't that buy ye a right big slice o' kidney pie?" I see Flick and Scut turn and run down the street toward Paternoster. Ah, yes, two fleet Shanky messengers bearin' the news.

The man who spoke and two other very tough-looking gents gather, then take off toward Saint Paul's. I chuckle to myself: *You're real good, Pigger, at kickin' kids around—let's see how you handle those three.* All have swords and I think I see pistol bulges under their long black coats.

They ain't the only ones interested, neither. Other groups of men confer and then take themselves off, intent on some mission.

Now there are also folks standing about who look at me in a curious way—thems must be the ones what can read and are wonderin' why I'm sayin' the words I am whilst pointing at a poster advertising an auction of yearling horses. But I put my finger to my lips like it's all a big joke, and they don't say nothing, as it ain't their business, anyway.

Well, the upshot of it was that Pigger had to light out of town, fast. In fact, we never seen him ever again. It's said that he got nabbed for stealin' a hog up north and got himself hanged for it. Though how the constables up there could tell him and the pig apart, I don't know. Maybe they hanged the hog and roasted Pigger... There's others who say he got a job in a circus as a geek, sittin' in a cage, bitin' the heads off live chickens, which seemed to me to be much more likely, that bein' the vocation I always felt he was born for. I don't know. All I know is we was deprived of his company from then on and we rejoiced in it. A cove named Natty B. Matt took over the Shanky Boys, and though he wasn't exactly a stand-up citizen of the streets, he was a practical fellow and we got along with him. Peace returned to the streets of Cheapside.

I, too, had to lay low for a while, 'cause of bein' guilty of spreadin' false rumors and other falsehoods, but it was worth it—Charlie didn't get hanged for murderin' Pigger, and Polly come walkin' back into our kip, thumb in mouth, the next day, as if nothin' had ever happened.

I lay low by going up to the rooftops again. Some of those blokes who went after Pigger to get the reward was now lookin' for me, for sendin' them on a wild-pig chase, so I figured high up was the place for Little Mary Faber to be till they cooled off a bit. I had a special place that I liked, a roof where the tiles came together twixt two gables and made a rain gutter. I could sleep there without worryin' about fallin' off, and I could watch the goings-on of the city from that perch high above. Judy or Nancy would come up each night to stay with me and bring me news of the gang's activities, and maybe a bit of food.

It warn't so bad, and after a while, when the heat was off, I went back down to join my friends in our kip.

"And that's the end of that story," I say, taking another invisible bow.

"Jacky, weren't you just the cleverest *thang*," I hear Clarissa say by way of snide comment on my little tale.

My face burns at that, but I say, "How 'bout a round of applause for our Hughie here for bein' the real hero of the piece?"

"Hear, hear!" and hands are clapped together and I'm surprised to find that some of the girls know how to whistle.

When the cheering subsides, Hughie, who I know is blushing mightily back there in the hatchway, says, "That was real nice, Mary. Now tell us about when you had the baby."

Well, *that* gets a rustle out of the girls, for sure.

"Yes, *Ma-ry*," comes Clarissa's slow drawl out of the gloom. "Please do tell us about when you had the *bay-bee*."

I heave a sad sigh. I hadn't told anybody about Jesse, not even Amy. He was just the *best* little boy, and it was true that, for a short while, he was mine.

"Well, of course, I didn't *have* a baby—I was only about eleven at the time. I found him in a garbage can."

I get up and start the story.

I WAS OUT on my own that day and I thought I'd check out a rubbish bin where I'd found some pretty decent apple cores the week before. I slipped up the alley and was on the pile in a minute, tearing away at the useless stuff, when I pulled away a bundle of dirty rags, and there he was. I don't know how he got there—prolly left by Muck to die after he'd taken the poor dead mother off to the anatomist's to sell. I know his mother wouldn'a left him in a garbage can if she could help it.

I don't know how he got there. I only know he was there and reaching up at me and sayin', "Ma-Ma..."

Chapter 44

I'm down at the Rat Hole again that night, having been awakened at one fifteen and ready in my black rig to go out at one thirty. We've found this is the best time for me to be out 'cause the watches have changed and everybody's back to sleep—including most of them that's on watch.

I gave Clarissa a good shake on my way down, and I soon find her here by my side in the candlelight as I make ready. Beatrice, who had been on watch on the Stage, had lit the candle and taken down the Rat Hole boards before I got there. Then she had gone back up on watch. *Good girl.*

"What are you plannin' to do out there tonight?" Clarissa demands.

"I've got to start disabling the other lifeboat so's the crew won't be able to chase us when we make our break. That ship we saw yesterday showed us that we've got to get moving on this or things will get out of our control and we can't have that. The fuse is five links from being done. We could go the day after tomorrow if the weather holds."

"I'm going out with you," she states firmly.

"No, you are not. You don't have a black rig and there's no time to make you one. Besides the *Bloodhound* only needs one Black Ghost."

"It's not fair that you should have all the glory."

Glory?

"Look, Clarissa, I know you are brave and bold, but this is not the time for it. Too much is at stake to pander to your sense of adventure. Your time will come, believe me, when we break out. Haven't we talked about your role in that enough?"

"*Humph,*" she says. "A little bit of playactin'...hardly seems heroic enough."

"The success of the whole venture depends on that bit of playactin', Clarissa, and don't you forget it. You've got the starring role and, if you must know, I'm a bit jealous."

She smirks at this. "Yes, you would be, wouldn't you, bein' the shameless show-off hussy that you most plainly are."

"Come on, Clarissa, we're all in this together, and when this is over and done with, we can go back to being the best of enemies."

"Well, still, I'm going with you to the top of the first ladder, anyway. I will act as sentry. No one will see me there," she says, and I have to agree to that. "What do you plan to do in the boat?"

"I plan to drop the oars over the side and slit the sails so they cannot follow us by either rowing or sailing. I would get rid of their rudder, too, but as that hangs outside the canvas covering, the fact that it's missing might be spotted, and so we can't chance it. No, the rudder will have to be the last thing to go, on the night before we escape."

"Suppose they discover the slit sails and the missing oars?" she asks. "Won't they blame it on us? Won't they conduct a thorough search?"

"No, they will blame it on the Black Ghost. He's gonna leave footprints there tonight. I'll explain later. Come on, let's go."

I get into the lifeboat without incident. Leaving Clarissa on the lower level with a warning not to do anything daring or stupid or both, I gained the deck, looked, and saw that the entire watch was huddled on the quarterdeck, no doubt a bit fearful of going off alone to possibly encounter either a ghost or a once-human heap of seaweed, neither of which would be much to their liking. As before, I loosen the line holding down the canvas cover and crawl in.

From the inside, I slacken the canvas on the outboard side and carefully put five of the six oars over the side—they are long enough so that I can just about touch the water with them, such that when I let them go, they slip into the water with nary a sound.

Having done that, I pull out my shiv and silently but thoroughly slice up the mainsail and the jib. That job finished, I put my shiv back in my waistband and pull out the oilskin wad I had also tucked in there before leaving the Hold, then open it up. I'm glad enough moonlight is shining in so I can see to do this work.

Earlier in the day I had taken a rag, soaked it down good, and on it I sprinkled the powder I'd made by crushing the red cake of dry watercolor from my miniature-portrait-painting kit. I added a touch of brown pigment to bring the color to reddish-brown, the same shade as dried blood.

Then I folded the rag and mashed it and kneaded it till the color started to seep through. Opening it back up, I saw that I had a nice, blood red printing pad. I wrapped it in the piece of oilcloth where I stored my brushes and put it away for later.

Now I lay the open ink pad on the lifeboat's rear seat and ball up my fists and start making baby footprints—I take my clenched right fist and press its right, or pinkie, side onto the pad and then push it down on the deck. Then I put the tips of my right-hand fingers on the pad and then push them all down, in a slightly curved way, on the top of the print I had just made, and behold, a perfect little child's footprint...or a perfect little ghost's...

I do the same with my other hand and place this print to the left and a bit ahead of the other one for the left footprint, and so on up the deck from the rear seat to the next, and then on top of that seat. Then I stop, as if the creature who made these tracks disappeared into thin air.

I learned this little number from Rooster Charlie back in the Blackfriars Bridge days. *Oh, Charlie,* I think fondly, *always the trickster you were, always laughing and joking to give us cheer when we was all gathered together in the kip and maybe down a bit on account of bein' cold and havin' nothin' to eat. You, Charlie, who said, "Now, ladies, you never can tell when these little tricks'll come in handy..."* Right you were, *Charlie, and right you are...*

I refold my pad and stow it away. I retie the boat's outer canvas and peek out through the opening on the near side, the way I had come in. I see no movement. The coast being clear, I crawl out, tie down the canvas, and head back for the hatchway.

There, I say to myself, *by leaving tracks I have covered my tracks.*

I slink around the corner of the hatch and *Damn!* I am confronted by two men who have plainly gone up on some errand and were afraid to go alone.

"Good God!" gasps one. The other is scared speechless. I see only eyes wide with terror.

I am just as terrified as they, but I make myself think, *You see them as men, but they see you as a black shadow, a black demon,* and I reach up and pull myself to the ratlines, curling my arms about myself in imitation of a black spider. I twist those same arms in weird ways, and I reach deep down in my throat and rumble out, *"Taboo...taboooo... taboooooooo..."*

They cannot move.

I, however, can. After I have uttered the last *taboooooo,* I leap from the rigging to the rail, and then, seeing them transfixed, I drop over the side.

I do not, however, drop into the ocean. No, I drop onto the anchor, which I know is hanging there by the side. I quickly clamber up the anchor shaft and onto the chain and into the hawsehole, the opening in the bow where the anchor chain is drawn. It's a very tight squeeze and I leave a good bit of skin with the barnacles that cling thereto, but I make it in. Sitting on the pile of chain, I put my ear to the hawsehole.

"D-d-disappeared, it did, right into thin air. You saw it, don't say you didn't."

"Nay, I saw it go right down into the sea, and it grinned a hideous grin at me as it went under and...*Oh, my God! We is lost! We is lost! We seed it, we did! We seed the Black Ghost, we did!"*

And chaos rules on the *Bloodhound*.

These two run back to the quarterdeck, shrieking out their story, and the ship's bell starts ringing and ringing, and I know a very unhappy Captain's gonna come roarin' out of his cabin, shoutin' out death and destruction to any who would disturb his sleep. I climb blindly over the piled-up chain in the anchor-chain locker to find my way to the door, where I can see light around the edges, and I wait there, crouched and fearful, 'cause I know the whole crew has been roused. A lamp has been lit in the kitchen and I hear shouts of *"Muster on the quarterdeck!"* and feet pounding out of the crew's berth. Then, when I don't hear nothin', I wait for another second, open the latch, which, thank God, opens from the inside, too. When I look out, there's no one around.

I bolt down the passageway and down the ladder. Clarissa is still there.

"Damn!" she says. "What happened?"

"I got spotted! We've got to hurry! They're mustering the crew, which means they'll muster us, too! Hurry!"

We go through the storeroom and worm our way through the Rat Hole and hear the other girls starting to wake up from the noise outside.

Beatrice is there with the candle.

"Get the boards up quick!" I say, and pull off my hood and black shirt. "They'll be down any minute!"

Clarissa and Bea get the boards up with one screw in the end of each, 'cause there's no time to do the others. We keep a little puddle of candle wax mixed with candle soot and brown color from my painting set next to the boards. Clarissa and Bea each take some up and thumb it into the screw holes to hide them.

Meanwhile, I'm strugglin' out of my black boots and stockings when I hear, *"Lord, save us!"* from above and I know that Sin-Kay and who-knows-who-else have entered our Hold.

"Bea," I whisper, "leave the candle and get back topside! Cause confusion! Give us some time!"

She nods and goes to do it.

I pull off my black top and gather everything into a bundle and hiss to Clarissa, "We've got to get this stuff into the hidey-hole!"

The top board to the hidey-hole cache is off and I cram in my black rig.

"Inspection line!" roars Sin-Kay from up above. "Now!"

There are sounds of great commotion overhead. Feminine cries of *"Oh, my Lord,"* and, *"Saints preserve us,"* and, *"Please, God!"* are heard, as well as Sin-Kay's *"Dammit! Line up! Get up from there! Get out of my way!"*

The girls are doing a good job of obstruction, but will it be good enough, will we have time, will...?

My burglar gear bein' in, I spit on my thumb and forefinger and snuff the candle and throw it in with the rest, and we put the top board back on. Screws in, sooty wax over the holes.

Now for my drawers and undershirt. It's dark, but I know where I left them and I feel around and find them.

"Hurry!" whispers Clarissa.

I figure out which one is the drawers and I try to pull them on, but I get them backward and have to twist them around and try again. I get them on.

"There's two missing," I hear Sin-Kay say. "That goddamned Faber and Howe, the two biggest troublemakers of the bunch!"

"Let's check down below," says a rough voice I recognize as belonging to Captain Blodgett.

Uh-oh...

The light of the lamp starts swinging toward the edge of the Stage.

"They'll wonder what we're doing down here," whispers Clarissa. "They might decide to look at things real close..."

Legs are seen on the stairs down into the Pit as the hand bearing the lamp comes down. No time for the shirt. I reach out and grab hold of her hand.

"They ain't gonna wonder about nothing," I whisper and fling myself down on my back. "C'mere! Lie down on top of me! Put your arms around me!" I know she does not understand, but she will.

I pull her down on me and I wrap my legs around her waist. I put my left hand on the back of her head and pull her face toward mine as I see the lamp bearer reach the bottom of the stairs. Then I push her mouth on mine and close my eyes. I feel her tighten up under my grip, resisting, but then...

Then I hear, "Wot the hell!" and I pop my eyes open in mock surprise to see Sin-Kay, Captain Blodgett, Chubbuck, and Sammy Nettles standing there looking in at us.

I release my hold on the back of Clarissa's head so she is able to lift her face from mine.

"Lookee there, lookee there," says Nettles, gleefully.

"What the hell is going on here?" says the Captain.

"We are particular friends, Captain Blodgett," says I, pretending to breathe hard. "We are merely looking for a bit of privacy so as to give each other some comfort."

"*Peculiar* friends if you ask me," says the Captain, which

seems to me to be a perfect case of the pot calling the kettle black, but I let it go. "Chubbuck, check it out back there," barks our Captain.

I hold my breath as the Bo'sun parts the washing hung there and goes back by the Rat Hole and the Powder Hole and the hidey-hole, to inspect, but as he expects to find nothing, he discovers nothing. *What could a bunch of silly females be up to?* would go through what passes for his mind.

"Nothin'," he says, coming back out from under the Stage.

Sin-Kay crouches down and steps under for a look. He comes back out and as he does, a hanging petticoat brushes by his face. He looks startled. He takes the garment and holds it to his nose.

Uh-oh . . .

"Soap. This rag has been washed with soap," he says, glaring down at me. "Who gave you the soap? You know that was forbidden."

I think fast. There must be an answer other than that we've been getting it from the storeroom on our own. There is . . .

"Nettles got it for us," I say. "He said if I showed myself to him in the altogether, he'd get us some soap. I did it, and he got it for us."

"That's a lie!" shouts Nettles. "That's what she's been doin' to get —"

But the back of the Captain's hand catches Nettles across the mouth and he don't say nothin' after that, he just falls back and whimpers, his hands over his sore and now quite bloody mouth.

"Go back to my cabin, Sammy," says the Captain. "I don't want you messin' around down here anymore. Sin-Kay, I don't want him down here again. These vile vessels are a corrupting influence on the boy. Get along with just the Dummy. If need be, I'll assign another sailor to the duty. Now I'm going up to talk to the crew. About them seein' things and such." He heaves a heavy sigh, and I know he wishes this voyage were over. "Everyone's accounted for. There ain't no ghost. Let's all get back to sleep. That's what I'll say. Let's all get back to sleep."

With that, he turns and leaves, with Chubbuck and Sin-Kay following him.

There is still light from their lamp as they go out, and I see many curious faces hanging down over the edges of the Stage and Balcony, looking at Clarissa and me lying there still, one on top of the other.

"You can get up now," I say, and then add huskily, "if you want to." At that, Clarissa leaps to her feet and makes a big show of spitting and retching and wiping off her mouth for the benefit of our audience. Then she stalks off and the total darkness falls upon us once again.

But I do not act as she does. I slowly put my shirt back on and I lie back in sweet relief at how things turned out for the best this night, and I say to myself, *Hey, I've been kissed by worse.*

Chapter 45

"We could be gone tomorrow, if the weather holds," I say, in conference with Clarissa and Dolley.

"Good," says Clarissa. "The sooner the better. The summer social season is about to begin and I do not want to miss it."

"I'm sure they will cancel the entire season if Miss Clarissa Worthington Howe is not able to grace the proceedings with her divine presence," I say.

That gets me a glare and a low growl from Miss Howe, who is still smarting over the teasing she's been getting concerning our little embrace of the other night. In fact, Rebecca had to be saved from physical harm when Clarissa went after her this morning because of that whole thing. Rebecca was performing that bit of pantomime everybody knows: She turned away from the audience and wrapped her arms about herself and ran her hands slowly up and down her back so it looked like someone else's hands were doing the caressing. Well, Rebecca was very good at it and she did it standing up on the Balcony while all the rest of us were down on the Stage, waiting for breakfast. All eyes were upon her as she did the bit, all the while moaning "Oh,

Jacky…Oh, Clarissa…" Clarissa almost got to her before cooler heads intervened.

"I don't know, though," I say thoughtfully, back on the subject of the weather. We're sitting on the Balcony looking out at the sky. "See that big area of clouds there, the ones with the little bumps on it that look like scales on a fish? They're called 'mackerel skies.' And see those high, long wispy ones? They're called 'mares' tails.'"

"So?" says Dolley.

"So sailors got a saying: 'Mackerel skies and mares' tails make tall ships carry low sails.' It means we're in for a blow and it's almost always right," I say. "But we'll see. If the weather holds, I go out tonight and disable the rudder on the other lifeboat and we'll go with the Plan in the morning. All agreed? Good."

But the damned weather doesn't hold. By noon we have whitecaps and by the time the flaps come down, the wind has whipped up into a full gale. We ain't goin' nowhere to-morrow. I sigh, resigned to yet another day in the belly of the *Bloodhound*. Ah, well, think about the story you will tell tonight, I say to myself. That'll keep you occupied, and the tale will keep them occupied, as well. They know we are going soon and they are about to jump out of their skins and we can't have that.

I REACHED INTO the trash pile and picked up the baby. I expected him to start screamin' but he don't…

He just looks at me and gurgles. Spit runs down his chin and onto the little dress he's wearin'. It's got a little

J on it in blue thread. *Must be his initial,* I'm thinkin'. *Wonder why Muck let him keep the dress?* He's got a nappy on, too, and it ain't very wet yet, so he must not have been in the rubbish for very long.

I hold him to my chest and put my right forearm under his bum and he nestles his little face into my neck and...

"All right, Clarissa, if it makes you sick, don't listen then."

And he puts his thumb in his mouth, and I head back to the kip.

Judy and Nancy are in the kip when I get there and they look up in wonder at what I'm carrying.

"Coo," says Judy. "Look at that. Mary's got 'erself a baby. Whatcha gonna do with it, Mary?"

"It ain't an *it,* it's a *he.* His name is Jesse, 'cause of the *J* there on his chest, see?" I say, then sit down on the edge of the stone platform that serves as the gang's bed at night. "I'm gonna keep him, is what I'm gonna do with him."

I set him on my knee and bounce him a bit. "Look at what a good baby he is, no crying at all, and him just a simple orphan like the rest of us. I can tell you, when I was in his place and first brought into this kip, I was crying like any ten babies."

"Any twenty," says Judy, who was there at the time.

"Well, he'll be cryin' soon enough, when he gets hungry," says Nancy. "I had a little brother...once." So she knows, and she don't have to say it.

Sure enough, the little bugger starts rummaging

around on my chest. I pull down my shift and he fixes his mouth on what there is of me, which is nothin' and he gets nothin'.

"Here. Let's try 'im on Nancy," I say, and pass him over to her. She's started to come out a bit on top, you know how we swells up a bit in the beginning.

She pulls down the top of her shift and Jesse clamps on but all we get is an "Ouch!" from poor Nancy, and all he gets is nothin'.

Just then Charlie, Hughie, and Polly come back in for the night.

"Good God, what the hell is that?" says Charlie upon seein' Jesse. "And what are you doin' with it?"

"Tryin' to feed 'im, is what," I says. "And 'is name is Jesse and he's the newest member of our merry band."

"Were dumber twits than you two ever born?" says Charlie, all incredulous at seein' what we been up to. "You've got to *have* a baby before them milk things start up, don'cha know that? Don'cha know anything?"

"I have a baby. He's right here." I pull Jesse off of Nancy and hold him up to prove my point.

"No, no, you stupid twit. The baby's got to grow in your own belly and come out of that same belly for that to happen," says Charlie, steamed. "And I'll tell you another thing—*I* says who's gonna be a new member of the gang, and not you."

"Oh," I reply. I wasn't too clear on how all that stuff happened then, so I let the feeding bit go, but...

"Rebecca, please, if you want to find out all about that stuff, I'll tell you tomorrow, not now. All right? Good. Now, hush."

But I don't let it go completely. "He could be a help to us, Charlie, like in the beggin'—a big-eyed, beautiful boy like him next to our Polly? Who could resist?"

Hughie kneels down by him and lets Jesse grab his big fingers in his tiny hands. "I like 'im," says Hughie, grinning hugely. Everything Hughie did was huge.

"Christ, Mary, what next?" says Charlie. "Last year it was them three kittens..."

"Right, and I raised them up proper, with no cost to the gang, and now all three are off leading good cat lives. And they gave us all a bit o' joy when they was here. I remember you playing with 'em, too, Rooster Charlie, and don't say you didn't."

"But you don't know nothin' 'bout raisin' babies, Mary, you don't. You think you know everything, and don't deny that, but you don't know how to raise babies," says Charlie, his mouth a grim line of certitude.

But I am stubborn. "What should I do? Put 'im back to die so's Muck can cart 'im off to Dr. Graves's Fine Exhibition of Guts in a Jar? Should I do that, Charlie Brewster? Should I?"

"We could leave 'im on a doorstep," says Charlie. "See if someone takes 'im in."

"They won't do that, Charlie," I says. "They'll think that he has diseases, since he comes from the likes of us. Nobody's gonna take 'im in 'cept us, and that's the truth."

"Damn!" Charlie groans. "We ain't got trouble enough..."

"But Jesse ain't got no diseases, do you, baby?" says I, taking him back from Nancy and holding him tight.

"No, you don't. You're just the best baby that is, and don't you pay that Charlie no mind. You're staying here with me, or"—and here I lean into it—"the two of us will go off alone, together."

Charlie rounds on me. "A threat, is it, Mary? Well, let me tell you this: You're a valuable member of this gang, but you ain't all that rare a thing, and if that brat don't pull 'is weight, and if you slack off in any o' your duties, then you can go, and to hell with both of you!"

"Fine, Charlie," I say. "Has anybody got any food?"

Charlie grumbles but opens his sack and pulls out two-day-old meat pies, a bit of sausage, and half a loaf of hard, stale bread. *Quite a haul,* I thinks to myself, and it could not come at a better time.

Charlie divides up the stuff in the usual way—carving everything into as equal portions as can be made, then turning around and calling out names as someone else points at one portion or another.

"Polly," he says, and Polly goes and gets hers.

"Mary," he says, and I lean forward and gather up my share.

While the other names are being called and their portions taken, I take a piece of the meat-pie crust and hold it up to Jesse's lips. He don't do nothin', he just shakes his head and turns away.

"Ain't been weaned yet," says Charlie, observing all this. "You'll see...It ain't gonna be easy."

We have a broken bit of a crockery jug that we keep water in, water we get from the horse trough up on Creed Street. I reach for it, lift it, take a sip, hold it, and then take a bite of the meat pie. I chew it up until it's a pasty glop in my mouth, and then I hold Jesse's lips up to mine and push the chewed-up mess out with my tongue. His lips worm around mine and he takes the food in. When we're done with that, I chew up another batch.

As I'm giving it to him, I see that Charlie is watching me doing it. I know as leader of the gang he's got to be hard sometimes and he knows it, too. But now he heaves a great sigh and his face softens, and as night falls and Jesse is full and burps his contentment and we get ready to go to sleep, Charlie says, "Mary, Mary, quite contrary, what are we gonna do with you? You're just too soft-hearted for this life we lead, is what it is." He says that and he puts his arm around my shoulder. "Here, let's put him between us as we go to sleep. Then we'll see what tomorrow brings. No promises, now, but we'll see."

As I lie there in the darkness under the bridge with Jesse sleepin' peacefully by me in the crook of my arm and Charlie near on the other side, and Hughie's broad back up against me on my right, the rags and straw pulled over all of us, I think about the way of things and the feel of Jesse's lips as he took the food from my mouth, and I think about how you can get real close to someone when you do that and you...you...you... sleep...

Chapter 46

It is morning and Rebecca will not be put off. "I want to know about those things and I want you to tell me," she announces firmly.

We're being tossed around ferociously by the storm, but only a few of us are stretched out sick. The girls have been told that they are going soon, and now this storm comes to delay things. Still, it's better that they lie here listening to my stories than be out there in a small boat. Had we left earlier, we surely would have been lost.

There will be no Dance class this morning, so I might as well grant Rebecca her wish.

"Very well," I say, "Mother Faber will now conduct a class in The Nature of Things." I'm seated cross-legged on the edge of the Stage, having just finished my bowl of cold gruel. I pat the deck next to me. "Come, Daughter, and sit." She plops down next to me and waits, wide-eyed in anticipation. I look at the child and think, *Oh, sweet Rebecca, you ain't gonna like a lot of what you're about to hear.*

I clear my throat and begin. "In the mature male of our species—"

"Speak up down there," I hear someone on the Balcony

say, and I hear someone else say, "Yeah. We certainly don't want to miss any of *this*."

Hmmm...I realize from the silence in the Hold that all of them are listening, and I bet a good half of them are just as ignorant as Rebecca about how a baby gets made and how it enters this world. All right, then. I raise my voice to be heard over the howl of the wind outside and begin again.

"Very well. *Ahem*. Things Your Own Mother Should Have Told You But Plainly Did Not, part one. *Ahem*. In the adult male of our species, there is..."

I don't have a blackboard or a drawing pad, so I make do with my left hand's thumb and forefinger making a circle and my right hand's forefinger going in and out of that circle again and again—just like Mrs. Roundtree instructed my younger and very worried self a few years back, when I didn't know anything about this stuff, either.

I cover the basics first, about how the baby gets in there in the first place and what happens after that, and then I tell about the other games that people play when they're of a mind to be a bit naughty, and for that I hear *"Eeeeeee-uuuwww!"* and *"I would never do that!"* and *"That's disgusting!"* and *"I think you're making all this up!"*

"Oh, nay, Sisters, I am not. I got this straight from a Mrs. Roundtree on Malta, and she was *definitely* an expert in this field."

"But how does the baby get out of there?" asks Rebecca, perplexed.

I take a breath and quickly tell her, and her jaw drops in disbelief, as girls' jaws have for thousands of years upon receiving that particular bit of information.

"But it can't—"

"Oh, yes it can, dear, believe me. I was midwife to the Captain's wife on the *Pequod,* when she had young Prudence in the midst of a storm very like this one, so I've seen it done with my own eyes."

"Lord...," whispers Rebecca, still stunned.

"Cheer up, lass." I chuckle and clap her on the shoulder. "That sort of thing is a long way off for you."

I stand and say, "Today's lecture is concluded. Thank you for your attention. And, in the spirit of dear old Mrs. Roundtree, each of yiz owes me a shillin'."

Today, for the first time since work on the Plan was begun, there is no one working on any part of it—the fuse is finished and there is no more carving to be done. Even the Dianas do not hunt, because Cookie is not cooking since they don't light the kitchen fires in a blow like this, which is why our gruel was served cold this morning. So no roasted millers today—though probably we'll still liberate a few more bottles of wine, as we have become used to rich living. Some crackers might settle some queasy stomachs, too. While I'm thinking on this, I reflect again on how lucky we are not to have gone several days ago and so gotten caught up in this storm. But the fuse was not done yet, thus we did not go to our doom. Now, however, the fuse is done and coiled and stowed and waiting in the powder magazine for the right time. That will be when the weather lets up, if it ever does.

The day drags slowly on.

Constance Howell's Bible reading was that part in Genesis where God kicks Adam and Eve out of Eden for being bad, and it being mainly Eve's fault, He tells her He's gonna punish her by making it so that it hurts like hell when she and all her descendants have babies—and so it is to this very day, thank you very much, Eve. Which I thought was a rather nice follow-up to my little lecture of the morning. Course I know she chose that bit to show what indulging in any of that nastiness I had been tellin' them about would get you, which is screaming your lungs out on the birthin' bed, but, hey, that's all right.

The flaps come down on yet another day at the Bloodhound Academy, Hepzibah leads us in a nice rendition of Anerio's *Venite ad Me Omnes,* and then I continue my story.

I HAD TOLD you before of the place high on a rooftop that I used to favor when I had to hide out for a bit, it having a nice safe rain gutter between two gables for sleepin' in and a good view of what was happening in the streets, but there was somethin' else about the place that I liked, as well. Off the back of this building I could look down into this square where there was a small house in a neat yard. A man lived there with his wife and baby son. The husband must have been a clerk or something, 'cause he wore a suit of clothes every day when he went out, and not workingman's garb. She was a pretty, young thing, bustling about, sweeping off the front steps, or washing windows, or hanging out laundry. When she hung out the wash, she would have the baby in a basket next to her and she would sing to him and laugh, and the baby would chortle back at her, waving his arms and legs about as babies will do when they are happy. I think I liked watching this family 'cause I imagined myself bein' one of 'em, and bein' cared for and all. They used to get dressed up on Sunday mornings and go down to Saint Paul's for church. I know, 'cause I followed 'em down there once.

Anyway, it was to that rooftop, up above that family's house, that I hied myself the morning after bringing Jesse to the kip. When I had woken up, a quick check of Jesse showed that the boy needed to own more than one diaper, and I meant to get him one. So, leaving him in the care of Nancy, up to the rooftop I go.

Peeking over the edge, I see that, indeed, the young wife has hung out six nappies, all in a row on a line. Making sure there's no one about, I jump from this roof to one lower and then one lower than that, and finally I shinny down a drainpipe to the ground, right next to the clothesline. I, quick, run over, grab one, pull it off, and then run like hell. Sorry, Missus, but as you had six or more, me Jesse had only one. Now two...

"Yes, Connie, a thief as well as a tramp, and you already knew that. May I continue?"

Back at the kip, me and Nan take Jesse down to the Thames and wash off his bottom and rinse out the nappy he was wearin' when he come to join our merry band. I took off my shift and dried him with it and then carried him back to the kip. It bein' the middle of September, things was right warm, so it was no hardship to any of us. Then we put his new nappy on him and tied up the sides and hung up the wet one in the kip, and I hung up my damp shift next to it.

There's three whistles—our gang's signal—and Charlie comes back into the kip, with Judy and Polly. He sees the laundry hangin' there.

"Christ. A bloody nursery…That this should happen to a man of my stature…," he says, and tosses a bread roll at each of us. Inside each roll is a bit of sausage. Such riches.

"Where'd you get this, Charlie?" asks I, lookin' at the wonderful roll in my hand.

"Benbow's had some heavy work to do, lifting stones and such, so we traded Hughie for the day in exchange for this grub. Lay to. Hughie's gettin' 'is at the job."

And we do…

"And yes, Hughie, once again you saved the day."

I chew up a mouthful and reach for the water jug, but Charlie stops my hand and says, "You swallow that, you," 'cause he knows what I'm up to. "Now."

I pretend to swallow, then take the jug, chew up roll and sausage and water, and tongue it out to Jesse's waiting mouth. Charlie snorts and goes over to sit down and eat his portion.

When me and Jesse are done, I pat his back and he burps and then puts his face on my shoulder and goes to sleep, just like that. He is an awfully good baby.

After all have eaten, Charlie stands back up and grabs my shift and throws it at me. "C'mon, you," he says. "And bring the damn kid." I slip on my shift and hoist Jesse onto my hip and follow Charlie out and up North Bridge. I'm a mite fearful, 'cause I know Charlie don't approve of me havin' this baby at all, and so I clutch Jesse a little closer to me as we walk along.

Charlie don't say nothin', which is not a good sign. We turn right on Ludgate and there's a bit of a crowd there among the vendors' stalls.

"Try 'im here," says Charlie, and he goes to lean against a wall.

I go out and get to work.

I put my hand out and say, "Please, Mum, please! Jesse here's gonna die if he don't get some milk," and, "Please, Sir, can you see it in your heart to give us a penny for Jesse's milk, please, Sir?" "Oh, Missus, you got a young one just like mine—please, a little somethin' for some milk," and on and on.

Finally someone pushes a coin into my palm and I look at it and it's a ha'penny. Not much, but somethin'. "Oh, thank you, Missus, thank you..."

Charlie comes up to us and says, "All right, we're done here. Let's go."

And so we walk, not back to the kip as I would have thought but up Old Bailey and up to Newgate. Charlie don't say nothin' for a long time and I don't, neither. Jesse coos by my side, lulled by the rollin' action of my hip.

"You know, Mary," says Charlie, finally, "you are a very valuable member of our gang, and you are very dear to me, as well." He lets that hang for a while. "But now you seem intent on starvin' yourself to death on account o' this baby." Another pause. "Now, you got to know that this baby is going to die, anyway, 'cause he's got to have milk, and not just bread mixed with your spit is gonna do it, and we don't have any milk. You know that, don't you, Mary?"

"Yes, Charlie, I know that, but I ain't givin' up hope yet. I still think he could be valuable to the band in the way o' beggin', I do," says I.

Charlie sighs and we continue on.

"We're gettin' right close to Shanky turf here, y'know," I says, lookin' around for signs o' the scum.

"I know," says Charlie, "but we're here now. Good day to you, Mrs. Little!"

I'm shocked to see Charlie bowing low to a woman sitting on her front steps, with an infant on her huge left breast, who is sucking, quite happily and quite loudly, away.

"Ah, and if it ain't Rooster Charlie Brewster, his ownself, God's gift to the streets o' Cheapside," says this woman, two hundred and fifty pounds if she's an ounce. "And I see you got yerself a brat. Ain't surprised at that, I ain't."

"Ah, well, Missus, that we do, and he's sore in need o' that product that you can so amply provide."

"Get on wi' you, Charlie. I can't afford to take in un-payin' clients, and I know you ain't got a pot to piss in nor a window to throw it out of," says the woman. "My girls 'ere, Thelma on the right and Betty on the left, are me sole support in this hard world. Can't expect me to give it away, now, can you?"

"Please, Missus," I pipes up. "'E's gonna die if he don't get some."

"Now, now, dearie, you save that guff for your marks or your nobs, not for me."

"Give me the coin," says Charlie to me.

Surprised, I hand it over. "That's gang money, Charlie, I don't expect you to—"

"We wouldn'a got it 'cept for the kid," says Charlie, flipping the coin in the air and catching it right in front of the woman's nose. "So, what, Mrs. Little, would be the charge to put this wee one on one o' your girls for a bit?"

"The charge, Charlie, is one shillin' a week."

My heart sinks. One shilling. A king's ransom to us.

Charlie nods gravely. I think he brought me and Jesse up here so we could see the desperation of our situation. "But what will one ha'penny buy right now?" he asks, holding up the coin.

"Oh, give it over, and give 'im over, too," says Mrs. Little, taking the coin and taking Jesse as I hand him to her.

She pulls down the right shoulder of her shirt, exposing the breast named Thelma, and Jesse clamps right on, his little hands pumping away.

"Oh, he's a greedy one, he is," says Mrs. Little.

"Charlie, I'm gonna love you forever," says I, my eyes filmy with tears, and I means it.

"Awright, that's it. That's one ha'penny's worth an' more," says Mrs. Little, and Jesse's mouth come off her with a loud pop!

She hands him back to me and I thank her and I hold him to me.

"Pat 'is back to burp 'im, dearie, or he'll spit up all that good pap you just paid for," says Mrs. Little, and I do it and he does burp. I can smell his breath and I reflect—today, into his mouth I have put bread, sausage, water, spit, and a good deal of Mrs. Little's bounty, and still his baby breath smells as sweet as any flowers. I hold him to me as we leave Mrs. Little.

"So you see, that's the way of it," says Charlie, his

arm around my shoulders. "We can't do a shilling a week, and unless you can figure another way..."

I know the truth of what he's saying, but I will not accept it, not yet I won't, now that Jesse's got a full belly and is good for another day, at least. Then I look up the street and see the hated gates of Newgate Prison. There are some black-clad people outside the gate, and it seems they are being refused entrance to the place.

"What's that about, Charlie?" I ask.

He looks over and says, "Quakers. Do-gooders. Prolly the turnkey won't let 'em in 'cause they make trouble."

"Come on, Charlie, let's go over there," I say, and head up the street. Charlie sighs and follows.

There are five of them. Four men and one woman, a young woman of about twenty-one. They are all dressed in that plain Quaker garb—black suits on the men, a black dress on the woman, white starched collars on all. They seem angry at being denied admittance.

I take Jesse up to the woman and say, "Please, Mum, I got this here baby and he's gonna die if he don't get milk regular and I can't give it to him, but there's a woman up the street who can for a shillin' a week. Oh, please, Miss, I know you Quakers do good all over the world. Can't you do good for this one poor little tyke what don't ask for much and—"

"Come, Elizabeth," says one of the men. "You, girl, get away, please."

"Aw, Miss, I know you're tryin' to help those poor wretches in the prison there, but why not help this poor little wretch out here, only one shillin' a week and you're sure to go straight to Heaven for it, I know you will, I—"

"Be off, girl, we are on important work here," says another of the men, severely.

"What could be more important than baby Jesse here?" I wail, tears pouring out of my eyes. "Look at 'im, he's a good baby, he's—"

"Elizabeth."

"One moment, please, Friend Fry," says the young woman. "I will speak with the girl." She stoops down to talk to me, eye to eye. "How came you by this baby?"

"I found 'im in a rubbish bin, Miss. No one else wanted 'im, but I did and I'm tryin' to keep 'im alive, but I can't without milk, I can't..."

She seems to be considering this and I look over at the prison and I say, "I can get in there anytime you want, Miss, really, I can. Me and me pals have always gotten in there. And...and...if you need messages passed back and forth, I can do it and...and I can read and write, and if you want to pass a message to one what can't read, then I can read it for 'im, and if you need word from some cove inside what can't write, then you can give me a piece o' paper and I can write down what that cove had to say and bring it out to you, and—"

"All right, child, enough," says the young woman, rising. "Where is this wet nurse of yours?"

"Right up the street there, Miss. Her name's Mrs. Little, and bless you, Miss, bless you."

We walk, an unlikely parade of Quakers and urchins, up the street, and the young woman confronts Mrs. Little.

"My name is Elizabeth Gurney. Will you feed that baby for one shilling a week as this child states?"

"I will," says Mrs. Little.

"Good. Then do it," says Elizabeth Gurney, opening her purse. "And you," she says to me, "how may we contact you when we need your services?"

And so began my time as messenger for the Quakers, or Society of Friends, as they preferred to be called. It was easy for us to worm our way into the prison. Heck, we had always done it...Well, the others done it, but I always held back 'cause I couldn't stand to see the poor condemned criminals in there, waiting their turns to be hanged. Oh, it warn't the criminal part that bothered me—after all, I was a criminal, too—no, it was the hanging business that got me. Y'see, I've always had this fear, this dread that bein' hanged was gonna be my fate at the end of it all—and given my way of life and all that, it wasn't such an out-of-the-way suspicion. But I felt that it was my duty, since I was the one what brought Jesse into our midst, and so I had to go down into those dank tombs and do what was asked of me.

"And such horrors did I see there that I cannot relate them to you, my sisters, for fear of destroying the sweetness of your sleep."

Anyway, with Mrs. Little and her Thelma and Betty, and my chewed-up bits of food to get Jesse fully weaned, the little lad prospered. He became the darling of the kip, the pride of the gang, and the joy of all, for he was just the best baby—he seldom cried and never complained. When his teeth started coming in and hurt him in doing so, Charlie went out to see the Dodger and came back with a bottle of Mother's Little Helper, and we rubbed it on Jesse's sore gums and it fixed him right up—made him sleep good, too, with a little smile on his face.

"And I know that you loved the baby, too, Hughie, from the way you played with him and rode him around on your shoulders. You was big, Hughie, and you could be rough, but none could have been gentler with Jesse."

But, no, it was not to last, for October turned into November and November into December and Christmas was around the corner and the land was turnin' to the cold, and one night when Jesse was between Charlie and me in bed in the kip, the rags and straw all pulled up, but not doing much good, Charlie said what I feared but didn't want to hear. "You know, Jesse ain't gonna make it through the winter. It's just gonna get too cold. He'll start shiverin' one night, catch the chill, and be dead in the mornin', and we'll just have to take him down to the Thames and float 'im off."

I sniffle and gather Jesse to me and say it ain't gonna be so, but I know what Charlie says is true. We ain't gonna be able to keep Jesse warm enough, what with the gang going from blacksmith's hearth to Saint Paul's basement crypt to any of the other dodges we did to keep ourselves alive through the cruel winter.

I'm thinking mightily on this problem, but I come up with nothing.

"What's that, Helen? Why not take him to an orphanage? Oh, Sisters, there were no orphanages, or none where a street kid could be dropped off. Don't you think we might have gone to one if we could? Nay, it was live hard and die young for such as us, make no mistake about that."

The wind come across the Thames real cold on this particular day, and I set out to get Jesse a blanket—if I could find one—to hold off the inevitable a while longer, and so I went back up onto my perch above the little family that lived so happily down below to see if they could spare a blanket, as they had once spared a diaper, and when I got there, I was met with a great shock.

As I looked over the edge, I saw a black crepe ribbon on the door, and even as I looked, the door opened and people came out—first, the young husband, then the wife, who was being held up by an older man and woman, and then others, bearing a small white coffin. I knew they were going to Saint Paul's, and all would come back, except for the coffin and the child held inside it.

I sat there for a while, looking down. There was wash on the line in the cold December air—the young woman's mother must have come to her daughter in her time of grief to help where she could, and what she could do was cook and console and do the laundry and hang it up outside. What else could she do, except the homey things that might bring some comfort to the bereaved girl?

I looked at the wash flapping in the breeze. I looked at the black crepe ribbon. I thought about the young family I had so admired, so envied, so loved.

Then I went down and stole the baby's blanket.

Chapter 47

I‌t was a nice blanket. It was a light blue, with pink needlework along the edges and tiny white flowers in the center and...

"Do you want me to go on? I told you I was a criminal, didn't I? Yes, so you should not have been so shocked at my action. And I might have had some other use for the blanket in mind. Maybe I had a plan forming in my head—did you think that might have been possible, oh, you who are so quick to condemn me? Shall I go on? All right, then..."

I kept an eye on the young man and young woman who had lost their baby. He went out each day to work and his wife resumed her chores, she did, but she did it without joy. She no longer sang, and sometimes, when she thought no one was around, she'd sit down on her steps and cry, rocking back and forth in her grief.

On the Sunday following the funeral, I took Jesse up for his breakfast at Mrs. Little's and then left him in the loving care of Judy, happily snugged in his new blanket. Then I went to check on the still-grieving parents to see if they would keep on going to church, now that God had taken their joy. They did, a downhearted two instead of a joyous three, but they did. And I had to know that.

"No, Rebecca, I couldn't just walk up to them and give them the baby. Don't you think I would have done that if I could, for Jesse's sake, as it was growing colder by the day and we'd see no more warm days till spring? No, the husband would have taken one look at me in my rags and filth, and he'd have refused to take him in. The same with leaving Jesse on their steps and knocking on the door and running away. Nay, there had to be another way to do it. Now, dear, pray let me continue."

Saint Paul's Cathedral sat like a huge fortress in the middle of its own open square, with no other buildings near it and no way into its fastness. Or so thought the smug bunch of tightfisted priests who ran the place, the same bunch who would not let us in the door for services, nor give us any money from the poor box, though you'd be hard-pressed to find anyone poorer than we were. The cheap sods.

It serves them right that the Rooster Charlie Gang found a way in.

There is a graveyard on the river side of the cathedral with the usual gravestones and markers, and a few of them are those little stone houses—mausoleums, I think they're called—where people stick the bodies of their dead 'cause they don't want to put them in the ground with the poor folk.

Anyway, about two years before, on a warm summer's day, when Charlie and me is out on our own tryin' to scare up a little action, we go up a side alley and come out on that graveyard. We go to cut across it on our way to the Bull and Boar Tavern to see what's shakin' there, when we see this bloke dressed in a long priest's cassock come walking through the yard toward us. Charlie grabs my arm and pulls me behind a large tombstone so's we can watch and see what the fellow is up to.

He walks along, then he stops in front of one of those mausoleums, one that's got some bushy trees around the doorway, hiding it, like. He looks about him, as if to make sure no one is about, then he steps behind the bushes. We hear the faint jingling of a ring of keys, the creak of a door opening and shutting, then silence.

A slow grin works its way across Charlie's face. "It's a priest hole," he says.

I ask what that means, and Charlie explains, "It's from back in the old days, when Protestants were runnin' around killin' Catholics and vice versa, all in the name of God, of course. Sometimes a churchman had to get out quick and secretlike, before the mob nabbed 'im for a roastin'. So a lot o' churches, and even some houses, had secret escape tunnels, called 'priest holes.' Get it?"

I got it, and Charlie got out his little lock-pickin' kit he kept tucked in his blue vest, next to his shiv, and we creep over and duck into the bushes where we saw the man disappear. Charlie runs his hand over the door and peers at the lock, and then chooses a pick and sticks it in.

"Are you sure about this, Charlie?" I say. "What if he's in there?"

"Wot? In there payin' a visit to 'is great-great-grandmum? Nah, 'e was out gettin' 'imself a nip, 'e was, or else 'e's got a lady friend out there somewhere 'e don't want 'is vicar to know about." He pulls out another pick and puts it in next to the first. "Ha!" he says as the lock clicks and the door swings open. "I knew it'd be easy. I mean, who wants to break into a crypt? Come on."

We step inside. With the door open and letting in some light, we can see that there is an opening in the floor and stone stairs leading down into darkness. There does seem to be a few real tombs in here, as well, and on top of one sit several oil lamps, along with a flint striker. Charlie takes a lamp, lights it, closes the door, and heads down the stairs, with me followin' a bit fearfully, I can tell you.

The stairs go down about twenty feet and then there is a door. This door is not locked and Charlie carefully looks in. "Good. It's what I thought it would be. It's the catacombs." He opens the door and we go in.

It is a long, long tunnel of stone, probably as long as the church itself, and on either side are shelves, and on the shelves are stone coffins, and on top of some of them are dead bodies just laid out in the open. Charlie's lamp shines on the face of one whose head is to the side so the gaping eye sockets of the skeleton look right at me. I whimper and grab on to Charlie's hand.

"Now, now, Little Mary," he says, soothingly, "these churchmen won't bother you. It's the ones upstairs you've got to worry about." But I ain't convinced... There's one what ain't been dead too long, his eyes sunken, the skin on his face like brown leather. Oh, God, there's one that—

But finally we come to the end, and there's another flight of stairs going up, and up them we go. When we reach the top, there's another door, and Charlie puts his ear to it and listens. Then he opens it. He puts the lamp down on the top step and steps out, with me hangin' on to him like a leech.

We have come out into the great, silent cathedral itself, in an aisle to the side. Light pours in through the grand stained-glass windows and the row of windows that go around the base of the great dome high overhead. Charlie heads down the aisle toward the entrance, toward where he knows the poor box will be. There's a foyer, and there's the box. Charlie sticks his hand in. "Damn!" he hisses. "Cheap bastards prolly don't let the money stay in there for even a moment 'fore they pulls it out and go spend it on themselves! Come on, let's see what's behind those doors."

We go back down the aisle and Charlie opens the door at the end of it. "It's where the altar boys hang their robes. Nothing for us there. Let's check the other one."

We cross in front of the huge altar with all the fine things on it and around it. It was probably the richest-looking thing I had ever seen in my life up till then. There's statues there, too, and they're very realistic. That's gotta be Mary and that Joseph, and there's Jesus in His cradle. Charlie's reaching for the handle on the other door when—

"What! Thieves! How the hell did you get in here?" shouts the man who comes out the door to gaze at us, astonished.

"The front door was wide open, Guv'nor!" says

Charlie, backing up. "We just come in for some spiritual guidance!" The man charges.

"Run, Mary!" shouts Charlie, making for the front door, but he don't have to tell me, as I'm leaping across pews and down aisles in my desperation to get away.

We make it to the foyer and have the door open, when the man catches both of us by the neck and shakes us about violently. Then he kicks open the door and thrusts us down the stairs.

"Gutter scum!" spits the man as he glares down at us sprawled on the cobblestones.

"Peace be with you, too, Brother," says Charlie, sitting up and then getting to his feet. He reaches down and pulls me up, and grumblin' about the milk of human kindness and all, we head on down to the Bull and Boar.

So, though we didn't get anything we could sell or eat that day, we got something even more valuable—now we knew how to get into the place, anytime we wanted. And some of the times we wanted to were on those nights, in the dead of winter, when it got too unbearably cold to be out and huddled about the banked fires of the blacksmiths. On those freezing nights, our gang would creep into Saint Paul's through the priest hole to find some warmth, and we were grateful for it.

On this morning, this morning of Christmas Day, I take up Jesse and have him say good-bye to the Rooster Charlie Gang, there under Blackfriars Bridge. He giggles and coos and waves his arms about as Judy and Nancy each kiss him on the forehead and say, "Good-bye, Jesse," and brush away tears from their eyes. "Bye, baby," says Polly, hardly more than a baby herself. Jesse grabs one of Hughie's big fingers as he pats the boy on his head by way of farewell. Then Charlie and Jesse and me leave the kip and head up into the town.

I had gone down to the river this morning and washed my face and hair as best I could with a bit of soap that Charlie had got from somewhere. Then I went back to the kip and Judy combed my hair out straight with the comb that we had borrowed off Mrs. Little last evening, when Jesse had his last supper with her. We then put some Mother's Little Helper on his gums and gave him a little sip, besides, right out of the bottle.

Jesse falls into a sound sleep as Charlie and I walk along. We go up Earl to Saint Andrew Street and then up that alley to the churchyard of Saint Paul's Cathedral and to the entrance to the priest's hole. Charlie opens the door and lights the lamp and leads the way through the catacombs to the door at the other end. Again he listens, then opens the door, and I step through, holding the wrapped-up Jesse in my arms.

"Good luck, Mary," whispers Charlie.

"Thanks, Charlie. You'd best go back now," I whisper in return. He nods and retraces his steps out of the church.

It's a good hour before Christmas service is to begin, and there is no one in the great room. I can hear the priests off in their vestry, prolly puttin' on their gear.

I hurry down the aisle to the little room holdin' the altar boys' robes. I put down the slumbering Jesse, choose one of the garments, and pull it over my head. I pick Jesse back up and head for the altar, my heart thumpin' madly in my chest—to get caught now would ruin everything.

I dash across in front of the altar and see that they have now placed the Nativity scene directly in front of it. I, quick, pull the statue of the Baby Jesus out from under his swaddling clothes, say, "I'm sorry, Jesus, but I think You'll understand," and I put baby Jesse in the cradle in His place. I rush the Baby Jesus statue back into the robe room and stick it under some velvet material that lies folded on a shelf.

I go back to Jesse and tuck him in carefully. He certainly is sleeping soundly. I lean down to plant a last kiss on his brow and then turn to go make myself scarce. I figure I'll head up into the choir to watch what happens from there and—

"You, there, boy. What are you doing?"

I freeze. There is a man standing there. A man in church robes. A deacon or a sexton.

"I-I was just giving my devotions, Sir. To the Baby Jesus," I stammer.

"Who are you? I've not seen you before." He peers at me closely.

"I've come in from the country, Sir. I'm Henry Hatfield. I'm with Father Philpott. To be here on this special day. The Reverend Philpott's off having his breakfast, Sir."

"Ah. Very well," he says, apparently satisfied. "Well, let's get started, shall we? Open the Gospel to Luke 2:1. Then we'll bring out the other things."

What other things? I'm thinking, as I go up on the altar and open the Bible and feverishly flip through. Ah, there's Luke...I thumb through three pages and there it is, Luke 2. As I'm doing it, I see some other boys come in and go to the robe room and put on their vestments. Hope one don't notice his is missin'.

I can hear the crowd gathering outside, and the church bells are starting to ring. The boys, now robed, come up to me and ask who I am and I say, "Henry Hatfield, in from the country to help out," and they say, "All right."

"We will have a Processional, of course. You—country boy—you're the smallest. You'll lead. Get the things."

I'm numb with terror, but I notice one of the boys going toward a cabinet and I follow him, hoping...Yes, he reaches in and hands me this large, long silver cross. I take it.

Churchmen are beginning to come in and take their places on the altar dais. The choir is up in the balcony, tuning up. A man goes to the great organ by the altar.

"Open the doors!"

I hear the crowd begin to pour in and take their places in the pews.

"All right. To the foyer. Places, everyone!"

Places? What places?

From the way the man in the center of a small group is dressed, he must be the head man. I go and stand in front of him, desperately clutching the cross, which must be quivering in my hand.

Hands take me by the shoulders and turn me around, facing the altar. I guess they're figurin' me for a country rube, which, for once, is good. A bell sounds, the organ blasts out, the screen in front of me opens, somebody nudges me from behind and I start walking down the aisle, my robes swaying gently back and forth. The choir starts singing:

Ades-te fi-del-is, lae-ti tri-um-phant-es!
Ven-i-te, ven-i-te, in Beth-eth-le-hem...

I get down to where the Nativity scene is and don't know which way to go, so I just go around on the left, figurin' the man behind me will want to go up where the Bible is, and since the heavens don't come crashing down and nobody yells at me and pulls me the other way, I guess I was right. I go over and stand out of the way and my breathing returns to normal. Sort of normal. I steal a look down at Jesse. He is still quietly asleep.

I chance a look over the congregation and... There! There, dressed in mourning black, is my young father and mother, on the aisle four rows back.

After the choir gets done beltin' out the "Adeste Fidelis," which I didn't know then but which I sure know now, and all goes quiet, the congregation gets to its feet and the head bloke stands up and goes over to the stand that holds the Bible.

He takes a deep breath and begins to read.

"'And it came to pass in those days, that a decree went out from Augustus Caesar that all the world should be taxed. And all went to be taxed, each to his own city.'"

I'm standin' there, holdin' on to my cross for dear life and hoping this all works out.

"'And Joseph also went up from Galilee, out of the city of Nazareth, into Judea, unto the city of David which is called Bethlehem, to be taxed with his espoused wife, Mary, being great with child.'"

Come on, Jesse, this'd be a good time to wake back up, I'm thinking.

"'And so it was, that, while they were there, the days were accomplished that she be delivered...'"

Come on, Jesse! Ah! I see a stirring! I see a little fist poking out of the blanket and waving about!

"'And she brought forth her firstborn son and wrapped him in swaddling clothes and laid him in a manger.'"

"Wah!" shouts Jesse, and he starts tossing his swaddling clothes aside there in his own little manger. "Wah!" Oh, and he's got a pair of lungs on him, he has! Good boy! I know from his tone that he's got Mrs. Little's Thelma and Betty more on his mind than scripture, but, hey...

The priest stares in amazement. He's a stern-faced type that looks like he don't believe much in miracles, in spite of his line of work.

There is a common gasp from the congregation. I watch my chosen parents over in their pew. *Come on, little mother, come on...*

She does. She walks timidly out into the aisle and her husband follows her.

"Whose baby is this?" bellows the priest. "Whosoever it is, come and take it up now!"

That ain't no "it," I think, a trifle resentful, *that's Jesse.*

The wife comes up and leans over Jesse and touches his blanket.

"Oh, look, Joseph, it's our baby's blanket," she says to her husband.

"If it's your baby, Madame," roars the priest, angry that he's been topped in this show, "then take him up now!"

"Oh, can we, Joseph?" she asks, the tears plain on her face.

The young man nods and she leans down and takes up Jesse and wraps his blanket around him, then the family walks down the aisle and out of Saint Paul's Cathedral, clutching their little Christmas miracle.

After the service was over, I stood with the others and handed back my silver cross, and turned to go, but I stopped when I saw the man I had first seen when I'd entered the church, who now was putting coins into the hands of the altar boys. "Good job, lads," he said, and then pushed a coin into my fist. I looked at it. It was half a guinea, more than I ever seen in the world.

I said good-bye to the other boys and thanked them for showin' a country bumpkin the ropes and slipped out the front entrance. On my way back to Blackfriars Bridge, I sold my robe for twelve pence, and I bought five full meat pies and a big wedge of cheese, and then slipped back into the kip.

We ate hearty that night, even as we mourned our lost member.

Oh, I kept track of Jesse over the next year or so, till I left Cheapside... From my rooftop I watched him take his first few steps, heard him say his first word, and watched him grow straight and strong. I heard his mother laugh again and I heard her sing to him. He belonged to them now and not to me, and that was all right. He was safe now, as safe as he could be in this world.

Jesse was just the best little baby...and for just a little while, he was mine.

Chapter 48

They all knew I was a bit drained last night from telling Jesse's story, and after I finished and had crawled back up into my kip and burrowed in with Annie and Sylvie and Rebecca, and was silently—well, maybe not so silently—crying in the dark, Hepzibah Van Pelt spoke up softly and said, "Can we sing you that song, Jacky, the 'Adeste Fidedis'? Will that make you feel better?"

I sit up and say, "I'd like that very much," and they do it, and it does indeed soothe my soul. When they are done, I ask her if they would also do that Nobby Patches song. "The choir at Saint Paul's sang that song, too, on that day."

"Nobby Patches?" asks Hepzibah, confused. "I don't think I know that one."

"Yes, you do. I've heard you do it. It's the one that goes...," and I hum a bit of it.

"Ah," she says. "'Dona Nobis Pacem.' Of course." She taps a stick or something in the darkness and says, "All right, girls. Altos will begin, then the sopranos will pick it up after they finish the first round, and then the contraltos will come in. Ready? One, two, three..."

And the sound fills the Hold. There are only three words in this song and they are all contained in the title, but it is one of the most beautiful, soul-soothing pieces of music I have ever heard. I'm with the sopranos now, and I sing with them:

> *Dona nobis pacem, pacem.*
> *Dona nobis pacem…*

It means "Give us peace," and it does give me peace, and I put my head down and sleep.

Peace comes to the ocean, too, for when we awaken in the morning, the sea is calm.

Chapter 49

It's been a few hours this morning since Sin-Kay had inspection and Hughie doled out the burgoo, hot this time. There's been no sign of Nettles since that night when the Captain whacked him one and told him, in no uncertain terms, to stay away from "those vile vessels," which is just fine with us vessels.

Dolley and Clarissa and I confer under the Stage, and we all agree that it is time to go. We also decide that this day should be spent drilling the girls in what parts they are to play in the breakout, so that no mistakes, no stumbles, no false moves are made when so much depends on things going just right.

We call the girls down by divisions and go over with them their parts in the Plan.

"When you hear me call out, 'Plan A...Ready!' Cloris and Frances will go to the Rat Hole and take down the boards. Bea and Barbara will go to the Powder Hole and open it. Abby and Helen will be wearing the wires around their waists and will go to the gate and wire it shut. When the Powder Hole is opened, Dorothea and Ruth will pull out the fuse and lay it out straight on the deck. Annie and Sylvie will each take one of the short-fused bags and put them up on the aft Balcony for me and Clarissa to throw if we have to go to Plan B. Wilhelmina will light two candles—one she will place near, *but not too near*, the end of the fuse. The other, she will place on the aft Balcony near the short-fused bags. Lissette will reach in the Powder Hole and start passing the water bottles out to—no, no, Lissette, just the water, not the wine—to Priscilla, who will pile them next to the Rat Hole. Connie, you will prepare Elspeth, and Martha, you will take charge of getting my seabag out. All will gather under the Stage and wait for the next signal. Everybody got that?"

Seeing nods all around, I continue.

"When you hear me shout, 'Plan A...Go!' Dolley will go through the Rat Hole first. She will have my shiv and a file and she will open the outer storeroom door. She will then proceed up the passageway and out onto the deck, followed by Katy and the Dianas—Chrissy, Hermione, Minerva, Rose—who will take care of any of the crew who might not have fallen for our diversion, and then they'll stand guard as the rest of you get in the boat."

I turn to the two experienced sailors. "Hyacinth, you'll be next out. Run to the boat first and pull back the canvas. Make sure Hughie gets the boat down and helps you get the sail up. Then Cathy, you jump in and take the tiller and be ready to steer away from the ship as soon as all are in the boat." More nods.

"So that we avoid confusion at the Rat Hole, after Cathy, the rest will go through in the same order as you did Sin-Kay's inspection line. That means Rebecca will be next, then

Ruth, and so on, all except for Dorothea. Each of you who are not in charge of something else, grab a bottle of water as you go through. Remember, if you meet a member of the crew, break the bottle on whatever hard thing is close to you and ram the jagged edge up under his chin.

"Dorothea, you will be the last through the Hole. You will light the fuse. Leave as soon as it catches, and start counting in your head, one one hundred, two one hundred, three one hundred, and so on till you reach fifty. By that time you'll be in the boat and then you'll call out the numbers loud and clear so we'll be able to hear them up on deck. Let nothing distract you from that, Dorothea. It's so very important."

Dorothea takes a breath and nods. I put my hand on her shoulder. "Brave girls, all of you.

"We'll go right after breakfast when the hooks come down. Make sure you eat every bit of food and drink all the water. When you get up tomorrow, put on your dresses and shoes and stockings, too, as you will need protection from the sun when we get out on the water. But when the time comes to jump in the boat, knot your skirts up around your waists so they will not get in your way. Are we all clear?"

There are nods all around. Clarissa nods, too, looking straight at me. I know, and she knows, too, that she has one of the more difficult parts to play in this game. All will be in danger, but she will be in danger alone.

"Good. Now let's crack out our last bottles of wine, have some of those fine soda crackers, and enjoy our last snack here in the banquet room of the Hotel Bloodhound. What say ye?"

———

That afternoon, we have each of the girls come before Dolley and Clarissa and me, down under the Stage, to have them recite to us *exactly* what their role is when we break out. All of them know that tomorrow is probably the day, but we remind them that you never know what might turn up—the storm might return, they might not put the hooks down tomorrow, a lot of things—but I know that since I am going out tonight to complete the disabling of the other boat, tomorrow must be the day.

When Rebecca comes up before us, she pouts and says she wishes she had something more adventurous to do than just carry out a water bottle and jump into a boat.

"There will be adventures enough when all this happens, believe me, Rebecca," I say. Her eyes are shining, feverish with excitement over the coming breakout. *Hmm...*Maybe a little too feverish.

"Come here, you," I say to her and put my palm on her forehead. It's warm, but maybe it's just the excitement... We'll see.

We got through the rest of the day as best we could. We did the Dance, we did the French, and we did the Science, but we were all jumpy. It was almost a relief when Connie read her verses and the flaps came down.

There was no story tonight, no. I think I'm storied out... Instead I sat with Hughie for a long time and told him some more about the horses at the Lawson Peabody and how he was gonna take care of 'em and all... *"Now, that Daisy's a sweet little thing and no trouble at all, but that Samson, oh what a hammer-headed bully he is—prolly take a special bridle, a hackamore, don't you think, Hughie? Aye, I thought so...,"* and how he'd have his own little room with curtains and stuff and how we'd have picnics on the Common. Amidst all this, I kept going over and over what his job in the upcoming breakout was to be, *had* to be—*"When you hear me shout 'Hughie! Go, go, go!' you've got to go up on deck, help Hyacinth haul up the sail, take the ratchet and lower the boat down. You got that, Hughie? Remember, Hughie, when you hear..."*

When I climb back up into our kip, I reach over to feel Rebecca's forehead. Still warm. *I'm all right,* she murmurs, awakened from sleep by my touch.

I don't know...

At one thirty I am awakened by the watch to go out on my last foray. I rub the sleep from my eyes and listen to those about me. I smile to think of how they all said they would not sleep a wink this night of nights. But it seems they were wrong.

I climb down and feel my way to the Rat Hole. I've done it so many times now, I think I could make it there without my hands stretched out in front of me. Caroline has opened the Hole for me and I thank her and send her back up on watch.

I don't wake Clarissa—why bother? I'll be out and back in no time.

I'm right. I'm back in the storeroom inside of ten minutes.

I had crept out, gotten into the crew's boat—it's hard for me to call it a *life*boat, considerin' all I've done to it—and did what I needed to do. I unhooked the rudder, lifting it up and out of its pintles, and tied a line around the tiller part—line I got by cutting off the jib halyard—and gently lowered it into the water. It made nary a sound as it slipped into the sea, and I made nary a sound as I slipped out of the boat, through the hatch, down the passageway, and back into the storeroom, patting myself on the back for a job well and completely done.

Then I freeze.

What's that? I stiffen and a chill runs up my spine. *Oh no! There's someone in here with me!*

I hear the striking of a flint and an oil lamp blazes into light.

My heart sinks. There in the glow of light from the lamp, standin' between me and the Rat Hole, is Sammy Nettles.

"Hey, hey, hey, if it ain't Smart-mouth herself…Ain't that somethin'? Ain't that really somethin'. Yer that ghost that's got ever'one scairt, ain'cha, girly? Well, you don't scare me none, no you don't, 'cause I always knowed it was one o' yer bunch what was doin' it. A ghost? Shee-it, no, just a skinny girl all dressed in black…Sheee-it…"

He stands there giggling while I stand transfixed with fear and despair— *We are lost!*

"Y'see, I got holes o' my own, there on the other side of the Hold, cracks that I can peek through. Yes I do, just like I know you all got holes, and I been keepin' my eye on all of yiz, yes I have…and I know how you got over here, too, yes, I do."

All our plans! All our preparations!

"I ain' gonna tell Captain just yet, girly, oh no, I'm not. First we gonna have some fun…" He giggles and snorts some more. "You just stay right there on your knees…"

Snap out of it! You've got to think! You've got to—

He puts the lamp down on the workbench and takes a step to stand over me. "That's good. That's real good..." He chuckles some more and then says, "Y'know, I'm glad it turned out to be you—that blondie's prettier, but you'll do 'cause you got such a smart mouth on you, don't you. Oh yes, you do..."

With that he loosens his belt and opens the front of his pants. I jerk back, but he puts his hand on the back of my head and pulls me forward.

My mind is reeling in desperation. *If I come up with my shiv and stick it in his gut, he's sure to cry out and we'll be discovered and all will be lost!*

"C'mon, girly. Let's do it now. Let's see just how smart that mouth really is..."

Oh, God! Even if I do what he so plainly wants me to do, he'll still tell the Captain! I've got to do something, I've got to—

But I don't have to do nothin'. Or not much, anyway. A loop of light line snakes out of the darkness behind him and goes over his head and drops down to his neck before it is pulled tight, oh, so very tight, by two small white hands on either side of his neck. His eyes go wide in surprise and then start to bug out as the small but apparently quite strong hands pull the cord even tighter, shutting off his breath.

He makes some gurgling sounds and tries to get his fingers under the noose that is strangling him, but it is too tight and he just can't do it.

Nettles's legs kick and thrash about until I throw my arms about them and hug them tight to me to quiet them and to keep them from raising the alarm. At first, I feel them kicking hard, then they slowly weaken, and then they go limp and just quiver, and then…nothing. I relax my hold on his dead legs and he slips down to the deck.

Clarissa Worthington Howe stands there shaking, the end of the garrote still held in her hand.

"Is he dead?" she asks.

"I think so," I say. Nettles sure ain't movin' anymore.

"I…I never did anything like that before," she says. "Never killed anyone before…"

I get to my feet and put my arms around her and hold her close to me. "*We* killed him, Clarissa, we both did," I say, to take some of the load off her. "It had to be done. Try to put it out of your mind now."

I hold her there in the darkness and gradually her trembling subsides and then stops. She stiffens and stands straight and shrugs off my arms.

"Come on, we've got to take care of him and then get back," I say, kneeling back down next to the body.

We roll Sammy under a shelf and cover him with some pieces of canvas that we find. Then we crawl back into the Hold, taking the lamp with us, and button up the boards.

In the light of the lamp, I watch Clarissa get back into her kip and crawl over to Lissette, who is sleeping sitting up, with her back to the wall. Clarissa puts her head in the French girl's lap and closes her eyes. She goes to sleep immediately, breathing gently in and out, her breath making a curl that has fallen across her cheek flutter slightly. She sleeps like a baby.

What a piece of work you are, Clarissa.

I lie awake in the dark, unable to get the thought of Sammy Nettles out of my mind. Sure, he had it coming, but to have held on to his legs like that and to have felt the very life go out of him…Well, sleep will not come easy this night.

We've got to go tomorrow, now, 'cause they'll be looking for him and they will find him. And in their search, they will also find evidence of our preparations and all will be lost. Yes, tomorrow we go.

The die is cast.

Chapter 50

In the morning, just as the first light of dawn is breaking, the watch wakes me and I awaken Clarissa and we both wake Dolley and the three of us quietly rouse the rest of the girls and tell them that Plan A is on for real today and there's no going back now—"*'cause we killed Nettles last night when he caught us out of the Hold, and it won't be long before they find his body*"—and they are to make themselves ready. And while they are quiet about it, the Hold positively hums with excitement. *It's on!*

No tears are shed for Sammy's departure from this world.

Then the flaps go up and Hughie rises to go get the burgoo. When he comes back, Sin-Kay is with him and a quick inspection is held. Sin-Kay has lost patience with us and wants only for this voyage to be over, and he takes the roll and is gone very quickly.

The burgoo and water are given out and everyone eats and drinks, every spoonful, every drop...*everyone except Rebecca*.

Last night, after I had climbed back into our kip, I felt Rebecca's forehead again...*Uh-oh*...I then slipped my hand under her shirt and found her chest soaked with sweat.

Damn! I lay down next to her and held her to me, for I knew that after the hot sweats come the chills, and indeed, they did come. I begged Annie and Sylvie to look after her on this day, to make sure she got through the Rat Hole and made it to the boat, and they, of course, gathered her shaking form to them and vowed they would. *Damn!*

The girls get dressed as excitedly as they ever did for any high tea, and for the first time in a long while, they put on their stockings, their shoes, and their Lawson Peabody School for Young Girls uniform dresses. Everyone, that is, 'cept me—I shove all my extra stuff in my seabag, 'cause I got to be able to move free.

We are ready to go. *Come on, Mick and Keefe.*

While waiting for the hooks, I look over at Connie, who is sitting by Elspeth, and I know she is trying to raise Elspeth's spirits enough to make the crawl through the Hole and the dash for the boat. Annie and Sylvie are doing the same with poor Rebecca—they have gotten her dressed and she is at least able to stand, however shakily.

All the girls are jumpy, ready to leap out of their skins. I think for a moment, and then say, "Connie, if you'd like to offer up something now, feel free..."

She looks at me, rises, holds out her hands, palms up, and looks heavenward. "Lord," she begins, "You, who delivered the Hebrew children out of bondage and then led them to the Promised Land...You, who delivered Daniel from the Lion's Den...You, who delivered Shadrach, Meshach, and Abednego from the Fiery Furnace...You who delivered all those of Your children, maybe, just maybe, You can find it in Your wisdom and mercy to deliver the girls of the Lawson

Peabody from their own bondage, so that they can continue to serve You, each in her own way. Amen."

There is a chorus of amens. Heartfelt ones, I believe.

Good job, Connie, I'm thinkin'. *Short and to the point.*

The top hatch opens and the hooks come swinging down! *Glory be!*

"Hooks coming," says Julia on lookout. "Captain's on the quarterdeck."

It is the signal to start Plan A.

Clarissa stands and looks at me hard and her look demands of me, *You swear you will cover for me?*

I nod. *I will, Sister, I swear.* The hooks are all the way down now.

"Very well, then." She goes to the bars, takes a deep breath, and screams out, "Captain! Come here! I wanna bath!"

"What the hell?" we hear the Captain say, and hear his footsteps approach.

I jump down into the Pit and call up to Mick and Keefe as I hook the first tub, "Mick! Keefe! She's gonna do it! Blondie's really gonna do it."

Their heads appear over the side of the top hatch.

"Wot?"

"Blondie's gonna take a bath right out there on the deck! Tell Cookie and the others!" Their heads disappear and the sound of running feet is heard as the word is spread.

"Now what do you want?" demands the Captain.

"I have to take a bath. I'm getting a rash. No sultan's gonna want to buy me if I have a rash. He'll think I'll give him a disease," says Clarissa, firmly.

"We ain't got a bathtub, so you can't have one. Now, shut up."

"You got a hose right back there. I've seen it. I'll bathe right there. You got some soap?"

I think the entire crew is now back aft of our cage, listening eagerly to this exchange. Sin-Kay then appears on deck.

"What is this, then?" he asks.

"Blondie there wants to be hosed off on the fantail," says the Captain.

"I absolutely forbid it!" says Sin-Kay. "I am in charge of the cargo!"

There is instantly a loud *"hmmmmmm!"* from the crew. The Captain looks around at his increasingly mutinous crew, and I know what is going through his mind—he's got a crew half out of its collective wits with superstitious terror over the sightings of the Black Ghost, he's got men terrified of being turned into giant seaweed sponges, he's got sailors worried he's gonna kill 'em at the end of the voyage—he's got to figure, *Hell, why not toss them a bone, and keep 'em happy?*

"And I am in charge of this ship!" says the Captain to the outraged Sin-Kay, "as I have informed you before." He strides to the gangway. "Bring her up! Pump up the hose!"

There is a mighty roar of approval from the crew.

Sin-Kay, plainly outraged, comes down the hatchway and opens the cage door. "All right, you," he snarls. "Get out here."

Clarissa takes one last look at me, straightens her back, puts on the Look, and goes out the door.

Take it slow, Sister, take it real slow.

Sin-Kay locks the door and follows her out of the hatchway.

"Plan A...Ready!" I shout and everyone flies into action. Abby and Helen are at the gate, whipping the wires from off their waists and lashing the gate shut. Then they join the others, who have rushed down under the Stage to carry out their own parts.

I go down there myself and see the boards coming off the Holes. I take my seabag and before handing it over to Martha's care, I withdraw from it my sword Persephone, sleeping silently in her sheath. She who had lain there quietly the entire time we were here, taking up the whole length of the bag. She will not be quiet now, oh no. I strap her harness around my waist and go back out and up on the Balcony and look aft.

As I look out, there is a roar from the crew. I guess Clarissa has taken off her dress.

I turn around. Annie and Sylvie each throw their bag of fused powder up at my feet and then go back to Rebecca. Wilhelmina carefully places a lit candle on the Balcony, next to me. All that would have been for Plan B, if the ruse with Clarissa hadn't worked and they didn't let her out to perform her little...diversion...and we had to blast our way out. But that, thankfully, did not happen.

"Plan A...Go!" I shout and run back down to the gate and say to Hughie, "Hughie! Go! Go! Go!" He looks at me, shocked, scared, and not moving. "Hughie! Get to the boat! Go! Go! Go!" Then he nods and goes up the stairs and— Sin-Kay had locked the upper door when he went out. Hughie rattles the door. *Damn!*

"Hughie! Break it down! You can do it! I know you can!" I cry desperately. "Come down to the bottom of the stairs and take a run up and put your shoulder to it! Please, Hughie, try!"

He lumbers back down, turns, and charges up the stairs, and Hugh the Grand crashes through the top door as if it were made of straw. *Hooray, Hughie!*

I go back down to look under the Stage. The girls are going through. Dolley and the Dianas are already gone. There goes Cathy, grabbing a bottle of water on her way out. Now Annie and Sylvie are guiding Rebecca through, now Sally, now...

There is another roar from outside. I can only imagine that Clarissa is playing her part well.

There go Caroline and Frances and Julia, and now Dorothea is bending down to light the fuse. It catches and I see her mouth working *one one hundred, two one hundred, three one hundred,* and then she, too, is gone through the Rat Hole.

I look about me. I am the only one in the Hold of the *Bloodhound,* and it is weirdly quiet, the only motion being the white rags hanging under the Stage, swaying slightly with the motion of the ship.

In the hurly-burly of getting the Plan in motion, there was no time for doubtful thoughts to creep into my mind and to sap my spirit, but because I am alone in the now-quiet Hold, such thoughts do come to me and my heart starts to pound and my knees start to shake. *Oh, to hell with it! The Plan will either work or it won't and there's no stopping now. We have everything to gain and nothing whatsoever to lose.*

Another cheer from outside. I go over to begin my climb up the tub rope.

Then I see the tub starting to lift. *Christ! I thought I'd have to climb the damned thing, but what the hell, I'll take the ride.*

I run over to it, leap to catch the rope, swing my feet onto the edges of the hole, straighten up, and wait as I am cranked, legs trembling, into the blessed sunlight for what may well be my last fight on this earth. Or rather, on this sea. The absurdity of it strikes me: the knight-errant Lieutenant Jacky Faber, Royal Navy, sword in hand, being lifted up to the field of battle, riding not on noble steed, but on the lip of a chamber pot. It is somehow fitting.

When my feet are level with the hatch top, I step off onto it and blink for a moment as my eyes get used to the sunlight. I see Mick's back, his hand still working the ratchet that lifted me up, his head turned, gazing aft. There is yet another cheer, but it is not for my grand entrance, oh no, it is not for me, and for once I don't mind. The cheers are for Clarissa, and I see her there, seated on a bollard, languidly peeling off her second stocking and tossing it aside. Clarissa may be an aristocrat, but right now she is showing a part of her that is pure pagan temptress. There is not a single pair of eyes on me, or anywhere else, for that matter.

Clarissa Worthington Howe rises to her feet, arches her back, and puts her hands on the hem of her undershirt. Then she slowly, slowly pulls it up. The crew sucks in a common breath.

I look back at the lifeboat. I see Dorothea getting in, her lips moving in her careful count. I turn back to face the crowd and draw my sword. I hear the soft sound of Katy's bare feet on the hatch top as she comes up on my right side.

Then Chrissy comes up on my left. Both of them have arrows nocked and ready.

Clarissa puts her hands on the waistband of her drawers and slowly, slowly pulls them down, and then off.

"*Fifty!*" comes the call from Dorothea. "*Fifty-one...fifty-two...*"

"Clarissa! Now!" I shout and there is a pink-and-white blond blur as she leaps up and dashes past me on her way to the lifeboat. All heads turn to watch her go and their gaze falls on me.

"What the hell?" is the most common of the expressions of surprise. "The girls are out!"

"Listen to me! All of you!" I shout. "There is a fuse right now burning down in the powder magazine! Lift your noses and perhaps you can smell the burning powder..."

"*Fifty-three...fifty-four...*"

"It is a timed fuse, and when that girl gets to one hundred, the powder's gonna blow the guts out of this ship and send it straight to the bottom!"

"Like hell it will," says Bo'sun Chubbuck, swinging his club as he comes for me.

He doesn't reach me, however, for Katy's bow twangs and she puts an arrow in his throat and another quickly follows into his belly. He doesn't seem to notice that one so much as the one in his neck, which he bats at as if it were a bothersome bee instead of what will be the end of his life.

"*...fifty-five...fifty-six...*"

The crowd seems stunned into inaction. Then the Mate Dunphy gathers up his courage and says, "I'll get that damned fuse!" and he would easily have done it, I'm sure, since he had a good forty seconds to get down below and pull it, if Chrissy hadn't stopped him with a shaft in his side as he tried to run past her. She did it as coolly as if she were setting out plates for a tea party for her dollies. Katy and her girls have been practicing shooting and re-nocking and they can do it with amazing speed. When Dunphy pitches over and falls to the deck, Christina King of the Beacon Hill Kings puts another arrow in his chest.

"...*fifty-seven...fifty-eight...*"

"Sailors!" I cry out to the stunned crew. "You may yet save your lives! You have time to get in that lifeboat there! You have no weapons, you cannot take us! The Captain was going to kill you anyway, you know that! Why try to save him and his lousy ship?"

"...*fifty-nine...sixty...*"

I see Mick down below me, looking up all stupid.

"Go, Mick! Keefe! Run! Save yourselves!"

"...*sixty-one...*"

That does it. Those two break and run for the boat and the rest of the crew follows them, frantic to get off the ship. The first ones there let loose the davit lines and the boat plunges down and men pile in, crawling over each other in their haste. I'm sure there were some who thought to get in our boat, but the sight of Rose, Hermione, and Minerva with drawn bows and arrows pointed right at them made them reconsider and flee back to the boat we had provided for them. I look around and see that there is one sailor, Carruthers, I think, kneeling on the deck, blood running out of his neck and over his hands. I look in the boat, where delicate little Julia Winslow sits with a strange expression on her face and a jagged, bloody, broken bottle in her hand.

I turn back to check the action on the quarterdeck.

"...*sixty-two*..."

"This is not happening," says the Captain, shaking in rage and disbelief. All this time, he has been standing there, stock-still. Then he runs down into his cabin.

What? Does he think that will save him?

"Katy. Chrissy. Get back to the boat. Help your other Dianas cover the retreat."

"...*sixty-four...sixty-five*..."

They immediately turn and go and I'm about to follow them, when a purple-sleeved arm goes around my neck and a pistol is pressed against my ear. My heart sinks. It is Sin-Kay. I hadn't counted on him doing anything in the fracas, but he had been hanging back, waiting for his chance, and I guess he found it and I am that chance. I am held fast.

"You scheming bitch. You think you have triumphed, but you have not," he hisses in my other ear. "We are going over to that boat. You are going to tell those girls to drop their weapons. We will then get in that boat and we will sail away. *I will not lose my cargo!*" He grinds the barrel hard into my temple. "Do you hear? Now move!"

I'm trying to get my sword around on him, but I can't. *I can't*—he's holding me too close—and he begins to shove me toward the boat, then...

"What? Hurt Mary? Mister hurt Mary?" cries Hughie.

Uh-oh...Hughie has gotten out of the boat and is coming toward us, pointing at Sin-Kay. "No, Mister, don't hurt Mary. Stop, Mister..."

"Get the hell away from me, you idiot, damn you!" yells Sin-Kay, but Hughie doesn't get the hell away. What he does is clamp his massive paw around Sin-Kay's neck and rips him off me. As I spin away, Hughie wraps his arms around Sin-Kay's, pinning his arms to his sides.

"...*seventy-two...seventy-three*..."

The pistol fires, and Hughie jerks. A strange look comes over his face, a look of bewilderment that changes quickly to anger. Hughie squeezes, his left hand grasping the wrist of his right. Sin-Kay gasps, his breath gone, his face swells, his eyes bulge. Hughie squeezes harder.

Then there is a sickening *pop*.

I know it is the sound of Sin-Kay's lower spine snapping.

"Hughie! Get back to the boat!" I plead, shaking him by the shoulder. "Go now, Mister's done!"

Confused, Hughie steps back, releasing his hold. Sin-Kay slumps to the deck, his legs flop around, all useless now. And—*Oh, Lord*—there is a spreading red stain on the front of Hughie's shirt. I choke down a sob and shove him back toward the boat. He goes.

"...*seventy-eight...seventy-nine*..."

Sin-Kay raises his torso by pushing up with his hands. Sheer terror is writ large on his face, as he knows full well that he is now a dead man.

"Enjoy your time in Hell, *Jerome*." I sneer down at him, and staying well clear of the clutch of his hands, I turn to go to the boat. I wish I could be more gracious in victory, but I can't.

On my way over the hatch top, I see that the crew's boat is filled to overflowing, and, *wonder of wonders*, there's Nettles, staggering out of the hatch, holding his head and moaning. We didn't kill him after all—the scumbag just went into a coma and he woke up just in time. *Glory be*...

He lurches forward and falls into the boat, just as it pulls away from the side.

"...*eighty-one...eighty-two...*"

Time to go. *Farewell,* Bloodhound.

I see that Hughie has gotten the boat down to the water, and I'm almost to it, when I find that things ain't over yet. Captain Blodgett has come out of his cabin, and aside from a crazed look on his face, he bears two pistols in his hands.

Uh-oh...

"Katy, get your girls in! Cathy, pull away and lay off! Pick me up in the water! Do it, now!"

Katy sends me a sharp look, but she follows orders, and I turn to confront the Captain.

"...*eighty-six...eighty-seven...*"

There's still time for him to get down and pull the fuse, and I can't let him do that. I run back over the hatch to face him and he levels a pistol at me and fires. I fall on my back and the bullet whizzes harmlessly across my chest. I drop my sword and roll over and over across the deck. He fires again, and again he misses, for it's hard to hit a moving target, no matter how close. Seeing me down, he lunges for the hatchway.

I scoop up Persephone and beat him to it, holding the point of the sword next to his neck.

"Whip me, will you?" I say as I thrust, but he brings his heavier sword up and deflects it.

"...*ninety-two...ninety-three...Jacky, come on!...ninety-four...*"

Captain Blodgett knows he has no more chance at getting

at the fuse. All he wants to do now is kill me, the cause of his ruin. He snarls and raises his sabre and comes at me. I crouch down and assume Position Four and wait for it. When he brings his sword down, I drop the tip of mine and entangle his blade in an envelopment parry, ending up in Position Six.

"...*ninety-six...ninety-seven...*"

He recovers, pulls back, and thrusts, in Four. I try a beat parry by knocking his blade to the side, but I don't have the strength to do it, so I don't knock it out of the way far enough. The point of his sabre goes into my left thigh, high up.

Yeeow! Damn!

I fall back, clutching my leg. *Son of a bitch!*

"...*ninety-eight...ninety-nine...*"

I've had enough.

"You've won this duel, Captain, but you have not won the war. Now, witness your judgement!"

"...*one hundred!*"

With that, I dash to the side and dive over, leaving the astounded Captain Blodgett looking helplessly after me.

The explosion comes as a tremendous, dead *thump!* when I am in midair, and after I penetrate the warm, clear, blue-green waters of the lower Atlantic, I open my eyes and look back upon the death throes of the *Bloodhound*.

The blast had opened up the middle, and the ship was already headed down. Even in the space of one held breath, I saw the nose go under and then the stern and then the entire ship.

Go down, Bloodhound, *you vile and filthy thing, go down. Go down, you purveyor of human flesh, you destroyer of men's souls, go down, go down, oh yes, go down to the very depths of Hell, itself. Go down...*

It is strangely quiet now, down here under the waves, after the tumult of the past few minutes. Strange, too, is the aspect of the *Bloodhound* as it sails down to its watery grave, for sail down it does, all its rigging and sails perfectly set as it goes farther and farther down into the deep blue-green sea, leaving a trail of oddly beautiful sparkling bubbles as its last wake.

It leaves some other things as well. I see Sin-Kay, clear as day, holding his breath and trying to claw his way back to the surface with his still-good arms. And I see as well a layer of dark and sinister shapes down below the fast-disappearing *Bloodhound*, a layer of gray that begins to move and separate and become the individual, massive sharks that follow ships like these for whatever they can pick up. They come up to feed.

Sin-Kay almost makes it to the surface before one of the brutes, which has got to be twenty feet long, comes up and goes at him. Considering the shape he's in, I don't know if he can feel anything when the first shark takes off his leg... Maybe not, but I guess we'll never know that. The second one takes off his right arm, and then another cuts him off at the waist, and from then on it is all just guts and plumes of blood in the water. The last thing I see is his face, which bears that look of complete and total surprise that many men wear when the unthinkable, their own end, becomes certain.

Captain Blodgett fares no better. He struggles, but the sharks, now in a frenzy, take him apart piece by piece, and then turn to the still forms of Dunphy and Chubbuck and

Carruthers, floating arms-and-legs out, like leaves in a gentle breeze, putting up no fight at all.

It occurs to me then that, however oddly beautiful the scene of the *Bloodhound* sailing down to oblivion, I'd better be getting the hell out of there, considering that blood is curling out of my own dear leg. With regret, I drop the sword Persephone and see her sink, and hope that perhaps her namesake will pick her up when she reaches the lower depths of Hades, and then, *Good God, one's comin' up at me!*

I forget idle thoughts and scramble for the surface. My head breaks through and I look around for the boat.

"There she is!" shouts someone, and I twist in the water and see the boat and start pulling for it. *Oh, please, God, not me legs!*

I reach the boat and Dolley puts an oar toward me in the water and I fairly scramble up the length of the oar and into the boat.

Just as I do, a huge black form, topped by a triangular fin, surges out of the water next to the oar, its back easily as broad as our boat. I frantically reach down and find that my feet are still there.

Thank you, God, oh, thank you.

"Set course 290 degrees," I gasp when I've recovered my breath.

"Aye, aye, Sir," says Cathy Lowell, mocking me a bit and looking down at the compass she holds in her hand. I had taken it from my seabag and given it to her this morning. She puts the tiller over.

The course takes us close to the crew's boat, which is a hive of activity. The Dianas take up guard positions to make sure the crew doesn't try anything. But they needn't have worried. All is confusion and despair on that boat. They've already discovered that I removed their rudder, most of their oars, and that all their running gear has been chopped up into useless lengths. The sails are in tatters. There is a squeal from one of them as he discovers the bloodred footprints. I'm sure the Legend of the Black Ghost will not fade quickly from their minds. It will certainly ruin their sleep tonight.

There are hissing bubbles burbling up between our two lifeboats, those bubbles being the last dying breaths of the *Bloodhound* as it slips even farther down into the dark at the bottom of the sea.

"Cheer up, lads," I say as we sail up to them, all shipshape and Bristol fashion, our sail tight as a drum. "You are clever fellows. You'll rig up something. I've even left you with one oar to maybe rig as a rudder. You might even survive long enough to be picked up by a passing ship. Who knows, you might even live to tell the tale of how you were bested by a bunch of little girls. But I doubt you'll tell that tale, even if you do survive. G'bye, Mick. G'bye, Keefe. G'bye, Cookie. I do hope you make it, I really do. But there's one thing I want you to do for me, in payment for all I've done for you."

They look at me stupidly.

"When it comes right down to it and things are bad, as bad as you know they can get when you're cast adrift at sea, do this for me...*eat Nettles first!*"

Every head on the boat swivels to look at Sammy Nettles, who has recovered enough to gaze about at all the faces staring at him to say, "Wot?"

"You must admit," I say in parting, "it's tradition."

We pull away and we see the crew of the *Bloodhound* no more.

Chapter 51

I hoped that Hughie's wound would be superficial, but alas, it is not. I wished that Sin-Kay's bullet had gone through the meat on his side, but when I open Hughie's shirt, I find that it had not—it had gone straight into his chest and stayed there. A little bit of blood has already trickled out of the side of his mouth. *Oh, Hughie, no...*

I pull his shirt back down and sit on the seat and pull his head over into my lap and stroke his hair. He sighs, contentedly. I don't think he's in a lot of pain, and that's good. The girls near us in the boat have seen what has happened to Hughie, and Sally puts her hand on his shoulder to lend him solace. Others do the same, murmuring comforting words.

"Tell me another story, Mary," he says. "About the gang and all..."

"All right, Hughie," I say. "Once upon a time there was a boy named Hugh the Grand and he was in a gang and one day he saved his whole gang, yes, he did, and he kept them from harm, 'cause he was the biggest, bravest boy there ever was..."

"A good one, Mary," he says. "I know I'm gonna like it..." And then he relaxes, lets out his last breath, and dies.

I put my face down in his curly locks and let the tears flow. *Good-bye, Hughie. I hope they have pretty little horses where you are going. You were always just the best boy...*

After a while I say those words I have heard so many times before—*We commend his body to the sea, and his soul to God*—and we gently put him over the side. The last I see of Hugh the Grand is his white shirt twinkling down through the clear blue-green water as he sinks.

After the funeral, I shake my head to clear it of grief—time for that later, and there is work to be done. Rebecca is sick, Clarissa is naked, my leg is bleeding, and the sun is beating down.

I see Rebecca nestled in the crook of Annie's arm, asleep, so I take care of the Clarissa problem first.

Anyone else on this boat, 'cept maybe me, would be huddled over, trying to cover her nakedness with crossed arms, but not Clarissa—she leans back, puts her elbows on the gunwale behind her, closes her eyes, and raises her face to the sun and purrs, "Oh, that feels *soooo* good after being in that hellhole for *soooo* long."

As I rummage through my seabag for something to cover Clarissa, it occurs to me that there are probably some on this boat that wouldn't mind terribly being back in the Hold of the *Bloodhound,* for the ocean sure looks a lot bigger when you're on it in a little boat like this.

"How...how far are we from land, Jacky?" asks Priscilla. The ocean swells roll under us and they are smooth and slick and calm, but they are big, and this boat is very small.

"I'd say about two thousand miles..." There are more

than a few gasps. "But we're not heading for the land—we're heading for the sea-lanes, where we hope to be picked up by an honest merchant or warship and returned home."

I find my old sailor togs and toss them to Clarissa. "Here, Eve, cover thy nakedness, or yea and verily, thy pinkness shalt be fried to a crisp red." She catches them and puts them on.

"Yo, ho, ho," she says when she has them on, the white duck pants and white top with blue flap. "I rather like it. I wish I had a mirror."

"Besides," I continue, "Captain Bligh of HMS *Bounty* was put in a boat very much like this with eighteen of his loyal men, when he was mutinied against back in '89, and he sailed that boat through the South Pacific three thousand eight hundred miles to safety. Maybe we will do as well as old Bligh."

"It is up to Providence, now," says Connie. "We shall have to pray."

"Oh, we will do that, Connie, loud and long, but first we have to take care of some things ourselves," I say, and dive back into my bag. While my hands search, I say, "We must have every girl learn to sail this boat, and we must do it quickly." I find what has to be my last piece of paper and the only pencil now and say, "Pass these up to Priscilla if you would. Thanks."

She takes the paper and waits for instructions.

"Priscilla, if you would set up yet another watch rotation, three girls to a section. Two of them will sail the boat, one on tiller, one on mainsheet, as Cathy and Hyacinth are doing now, while the other one will constantly scan the horizon for any ships. We want to see them before they see us, 'cause we sure don't want to be picked up by a nasty pirate after all we've been through." Priscilla puts the paper on the seat next to her and starts writing down names.

"Dorothea, wait...Here." My hand goes back in my bag and pulls out my long glass. I pass it over to Dorothea.

"It's best to use it standing with your back to the mast to steady yourself...and, Dorothea, we are looking for ships, not birds." She smiles and stands and does what I've suggested. I know she is delighted to once again have a telescope in her hands. "Dolley, what do we have in the way of water and food?"

It turns out that we have twenty-one wine bottles full of water and two tins of soda crackers, and that is worrisome— we can go maybe two weeks without food, but there's only enough water for about three days, and that's giving each girl a scant five ounces a day. Sure hope it rains, but there ain't a cloud in the sky.

"Now we've got to rig this canvas as a cover, so it can get some of us out of the sun, but first—"

"Jacky, your leg...," says Sylvie.

"I know. In a minute." I step over to take a look at Rebecca. "How is she?" I ask Annie.

"The same. She was able to crawl through the Rat Hole and then stand, but Sylvie and I had to carry her to the boat," says Annie. "She's about out now."

I put my hand on her forehead—still feverish. I lift her upper lip and look at her gums—they're healthy and pink, so it ain't scurvy. I'm thinking jail fever—typhus...*Damn*...

"Try to get a little water down her," I tell Annie, and to the others I say, "and as for the rest of us, I think we should take no water today because we only have enough for a very short time." There is agreement to that. I go back to my seabag, and once again open it.

I pull out the oilskin packet I was looking for and open it. Lying there, with the bright colors of their feathers and the brass gleam of their hooks and looking just as resplendent as the day they were made, are my fishing lures. All except for one have a small, twenty-five-foot coil of light but strong line attached to them. *Thanks again, Tilly.*

I'm thinking this is a job for the Dianas. I see Katy up toward the bow, her bow still in her hand. I call her name and she makes her way back through the ranks of seated girls.

"Take these, Katy, and get them in the water. Tie the end of each line to a cleat and put a girl on each one, and have her pull on the line and then…"

"I know how to jig for catfish, Jacky," she says, almost smiling. "Don't worry. And if we get a big one and he's givin' us trouble, well, we still got some arrows left." She goes to set the lures.

I sit back, feeling a little weak, but I must push on. "Dolley? My shiv, please." She pulls it from her waistband and gives it back to me. I look at my old shiv—Charlie's shiv, actually—and the cock's head I had carved in it long ago in Charlie's memory, and wonder at the places that knife has been, and the uses to which it has been put. Then I reach down and cut off the left leg of my drawers, high up and close to my crotch, and look at the wound.

It's a mess, but it could be worse. I take the cutoff pant leg and dip it over the side and start to clean the blood off my leg and, *"Yeow!"* when the salt hits the wound. *Damn!*

"Wait. Let me do that," offers Sylvie. The cut is about two

inches long and who knows how deep. The damn thing hurts like hell.

"Did it go all the way through?" I ask, and she reaches around to feel the back of my thigh.

"No, but it looks deep enough."

Indeed it does. The cut itself is not bleeding all that much, just seeping, really, but the lips of the wound are far apart and I know they will not come together on their own.

"Ruth," I call. "Do you still have needle and thread?"

"Yes, I do, Jacky," she replies.

"Then come here, if you would."

I stuck the wadded-up piece of my drawer leg, which will later serve as a bandage, into my mouth and clamped down hard. Annie and Sylvie each held an arm, and Martha and Dolley each held a leg. Ruth leaned forward with her threaded needle... and the job was done. They were brave—I was the only one to faint.

It was strange to have four o'clock come with no flaps coming down to shut off our light. We got to see our first sunset since our abduction and it was a glorious one—all streaks of pink and white and purple that deepened to red and blue and gold before going dark. We had Connie's reading, and yes, she somehow managed to get out of the *Bloodhound* with both the Bible and Elspeth, and even a bottle of water. Then, in Chorus, Hepzibah led us in the "Song of the Hebrew Children," which we sang out in great hopes of a similar deliverance, out over the rolling waters from our tiny little boat right in the middle of the great big sea.

Chapter 52

I have always been a quick healer. I bounced back from the beating I got from Bliffil back on the *Dolphin,* my eye recovered when the drunken Gully MacFarland closed it up for me with his fist that time in Boston, and I did not suffer the dreaded infection from that splinter I took in my butt when on my beloved *Emerald.* Yes, I have been blessed with a hardy constitution and a tough body resistant to the physical ills that have felled others much bigger and stronger than me.

But not this time. Count on that damned Blodgett to have a dirty sword!

On this second day, the wound starts to fester and I begin to feel feverish. I take off the bandage and look at my leg and it has grown fiery red around the wound. Streaks of red course across the whiteness of my thigh. The skin begins to get tight, and it throbs, oh, it throbs and throbs…

On the third day, we are out of water. We have long since eaten the crackers. It has not rained. We have spied no ships. The wind is light and we do not make much progress north. I hurt, oh, I hurt so much…It is hard for me to keep my mind on my duties, but I try, and I try not to cry or whine. I see that the watches are observed and the girls are learning their small-boat seamanship. The lookouts are diligent in their search for ships. Rebecca is still down, and now there is no water. I despair for the child. I despair for myself. I despair for all of us. *Have I done wrong in planning all this?*

The skin on my thigh has become tight as a drumhead and it is now a dull color of purple gray. I have decided I do not want to live without my leg, but that doesn't matter, 'cause no one here knows how to take it off, anyway.

On the fourth day, lips are beginning to crack, and the girls have to be warned over and over that drinking the salt water means death, pure and simple, but the temptation is great, I know…All that water, and not a drop to drink…I start drifting in and out of consciousness, and then…there is a cry from up at the bow, which brings me back awake.

It is a fish! Katy has caught a fish!

I make myself sit up and look. I see that it is a dorado, one about three feet long. *Glory be!*

"Katy!" I croak. "Come here and take my shiv!"

She comes back to get it while the fish flops around up forward. Two girls immediately jump on it to prevent it from getting away.

"Pop out the eyeballs and slip them down Rebecca's throat. Sailors have told me there's good water in them… not salt. Do it." She does, and the orbs go over Rebecca's lips and down her throat. Her tongue comes out to lick her lips. *That's a good sign,* I think…*Hang on, Rebecca.*

"Now slit the belly from the throat to that hole back in the back. Good. Spill out the guts. And see that dark red thing there? That's the liver. Cut it up and put a slice down Rebecca and then each of you have a bit. It will give you sustenance. Then cut the flesh from the bones and chew it raw. You could dry it in the sun to cook it a bit, but you'd lose the moisture, so don't do that. Maybe later, if you keep catching them...maybe..."

I put my head back down and close my eyes and drift off again. I have a dream about my mother lifting my head and holding a glass of cold milk to my lips, but then I open my eyes and it's Clarissa pushing a bit of the fish liver into my mouth. It's good and I swallow.

"Thank you, Sister, but you shouldn't waste it on me, 'cause I don't think I'm gonna make it." I hear someone say, *"No, no, don't say that, you'll be all right, you'll see..."* I run my tongue over my parched lips and say, "When I die, cut me open right here"—and I lift my finger and run it down just under my ribs on my right—"and you'll find my liver." I think back to the *Dolphin* and to Tilly with his anatomical charts. I can almost smile—funny how things come in handy. "Take it out and cut it up and each of you eat some of it. No, no...don't protest. It's what is done in situations like this—none will think less of you for it. It's a grand naval tradition..."

I'm about to slip off again, but then I hear Elspeth speak and it jolts me awake.

"No. No, it should be me...to me that you do that. I...I don't deserve to live, so just do it..."

What?

I lift my head. "Do you really mean that, Elspeth?"

"Yes...It should be me...It will be me...I can't...I can't live with myself anymore..."

I must do this thing, and I must do it now.

"Help me sit up," I say, and Sally and Rose put their hands under my back and gently lift me up. *Damn, that hurts! Stupid leg!*

"Elspeth. Come over here and kneel before me. Who has my shiv?"

Elspeth rises, looking desperate and scared, her eyes pools of deep despair. She stumbles her way back through the ranks of girls seated at either side, holding her hands crossed on her chest so as not to touch anyone for fear they will shrink back from the touch of the Judas, the pariah.

She gets to me and sinks down between my knees. Katy hands me my knife.

"You are willing to give your life for your friends? Of your own free will?" I ask.

She nods, sobbing.

"Say it."

"I...I will give my life for my friends."

"Very well. Bare your breast."

She reaches up with trembling hands and pulls her dress and chemise down over her shoulders. I put the point of the knife on her chest where I know it can slip between two of her ribs and into her heart when I push.

She is shaking with fear and anguish, her mouth pulled down in a grimace that exposes her lower teeth, but she does not pull away. Instead, she puts her hands together and her lips move in prayer.

"Say your last prayer, Elspeth Goodwin, and when you are done and say 'amen,' I shall thrust."

Tears pour from her eyes as she says, *"Now I lay me down to sleep, I pray the Lord my soul to keep, and if I die before I wake, I pray the Lord my soul to take...Please, Lord, save my friends...Ah—Amen."*

She closes her eyes and waits for the thrust, finally at peace now, I believe.

I thrust.

But I do not thrust into her heart. No, instead I lift the point of the blade and thrust it up into her hair and cut from it the hated blue ribbon. I lean over and kiss her glistening forehead.

"You have redeemed yourself, Elspeth Goodwin, you have atoned. Now rise up and go and live your life." With that I throw the ribbon of shame into the water.

Gasping, Elspeth rises and her sisters' hands reach out to her to comfort her and to take her back into their loving company.

I look down at my shiv in my hand and at that cock's head carved on it, and as I gaze at it, I'm amazed to see the head, with its red coxcomb, suddenly turn and fix me with its beady eyes. The beak opens and the cock says, in Rooster Charlie's very own voice, "I knowed you wasn't gonna do that girl that way, Little Mary. You was always too soft-hearted for work like that, you know you were."

The blade falls from my hand and clatters to the bottom of the boat.

I think it best that I lie back down.

Chapter 53

Days turn into nights and nights to days and the sun, the sun always beats down, drumming on my forehead and beating on my eyes through my thin closed eyelids. I can't shut it out, I can't, I can't...I turn my head to get away from the sun and look out over the water and the sun becomes a crazily blurry disk in the sky and I blink and then I blink again, not believin' what I'm seein'. 'Cause when I look below the sun, there on the waves is a boy dressed in ragged white britches and a bright blue vest, climbing up and down the waves as if they were small hillocks in a gentle meadow in England and he waves to me and I ask, *"Charlie, is it you?"* I see that it *is* Rooster Charlie, of all people, out walking on the water as if for a stroll down Bride Street in Cheapside, laughing and tossing his red mop of hair to the side like he always did and calling out to me, *"Mary, Mary, quite contrary, why can't you button your lip?"* and he's got his arm around the shoulder of his great and good friend Hugh the Grand. *By God, it's Hughie, yes, it's you,* big and bold as life again, and there's Ned, good Ned Barrows, my brother midshipman and bold knight-errant who stood guard outside my doorway on the *Wolverine* to keep me that night from harm, now grinning and waving his hat at me. *"Ahoy, Jacky! Ahoy, Puss-in-Boots!"* and *what?* No...not Mum and Dad, and Penny, too? *Oh, Mum, I missed you so!* and her reaching out her hand to me, tears of joy runnin' down her face. And I taste my own tears runnin' into my own mouth right now and Benjy, him of the Dread Brotherhood of the *Dolphin,* lookin' not a day older than the day he died. Died? *Yes, you died, Benjy, you did. I saw it with my own eyes. You've all died, all of you, you've...*

Is this it, then? Is...is this the Heavenly Chorus? *Come down, Angel band, come and around me stand, bear me away on your silver wings to my eternal home.*

Is this the rush of wings that I hear? Is it...

No, it's not. 'Tis not the whirring of angel wings, no, not of wings, but the flapping of a large, slack sail hanging above me. I come to my senses long enough to realize that I am being put on a pallet, strapped in, and hauled aboard a ship. In the blur, I think I can make out the red, white, and blue of the Union Jack floating from the masthead. I know I am being taken aboard a British warship.

Then I know nothing for what seems a long, long time.

Chapter 54

The first thing I see upon opening my eyes is Annie, faithful Annie, sitting by my side and holding my hand. On the other side, I see the bowed head of Constance Howell. It appears she is praying over me.

I seem to be lying in a small room, maybe an officer's berth, on a large ship. I know it is a ship because I can feel it moving under me. It is a very pleasant room, with a port-hole that is open. Its curtain blows gently in the breeze. From the outside I think I hear male voices as well as those of my sisters. All seem happy and are laughing.

I am covered by a sheet, and my arms, which are bare, lie by my sides, on top of the cover. *Thank you, God,* I think as I look down and see that both of my legs are still there. Then, though I am weak, I find I can lift my hand to place it on Connie's head, and say, "Thank you, Sister."

Her head jerks up. "Praise God!" she cries, and she runs from the room, I suspect to tell the others.

"Oh, Jacky, I'm so glad!" cries Annie, tears in her eyes. "I'll get the doctor!"

While there is no one in the room, I cautiously lift the sheet and look under. Peering from left to right, I see my bandaged leg, then my little puff of maidenhair and then my blue tattoo. Nothing else. No clothes, no drawers, nothing. *Damn!*

But maybe they didn't get the word on my being wanted by the Crown, maybe they didn't get my description. Maybe they were off on isolated duty. Maybe...

The ship's surgeon comes to me, lifts the sheet, examines the wound, and pronounces that I shall get well because of the indisputable evidence of "Laudable Pus" and other such disgusting things. I thank him for his kind ministrations and I especially thank him for saving my leg—many a naval surgeon would have just hacked it off upon seeing the mess it was in, but he did not, and I will be forever grateful to him for that.

I now have a string of visitors. Annie, of course, and Sylvie are the first to come to my bedside. As soon as we had hit the civilization of the British ship, the serving girls instantly reverted to their servant status. Sort of. Katy announces that she's quitting the serving trade—*I don't belong there and I don't belong in Boston. I'm headin' back West... jes' to see what I can find...*

And then, to my great joy, I see Rebecca come running in, fully recovered... well, more than fully recovered—she has taken my sailor togs from Clarissa and is making a great pest of herself by climbing all over the ship, taunting her sisters by sayin' she can climb the rigging as well as any old Jacky Faber. Well, we'll see about *that*.

They all file by and take my hand. There's Dolley, and Rose, and Dorothea, who, of course, has tales of wondrous birds she has spotted from the foretop and won't Mr. Sackett be amazed. *That he will be, Dorothea, if only to see you back.* And Lissette and Helen and Abby and all the rest.

Then it's Clarissa who stands by my bedside to look down at me. She's been into my seabag and has put on my blue dress, the one I modeled after the one Mrs. Roundtree was wearing that time back in Palma. She is powdered and her hair is freshly washed and combed and put up and she looks absolutely magnificent, damn her to hell. I have heard that the ladies of the Lawson Peabody have been invited to dine with the officers this evening. More than one will lose his heart to this one, this evening, count on it. Even Rebecca has a fourteen-year-old middie panting after her.

"You know, Jacky dear," says Clarissa, "I really am glad you are not dead. I did not think I would ever say something like that, but it is true."

She pauses for a while, as if to collect her thoughts, and then says, "It has nothing to do with you, or with what we just went through—however, I have decided to give Angelique back her time."

"You mean you're going to free her?"

"That is what the phrase means," she says, flipping back a perfect curl. "I don't know what I can do about her mother and brother, since they are not directly owned by me, but I will try."

"That is very commendable of you, Clarissa."

"No, it isn't. I only do what pleases me and that does please me. And it does please me that you are not going to die, at least not yet, but…"

She leans over me and smiles and says in a low whisper, such that I can feel her breath on my face, "But you have to know this, Jacky dear…Back there on the boat? There is a part of me that would really have enjoyed eating your liver."

With that she brings down her perfect lips and plants a kiss on my forehead, then swirls from the room.

She has on my dress, and she looks magnificent in it. There is to be a party, where there will be many beautiful young midshipmen and officers. And I can't go.

Damn!

Petite and delicate Julia Winslow comes in, too, to sit with me a bit. I notice that someone has gotten the blood off her dress, the blood of the sailor whose throat she cut. When she leaves, Elspeth comes in, the last to visit.

She has regained her color, and some of her spirit. The other girls have been very kind to her, and the prospect of once again seeing her beloved Boston and her doting parents has restored her to something like her former self.

"Will you be all right, Elspeth?" I ask, squeezing her hand.

She nods and replies, "Yes. Thank you," and then she goes to join the others getting ready for the party.

I watch her leave and reflect on things. I think of her and I think of Julia. I think of the Dianas, too. I know there will be many accounts about our adventure—tales of fortitude, of suffering, of privation, and of bravery—but also I know there will be other stories, tales left untold, that will be better left in the dark, dank, and now forever silent belly of the *Bloodhound.*

PART IV

Chapter 55

The HMS *Juno* was bound for New York and that is where we went, but Captain Rutherford decided to take us on up to Boston, us being frail females and all and very much in need of their protection. There was a bit of business they had to do in New York and then we would be off.

I was afraid that bit of business would be me, but nothing seemed amiss in that regard. The girls were all good and careful in calling me Nancy Alsop, as instructed back on the lifeboat, and so I began to breathe easy.

We docked at Fulton Street Wharf and it was good to see the land again. We were astonished at the size of the city as we were warped in, but we were even more astonished to see Henry Hoffman, on his horse, come riding up the pier. *Our Henry Hoffman? Can it be?*

It is.

I looked at Sylvie and Sylvie looked at nobody but Henry, who, it was plain, did not know we were on this ship. I thought about it and began to suspect that he was sent down to New York to see if any news of our fate came into this port. He did not look particularly hopeful as he approached the gangway of the *Juno* as it was put down to the dock. His head was down as he walked up.

Ever the dramatist, I had shooed every one of the girls back from the rail so as to preserve the surprise. Annie and Rebecca had to tightly hold Sylvie back in a side passageway.

Henry gets halfway up the ladder, and I tell Sylvie in a whisper, *"Go back to Boston, Sylvie, and tell our story. But in your happiness, remember this—be kind to everyone in the tellin' of the tale. Do you take my meaning?"*

She looks at me and then at Elspeth. She nods, her chest heaving with excitement.

I put a kiss on her forehead. "Go then, Sylvie, and we wish you the greatest joy," and we let her go.

Henry Hoffman reaches the top of the ladder, and then his fondest dreams come true. Sylvie Rossio leaps upon him, covering his face with kisses and crying, "Henry, oh, Henry, how I have missed you so!"

Henry near faints away, but he doesn't. He gapes at her. He gapes at all of us standing there grinning.

"But, but, I should find out what—"

"Henry," I say, "your Sylvie knows the whole story. Put her on the back of your horse and fly to Boston and let her tell the tale. It will ensure that we have a proper reception."

I *do* like a proper reception.

The two of them race down the ladder and Henry leaps on his horse, then reaches down for his girl and pulls her up. She wraps her arms around his waist and buries her face in the nape of his neck and they are off.

I reflect to myself that those two will be married very soon. Maybe even tonight...

Chapter 56

Lieutenant James Emerson Fletcher
The Pig and Whistle
State Street, Boston, Massachusetts, USA
July 2, 1806

Miss Jacky Faber
On Board HMS Juno
Off New England, USA

My Dearest Jacky,

You cannot imagine the joy. The joy of knowing that you are alive and well, the joy that I will see you on the morrow, and the joy of knowing that you will indeed be reading this letter and all the others I wrote in those hours and days of sorrow and desperation during your absence and presumed loss.

To ease the agony of waiting these last hours before your arrival, I will write down an account of How the Blessed News of the Deliverance of the Girls of the Lawson Peabody Was Brought to Boston. I know our children will delight in the story of How Their Mother Saved the Day.

I was walking this morning in my usual state of deep melancholy when I encountered John Higgins, who was coming out of the courthouse, no doubt on another of his sleuthing errands, and we agreed to go up the hill to call on Mistress Pimm, to see how she was bearing up. We walked in companionable silence up Court Street to Tremont and then on to Beacon Street. We were just approaching the school when we heard a clatter of hooves and a hallooing behind us. We turned and saw a horse and rider, and when he got close enough, I recognized Henry Hoffman, who I had supposed was still in New York. Then I noted that he had two arms about his waist and then the head of a black-haired girl looked out from around his shoulder and for once the unshakable Higgins stood open-mouthed in wonder.

"It's Sylvia Rossio! One of the girls who was taken!" he gasped.

A spark of hope ignited in my heart.

Henry came abreast of us and reined in the horse. "They're safe!" said this Sylvia. "They're all safe!" And sweet relief flooded my mind. "Come! We must tell Mistress! We must tell everybody!"

Higgins's rock-hard reserve returned to him. He allowed himself a slight smile and said only, "Hmmmph....I wonder what took her so long?"

I, on the other hand, threw my hat into the air and went whooping up the street to follow the bearers of Glad Tidings into the Lawson Peabody.

When I go through the door, the place is already in an uproar. We encounter Mistress Pimm in the hall, and Sylvia cries, "Oh, Mistress, they're all safe, every one." Mistress's expression does not change. She nods and says, "Good. Then we shall be able to resume classes next week. I shall inform the faculty. Shall we all repair to the drawing room, where Sylvia can tell us her story? Ruby, tea for all, please. Betsey, please stop crying. Peg, please join us, as well. Oh, yes, and please get Angelique. She will want to know, too. It is good to see you again, dear," she says to Sylvia and leads the way into the room.

The tea is served and the girl Sylvia stands up and tells the tale. There is shocked silence when she relates how you all were taken and brought so low, and later, when you, yourself, were so cruelly flogged. I could not believe it. I still burn with fury when I think on that atrocity, and my only wish is that Captain Blodgett were still alive so I could hunt him down and kill him. Mistress Pimm, upon hearing that account, stood up, took her rod, and broke it across her knee, saying she would never use a rod for punishment again.

Word is sent to the courthouse and bells are rung and people run out to see what the fuss is—the last time it was rung it was for a certain fire, you might recall. Joyous parents are informed of the happy news and are invited for a retelling of the story this evening.

I count the slow minutes, and the even slower hours. I know I shall not sleep tonight. I know also that I will never let you out of my sight again.

Your Most Devoted & etc.,

Jaimy

Chapter 57

We sail into Boston Harbor, all of us up on deck, with all flags out and flying. It is an absolutely gorgeous day—the sun is shining, the breeze is cool and light, and the sky is blue. As we stand into the harbor, we are met by a multitude of small boats, all the people within them *halloo*ing and waving and blowing horns. One of the boats is the *Morning Star*, with Jim Tanner at the helm, cheering for all he is worth. My chest tightens at the sight of both of them. I wave back joyously. Fireworks are set off and brightly colored smoke bombs are exploded and we can hear bands playing on every jetty that we pass. We all stand on the deck and wave and *halloo* right back at all of those who came out to greet us on this glad day.

As we approach Long Wharf, for that is obviously our destination, Dolley, Clarissa, and I stand together, back from the others. We had decided that our last act as Division Officers would be to designate ourselves as the last ones off. It suited Dolley's sense of rightness, Clarissa's sense of aristocratic privilege, and my sense of the dramatic.

Dolley, like the others, is in school dress, the clothing in which we all were taken. Clarissa, having no dress, or any other clothing, for that matter, it having been left on the deck of the *Bloodhound,* is dressed in my maroon riding habit. She looks splendid, and how could I deny her? It is her way, I know that now, and I know we could not have gotten through what we did without her. So let her preen—she has earned it. I thought of wearing another of my fine outfits that were stuffed down in my seabag, but, no, best to remain modest for a change. I'm wearing my school dress, too, newly cleaned and pressed, as best the HMS *Juno* could do it.

I look around at the scene and know the Captain of the *Juno* can't wait to be rid of us and had bent on all sail to get us up here with the last bit of speed the ship would bear. Discipline on the ship, as far as the midshipmen and junior officers were concerned, had gone completely to hell— many of our girls had been flirting outright with the young men, and the young men, astounded at their luck to find thirty or so young women in various states of undress in the middle of the ocean, were certainly easy prey for their charms. I'm sure many pledges of undying love and devo- tion were exchanged, and who knows, some of them might turn out to be true. Even little Rebecca's thirteen-year-old self has found a midshipman near her own age, and they have been holding hands and making cow-eyes at each other these past precious days.

I look upon my Sisters and reflect that many of the par- ents of these girls are going to be more than surprised by the daughters returned to them, as they will not be the same giddy girls that gaily left on that fateful day. They may very well not accept anything that their families, their society, or even their own individual fates merely hand to them. They will be trouble, mark me on that.

The instant the *Juno* is warped to the pier and the first line is thrown over, a flag is hoisted on the masthead of the Customs House and immediately every church bell in the city peals out and the bells do not stop.

The gangway is lowered without great ceremony, and the girls swarm off the *Juno*, having been formed up in the last muster of Sin-Kay's alphabetical line. They don't mind, for it gives them great joy to see little Rebecca run down the gangway into the arms of her family, then Ruth, then Sally, then all the rest. There goes Annie and Helen and Dorothea and... *There's Higgins!*

Oh, God, *Higgins,* and Peg and Mistress beside him... and then Connie and Martha go down and... *There's Amy and Ezra!*

And there... *No, it can't be.* There, next to Higgins. *Oh, Lord, it's Jaimy...* Good God, it's really Jaimy, standing there smiling up at me and reaching up his hand, and the tears pour out of my eyes and down my face and they are tears of absolute joy.

My happiness is complete.

Clarissa, standing next to me, notices. "So that's him, eh? Well, he looks presentable... Good chest... fine leg..."

Then it's Dolley's turn to leave the ship, and a great cheer goes up from the girls as she goes down the gangway.

Dimly, I sense Clarissa looking at me. "Well, even though I owe you one in that regard, I might let you keep him." And with that, she turns and goes down the gangway, head up, the Look in place, to the cheers of her Sisters.

I have not been able to take my eyes off Jaimy's as I float, as if in a dream, to the gangway. I put my foot on it, and then...

And then two bayonets cross in front of my chest and I hear the Captain intone, "Miss Faber, by order of His Majesty, King George the Third, you are under arrest on the charge of Piracy!"